Black's Magic

By
MJ Walker and Val Brown

ISBN 0-9755739-2-6
First Printing 2004
Cover art and design by Anne M. Clarkson

Published by:
Dare 2 Dream Publishing
A Division of Limitless Corporation
Lexington, South Carolina 29073
Find us on the World Wide Web
http://www.limitlessd2d.net

Printed in the United States of America and the UK by

Lightning Source, Inc.

IV

Acknowledgements

Val Brown and M J Walker would like to send a big thank you to all those who helped make this possible. To Reagan, Jane and Hilary for assisting in the editing of Black's Magic. To Maya, Tim and Michael for providing much appreciated information and to Sam, Anne and the Limitless team for their hard work and dedication.

Special Note

We would like to remind you that some of the words in this book may not always look 'correct', depending on what part of the world you call home. Our authors are international and we have elected NOT to change the spelling or wording that they use and which is considered correct and appropriate in their homelands. It is the opinion of the publishers that changing this would alter the author's voice and deny the work the international flavor and appeal that made us choose to publish it in the first place.

Chapter 1

High thread count, smooth texture, taste of basic fabric paint...hmm, my guess is a hand-painted silk scarf. By the taste of the pigment I'd say East Indian, more than 30 years old. Guess that seminar on Asian Craft Construction has finally come in handy.

Figuring out what was being used as a gag and blindfold, however, did Skyler Tidwell little good in actually getting rid of the things. For the thousandth time she tested the ropes binding her wrists and ankles together and wondered when she would find out what exactly had happened to her and why. She could tell she was in a vehicle and that it was moving, but basically that was all. *Oh, one other thing* Skyler thought as she was bounced yet again, *this road is in desperate need of repair.* It was a perplexing puzzle and the one thing Doctor Tidwell detested was a puzzle. She ran it over in her mind one more time, looking for the elusive clue that would let her figure out what the hell was going on.

It had been early evening when Skyler arrived at Wellington University. After a brief stop to check in at her hotel, she had taken a taxi immediately to the centuries-old institution. It had been two years since she had last seen her mother and Sky was pleased when her mom suggested they get together at the University located just north of London. "If you're going to be in the same hemisphere as I am, you might want to drop by," her mother, the eminent Dr. Marlene Tidwell, had joked. The jest covered a very real longing to spend more time with her daughter.

Her mother was on a sabbatical from Eastern College in Pennsylvania where she was a tenured professor of Biology and was "on loan" to Wellington for a research project in genetics. Skyler wasn't completely sure of the nature of the project, but she was under

1

the impression the combined American and British governments were bankrolling it. Whatever it was, her mother was enjoying the time being spent on the project, telling her daughter that the stimulating research was "keeping her young". Not that her mother needed to worry, she retained the good looks of a woman many years her junior, obviously favored by the genetics she now studied.

From her cocoon of darkness, the younger doctor reviewed her present circumstances again. She was less than thrilled and was becoming more and more frightened. *It won't help, Skyler Jane Tidwell, so just calm yourself down. You've got a good mind, so use it. If you lose your cool you'll have no control whatsoever. Okay, I don't know what's happening now so I'll try to think about something I know everything about. Calm down, calm down...* Skyler let her thoughts drift to her own life, to combat the rising feeling of panic that at times was threatening to swamp her.

Sky's family lived in the Philadelphia area where her mother had been hired as an associate professor at Eastern College. Skyler's father was a police officer and had been her best friend. *So middle class,* she thought and smiled a little, though the gag made it difficult. *Swing set in the backyard and a puppy in the house.*

Skyler remembered the golden lab with great fondness. *I sure miss you, Tess.* Her mother got the puppy from a co-worker shortly after it was weaned and brought it home in a box for Skyler. The excited child pulled the dog from its blanket draped home and said, "Welcome to my house, Tess!" Marlene Tidwell was astonished that her daughter had decided on a name so quickly and asked her about it.

"Her name is on the box," the child said simply as she hugged the puppy close. Marlene flipped the lid back to see the label on the box she had obtained from work...***100 Test Tubes***. Tess Tube was the dog's name from that point on though it was rarely called anything but Tess.

The defining moment of Skyler's childhood took place when she was six years old on a cloudy and cold Monday afternoon. Even now the memory caused her to shiver and not only in remembrance of the weather that day. She had come home from school and settled herself in front of the television to watch the afternoon cartoons. Her mother had finished early at the college and was in the kitchen chopping vegetables for a soup. The volume on the television made it impossible for her to hear the knock on the door.

Skyler opened the door to greet two somber faced men, one in a heavy topcoat and the other in a patrolman's uniform. The one in the topcoat spoke first.

"Skyler? Remember me? I'm Lieutenant Simmons, I work with your dad."

Marlene entered the living room then and came up behind her daughter at the door. When she saw the visitors on the front porch of her home, the smile slipped from the face of the biology professor.

Skyler's father had been killed in the line of duty. It happened trying to protect a small child who had become trapped in the crossfire of rival gangs bent on ownership of an insignificant inner city park. The little girl had survived the furious assault, but Officer Jerome Tidwell had not. At the funeral Skyler held her mother's hand as tears slowly streamed down her cheeks. Her father had been her hero, but now he was gone and from that point on it would be just Marlene Tidwell and her rather serious blonde headed child.

They had been a tight-knit twosome, even through Skyler's attendance at Eastern. Being something of a child prodigy, she had graduated high school at age 14 and went directly on to college. She had a huge capacity for knowledge and a fantastic memory that was as close to photographic as you could come without actually earning that label. She immersed herself in academia, all but ignoring the social aspects of life. After all, dating was bound to be a problem for a sixteen-year-old taking courses in such arcane subjects as Pre-Columbian Archeology in South America and Mummification Processes of World Peoples. Study became a substitute for companionship and books replaced the need for friends.

Flying through her college curriculum, Skyler continued on to graduate studies, receiving her Masters Degree at age twenty-one and her Doctorate at twenty-four. Her fascination with everything from Geology to Psychology made it difficult to narrow her focus down and when she finally graduated, Eastern College issued its first ever advanced degree in the nebulous area of "Human Studies". Skyler called herself a jack-of-all-trades; "egghead" and "professional student" were the less flattering names given to her by some of her fellow students. The scholar didn't care though, all aspects of human behavior and human endeavors fascinated her.

In the two years since Skyler had last seen her mother she had been both traveling and working on projects important to her academic and professional career. The twenty-eight year old had supervised the excavation of an early man site near Olduvai Gorge in Africa, studied Sherpa populations in Nepal and catalogued destruction of crucial rainforest in the Amazon basin. Each project may have seemed completely different from the other, but they all fell into Skyler's area of expertise, or at least one of her areas.

Finishing up a recent six-month survey of disaster relief effectiveness among sub-Saharan nomadic populations, Skyler was now ready for a stint in the more populated and civilized British Isles. After taking some time off to complete her blistering report to the United Nations for their failure in the area of African disaster relief, she was scheduled to oversee the excavation of a newly discovered area of Roman ruins in the northern part of the country. It seemed that an industrious farmer sinking a new well had possibly discovered the first true temple to Artemis in England. Skyler was excited by the new project and couldn't wait to share the news with her mother. It was this that had led her to the campus where her mother's lab was located.

Skyler was feeling good, and if she had been given to noticing that sort of thing she would have to admit she looked good too. The North African sun had graced her features with a deep tan that accented her emerald green eyes, and her blonde hair was streaked with sun coaxed highlights. The relatively rugged living conditions had subtly toughened her up and the perennial scholar now had an appreciation for the definition her form had taken on. She liked the way she fit a little more snugly into the black jeans, green polo shirt and black suede jacket she had chosen for the meeting.

Being dropped off at the main gate to the university, Skyler was surprised to find the campus quiet and sparsely populated until she remembered the students wouldn't be returning from the Christmas break for another week. The sun had set by the time she found a security guard to ask for directions to Newton Hall, the building in which her mother's lab was located. She laughed to herself at the term "security guard" as the elderly man gave her the guidance she needed. It was obvious this sweet grey-haired gentleman was more of a rattle-the-doorknob-to-make-sure-it-is-locked kind of watchman than a security guard. Fortunately, by the look of the sleepy campus, it didn't appear that his services were needed in any other capacity.

Skyler headed for the large brick building that housed the Physical Sciences Department. As she walked, automatic lights began flickering to life, illuminating the cobblestone path but sending adjacent objects into shadows. She hurried along toward the brightly lit building; her mother had assured her that working late was commonplace and she would have no trouble finding someone to point out the genetics lab once she was inside. Her hand was reaching out for the handle to the door when a voice called out to her.

"Doctor Tidwell?" Skyler turned to see a pleasant looking, red-haired young woman smiling at her.

"That's right," Skyler replied, thinking her mother had sent someone to watch for her. At her words she felt, rather than saw, movement behind her. Then several things happened all at once. Her arms were grabbed; she was shuffled out of the light of the doorway and then total darkness descended as something was placed over her head. Her vision was obscured and as she opened her mouth to cry out, a smothering hand was clamped over her mouth through the material. Screaming was forgotten as breathing took precedence. The doctor pulled air through her nose in a panic as she felt a sharp jab to the inside of her left arm.

Skyler felt heaviness in her limbs and the hand across her mouth now seemed to be holding her head up as it lolled forward. The doctor dimly recognized the agent being used to drug her from a course she had taken in Applied Pharmacology, but that was as far as she got before slipping completely into unconsciousness.

And then what? Skyler thought. *I don't have a clue. How long was I out? Where am I and for God's sake, why is this happening to me?*

For all her education she didn't have an answer to that one.

****

On the rocky coastline off the southern edge of Cornwall, a statuesque lighthouse stood on the crest of a large cliff. The tall cylindrical building, painted with highly visible red and white stripes, was the only notable feature on an otherwise banal landmass. Stretching out as far as the human eye could see and spanning around three quarters of the building was the English Channel, a large mass of water separating the British Isles from the rest of Europe. To an onlooker the site would appear to be abandoned, both lonely in the lighthouse's singularity and in its situation, but to one person it was home. A closer inspection of the area would reveal well maintained areas of shrubbery and flowers, hand-built wooden furniture for hot summer days and even worn and muddy boots by the doorway. A wooden structure, which would seem nothing more than a small shack was actually the doorway to an underground garage. The facility was only one small part of a larger compound, but it housed three cars, one motorbike and two bicycles with enough tools to preserve the upkeep of them all. The lighthouse was in perfect working order and on dark nights its light beamed proudly as a warning beacon for all passing ships.

It was mid-morning and the sky was littered with dark winter clouds. They stretched out across the sky, covering a once brilliant blue with a dull and ominous grey. A distant rumble rolled over the land signaling the coming of a heavy storm. Seagulls that had been soaring through the air began heading towards sheltered land as the atmosphere flowed with an eerie calm.

From a distance the sound of an approaching vehicle began to increase. Out along a single, well-worn and narrow road a navy blue SUV rose over the horizon and made its way towards the lighthouse. The crunch and grind of dust and rocks grated under the 4 x 4's thick, heavy wheels as it made a speedy climb towards home. The vehicle never decreased its speed as it neared the wooden shack and instead a quiet beep floated unheard over the land as a remote door was activated and garage doors opened. The 4 x 4 skillfully manoeuvred its way through the doors, which closed behind as it travelled down into the underground garage and screeched to a halt beside a black Audi TT convertible. The engine died as the sole occupant of the vehicle opened the door and black booted feet hit the ground.

Addison Black climbed out of the Range Rover and closed the door behind her. She pulled off black shades and slipped one arm into the pocket of her tight blue Levis as she headed towards two metal doors. The door on the left led to the rest of the underground facility and required an eight-digit password and fingerprint scan to enter, while the right door lead to the lighthouse. Addison took the right door. She slipped a small silver key into the lock and opened the barrier, taking the steps two at a time until she reached the upper door of the narrow corridor. After keying in a smaller, four-digit password she stepped into the main building.

Once passing through the door and stepping immediately into the kitchen, Addison slipped off her black leather jacket and draped it across the back of a nearby chair. She held out her arms and stretched quickly before scanning the room. Usually by now she would have been greeted.

"Spike?" Addison called, her inquisitive eyes searching. "Hey you little beast, where are you?"

Hearing nothing, Addison stepped further into the kitchen and kicked off her boots. Socks still in place she padded across the black and white tiled floor to the spiral staircase. Ignoring the black iron banister, the ebony haired woman climbed the steps to the first floor sitting room of the lighthouse.

"Spike?" she questioned, spotting a peculiar looking lump under the cream throw over her settee. Knowing Spike was hard of hearing, the woman stepped a little closer. "Don't tell me you are angry at me for staying out all night? I know Jenny came to give you a walk early this morning, you little mutt."

Addison sat down beside the covered lump and immediately noticed a response. A tiny head lifted under the blanket and struggled to free itself from the cover's confines while Addison chuckled at the dog's antics. After seconds of the small dog stumbling around, Addison took pity on the whimpering mongrel and pulled the throw from Spike's head. Immediately a tiny black dog, with gray speckled flecks on its head, bounced into her arms.

"Hey, I see you missed me, girl!"

Spike barked, jumping around frantically upon Addison's lap as she tried to lick every available inch of skin. Unfortunately, due to an unnaturally small stature, that was nothing higher than her stomach.

"All right, calm down, girl." The black dog settled immediately into Addison's lap. "Good girl," she said and began stroking her hand over Spike's head. "Oh you would have liked the one I had last night, girl. Uh huh! She had magnificent breasts..." Spike looked up at Addison, unimpressed. "Not a breast girl? Okay... well she had legs that could wrap around your body twice... and a tongue that could scramble eggs at fifty paces!" Spike yawned and placed her head back upon her mistress' lap. "Well think what you will, Spiky, but she was one hell of a sexy lady. An off-season tourist," she added. "We spent last night in her hotel room and let me tell you... there was very little sleep involved!"

With a disinterested huff, Spike rolled onto her back as Addison's hand mindlessly wandered to her stomach and commenced a gentle tickling. Resting her head back against the sofa, Addison's dark eyes moved to the television unit on the opposite side of the room. Sitting upon the television set was a medium sized photo frame holding a portrait of four uniformed soldiers. Though from her distance Addison was unable to make out the four smiling bodies, from memory she knew the colour print by heart. The picture was of Addison with the three other members of her four-man fire team. At the age of twenty-one Addison had joined the Royal Marines, her decision to do so being one initially made out of a desire to leave her past behind. Addison was the only child of equally abusive parents who found the quest for their next drink favourable over the welfare of their child. She grew up in a small three-rise block of flats owned by the city council and positioned in a neighbourhood reputed for its high crime rate and grotty appearance. It was an estate in which just living there alone was a strike against employment opportunity. The only way many youths attempted to earn money was by turning to a life of crime.

It was a direction that Addison herself had turned to. Accompanied by a gang of five friends from the same neighborhood, they started by stealing from shops and re-selling what they stole at half the retail price. Addison quickly earned the reputation as the girl to go to when something was wanted at a cheaper price, no questions asked. At the age of eighteen, Addison had become quite talented at avoiding capture, but soon the desire for more reared its head. Addison began stealing cars, first to smash into shops and steal the merchandise and then simply for the thrill of the chase. She began to love the high-speed chases the police would give when they came across the stolen vehicles. Action-packed chases down midnight streets, in cars or on foot, were almost nightly rituals. Never once did she get caught, often managing to disappear around an unexpected corner. The local authorities never had any idea of who she was. For three years that was her way of life. Continuing to live at home, she found her parents stole much of her own 'belongings' for the purchase of either cigarettes or alcohol. It was a vicious circle that found Addison's life in a rut. Then one evening, on the thirty first of October, something happened that changed her life forever.

Pushing the painful memory aside and holding Spike gently with one hand, Addison rose to her feet and crossed the room. She picked up the framed photograph and looked down at the smiling faces. The picture was taken the morning after the four friends has returned from a day's leave. They spent most of the day drinking and finished the night off by getting the Royal Marine crest tattooed on their upper arms. The day after the picture was taken they had all left for a six-month training period in the desert.

Training in the Royal Marines was one of the longest and most demanding infantry training regimens in the world. That was of no consequence to Addison. She had set her ambitions on becoming a Commando Soldier and nothing would dissuade her from the pledge she had made to serve her country the best way she could. Addison easily passed all series of tests of fitness, endurance and military professionalism and earned the right to wear the Green Beret and 'Royal Marines Commando' flashes upon her uniform. It was then that she joined the 45th Commando at Arbroath in Scotland.

Addison was also honoured to be awarded the Commando Medal which was given to any soldier who showed he or she possessed qualities such as leadership, unselfishness, cheerfulness under adversity, courage and determination while maintaining high professional standards during training. Those were considered qualities that defined the commando spirit.

Addison smiled down at her friends. They had been close during their time together. Addison had always found it easy to draw people by a unique and striking visual appearance that was a point of comment by everyone she met in her younger days. It was also lucky that the four did get along so well, as they not only trained together but also shared accommodation. Life as a Marine Commando was never plain sailing. It seemed that around every corner another hurdle was there to overcome and it was something each soldier cherished. Though there were few women in the Marines, Addison didn't come up against as much sexism as she anticipated. Her talents as a Marine Commando made sure of that. It was common knowledge among the ranks that Addison Black could take a man down with a single punch... and she had.

For six years Addison remained in the Marines, but soon she yearned for more, more of a challenge, something that could push her further and harder. She was given the opportunity to join the S.A.S., one of the most elite counter insurgency forces in the world. It was so secretive that many people weren't even aware at that time that such a team existed. Without so much as a chance for second thought, Addison agreed and passed the initial selection process easily. It was then that her instruction really started as she underwent such things as medical training, advanced weapons training and parachuting. The first phase was that of endurance, beginning with a week-long battle fitness course and then learning basic map revision, gym work, orienteering and many miles of running or marching while carrying up to sixty pounds in weight. Addison found the Endurance March, which took twenty hours to complete, the most gruelling by far. However, she passed the first test and went on to S.A.S. weapons training, languages and took a Mensa test to make sure she could adjust to the S.A.S. way.

The second part was the Jungle Phase and took place in Brunei at a British Army jungle training school. It was six weeks without a shower and, to Addison, the most uncomfortable part of the training. It was also the phase where many recruits failed, as getting ill was considered unsuccessful completion. Survival was the key and getting even a cold was failure. The last and most intense part of Addison's training was combat survival. One month of living off the land whilst using evasion and escape techniques, she also learned interrogation techniques from people who had been tortured. The final test was known simply as survival week. One week of trying to live off the land while being hunted down by Ghurkhas and Para's, knowing that if caught she would be interrogated. Eventually she was caught, and straight away Addison was blindfolded and taken to an unknown destination. Her wrists bound, she was kept in a small cage made from chicken wire. For forty-eight hours Addison was held and interrogated. She was allowed to give only four pieces of information; her name, rank, number and date of birth. The only other piece of information she was asked was her mother's name. For that she could only reply, "I cannot give you that information." For forty-eight hours she was asked the same question; she was beaten, starved and then she had been placed back in her cage that was then covered with corrugated iron and beaten with a hammer for over an hour. Still she could only reply, "I cannot give you that information." Addison received brutal punishment for her persistence. One moment that always stood out in her memory was when she was hit with such force that she fell to the floor and felt bones in her arm and cheek break… but still she denied them. Because of her strength and ability to prove she was not a security risk, she passed the last phase and was awarded her S.A.S. beret and a one-year probation.

By the time her one-year probation was over, something unexpected happened. General Blithe, a member of the British Military intelligence, otherwise known as M.I.5, approached Addison. A new, secretive division was opening within M.I.5 to be run by high-ranking individuals with top-level clearance, which wanted Special Operatives to work for the Government. These operatives, who were already highly trained in all areas and competent to work in the field alone, were required to serve the Military and Government on strategic missions. Whether they required information on other countries, kidnappings, rescues, surprise ambushes, or data hacking, each S.O. agent was required to be able to handle them all. Addison was surprised to hear General Blithe had been watching her career for many years and considered her an ideal candidate for this clandestine operation. She readily accepted.

Was she a spy, a mercenary or a soldier? That was unclear to even herself. She was known simply as Addison Black SO2, secret agent for M.I.5.

This was the position Addison had held for the last five years and at the age of thirty-four Addison felt she was only now just reaching her prime. The best part about her job was that she got to choose where she wanted to live and as soon as she found the lighthouse she knew that was what she wanted. The lighthouse was fully capable of working on its own; it didn't need a keeper and that suited Addison fine. The place was her own little oasis of solitude, away from the hustle and bustle of life and somewhere she could simply relax. Even the most hectic life needs the occasional down time.

Chapter 2

The vehicle Skyler was riding in came to an abrupt halt, bringing her out of her thoughts and back into the minimal input she was receiving from the world around her. Listening intently she heard two doors open, then slam shut and a pair of footsteps crossing graveled ground.

A door nearby opened and a rush of colder air fell across her. *In the back of a van or truck* she thought quickly before a familiar female voice reached her.

"Doctor Tidwell? The drug should have worn off by now so don't bother to feign unconsciousness. It will be much easier if you walk with us and not make us drag you across the ground. The stones will definitely mar your lovely face." An unseen hand touched her cheek and Skyler involuntarily pulled away.

A soft laugh floated through the blackness. "That's what I thought." There was a brief pause then the woman said, "She's awake. Get her inside. The blindfold and gag stay put until she's in the guest room." Skyler felt the ropes around her ankles cut loose and her upper arms were used to roughly pull her out of the vehicle. A burning pain started in her shoulders and the ropes dug into the wrists that were still bound behind her.

Her feet touched the ground and momentarily her knees threatened to give way as the aftereffects of the drug made themselves known. With an effort she remained upright and even moved without stumbling as she was propelled forward. Skyler couldn't shake the feeling she had heard the woman's voice somewhere before, then it struck her. *The red-haired woman at the university!* The voice had been tinged with a light Irish accent and it was that trait that the scholar remembered now. She silently congratulated herself on figuring out one part of the mystery and she felt better for it. In Skyler's world understanding always meant control, and control was the one thing she could never get enough of.

Through the soft material of her suede boots, Skyler could feel gravel give way to what felt like paving stones.

"Steps," the woman's voice came again, this time from behind her. Four short steps were taken with minimal problem and Skyler was once again out of the fresh air. The air was warmer indoors, but Skyler didn't notice as she was concentrating on memorizing the pacing and numerous turns they were taking. She had a feeling her hosts wouldn't give her much of an opportunity to leave, but you never knew when the information would come in handy.

She was pulled to a stop only to feel the floor suddenly drop out beneath her. It wasn't a long elevator ride down, but her heart sank with the cubicle as each second passed. The movement halted abruptly and Skyler was once again urged forward.

"In here," the voice instructed, and Skyler was moved to her left. The guiding hands left her arms and the sound of footsteps retreating preceded the sound of a door being shut and locked behind her.

"Let me make you a little more comfortable, Doctor," the woman's voice said, causing Skyler to jump a little. She hadn't realized the woman was still in the room. Bindings at her wrists were removed and the scholar drew her arms around to the front of her body to massage her forearms. The gag was removed followed by the blindfold. Skyler squinted and blinked sensitive emerald orbs against the light invading her eyes after being so long in the darkness.

The "guest room" was a small square room that resembled nothing so much as a bomb shelter right out of the 1950's with Spartan living quarters and bare bones furnishings. Skyler remembered seeing an exhibition of the shelters at the Smithsonian.

"Doctor Tidwell," the redhead began, "welcome to your temporary abode and I assure you if you cooperate with us, it *will* be temporary. Of course you must realize what this is about; we need the information you possess about Project Gemini. Tell us what we want to know and you will be released quite unharmed." The Irish lilt was deceptive in its soothing quality. If the reality of her kidnapping hadn't invaded her thoughts, Skyler could almost imagine this young woman leading a group of tourists through the Irish countryside.

"Look, Miss…" the scholar began.

"You may call me Brodie," the redhead supplied.

Nice name Skyler thought. *Nice everything right up to those baby blues.* If those blue eyes hadn't carried the dead gaze of the sharks Skyler had seen while scuba diving off the Baja Peninsula in Mexico, she might have thought the woman was attractive. But a shark was a shark, in or out of the water, and if the doctor learned one thing from her research in Mexico, it was you never trusted a shark. A four-inch scar on her lower left leg would always be a graphic reminder of that fact.

"Well then...Brodie...I'd love to help you out but I don't have the faintest idea what you're talking about. I don't understand why I'm here and I've never heard of any Project Gemini. So if you'll just let me get the hell out of here, we'll forget about this whole thing and I won't need to inform the police or the American Embassy."

Brodie laughed out loud and it momentarily softened the predatory look. "Doctor Tidwell, you amuse me. Even in the face of the facts you have a bravado that's quite admirable." Now the amusement fled from her eyes to be replaced by an undisguised snarl. "Do you really think we were unprepared? Do you really think we didn't plan?" She pulled an index card from the pocket of the pea coat she wore and began to read from it. "Blonde, green eyes, five foot four inches tall, one hundred twenty pounds, Wellington University, Newton Hall." She looked Skyler up and down. "Right woman, no doubt about it. Now if we could just drop the pretense, Doctor, and get down to business."

Skyler barely heard the last words. Her mind had already worked out the fact that it was her mother these people were after. It was her mother who was in danger and Skyler had merely been in the wrong place at the wrong time. *Or maybe the right place at the right time,* she thought. *If I hadn't been heading into that building when I was... Mom...in the hands of whoever these people are...*

Skyler's knees did buckle then, a movement Brodie misinterpreted. "Maybe I was mistaken, Doctor, maybe the drug isn't quite all out of your system." The redhead assisted the scholar to the metal-framed twin bed and lowered her down.

"Why don't you try to rest for awhile? I'll bring you something to eat and when you're feeling better, we'll have that chat. See? We're looking out for you." The attempt at a gracious smile fell short of her eyes giving her a wholly insincere look.

Instead of responding, Skyler merely nodded and slumped back onto the scratchy gray blanket covering the narrow bed. *I can't let them know they don't have the right person, not until I can figure out what's going on here.*

Brodie walked toward the door where she knocked and said a

few words through the thick wood. Skyler recognized the language, but not the meaning of the words. *Damn,* she berated herself, *you speak 5 languages and not one of them is Gaelic.*

The door was unlocked from the outside and Brodie left without another word to her captive. Skyler watched her go then closed her eyes bringing her hands up to massage suddenly throbbing temples. For the first time she acknowledged how wretched her situation was and a small tear of desperation slipped down her cheek.

****

Entering an efficiently organized office in the underground complex, Brodie moved behind a large oak desk and pulled a cellular phone from the top drawer. Pressing a pre-set number, she listened as the connection was made. She sat up a little straighter as a voice came on the other end of the line.

"We've got her...no, not yet but she will." From another desk drawer the redhead drew out a particularly lethal looking knife. Its polished steel reflected the ebony handle. "Oh yes, I can guarantee it. Professor Marlene Tidwell will tell us everything."

****

The sound of crashing thunder shook Addison from an unexpected slumber. Blinking bleary eyes, tired from little sleep, she yawned and looked down to the fidgeting bundle upon her lap. Spike loved the rain, she loved water in general and living by the sea for the little dog was pure heaven. Spike grew more excited, hearing the patter of rain upon the window of the lighthouse.

"Please not today, Spike!" Addison hoisted the scruffy dog from her lap and deposited her upon the floor. The black dog scrambled around her feet causing Addison to sigh. "Okay, but I stay by the door. You can frolic in the rain for as long as you like, but I refuse to get wet!"

Spike yapped with excitement.

"Let's go and find your ball, huh?"

Spike scampered off towards the stairs and Addison followed, continually amused as she watched the small dog bound up each mountainous step. Spike, however, still managed to reach the second floor of the lighthouse after Addison and she followed her mistress into the bedroom. Addison looked around the room cluttered with books piled high in each corner.

"Where's your ball, Spike?"

The dog ran off into the adjoining blue and white tiled bathroom and began her search. Shaking her head while deciding to leave Spike to it, Addison headed into the bathroom and switched on the small-boxed light above a wall mirror. She gazed at her reflection and sighed. Around her feet she felt as much as heard Spike continue her search for the infamous battered orange ball. Leaning forward, Addison opened her right eye wide with one hand while she used her finger to slide out a single contact lens. Placing the tiny coloured object in a special container, Addison then splashed her face with cold water. Picking up a blue towel that matched the colour scheme of the bathroom perfectly, Addison looked down at Spike.

"Any luck?"

Spike huffed and trotted back out of the bathroom, sniffing the ground diligently. Carrying the towel, Addison walked back into her bedroom. From the corner of her eye a small flashing red light caught her eye and she turned to her telephone and answering machine.

"You didn't tell me I had a message, Spike!"

Patting dry her face, Addison checked the message.

"*Addison, it's me,*" came a familiar voice from the machine.

Spike's ears shot up in recognition and her head cocked to the side intently.

"*If you really aren't there then call me when you can. I was wondering whether you wanted to go paragliding with us next weekend and I have a few new toys for you to try. If you are there then pick up the phone, you lazy arse.*"

Addison chuckled, "Only if you have managed to adapt an onboard vibrator for my car!"

"*I know you... you're there... pick up or this message will self destruct in five seconds...*" The male voice paused. "*Four... come on... three... pick up... two... you won't regret it... one...*" The voice paused again. "*Hell, I guess you aren't there! Okay, well call me when you can... bye.*" The line went dead.

Addison looked down at Spike's furry face. "I'll call him tomorrow!" Dropping the blue towel upon her unmade bed, Addison walked back towards the spiral staircase that stood at one end of the room. "Let's go find your ball." Scooping Spike into her arms, Addison jogged down to the ground level kitchen. Under the table she spotted a familiar object. "That looks suspiciously like a ball to me, Spike. What do you think?"

Spike wiggled in her arms, insistently asking to be placed back upon the floor. Addison did as requested just as the telephone began to ring. She picked up the wall-mounted device.

"Hello?"

"Addison, it's Perkins."

The ebony haired woman rolled her eyes. "I promise I only just received your message. I was going to call you."

"No problem, Addison," Samuel Perkins assured her. *"Listen, things have gone belly up in accounts. We need you to pack for a business trip right away. National, first class."*

Addison nodded, understanding the code behind Perkins' words. 'Belly up in Accounts' meant there was a kidnapping situation and 'pack for a business trip' meant she was to be sent on assignment. 'National, first class' simply meant the assignment was in the country and she was to travel at least half way by air. "Right," she answered. "Do I have a car on the way?"

"Be there within the hour."

"See you then, Sam." Addison hung up the telephone and looked down at a worried Spike. "Sorry, girl, but it looks like playtime's off!" Spike whimpered and dropped the orange ball. "I've got to go to work, but guess who gets to spend her time with a certain inventive scientist?" Once again Addison scooped up Spike with one hand and headed towards the door leading down to the underground facility. "Of course Sam doesn't know yet, but that'll be our little surprise!" With a chuckle Addison opened the door and trod the steps down towards her secured command centre.

Access to Addison's underground command centre was limited to only three people: General Blithe, Samuel Perkins and herself. Of those three people, each had their own eight-digit access code and fingerprints mapped into the security system. What was contained behind the steel door was both highly dangerous and illegal for the general public. For that reason, access into Addison's facility was restricted, clandestine and monitored through a direct link to M.I.5, Special Operations Headquarters.

Once again back in her garage, Addison placed Spike down upon the concrete floor. She quickly scampered off and disappeared under Addison's Audi TT. Her black coat blended into the shadows of the equally black car, but Addison could clearly zero in on Spike simply by the incessant sound of sniffing and eyes that glinted in the artificial light of the garage.

"Spike, if you create so much as a puddle near my car I swear I'll use your scruffy fur to mop it up!"

The warning was taken with little heed as the overly small dog continued to nasally cover the garage floor. With curiosity, Addison bent her head to the side to watch Spike in time to see her trot back out from behind the Audi with a large, gnawed bone in tow. It was twice as long as Spike and obviously heavy with one end dragging along the floor as Spike manoeuvred it over to Addison. Chuckling to herself Addison turned to the steel door. A large square digit pad was secured to the wall ahead of her, its access light shining a bright red. Beside that was a second pad in the shape of human hand, which too was shining a bright red. It was on this that Addison placed her left hand as she keyed in her access code. Once entered, her fingerprints were scanned before the access light flashed to a luminescent green and she was given ten seconds to enter the room.

Spike stood at the doorway ready and waiting to enter and as the heavy steel object moved open, Spike dragged her bone inside. Addison followed the dog, shaking her head in amusement as automatic lights flickered on, casting the room in a soft glow. While Spike dragged her bone to a specified corner of the room complete with tartan doggie bed, Addison stood by a large metallic table.

The room itself was rectangular in shape. A simple square steel table, dull from age and use, stood in its centre. Around the walls of the room were racks, cabinets, cupboards and shelves containing all of Addison's field gear. The wall to her left contained multiple racks holding all her weapons, pistols, shotguns, submachine guns, knives, and flash grenades. Though M.I.5 Headquarters did maintain a fully stocked arsenal, Addison kept a supply of her personally favoured weapons. Along the wall ahead of her stood a large wooden cupboard containing different types of combat attire from camouflage to totally black sniper's wear. Rows of shelves held many tools vital for use in the field including night vision binoculars, microscopic cameras, hand-held global satellite tracking systems, bugs, wires, multi-functional compasses and small explosive devices. On the wall to her right were many steel cupboards containing ammunition for each weapon Addison possessed. Whatever she needed, from tiny clips for her 'baby Browning' to larger clips for her submachine guns, Addison had them all. On the final wall behind Addison stood a large computer, a database connected straight to Special Operations Headquarters through which she could gain information and communicate with them through a secure line. It was a place where Addison would spend much of her time, often working all hours and even sleeping upon on an old futon bed beside the computer. The room, due to its somewhat clinical appearance of metal and soft light, appeared very cold. The walls being nothing more than ancient rocks that had been mechanically dug out of the cliff was warmed only by a single space heater in one corner of the room.

"Right, let's get to it," Addison said to an uncaring Spike as she walked over to the firearms. Her eyes scanned over the rows of dangerous weapons and zoomed in firstly on her favourites... two Beretta Brigadier 9mm steel pistols with black rubber grips; she would carry them in holsters attached to the back of her belt. Pulling them off the rack in favour over her Desert Eagles, as they were heavier, Addison placed them upon the table and turned back to the firearm racks, folding her arms. There were three basic weapons Addison would take on any major assignment: pistols, a shotgun and a submachine gun. She was, if anything, a great believer in being prepared for any situation. Unfolding her arms, Addison pulled a Spas 12 shotgun followed by an H&K MP5 A4 Kurtz submachine gun from the racks and placed them too upon the metal table. H&K submachine guns were standard issue weapons for the Special Air Service and Addison had become accustomed to their usage. Addison also preferred this submachine gun as it was around the size of an Uzi and therefore easy to carry upon one's person. Turning one last time to the racks, Addison took a Baby Browning pistol and small Colt Tactical Survival knife from their positions. She had several of these weapons as she found they were just the right size to attach to her boots.

Hearing an attention seeking yap, Addison looked down at Spike who was now scampering around her feet.

"What do you want, Spiky?"

Spike rose to her hind legs, looking up at Addison, with her front paws resting upon Addison's leg.

"Go and play with your bone."

Spike barked again forcing Addison to relent with a roll of her eyes. She scooped the tiny dog up and deposited her upon the table. Instantly Spike nestled into a comfortable position and closed her eyes. Chuckling quietly, Addison opened a tall standing cabinet. Inside the wide compartment was a row of combat attire. Pulling out her favourite black clothing, Addison placed them upon the table and turned to choose a pair of boots.

"Hmm," Addison tapped her lips in thoughts. "What do you think, Spike, the black ones or the black ones or should I choose the black ones?" Amused at her dry humour, Addison chose the closest pair of worn boots and turned to place them with the rest of her kit. What she found caused her to smile. Spike had abandoned her position upon the cold surface of the table in favour of the softness of Addison's clothing. Dropping her boots, Addison leaned forward until she was nose to nose with the dog.

"What are you doing?"

Comfortable eyes blinked open and the scruffy dog looked languidly at Addison.

"Move your furry arse, Spiky."

A tiny tongue poked out and swiped across Addison's nose.

"And that won't work, Mongrel. Now get off my clothes!"

As slow as cannily possible, Spike dragged her body from Addison's clothes leaving behind a scattering of short white hairs from her underbelly. Addison forced out a weary sigh and pulled the now marred attire from the table and exchanged them for ones sans dog hair. She placed them straight into a large duffel bag followed by the rest of her chosen equipment. She then added gun holsters, night vision binoculars, a small medical pack, several flash grenades, tape to bind ammunition clips, two black leather belts and two pairs of handcuffs. Although she had ammunition for all her weapons, she left them alone knowing she would get it from the Special Operations Headquarters. Weapons of either blades over six inches or any gun had for some years been illegal in England and although Addison was licensed to carry and use such weapons, she preferred not to do so when it wasn't necessary.

Once her gear was packed and ready, Addison looked down at Spike. "So, Spiky, are you ready to go?"

Spike scrambled to her feet, her small tail wagging back and forth. Slinging the bag over her shoulder, Addison picked up Spike and headed out of the secure room.

"Let's go and see if our car has arrived, shall we?"

19

M J Walker and Val Brown

Chapter 3

It was a fit of sneezing that woke Skyler from the uneasy sleep that had finally come over her. After a meal of soup and toast brought by the ever-watchful Brodie, the doctor had been surprised that no further interrogation had taken place. *Letting me get used to my captivity no doubt,* she thought.

The redhead had merely set the tray down and left the room. She returned to pick up the tray and point out the toilet facility, a metal commode that pulled down from the wall and reminded Skyler of every prison movie she saw in the "Movies of Incarceration Film Festival" she had attended at the college. It was partitioned from the rest of the room by a white fabric screen. Exiting with the tray, Brodie announced it was after three in the morning and therefore the doctor must be tired. Ominously she mentioned that they would "talk further in the morning." As the door closed and locked, the lights dimmed leaving only 2 small, recessed night-lights in the wall for illumination.

Curious about the sneezing, Skyler did a brief physical assessment of herself. There was no apparent fever, so she ruled out the start of flu. There was no chest congestion and she discarded the idea of pneumonia. She had no headache or sore throat, only nasal congestion. *Must be an allergy* she thought miserably. Realization of what she had just thought hit her like a ton of bricks and she sat up quickly on the edge of the bed. *Wait a second; I only have allergies to three things; that damn dust in the Egyptian tombs, yak fur and heather. The air is too heavy to be Nepal and I don't see a sarcophagus, so it's got to be heather.* Pulling the scratchy gray blanket up, she inspected it closely. *Mm-hmm, there it is, a bunch of seeds at the hem. Heather! They must have used the blanket outside at*

21

one time or another.

Let's see, heather seeds. Brodie said it was three when she turned out the lights so that means we travelled about nine hours because I was at the University at six in the evening. Nine hours by vehicle and heather seeds. Scotland, it has to be. That would explain why it was so much colder here when they took me out of the vehicle than it was when I was in London.

Making the discovery of her whereabouts elated the scholar. For the first time Skyler felt a tiny measure of victory in her quest to have some understanding of her situation. She now also knew something she was sure her captors would prefer she didn't know. *Well tough tuna boats, Brodie.* Skyler mused. *You're messing with Skyler Tidwell and you've got to get up pretty early in the morning to out-think a Tidwell.*

Even as the thought was drifting through her mind she felt the momentary bravado slipping. She knew where she was and had a good idea of what she was doing there, but that knowledge really did her little good. She was still a prisoner.

Removing the blanket with the offensive material, she carefully folded it and put it as far from the bed as possible. A small foot locker at the bottom of the bed yielded a yellow cotton blanket free of heather seeds and Skyler returned to the bed though she despaired of actually getting anymore sleep. *A plan, that's what I need* she thought. *I'm going to lay right here until I think of one.* With that she turned her considerable intellect to her dilemma.

****

The lights flickered on some hours later; Skyler couldn't be sure how many as there was no clock in the room. The doorknob to her room began to turn slowly. The unusual door was the one thing the doctor had remembered while she had been thinking. Instead of opening inward as most doors did, this one opened outward. Skyler pinned her hopes on that fact.

As the portal opened Skyler thought, *Plan A: escape,* and pushed against the door with all her might. Dishes flew from the tray Brodie was bringing in and the redhead crashed back into a large man standing behind her. Skyler took the brief opening and used it to her best advantage. She tossed the gray blanket she had discarded the night before over the two people in the hall as she pushed past them. She had thought about it and knew that every nanosecond might count.

Having mentally retraced her steps a hundred times, she took off unerringly toward the elevator. She knew this was when she would need some luck and no amount of planning could shake that fact. If the elevator wasn't on this level, she was sunk.

Luck was on Skyler's side and if she hadn't been moving so quickly she might have stopped to pump her fist in the air in victory as the elevator was not only on her level, but the door to it stood wide open. Dashing into the lift, she hit the button labeled Level 1 and prayed elevators in the British Isles were labeled the same way as in the States. The door slid shut soundlessly and Skyler took her first deep breath since pushing the door open. *Plan B: to the surface,* she thought. It was a little disconcerting getting to this part of the plan, for Skyler didn't have a clue as to what she might find up top. Trying to wrap her mind around the problem, Skyler barely noticed the car wasn't moving at all.

She realized it at once though when the door to the elevator opened and she stood facing a very angry, oatmeal covered Brodie. Behind Brodie was the man who had stood behind her at the door, but this time he held a very large, and very lethal looking handgun.

"Perhaps you will return to your room now?" Brodie said through clenched teeth as she motioned Skyler off the elevator and back toward her room.

"Let me guess, remote controlled elevator?" Skyler asked as she meekly returned to her room. In response, Brodie lifted up her hand in which she held a small silver box with several black buttons.

"Very astute, Doctor." Handing the remote control to her confederate she moved slowly toward Skyler. "You certainly seem to be as intelligent as the reports about you indicate, but I think I'm going to need to teach you a lesson you may not have learned in the academic world." With the speed of a striking snake, Brodie's fist shot out catching the doctor flush in the mid-section. As she doubled over and crumbled to the floor gasping, Skyler knew this lesson was far from over. *Plan C:* she thought as a booted foot caught her in the ribs, *get the shit beat out of me.* Except for pain, it was her last coherent thought for quite a while.

****

"She's been gone for hours and what are you doing about it? Nothing!" Marlene fumed. Her fair features were flushed with agitation in contrast with the distinguished older gentleman seated at the desk across from her.

General Blithe tried to comfort the distraught blonde woman. "I assure you, Professor Tidwell, we are not idle. Ever since Constable Barclay raised the alarm we have been working on your daughter's disappearance." The constable was old, but his eyes were sharp. As a retired S.A.S. agent, he certainly knew a kidnapping when he saw one. Though a little long in the tooth to stop the crime, the elderly gentleman provided the agency with excellent descriptions of the abductors and their vehicle. "As we speak, our best agent is on the way to London to assume charge of the investigation. Agent Black is top drawer, ma'am, and has my highest confidence."

The general was considerably calmer on the outside than he felt on the inside. It had been less than a day since Skyler Tidwell had vanished and he had already received a phone call from the American ambassador as well as a terse call from 10 Downing Street. The Prime Minister himself was reported to be taking "a personal interest" in the case and the General could well understand why after he had been briefed on the nature of Project Gemini.

"Professor, if I may ask you a few questions…how many people knew of your daughter's visit?" He stroked his brown moustache as he questioned the attractive woman. The general had difficulty believing the woman before him was old enough to have a daughter twenty-eight years old.

"Let me think," Marlene replied. "Skyler and I of course. Maybe one or two of my colleagues on the project, but nobody knew the specifics except she and I. We weren't sure of the time until the very last day."

General Blithe stood and moved around the desk. His intelligent brown eyes looked with sympathy at the American. "You're sure of this? No one but the two of you knew your daughter's schedule?"

"As far as I know," the professor returned. "Is that important?"

"Very possibly, doctor." He ran his fingers through his brown hair, long ago grayed at the temple. "If no one else knew she was arriving that evening, there's only one explanation."

The truth dawned on Marlene Tidwell. "They were after me."

"If that's true and your daughter was taken by mistake, that puts her in a very precarious situation." Mark Blithe reached out and placed his hand on the woman's shoulder.

She trembled a little as she said, "She'd be expendable." Her eyes closed against the anguish of that realization.

****

Strolling down the corridor of Special Operations HQ, Addison checked her watch. It was just now two o'clock and the smell of cooked foods floated down the narrow hallway. Although Special Operations Branch was a small and secretive unit within M.I.5, it employed some of the country's most elite soldiers and scientists. As such it needed the presence of a fully functional canteen, but unfortunately as no outside catering staff were allowed access into the highly secured building; dinners were limited to vending machines and a large selection of micro-waveable meals. This in itself caused a problem, as many of the employees were unhappy with the choice of nutrition on offer. To the soldiers this was of no concern; they could, and had, lived for months at a time on ration packed foods and nutrients off the land. For the scientists it was a different matter. They demanded a wider variety of more freshly cooked foods. It was, however, the scent of Chinese food that drew Addison towards the canteen.

With her black duffel bag over one shoulder and Spike in the other hand, Addison stepped into the spotlessly clean room. Although not a large area, there were ten tables each with four chairs around them and several vending machines along the nearest wall. Beside the hot drink machine stood a table holding two microwaves and beside that a chest freezer stocked full with ready meals. The room was empty apart from a single body sitting at the far table. Adorning the surface of that table were many foil cartons containing a selection of Chinese takeaway foods. The enticing smell, coupled with the person devouring the Oriental cuisine, drew Addison closer with a wry smirk.

Nearing the origin of the delicious scents, Spike began to whimper causing the sole occupant of the table to glance up in curiosity. Blue eyes narrowed upon spying the struggling Spike.

"Addison, I am not looking after that. She pissed in my favourite trainers last time you had me take care of her!"

"It was her way of showing you affection," Addison told Samuel Perkins with a laugh. The ex-soldier/scientist didn't appear convinced. "Hey, I told you Spiky needed at least two walks a day."

Samuel put down his chopsticks. The blonde man's eyes narrowed. Although he and Addison had never served together in the Military, they were close friends. Samuel had been recruited into Special Operations just after Addison and as such, his ranking within the Unit was SO4, a title that naturally he disliked immensely as this was the chemical designation for sulphate. For this reason Addison jokingly called him SO3 and a half. Samuel wasn't sure which name he disliked the most, but he took the jesting with the humour intended.

Addison dropped her duffel bag down onto the floor and sat upon the chair opposite Samuel. She held back the scampering dog eager for a taste of the highly scented foods. "Come on, Mate, you know you are the only one I trust with her. She likes you!"

"She likes my frigging shoes," the scientist groused.

Addison shrugged. "Same thing." Leaning over the table she swiped a piece of prawn toast from Samuel's plate. "Please... I don't want to resort to physical coercion here!"

"Like you would have a chance!"

Feeling the first flutters of a challenge, Addison arched her eyebrows. "Want to bet?" Giving the remainder of the prawn toast to Spike, Addison placed her upon the seat beside her own and reached out her arm, pushing the containers and Samuels's plate to one side. "I'll arm wrestle you for it. If I win you look after Spike, but if you win I will never badger you to take care of her again!"

"What kind of bet is that?"

Addison placed her elbow upon the table and held out her hand. "Come on, Sammy boy, put your balls where your mouth is!"

Samuel's features burned at the comment. "You're on!" Placing his elbow beside Addison's, they clasped hands. "On the count of three... one... two... three!"

And the challenge was on. Blue eyes burned into Addison as the couple strained against the strength of each other's challenge. Addison found her arm beginning to lower as a smug smile spread across Samuel's lips. Adding a little more muscle, she pushed their arms back to level pegging and returned his grin with one of her own.

"Do you really think I'm that easy?" she asked.

Samuel chuckled. "Some of the women around here might think so!"

"Bull... I never mix business with pleasure." Addison pushed a little harder.

"Apart from Kathy!"

Samuel had a point there. Of the few women who worked at Special Operations that she did find attractive, Addison had only shared an intimate encounter with Kathy. She blamed it on the fact that she had just returned from a rather rough assignment, which had left her craving for some much needed sexual stimulation. It was not the first time Kathy Bridges, from the armoury, had propositioned Addison, but it was the only time she had ever given in purely for lust.

"Like I was the only one," the agent returned, implying she knew of Samuel's tryst with her as well.

This time it was the scientist who pushed a little harder;

Addison's arm, however, remained steadfast. "Maybe we are more alike than you care to admit."

"Maybe. Except my hairline is not receding on top!"

"Bitch!"

"And that is just the way you love me!"

Samuel chuckled. "Damn right!" He frowned then. "You are aware that you are missing a contact lens, right?"

"Forgot it on my way out. I'll use one of my spares here. Now stop talking and let me beat you!"

"Never!"

Both agents continued their battle unaware that Spike had hopped up onto the table and was gingerly lapping at the corner of Samuel's plate. Her large round eyes remained fixed upon the battling duo as her tongue sought out the spicy cuisine.

From the doorway of the canteen two more gentlemen entered the room. Both were scientists wearing long white lab coats and sporting enquiring expressions. They approached Samuel's table together.

"What's going on?" a middle-aged man with a thick head of auburn hair asked.

"What does it look like?" Samuel responded through gritted teeth. A pink shade of exertion and sheen of perspiration coloured his cheeks. The contest was heating up and both challengers' arms shook with effort.

"Twenty pounds on Black," said the second scientist. "She will have him in no time!"

His auburn haired counterpart shook his hand. "You got a bet there."

The minutes seemed to pass a lifetime per second as Addison battled Perkins. There was no doubt in Sam's strength, he seemed to match Addison equally, but what he lacked was her perseverance. Over five minutes passed before Addison finally slammed Samuel's arm down. Much to her surprise almost seventeen voices simultaneously cheered and groaned as the contest ended. She looked around, bemused by the men and woman who were handing over and receiving small cash wagers.

Rubbing his aching arm, Samuel admitted defeat. "You know, I would have looked after her anyway."

Addison smiled. "I know, but this was much more fun!" She looked down at Spike who had just finished devouring the contents of Samuel's plate. "Spike! Bad girl!"

Rising to her feet as the dog jumped, Addison scooped up the tiny mongrel. "You are a naughty girl for eating that, Spiky!" Addison shook her head and kissed the dog's soft muzzle. "Anyway, I have to go now, little bit, but Sammy is going to look after you, okay? I will be back soon so be good!" Addison handed the dog over to a dismayed looking scientist. "Umm... a word of warning... Spike and spicy foods don't mix well!"

"What does that mean?" Samuel asked as Addison picked up her bag and slung it over her shoulder.

Addison patted her stomach then pointed towards Spike. "Just be prepared," she said, hearing Sam's despairing groan. Just before leaving Addison addressed the gathered members of the staff. "Thank you to all of those who had faith in me. I see your confidence was rewarded and I hope you have a drink tonight in my name! To those of you who didn't..." Addison grinned, "you should know I never lose... that's ..."

"Black's magic!" responded her fellow workers followed by a series of groans and chortles.

Addison winked, followed by a nod. "You know it," she said and exited the cafeteria.

Feeling slightly sorry for Perkins, the agent made her way down a long corridor. At the end was an elevator beside a stairwell. Opting for the stairs, Addison descended towards the basement level of the division. General Blithe's office was situated in this part of the building and it was standard procedure that she report to him for a briefing before every assignment. Unless otherwise stated, by the General himself, no other official could issue her an assignment.

Reaching the bottom step, Addison took a left through the grey walled hallway and stopped at the large door leading to Blithe's secretary's office. Beyond her room was the General's office. Stealthily she opened the door and peeped into the room. The secretary had her back to Addison and appeared to be profoundly engrossed in some matter of reading material. Addison crept silently into the room. Not even her breath made a sound as she skulked up behind the woman and looked over her shoulder.

"I heard reading material like that would make one go blind!"

The dark haired woman jumped and spun around in her chair. "Addison, you almost scared the life out of me!" She placed a calming hand upon her rapidly beating heart.

Addison looked down at the seated secretary and smiled seductively. Dropping her duffel bag she pulled the book from Miss Bakersfield's hand and read the front cover. It was an erotic lesbian tale that she herself was familiar with. "Really, Miss Bakersfield!

Reading such things during office hours? What will the General think?" Addison perched herself upon the edge of a large teak desk.

The secretary blushed. "Addison please... how many times do I have to remind you to call me Antonia."

With a sly smile, Addison placed down Antonia's book. It was so much fun to flirt with this woman even though she knew it was harmless. "Is that what you allow your closest... friends... to call you?"

"Possibly." Antonia leaned back in her chair and allowed her dark brown eyes free roam of Addison's body. "I take it you have an assignment?"

"Here to see the General," Addison replied, enjoying the secretary's perusal. She made a point of uncrossing her legs.

Miss Bakersfield nodded. "He isn't in his office. Apparently he's been in conference since before I arrived here this morning. I haven't seen him yet today. So... do you know what's happening? It must be a serious matter for him to be up all night."

With a shrug, Addison leaned closer. "You know as much as I, Miss Bakersfield."

Antonia was just about to respond when General Blithe entered his reception.

"Agent Black... I see you have arrived! Excellent. I am in conference presently and would like you involved. Can you come with me, please?"

Winking, Addison rose from the desk and approached her superior. "Yes, General... we have a situation?"

General Blithe nodded. "Indeed we do. Come with me and all will be revealed."

With a sharp nod, Addison followed the General back out into the corridor and down to a high security conference room. Mark Blithe held the door open and Addison walked into the room first. She was expecting to see the usual gathering of military officials perched around the room, but instead she found a woman sitting upon a luxurious couch by the right wall. She didn't recognise her and knew she had never been into the S.O. Headquarters before... the visitors card upon her jacket proved as much. Addison did, however, know that she was a woman of high standing within the military or government by the sheer fact that she was within the walls of Special Operations Headquarters.

Entering behind her, General Blithe closed the door. "Agent Black, I would like you to meet Professor Marlene Tidwell."

"A woman?" Marlene said unexpectedly.

Noting the American accent, Addison looked down at her own breasts, clearly noticeable due to the tight fit of her shirt. She then looked up at the General and shrugged before looking back at Marlene. "Since the day I was born apparently!"

Her remark seemed to break the tension in the air and the woman smiled. "I'm sorry, Miss Black, it's just that I guess I was expecting a man."

"I know, and they are always so disappointing... present company excluded of course."

Mark Blithe groused at his top agent's behaviour. "Shall we all sit down?"

"Of course." Addison sat upon one of the many chairs beside a large rectangular table that stretched across the length of the room. She positioned herself between Marlene and her boss who was seated at the head of the table. Trying to gain some understanding of the situation, Addison looked into the eyes of the other woman. An undeniable layer of trepidation was clearly visible and Addison realised that whatever the problem was, it was in direct relation to Marlene Tidwell.

General Blithe sat down. "Yesterday evening at precisely a quarter to seven, a Miss Skyler Tidwell was abducted from the grounds of Wellington University."

Addison nodded with complete attention.

"The abduction was witnessed by the elderly security guard on duty that evening. I am sure you are aware of Constable Barkley?"

Addison nodded again. He was well known in the S.A.S. for being the first soldier to receive a Victoria Cross for bravery and conduct in the field.

"Barkley witnessed the events but was unable to raise the alarm in time to stop Miss Tidwell from being abducted. He did, however, get the licence plate of the vehicle used in the abduction. Also, Miss Tidwell dropped her purse in the struggle, which he swiftly retrieved. So far we have heard no word from the abductors."

"And who is this Skyler Tidwell?" Addison asked.

"She is my daughter," Marlene replied.

Addison frowned. "If you don't mind me asking, Professor Tidwell, what was a young girl doing out alone at that time of the evening?"

"She is twenty-eight years old, Agent Black."

Addison's sheer surprise was shielded by her neutral expression. She had no idea the woman in front of her could have a daughter of such an age. The agent looked to General Blithe for answers.

"Skyler Tidwell was on holiday here, Agent Black, visiting her mother. She had only just arrived in this country and had travelled straight to the University to meet with Professor Tidwell. We believe

30

that Skyler was abducted by mistake with the belief that she was in fact her mother."

Addison addressed the blonde woman with a frown. "Why is it you would be the target, Professor Tidwell?"

Marlene rose to her feet. All the talking she had been doing since her daughter's disappearance was beginning to anger her. She didn't want to talk; she wanted something to be done. "I am a scientist working on a coalition project between Britain and the U.S."

"Which is?"

Marlene looked to the General and after receiving a nod, she continued. "It's called Project Gemini..."

The name was instantly familiar to Addison. She had heard many rumours pertaining to Project Gemini through her own sources. It was said Project Gemini started out as a breakthrough discovery during research on the tuberculosis bacterium. Addison wasn't sure what that breakthrough was, but she knew it was being extrapolated for use in cancer therapy research.

"But I don't understand," Addison pressed. "Why would anybody want to abduct your daughter... you? Project Gemini is a medical project... isn't it in the research of cancer therapy?"

"Yes," Marlene responded.

"Then who and why would anybody want to kidnap you?"

"The why we are unsure... as for the who, that I can help you with." General Blithe picked up a large manila folder and chucked it into Addison's lap. The agent opened Blithe's folder to the picture on the front page. Addison's eyes narrowed as she spied a familiar face,

"Agnes Brodie!" Her eyes scanned over the redhead's picture. Addison had long been familiar with Agnes Brodie. The woman of Irish descent had been linked with several terrorist organisations and although no damming evidence had ever been produced, Addison was positive of her guilt in several major incidents. Brodie was presumed to be in the arms and terror business simply for the money. There were extortionate sums to be made through the illegal trafficking of weapons and trading government secrets. That was not to say Agnes Brodie didn't crave the power as well. Like any megalomaniac with delusions of grandeur, Brodie was not adverse to violence and intimidation. Addison was positive that as a child she would have been the troublemaker in the playground who would beat upon other children and steal their lunch money. The agent wondered what Brodie's involvement was in this case.

"And she was a positive identification?"

General Blithe walked around the table. "By Barkley himself. If you look further along in the file you will find satellite images and pictures taken from a motorway service station on the M1 northbound. Thanks to Barkley's sharp eye and quick mind, we were able to trace the number plate and although it led to a dead end, we obtained these images of the light blue transit stopping for diesel in a monitored station. We also have images of the van entering and travelling through Scotland thanks to its irresponsible driver. The vehicle was captured going over the speed limit twice by two motion surveillance cameras first in Dunblane and then Badenoch. Addison studied the documents before turning to a large map of the British Isles. She strode over to the map and ran her index finger up along the route the abductor's van had taken. Reaching the last known point for the transit, Addison studied the Grampian Highlands. Her eyebrows furrowed together.

"Here in and around the Monadhiath Mountains, aren't there some abandoned mining caverns built within the hills? Are you thinking that is where they might be?"

"Intelligence believes so. We are focusing in on that area as satellite imaging seems to have captured movement in that area recently." Mark Blithe folded his arms over his broad chest. "It is obviously in Skyler's best interests for us to expect they have the worst of intentions towards her. As we have no idea what part in this Agnes Brodie plays, we can only assume there are high sums of money involved."

Rubbing the smooth surface of her chin, Addison nodded. She knew her job was to go in there and get Skyler Tidwell out with as little fuss as possible. The abduction of an American on British soil would be a high profile case and one they would want resolved quickly. What troubled Addison was that the motive behind the case was unclear. Why would Marlene Tidwell be the target for abduction? Unfortunately, although these thoughts did concern her, Addison knew it was her job to follow orders and not ask questions.

Noting the sudden silence within the room, Addison turned to Marlene Tidwell. The blonde research scientist was gravely silent, her hand covered trembling lips and her eyes glazed with unshed tears. Addison pushed nimble fingers through her hair and glared at the General. They both knew better than to be discussing the probabilities of a situation in front of the victim's mother. Scratching the back of her neck, Addison sat down beside Marlene.

"Professor Tidwell, I know it's a difficult time for you, especially facing the unknown, but please try not to worry."

"Try not to worry!" Marlene laughed quietly. "It's hard not to when all that's happened since my daughter's disappearance is a lot of talking by you people. I want to know when you are actually going to do something about getting her back." The older woman rose to her feet. "Lord knows what could be happening to Sky right now. I want my daughter back."

"That is why Agent Black is here, Doctor Tidwell. We will be sending her to locate and bring home your daughter. She is one of our most highly experienced operatives."

"And when will you be leaving to do this, Agent Black?"

"Just as soon as I have some visual and background information on your daughter, Professor Tidwell."

"Speaking of which…" General Blithe pulled a second, slimmer folder off the conference table. "Here is Skyler's file... background and visual data." He handed the folder to Addison and sat back down in his chair. "The picture was taken from her driver's licence and most of the information was taken from several university databases."

"Uh huh." Addison opened the folder. She scanned through Skyler's background as her brows arched higher and higher. "Blimey! If you don't mind me saying, Professor Tidwell, your daughter certainly gives the words 'eternal student' a new meaning!"

Marlene's features softened to a glow of pride. "She got her first Masters Degree at the age of twenty one."

Addison whistled in amazement. She herself had only just scraped through high school. Addison had hated school. She would attend as little as possible and it was a great surprise to everybody, including herself, that she even managed to pass her O levels. The agent continued to skim through Skyler's file in growing amazement at the younger Tidwell's academic achievements. *She has more letters after her name than in a Welsh village,* she thought wryly. Turning to another page, Addison found an enlarged scan of Skyler's driver's license. She gazed down at her scrawny, pimple covered features, wearing thick-framed glasses held together by clear sticky tape. *And sometimes the apple falls very far away from the tree!* Addison read over Skyler's license details.

"Hold on a moment. This license picture was taken in 1997. It's six years old. Don't you have anything a little more recent?"

"My daughter travels a lot, Agent Black. In recent years lasting memories like photographs have taken a back seat to our academic quests. This was the most recent picture we could find of my daughter."

"Right." Addison put down Skyler's file after memorising the information within. The assignment seemed straightforward enough. Go in, get the girl and get the hell out again. However easy it always seemed, any one of a million possibilities could always arise to make a difficult situation even more so. Addison had seen them all. From the highly dangerous, being chased by wild dogs and hunted by a group of vengeful terrorists in below freezing conditions with nothing to protect yourself but your own two hands, to the highly ridiculous; disguising herself as a clown in order to infiltrate a circus believed to be trading stolen arms around the country. Addison was careful never to go into a situation with any expectations, but there was one aspect of this case that did bother her. Agnes Brodie. She was a highly intelligent woman who seemed to lack basic human emotions. She was clinical in her approach to all situations and didn't appear to understand that life was a gift not to be abused. She didn't scare Addison, but she did leave her with an uneasy feeling. Brodie was capable of anything and that was her main concern for Skyler Tidwell.

Mark Blithe tapped the tips of his fingers upon the table. "There is one more thing. Due to the very fact that it appears Skyler's abduction was a mistake we are keeping this under very tight wraps. Nobody else apart from Downing Street and us know this and that is the way it shall stay. If it was to get out that this abduction was a mistake then not only could Skyler's life be in danger, but also it would be harder for us to zero in on the organisation responsible. Present conversation about this ends here."

Taking the General's hint, Addison rose with a nod. Much to Marlene Tidwell's relief, the time for talking was over.

Chapter 4

It was strange the things one found out from an expertly applied beating. *I never knew pain had a color* the doctor thought. First it had been a red in its intensity then faded a little to a purple as it settled into a steady dull hum of misery. Skyler had never been in a real fight and had never had the opportunity to explore the mysteries of an assault firsthand, but Brodie was giving her that learning experience now.

It wasn't during the actual rain of blows that Skyler learned the lessons; it was after Brodie left when the pain changed from a waterfall of agony to a steady stream of aching and soreness. She dragged herself to the bed from the floor where she had spent most of her time as Brodie beat her without mercy or any apparent emotion. If Skyler hadn't seen the clenching of the redhead's jaw she might have thought the beating was given in an almost clinical and detached manner. The doctor had seen it though and knew that a mighty rage ruled Brodie, no matter how hard she tried to hide it.

It was on the bed that Skyler's keen intellect went to work. She tried to use her mind to escape the throbbing sensations reporting for duty from her entire body. *No, correct that,* Skyler thought, *she didn't hit my face. So, Brodie, where did you learn to hit where it wouldn't show? Were you an abused child? Did you suffer corporal punishment at the hands of an over-zealous headmistress at a parochial school? Was it a rigorous gang initiation ritual? Guess what, Brodie? I don't give a fuck.* Skyler gave a little laugh at her attempt to employ the little used expletive. *Fuck? That's the best word your college-trained mind can come up with?* The short laugh cost her as a sharp pain issued forth from the area of her right ribcage. The doctor placed the palm of her hand against the offending area and shifted on the bed to relieve the

35

spasm in her side.

Panting from the exertion of reaching a slightly more tolerable position, Skyler knew a few things for certain. She hadn't cried out the truth of her identity during the beating, but she realized she could never hold out for long if the physical abuse continued. She wasn't cut out to withstand torture; that much was painfully obvious. *Don't laugh at that stupid pun, Skyler* she warned herself.

Turning her face to the bare wall, Skyler battled a sense of desperation she found trying to creep into her mind. *Don't give in, don't give in, that's what Brodie's counting on now. She knows I won't cooperate of my own free will and now she'll have to find a way to coerce me. Why do I get the feeling she's very good at finding those ways?* Skyler wasn't sure what could happen to change the course of events as she predicted they would play out, but whatever might happen, it would need to happen soon. The American felt a trembling set up in her limbs. *Shock,* she contemplated with some detachment. Gingerly she pulled the blanket up from the end of the bed and over her shoulders. As her head returned to the pillow she knew it would take a miracle to get her out of the mess she was in. *Or maybe some kind of magic,* she thought as the tears she had kept at bay since her abduction began to flow.

They weren't tears of sadness or fear. They were tears of pure anger. *That's another thing you taught me, Brodie and I'll have to thank you for it some time. Now I know what the need for revenge feels like.*

****

Marlene Tidwell just stared at the door as Addison departed the conference room.

"Well, she's certainly something," she said almost absently to General Blithe. "You say she's one of your top agents?"

"She's the best, Professor Tidwell," the general affirmed.

She turned her hazel eyes to the man. "Look, around our house two Doctor Tidwell's were a bit much. She's just Skyler and I'm just Marlene. Also around our house it was just the two of us. She's all I've had since the death of my husband. I can't lose her now."

"I understand," he said sympathetically. "Believe me, if there is anyone who can find and bring your daughter back safe and sound, it's Addison Black. I'd trust her with my life. I have done that very thing in fact. I'm alive today because of her."

"She saved your life?" Marlene was intrigued now. "Can you

tell me about it, General? Maybe it would help lessen this apprehension I'm feeling."

"First of all you might as well call me Mark, Doc...I mean Marlene. I can't tell you everything of course because pieces of it remain "Eyes Only" to this day, but let's just say hypothetically that there were some troublesome South American islands that my country was involved with. Maybe you could picture an intelligence mission to gather numbers on the opponent's troop strength and weaponry capabilities. It seems to be a routine mission until somewhere along the line inside information is passed. Information that puts almost all the team straight into the hands of a pack of mercenaries sponsored by the opposing government. A pack of very unfriendly mercenaries."

Mark Blithe's jaw clenched slightly at the obviously unpleasant memories, but within a moment he continued. "Know this, on a mission of the sort I'm describing, nothing can be allowed to prevent a successful completion. Nothing. That would include the loss of the rest of your team. The loss of a team isn't acceptable to Addison Black though. Single-handedly and without regard to her personal safety, she secured the release of the team and the...termination...of the mercenaries. Literally I was seconds away from death, but thanks to her I lived. She wouldn't take any credit for that mission either, but they insisted on rewarding someone. A promotion to general and a desk job, it makes me wonder if it was such a great reward after all." He paused here wanting the full importance of his next words to be completely appreciated by Marlene.

"Honestly, it is a rare female that is invited into this branch of government service, but Addison is that special one. She's fearless, inventive, focused and highly skilled. There is nothing she will not do to see your daughter returned safely to you."

Marlene digested the man's words. General Blithe had left no doubt of his implicit faith in the agent.

"Okay then, Mark, I'll have to trust your judgment on this. I just hope Skyler will be alright."

"She will be, Addison will see to it. Now, why don't you let me show you to the secured guest quarters here? You must be exhausted and we may not hear anything for a few hours at least."

"I suppose I could try to rest, but I can't guarantee I'll sleep. You'll let me know if you receive any word, won't you?"

"Of course I will," the general assured her and escorted her to the door. Prior to opening the door he stopped to retrieve a decorative wooden cane she had seen him use before. As he stepped into the corridor he walked with a noticeable limp and when he glanced at the

American he saw Marlene trying politely not to stare. Marlene realized she was watching the general's hobbling gait and reached for a subject.

"Um, Mark, can I ask you something about Agent Black?" At his nod, she continued, "Her eyes?"

A brief flash of alarm crossed the general's face. "I'm glad you didn't mention that while Addison was here, Marlene. She's a little touchy about that subject needless to say."

"I understand," the American said. She hesitated a little, slowing her step for the man who was making his way along rather painfully. He decided to enlighten the woman on the circumstances of his disability.

"You're very kind to pretend I don't have a terrible limp, Marlene, but it's quite all right. It's not a permanent wounding. Though temporary, it's courtesy of an adventure with Addison as well."

"Another hypothetical mission?" Marlene inquired.

"No, a scrum on the rugby pitch two weeks ago. Did I mention Addison **hates** to lose?"

Despite the gravity of her daughter's situation, Marlene had to laugh at that. Mark Blithe was a very nice man she decided and she found herself glad for his company. It was while she was thinking this that a tall man in a white lab coat rushed past them carrying a scruffy looking dog in what appeared to be a diaper.

****

Brodie slammed the door to the office. She had lost control with Doctor Tidwell and the one thing she despised was losing control in any fashion.

"Bitch! Why couldn't she just cooperate? Damn it, this is going to put my questioning behind schedule and I need that information!" Brodie thought about the money already on deposit in her numbered account in the Cayman Islands and knew if there were a screw up, she'd never see the rest of the promised funds. She needed to check in with her superior.

Retrieving the phone from the desk, she punched the pre-set number again. Her superior answered immediately.

"Brodie here. We might be a little longer in obtaining the information you're seeking. The good doctor isn't as meek a mouse as I thought she'd be…No, nothing like that, just a bit of spirit that needed taming." She listened then as a seriously displeased employer explained the consequences of failure.

"I understand. I'll start the interrogation later today…Right, did

38

you find out who they were sending?" As Brodie heard the name a flush crept up the back of her neck and she clenched her free hand into a fist. "Addison Black! Well, isn't that interesting? She's managed to throw a fucking monkey wrench into several of my plans before, but this time it's going to be different. Very different indeed." She disconnected after giving a promise of results in the near future.

Slipping into the chair behind the desk, Brodie thought with anger about the very charming and beautiful agent she figured would already be working on the case. Malice deformed her normally placid looks as she recalled their previous meetings. She had come painfully close to losing everything on several occasions and it was only her ability to cover her tracks that had saved her from being a permanent guest in one of Her Majesty's danker prisons.

"You'll get yours this time, Agent Black, because I'll be one step ahead of you. Don't worry though; I'm a gracious winner. I'll even get a little gift for you, Addison. Hmm, let's see, what would be appropriate for the S.A.S. agent who has everything?"

Pretending to ponder the question thoughtfully she tapped her chin with her index finger. "I've got it! A marvelous gift for Addison! How about one dead American research scientist followed by an international incident because of Agent Black's botched handling of the job? Why Brodie, you clever thing…it's just perfect."

****

Special Operations had its own unique exercise facility for keeping its agents in peak physical condition. From multi-gyms to a wooden dummy for martial arts training, everything was provided for the agents including a luxury tiled locker room. It was into this that Addison had retreated. She escaped for one last hot shower before dressing for her assignment. Sometimes an agent could go up to several months without the comfort of hot water for bathing, so it was Addison's tradition to have a hot shower before she departed on a mission. Once done, the agent padded into the empty locker room and slipped into a practical sports bra and matching panties.

Unzipping the main compartment of her large duffel bag, Addison reached inside the loaded container and pulled out a pair of thick, black combat trousers and a shirt. She held open the trousers and stepped into the legs, pulling them up around her hips. She neglected to fasten the row of buttons as the door to the changing room swung open and Samuel Perkins waltzed inside.

Pinning the man with an expression of faux indignation, Addison pretended to cover her chest. "Don't you know how to knock?"

"Oh, like you have anything I haven't seen before."

Addison swiftly coiled her padded, black shirt and flicked it at the scientist. "You have never seen mine before. Sod off."

Samuel pulled a round magnifying glass from his top pocket and held it up to Addison. He squinted through one eye and whistled. "Wow, through this thing you really do have sizable breasts. **That**, I have **never** seen before."

Swiping the magnifier out of Perkins' hand, Addison peered through the glass at the scientist. "This doesn't even work. It's broken." She gazed neutrally at his enlarged features.

"It certainly is not!" Perkins retorted.

Stepping closer, Addison held the magnifying glass up to the zipper of his pants. "It sure is, take a look at that."

Samuel looked down before realising what the agent was implying. "Okay, okay...!" He took the magnifier from Addison and slipped it back into his pocket. "Anyway, the reason I came in here, apart from letting you know Miss Bakersfield has Spike until I finish here this evening, is that I wanted to remind you to check by before you leave. I have a couple of things I think you may find will come in handy."

"Cool... does it have multi-speeds of vibrating pleasure?" Addison asked as Perkins stepped towards the exit.

"Ha, ha! You wish, Spy Girl!" Perkins backed up towards the exit. "Just you remember to make sure those little suction marks are covered before you leave this place!" Samuel pointed towards several little love bites adorning Addison's body. "At least I see the reason why you weren't there to answer your phone last night!" Perkins wiggled his eyebrows before opening the door.

Addison chuckled as the scientist left the room. Picking up a white tank top she slipped it over her head before shrugging into her black padded shirt. Addison fastened the buttons into place and tucked it into her combat trousers. Finishing the last button on her pants, the agent slipped the first belt into place. To that she added the holsters for her pistols at the back and slipped both Berettas into place. They were already loaded and she placed eight more clips into one leg of her trousers, four in one arm of her shirt and four pouches attached to her belt.

After Addison's quest to obtain a new contact lens, she had stopped by the armoury and loaded up on all the ammunition that she could comfortably carry. This included pistol clips, shotgun shells and ammunition for her H&K submachine gun. She had already taped the magazines together for swifter loading purposes.

Next, Addison slipped into her boots and secured the laces. To one boot she attached a knife and to the other, a Baby Browning pistol. This was smaller and she placed two more clips for that pistol in her other trouser leg pocket. Reaching back into her bag, Addison took out a second belt and wrapped it around her waist. This belt was different as it clipped to her first belt and had straps, almost like elasticised braces, which went over each shoulder. It was a holster specially designed so she could attach her Spas 12 shotgun to her back and submachine gun to her side. Both larger firearms in place, Addison filled a small backpack with a case of shotgun shells – a second case she emptied into the secured pocket of her three quarter length jacket – and bound H&K magazines.

Sitting on a dark wooden bench, Addison leaned her side against the grey wall of the changing room. Ahead of her she could hear the constant drip of a showerhead against the tiled floor. Addison took a deep breath. She felt a familiar flutter in her stomach. It was common for her to feel nerves before a new assignment and this was no exception. However well she performed in the field, apprehension was always present before an assignment. Addison believed it was what kept her alive. If she let her over-confident nature interfere with natural caution, she doubted she would still be alive today. Regardless of that fact, as soon as Addison got started, she appeared fearless.

Removing the remaining items from her duffel bag, Addison place them in either her small backpack or in strategic places upon her body. Once finished, she rose to her feet. Addison knew both General Blithe and Samuel Perkins were waiting for her. She had a flight upon a private military jet that would take her straight into Scotland where a Jeep would be waiting for her to carry out the mission. Slinging the backpack over her shoulder, Addison exited the changing room and headed towards Samuel's laboratory. Her booted footsteps echoed down the empty corridor as she passed several other labs. Each one contained groups of scientists, dressed in attire suitable for the conditions they were working in. Addison stopped by one window and looked in upon a group of three women and one man who were all dressed in bright orange jump suits. She tapped upon the window and waved, as four faces looked her way. Putting up both thumbs she indicated approval of their choice of colourful dress and received varying forms of obscene finger gestures in response. Addison placed her hand over her heart feigning hurt and the four laughed inside the soundproof room before turning back to their project. The four bodies gathered around an unusual metallic, oval object that seemed to be emitting a yellow, non-toxic vapour. Addison wondered what on earth they were up to now. As usual, it wasn't her place to ask questions, but she knew if she did ask them she could be pretty sure of an honest response. Addison was both liked and respected within Special Operations and for that she was privy to a lot of inside information. More information than she possibly should have known.

Samuel Perkins' laboratory was alive with activity. The room was large, about half the size of an aircraft hanger and possibly just as noisy. Scientists and fellow agents stood around the metallic room conversing with varying degrees of excitement. Venturing further, Addison sought out General Blithe. She noticed him standing in the far corner of the room beside Perkins. He stood tall; his arms crossed as he listened to Samuel speak animatedly about an unusual car in front of them. As Addison approached, General Blithe nodded to her in acknowledgement.

"Agent Black, are you prepared?"

"Yes, sir."

"Excellent." Blithe motioned towards the silver convertible in front of him. "What do you think? A completely new kind of vehicle designed by Agent Perkins himself. We begin tests today... as you can see it has attracted a lot of attention already."

Addison looked around the gathering of soldiers and scientists. "So it has. And it looks like I will miss it. So... is this your new brainchild, Perkins? Is this the car that you believe will be able to out-manoeuvre a Formula One racer?"

"Without a doubt, Addison! Can you imagine using one of these in a chase? You could catch anybody! I start remote control tests within the hour."

"And this is what you wanted to show me?"

"Ah, no. Actually I have two things for you." Reaching into his lab coat pocket Samuel pulled out a black watch. His smile was broad as he laid it out upon his hand for Addison. "What do you think?"

The agent seemed unimpressed as she answered him dryly. "Sam, it's another wristwatch. It's always another watch. What does this one do? Shoot a web like Spiderman?"

Samuel continued to grin. "Actually no." He moved closer and began instructing her on the gadget's functions. "As you can see, this looks like a normal watch, but if you switch this button here..." Samuel turned a small, silver catch. "It becomes a heat detection device." Addison watched as the screen turned red and the second hand of the watch began to rotate at a faster rate as many dots flashed on the circular face. "Any warm bodied presence within one hundred feet of you is detected by this. Pretty good, huh?" He handed it to Addison with a proud smile.

Wrapping the watch around her wrist the dark haired woman nodded, obviously impressed. "I have to admit it, Sam. This could be a very handy little device."

"Sure could." Next Samuel pulled two silver pens from his top pocket and handed them over to Addison.

"Why do I get the feeling I shouldn't click the top here?"

General Blithe, who had been quietly inspecting the car, now spoke. "Those were my idea. Imagine the power of a single stick of dynamite in a handy, everyday instrument and there you have the Sparky 2000. Press the cap and you have four seconds to run."

"Cool!" Addison studied the design. "Let's hope you don't get these mixed up with the ones you guys use to write our pay cheques every month, huh?" She slipped the pens into a pocket on her jacket's right arm. "Is that everything?"

"It is." The General handed Addison several sheets of yellow paper as he took Addison to the side and spoke quietly. "Memorise these on the plane up to Scotland. It contains more information on Skyler Tidwell that you can use to prove you are there to help her if need be. You also have the coordinates of your vehicle that's already at the airbase waiting for you. The usual packet of information has been provided. It is still unclear why Skyler Tidwell was abducted so while you scout the area, we will be doing some detective work on this end. There will be a radio in your Jeep to contact us, so use it. I mean that, Addison! My gut instinct is saying we have trouble brewing. I want you to make sure it is neutralised before you return. If you have to put Miss Tidwell on a plane and remain in Scotland to do it, then that is what you must do. Understand?"

"Yes, sir."

Mark Blithe nodded. "Good." He motioned to the far side of the laboratory where a uniformed officer stood at ease, waiting. "Corporal Sanderson is waiting to transport you to your jet." He held out his hand and Addison shook it firmly. "See you later."

"See you later, Sir." Addison nodded towards Perkins. "Later, Sam."

"See you later, Addison," Perkins replied.

It was common practice never to say 'good-bye' to a fellow soldier when they headed off on assignment. They felt it was bad luck to use such a phrase that had 'permanent' overtones. Their assignments were dangerous and usually life threatening. In just the same way Macbeth was never mentioned in the theatre, so a farewell was never uttered for fear it would be the last time you would see a person. The death of a fellow agent or soldier was a tangible blow to each remaining operative and as such, no lasting goodbye was ever uttered.

Securing the backpack upon her shoulder, Addison left to begin her mission. Deep within she began to feel her excitement building. The thrill of the hunt, the adrenalin of combat, this was what she did best and this was what she lived for. No matter what the cost, Addison would secure the safety of Skyler Tidwell and solve the puzzle of why she was taken in the first place. If there was one thing Addison would never accept – it was defeat.

Chapter 5

Flying had long been a great passion of Addison's. From the first moment she sat at the controls of a helicopter during her time in the military, she was hooked. The feeling of solitary liberation she gained from soaring up in the billowing clouds was something she had never experienced before. During her free time, Addison earned her glider pilot's license and logged many hours soaring above the French Alps, enraptured by their beauty and overwhelming presence.

On the flight to Scotland, however, Addison was the only passenger in one of the military's British Aerospace 125 business jets. It was a plane that seated up to fourteen passengers, but with eight of the seats removed she had plenty of room in the small aircraft. The agent took advantage of that fact by reclining her seat all the way back and closing her eyes. The only sound to penetrate her hearing was that of the plane's twin engines.

Living the life she did, dealing with the constant spontaneity, Addison had the ability to sleep anytime, anywhere. She often joked that she slept like a cat, able to nap at any desired moment in time. With an hour before the aircraft would land, Addison drifted into a light slumber.

For the most part, Addison rarely dreamed and never during a brief sleep. If she did, she never remembered. The ex-Special Air Services soldier was happy to keep it that way. Many of the incidents she had seen in her line of work were enough to haunt her waking hours; she was content for that not to pass over into her sleep as well. The kind of work she did was not for the slight of heart. Operatives chosen for the M.I.5's Special Ops branch were carefully selected. Not only were their physical skills a matter of consideration, but their psychological capabilities as well. If the slightest question hung over your head, it was a sword of Damocles and your rejection would be immediate. Addison was good; she was the best. Her psychological strength was as dominant as her physical abilities. She did have one downfall, however, that had not been brought to light. Addison had a heart. It was a beating zest for life that made her grieve a little for each life lost. She felt no guilt in her actions though. Addison was, after all, one of the 'good guys,' but deep down inside, when she was back at home, wandering the lone cliff tops with Spike, Addison mourned the lives she had taken. She was a human being after all.

The expected sound of a disembodied voice woke Addison swiftly. Dark eyes blinked open. It was the pilot's voice informing Addison that the plane was soon to be landing. She didn't need to be told to assume the correct landing position, it was generally expected she would do so.

Addison readjusted her seat and re-buckled the belt. Covering her mouth as she yawned, the agent looked out of the plane's window. She could clearly see the expanse of Scotland's picturesque landscape. Around her she saw the Highlands, while to her left she spotted a wide area of level land. This was to be their landing site. Nothing else marred the landscape except for a single four-wheel drive Jeep, especially built for the rough and rocky terrain of the highlands.

The Hawker Siddeley aircraft took a steep turn to the left as it began landing procedures. Addison continued to watch the ground below as it came ever closer. She folded her arms. It had been a long time since she had last been to Scotland. Her job had taken her to the furthest points of the earth, from the Falkland Islands to under the Arctic Ocean. She had seen an awful lot in her thirty-four years, but one thing she enjoyed was the fresh air and beautiful scenery of Scotland. Addison once convinced Samuel to accompany her on a rock-climbing excursion in the northern Highlands, but he had complained about how cold he was for the three days they were there. He had even made comments about the air being too cool and clean. Addison made a mental note that if she ever took him again, she would pack extra warm clothes and a canister of central London's vehicle exhaust fumes – just in case.

There was hardly a jolt as Addison's plane touched down smoothly. It ran along the open field at a decreasing speed, approaching a vehicle and its sole occupant who had been patiently waiting for Addison to arrive. In standard procedure, somebody would always be waiting for Addison with her means of transport. Any final information was given and then the agent was on her way. Heading out into the unknown was the moment she most looked forward to. She never knew what was around the next corner. Addison was ready and raring to take on any challenge heading her way.

As the engines died, Addison unfastened her seatbelt and rose to her feet. Grabbing her backpack and the weapons she had removed during her flight, she opened the airtight door and readied the steps. From the camouflaged four-wheel drive Jeep she saw a single body exit the driver's side and casually approach. Dressed in civilian attire, Addison only just recognized Sergeant Quinton Zimmerman, a rendezvous officer for the M.I.5, who still worked up at the Marine Barracks in Arbroath.

Quinton Zimmerman smiled as he spied Addison. His crooked bottom teeth and chipped upper tooth did nothing to mar the traditionally handsome blonde hair, blue-eyed looks. They had served together in the Marines and had become good friends during that time. "Agent Black," Quinton checked his watch, "Right on time... like I would have expected anything else."

"What's with the formalities?" Addison asked, as she took Zimmerman's offered hand and pulled him into a hug. "Please don't tell me the military life has finally made a gentleman of you? I thought we agreed that would never happen to us?" Addison pulled back and smirked.

Quinton laughed. "I fight it every day."

"That's my boy," the agent replied with faux pride. She approached the Jeep and opened the driver's door, slinging her equipment into the passenger seat. "Any final orders from the General?"

With a nod, Quinton pulled a small communication radio from his back pocket. "Yes, just one. General Blithe says use it or face the consequences."

"Which are?" Addison asked as a mischievous smile played around her lips.

"Something about you being Santa at the next Christmas party."

The smile fell from Addison's lips. "Threat received and understood." She took the radio from Quinton and pushed it into her pocket. "Whatever happened to the good old days of public floggings? That is what I want to know," Addison groused as she climbed into the Jeep and shook Quinton's hand. "See you later, mate. We will have to get together for another poker night."

"Strip poker?" Zimmerman enquired.

Addison winked. "If you're lucky."

"Good enough for me." Quinton stepped back as Addison shut

the door.

Addison turned to check the back of the jeep finding a few extra supplies, a canister of fuel, a camouflage jacket and several container items. Looking back, she waved as Quinton Zimmerman boarded the plane she had just left and closed the door. With the key already in the ignition, Addison started the Jeep's engine. It purred into life. Dipping the clutch, she placed the vehicle into first gear and started moving. A map had already been provided for her and was open on the dashboard. It was unnecessary as the agent owned her own digital appliance, but that piece of gadgetry was classified and owned by M.I.5, Special Ops. Checking her co-ordinates, Addison turned the Jeep towards a long narrow road and set off on her mission to rescue Skyler Tidwell.

Thumbs tapping upon the steering wheel, a song fluttered into Addison's brain and she was helpless to resist singing.

"Oh the Deadwood stage is a rolling on over the plains
Blah, blah, lalalalalalalalalaalalalaaaaaaa...
Beautiful land, no time to delay
So whip crack away, whip crack away, whip crack away!"

Suddenly remembering the bulge of the radio in her pocket, the agent realized she should call into Headquarters and confirm her position. She pulled out the small, grey device.

"Come in HQ, this is … Santa Claus … do you read me?"

Addison waited a moment before her call was received.

"Roger, Black, this is HQ." The female voice belonged to Meredith Nicks, Chief Officer for Communications. "We receive you. I am patching your transmission through to General Blithe's secured line for conference... over."

"Roger that." Addison waited for the general to speak. She put the Jeep into sixth gear as she sped along the empty road. She estimated it would be a two-hour drive to her next destination, weather and ground permitting.

"Hello, Santa," came the general's mirth filled voice.

"You are just plain mean," Addison replied. "You don't really want me to be Santa this year, do you?" Addison remembered what had happened to last year's Santa for the Military's Christmas party. After getting a little worse for wear the man had been stripped naked, tied up with a selection of colourful bows and deposited unconscious under the hotel Christmas tree. They were all staying at the inn for a long weekend. It has been quite a shock for the cleaner the next morning.

"If you don't use this radio I will put you forward, yes."

Sighing, Addison relented. "Okay, okay... this thing will never leave my side. Satisfied?"

"Yes, thank you."

"What else did you want?"

"Oh nothing," Blithe said. "I just wanted to make sure we were clear on the whole issue of communication. You know there could be a lot at stake if this isn't resolved, Addison."

"I know, sir. I'll contact you whenever possible."

"That is all I ask. Thank you. Over and out... Santa."

The line went dead and Addison chucked. "He always has to have the last word." She smirked wickedly. "I guess he still hasn't gotten over waking up to a shrieking maid and pine needles sticking up his butt last year!"

****

Skyler woke up to the sound of the door to her room being unlocked and opened quickly. An armed guard blocked the doorway, now ready for an escape attempt. He needn't have bothered. The American was in no shape to make another attempt to get away. She ached in places she barely realized she could ache. Nothing was broken but that didn't seem to make much difference, Skyler was effectively hobbled.

Eyes shifting left and right, the guard seemed satisfied and stepped aside to admit Brodie into the room. She carried a tray with breakfast items and a small basin. Walking to the table near the bed, she deposited the items there without ever taking her eyes off the American.

"Good morning, Doctor Tidwell. I hope you slept well," Agnes said with a smirk.

"Actually I was a little uncomfortable last night. Must have been the mattress," Skyler returned.

Brodie gave a small laugh at that. "You have spunk, Doctor. Usually that is a trait to be admired, but I hope you have come to realize that spunk is a potentially painful thing to have when you deal with me."

Skyler rose from the bed, suppressing a groan as she did so, not wanting to give Brodie the satisfaction of hearing her discomfort. She shuffled to the table and dropped into one of the two chairs there. Brodie slid the tray in front of her and the delicious aroma of hot oatmeal and thick slabs of crusty toast tickled Skyler's senses. She glanced up at Brodie in suspicion.

"Go on, it's quite safe I assure you," her captor stated evenly.

Skyler picked up a spoon, dipped into the steaming food and closed her eyes in appreciation of the thick, fluffy mixture. "The locals know their porridge, don't they?"

Skyler's eyes opened at Brodie's words and her line of sight was drawn to the small plastic basin. Brodie took the basin to the small sink near the pull down toilet. "Some soap, a toothbrush and toothpaste for your use. Don't waste them, you wont get more." Brodie returned to the table and sat in the chair opposite Skyler, watching her eat for a moment.

"You will be allowed time to finish your breakfast and refresh yourself then I will return to have that conversation I promised you before. I hope you will be in a cooperative mood, Doctor, and not force me to repeat our little lesson of yesterday. You have cost me valuable time and I'm not in a forgiving mood today."

Skyler made no reply, just bit into the warm toast, enjoying the texture on her tongue. She felt sure Brodie had something else to tell her because she made no move to leave.

"It will no doubt have crossed your mind that by now the alarm would have been raised and that the authorities would be searching for you," Brodie began. Skyler's curiosity was piqued, as that was exactly what she had been thinking.

"Well, you would be correct in that assumption." Brodie paused here and the blonde felt an unmistakable "but" coming on. She was not disappointed.

"But, we are not unprepared for that occasion. Just in case you foolishly think you should withhold information from me because of your imminent release I will tell you we know everything about their efforts. Even now we know the government has dispatched one of their top agents to locate you. Agent Addison Black is an old friend and someone who is owed a final payment on an old debt. We have tangled before but this time the outcome will be different. British Intelligence, what a curious oxymoron! I welcome the challenge, Doctor, because we will be prepared for it."

Skyler watched the Irish woman as she spoke and was very glad she wasn't this Agent Black, whoever he was. There was definitely bad blood between Brodie and the agent.

Brodie stood and moved away from the table. "You are not dealing with amateurs here, we have sources you could not imagine. You will not be liberated until we decide you will be. Tell us what we want to know, it is your only hope of leaving here alive."

So, she finally said it Skyler thought. *Talk about the Gemini project or die. What are you working on, Mom?* She looked at Brodie

50

with what she hoped was a thoughtful expression on her face.

"I see how hospitable you can be if I do something that doesn't set well with you, but what's in it for me if I help you? You have to realize I could never work in this field again once I compromised my position by giving you what you want. I would need some financial consideration. You know how important this information is," Skyler said. *At least I hope you do because I don't have a friggin' clue.*

Brodie stared at her as if trying to determine the honesty of the words. "Certainly, Doctor, I will check on what can be arranged. I'm glad to see that you have decided to be practical about the situation." The redhead leaned over the table and ran a fingertip softly down Skyler's cheek. "At least I hope you are being practical and that this isn't a ploy to gain a little time." Brodie turned her finger and ran the nail down the same place she had just caressed and extended it to lightly slash across Skyler's throat. "It would be a pity to have to mar such a lovely face."

She stood abruptly and moved toward the door. "Who knows, Professor Tidwell, perhaps when all this unpleasant business is concluded we could get to know each other better, maybe even become…friends." She knocked sharply on the door, spoke in Gaelic and turned to rake Skyler's body with a look that made the American feel somehow naked and dirty. "Yes, very intimate friends." The door opened behind her and Brodie exited.

Alone in the room, Skyler shuddered in revulsion. *A woman, yes… that woman? I'd rather swallow my own tongue.* Realizing the tongue in question was beginning to feel a little fuzzy, Skyler slowly got up from the table. Moving wasn't quite the agony it had first been and she made her way to the small sink without too much difficulty. Turning the faucet on she waited as the water warmed. She unwrapped the hotel-sized soap and wished there was a mirror in the room. *On second thought maybe that's not such a great idea, God only knows what I look like.*

She brushed her teeth and washed her face, feeling much better afterward. She glanced back to the door wondering how much time she had before Brodie reappeared and what she was going to do when the redhead did.

****

In the office, Brodie toyed with the knife she had pulled again from her desk as she talked on the cell phone.

"Yes, I understand. That's perfectly clear. No, there will be no

51

further delays." The other party hung up and the redhead clenched her jaw in frustration. There would be no money for Professor Tidwell unless it came out of the money Brodie had been promised. One thing Brodie did not do well was share and under no circumstances did she share money. *Sorry, Doctor, you'll have to do this with other means of persuasion.* A fly buzzed by her head, breaking her concentration, but reminding Brodie of another annoyance. Holding the cell phone in her left hand she punched in the now familiar number.

As the connection was made she came directly to the point. "What's happening there?" She listened without comment as information was passed.

"When did she leave?" Receiving the answer, Brodie consulted her watch and calculated how far her nemesis might have gotten in the allotted time. "Damn! Well, it makes no difference, even if Addison can find us she'll be too late." She broke the connection and decided it was time to get back to the doctor and begin the process of extracting the information that was required.

"Alas, Addison, by the time you get here, and I have no doubt you will, it will sadly be too late to save the late Doctor Marlene Tidwell. Of course I'll be here to greet you and I have such a welcome planned." With an almost invisible flick of her wrist, Brodie sent the knife hurtling toward the far wall where it stuck deeply into the plaster and neatly divided the unsuspecting fly in half.

****

Skyler had freshened up as much as was possible given the limited resources at her disposal. She sat at the table waiting for Brodie's return and hoped her new plan would work out. *Delay, delay, delay until this Agent Blackjack or whatever gets here. The way my luck is going he'll be more like Inspector Clouseau than James Bond. I need to be ready to try and make a break for it again, even if it kills me.* Skyler shifted on the chair and knew that a move to leave might very well lead to her death, but figured the redhead's revelation of earlier meant she was dead anyway. *Brodie is bound to realize soon that I don't know anything about Project Gemini. Or will she?* Thoughts began to fly through the scholar's head.

The opening of the door interrupted her plans. As earlier, the armed guard scanned the room first and relaxed after spotting Skyler sitting meekly at the table. He stepped aside and nodded at Brodie who was standing behind him holding several tablets of paper and a box of pencils in her hand. Moving past the guard, Brodie entered the room.

"Bad news, Doctor Tid..." The redhead's words were cut short by her scream as her right foot slid completely out from underneath her. The tablets in her hand didn't allow her to reach out and grab the door for balance and her left foot followed the right. She flipped backward and landed hard on the ground, striking her head on the painted concrete floor. Skyler never moved as the momentarily stunned guard recovered enough to move to Brodie's side and check his superior. She was quite unconscious.

He glared at Skyler who merely held her hands palm up and shrugged her shoulders, portraying the perfect picture of innocence. The guard kept his gun trained on the prisoner as he used his free arm to pull Brodie from the room. As the door shut and locked, Skyler couldn't keep a smile from her face and let out a quiet whoop of victory.

Paybacks are a bitch, aren't they Brodie? She thought as she tossed the bar of soap in the air and moved to clean up its residue from the floor. *Poor baby, I guess she didn't know most accidents happen in the home.* Skyler used a discarded towel to scrub away the last vestiges of soap then she gathered up the tablets and pencils.

Taking them back to the table, Skyler started fleshing out her next plan in her mind. When she had most of it clear in her mind she began to write. Line after line was filled and she stopped only long enough to think, *you better hurry up Agent Black, I can't keep thinking of things forever.* She turned her attention back to the tablet and began writing once again.

Chapter 6

It was obvious the further up and into the Highlands Addison drove, the colder it became. Clouds hung low in the sky and the agent had been driving through them for the past hour of her journey. She had been given clear information on the location of the abandoned mines, so she had a good idea of where to begin. There were four entrances. Each was connected by a maze of underground tunnels. It had been over a hundred years since the mines had been closed down. Records stated that some of the conduit tunnels had become unstable and after a serious accident in which over one hundred men were buried alive, the mines were permanently abandoned. It was, however, presumed there were still rich deposits of coal within their caverns.

With one hand guiding the steering wheel, Addison rechecked her map. She was almost a mile away from the southern entrance. It was time to hide the Jeep, as the rest of her journey would be on foot. Scanning the terrain for an ideal place to hide the camouflaged vehicle was not a problem. Addison spotted a small outcropping of coniferous trees to her left. They were shaped like two sides of a triangle and lightly cloaked by a mist of cloud, providing adequate cover for the Jeep.

"Perfect," Addison mumbled. She turned the vehicle towards the trees that reminded her of bare Christmas trees. They swayed in a firm breeze that drastically increased the cold atmosphere.

"Why couldn't she have been taken and held on some remote tropical island?" Addison steered into the tree's cover. "I much prefer working in a warmer climate." Turning off the Jeep's engine, Addison pulled the key from its ignition. It slid out with a metallic 'clink'. "I can think of a couple of more exciting ways to obtain rigid nipples, that's for sure."

As Addison opened the vehicle's door a howling wind greeted her. Its biting force rushed over the undulating crests of hills, rustling through crops of overgrown heather. Above her, the sky seemed indistinguishable through the grey mist of accumulated clouds. Evening was closing in and the temperature was rapidly dropping. Addison was positive that as night arrived it would dip below freezing; a weather condition she most despised while working.

Climbing from the Jeep, Addison closed the door. A resounding slam echoed over the hills and disappeared into the foggy distance. Addison looked around her, unable to see more than thirty feet ahead. An almost ghostly silence surrounded her, only fractured by the sporadic gasps of wind. From high above, an unexpected clap of thunder rumbled through the sky. Addison looked up towards the grey atmosphere.

"Typical!"

Striding around to the back of the camouflaged vehicle, Addison swung open the boot door. Quickly she reached inside and pulled her equipment closer. Venturing further, she pulled the backpack and weapons from the passenger seat. Opening her bag she added some packed ration food, a set of basic tools and spare combat jacket into the remaining space.

Once loaded with all necessary items, the agent closed and locked the Jeep. Another clash of thunder ricocheted through the sky above her and Addison detected the change in the air. Rain wasn't far away. Around her she heard the squawks of unseen birds as they fled the open space in search of shelter. Casting a cursory glance over the electronic map and compass, Addison set off to the northeast. She made sure her radio was switched off; she couldn't risk detection at this point.

She had been walking for almost half an hour when something captured her attention. She stopped suddenly. Her vision was severely limited due to the increasing fog and low clouds upon the highlands, so Addison had to rely upon her other senses. There was a particular scent in the air that seemed familiar to her. It was the aroma of cheap cigars, the kind her father used to smoke. Addison knew she was nearing the southern entrance of the mine. The agent proceeded with care. Using increased stealth and expertise, Addison followed the acrid scent in silence. It wasn't long before the aroma was accompanied by voices. Addison frowned as she crouched behind a large boulder. She could identify just two men, but what perplexed her was the fact they were speaking in Gaelic. Addison was familiar with many languages and was fluent in seven, but Gaelic was not one of them.

Kneeling close to the boulder, Addison looked over the grey stone. She studied the two men standing on either side of the mine's entrance. They were both dressed in Air Force blue uniforms and carried decent weapons. Each man held an Uzi submachine gun and had a high-powered pistol strapped to their right thigh. It was obvious to her that these men had some form of military or advanced arms training.

Addison watched them as they conversed and laughed with each other. The agent was biding her time. She hoped that when the rain came it would encourage both men to seek shelter. Addison knew in any operation such as this, at some point the alarm would be raised to an intruder's presence, but she wanted it to be when she was ready.

It took only five minutes for the rain to start and during that time Addison had tried to assess Skyler's situation. She knew Agnes Brodie was definitely not a second rate 'wannabe' in the world of terrorism. The armed men guarding the mine's southern entrance were testament to that. The taller of the two had used a remote, handheld radio to keep in contact with four different people during those brief minutes. All but one of the conversations was in Gaelic. The operation was well planned. It seemed that every so often each soldier on watch would call in to maintain open links and assurance of presence at station. During the one English spoken conversation, Addison had discovered Agnes Brodie was actually present within the mines. A slow smile of satisfaction spread across her lips. Addison had unresolved issues with the Irishwoman and she was more than willing to bring those matters to a head. However, Skyler Tidwell's safety was her primary consideration.

The rain started as a gentle patter. It did, thankfully for Addison, quickly gather speed into a heavy downpour. As the large droplets fell upon her head, the agent watched and waited. She was a little annoyed to see that only one of the guards entered the mine for shelter, but then considered it a good fate. It meant the retreating guard was leaving the post completely and only one would remain. It also happened to be the guard who held the radio. With only one man remaining, Addison realised it was in Skyler's best interest for her to get into the mine as soon as possible. That meant taking out the first guard.

Addison studied the mine's entrance. It was a wooden framed hatch, built vertically into the large grassy mound. Formulating her plan, Addison stepped out and around from the large boulder while the guard was facing the opposite direction. She jumped up onto a higher boulder on the hill and further still onto an even higher rock before leaping across and vaulting off one final flat stone. Addison jumped through the air and landed no more than a foot away from the guard. Hearing the movement, he spun around only to find his jaw connecting with a solid punch. As he stumbled backwards Addison struck him again, breaking his nose and then spinning around to deliver a roundhouse kick to the side of his head.

He collapsed, unconscious, to the ground.

Rolling her eyes, the ebony haired agent ran a hand through her wet, shaggy hair. Knowing she couldn't leave the guard in view she grabbed his legs and began to haul him behind a rock.

"You know..." Addison stated as she dropped his legs and unloaded the Uzi, throwing its ammunition into the distance. "If your mates are as easy as you, this will be a breeze." She threw the machine gun in the opposite direction and then pulled his pistol from its holster. Addison checked the clip and found it fully loaded. She slipped it into her remaining empty pocket. As a flash of lightening lit up the sky, Addison knew it was time she entered the mine.

****

It seemed apparent that the mine had undergone some major alterations. Addison wondered how long it had taken Agnes Brodie to secure the narrow passages and what had been her original intention for doing so? Had the abduction of Marlene Tidwell been a long standing and highly thought out plan? Who else was involved in this and more importantly, why?

Addison walked cautiously down the narrow, dugout passageway. Wooden beams reinforced the structure and along each side of the wall were recently installed, electric light fittings. They brightened up the underground tunnel considerably, though she supposed there was nothing that could be done about the dank aroma of the stagnant and sweet moist soil.

With her H&K set to burst mode, Addison kept to one side of the tunnel, the submachine gun pointing ahead as she approached a single door. On closer inspection Addison realised it was in fact an elevator. Releasing the gun to her side, Addison took a large chisel ended screwdriver from her backpack and pried the door open. She didn't want to electronically open the elevator in case it captured unwanted attention.

The shaft door separated in the middle and opened smoothly. Bending to her knees, Addison wedged the screwdriver into the bottom of the door and jammed it open. Taking a small but powerful flashlight from a clip on her belt, Addison shone it into the shaft. There was at least a thirty-foot straight drop to the top of the elevator's roof and it seemed the only passage to take. Half way down the drop, there was another shaft, but it was boarded up, Addison noted, from the inside!

Placing the torch between her teeth, the agent rose to her feet. With a light jump she leapt silently onto the lift's centre cable. It was a sturdy metal pulley designed to lift the elevator's weight. Feeling her muscles strain against the material of her shirt, Addison began lowering her body down the lift shaft.

The agent was slow and deathly silent. The only noise that greeted her ears was the sound of her own controlled breathing. It didn't take her long to reach the top of the lift. Addison stepped quietly onto the metal roof. She knelt silently and listened for any nearby sounds or voices. There was nothing. Confident the area was clear, Addison released the roof hatch. It lowered down into the lift, away from Addison. She leaned forward and looked through the compartment and out into a narrow passageway. That too was bathed in artificial light. Thankfully, it was empty. Holding on to the edge of the hatch, Addison leaned upside down and slipped into the lift. She flipped over and landed squarely on her feet. Readying her H&K, Addison stepped into enemy territory.

The first notable difference in this lower tunnel was the air quality. It seemed a lot thicker and a little less tolerable to breathe. The agent had no idea how miners had spent entire days down in places such as this, and in much worse conditions. Addison had been potholing for leisure twice, but it had never felt like this. It was as though the souls of all the men who had died so many years ago, lingered still.

"Okay, Skyler Tidwell," Addison mumbled. "Let's get you and get the hell out of this ancient grave."

****

The door to Skyler's room burst open with such force that the knob slammed into the shoddy concrete wall behind it. Skyler winced at the sudden noise and though she didn't look up from the writing tablet immediately, she prepared herself for the outburst she felt sure was to follow.

When no outburst was forthcoming she hazarded a glance toward the door. Brodie stood on the other side of the threshold, inspecting the portal closely. Satisfied there were no further perils to impede her progress into the room, she moved toward the scholar with a determined stride. Now attired in olive drab fatigues, Brodie resembled every inch of what she was, a heartless mercenary.

Brodie maintained a neutral expression on her face as she approached the table where Skyler sat, but her eyes gave away the fury within. Reaching out to the scientist, Brodie grabbed a handful of blonde hair and pulled backward forcefully. Skyler shrieked out in pain as her scalp was used to force her face up to within inches of a furious and deadly redhead.

"I don't know how you pulled that off, Doctor, but nobody plays Agnes Brodie for a fool. I've taken out people for less than that and as much as I want that information, I won't hesitate to kill you if you try anything like that again." Brodie punctuated her threat with the appearance of a large knife with a wickedly gleaming blade. She traced the cold metal slowly down Skyler's face and under her chin where it moved across her throat.

"Of course there are worse things than just dying outright," she murmured. "It would be such a pity to mar your lovely face, but don't push me, Doctor Tidwell, because you will find that it wouldn't bother me in the least to punish you in that fashion." Skyler trembled a little then, but it had less to do with Brodie's words than the glimmer of excitement she saw in her eyes. Brodie would not only disfigure or kill her with ease, she would enjoy it as she was doing it.

"I don't know what brought this on, Brodie," Skyler said, "but I thought we were going to work together on this. I thought we were talking about you arranging a financial arrangement for me in return for my cooperation. Maybe your accident made you forget?" Brodie released Skyler's hair and her head bobbed forward with the lack of traction. The redhead straightened up and sneered down at her captive. The American could only hope her face showed the innocence she was trying to project. Brodie stared at the blonde and Skyler knew she had to pull her last ace out of her sleeve.

"I mean, here I was, not sure if you were terribly injured or not and yet to show my good faith I started working on the information as you requested." Skyler pulled the writing tablet closer to her so Brodie could see what was written there. Skyler was about to take her last chance. If Brodie had any scientific background she was sunk and she knew it. She barely breathed as the redhead scanned the papers.

"What is all this?" Brodie questioned. "I can't make heads or tails of it." Skyler almost giggled in relief, but schooled her features. She cleared her throat and took on a scholarly tone as she said, "What is it? Well, obviously it is the heart and soul of Project Gemini. I thought you would have been more familiar with my work." Brodie looked uncomfortable with the criticism and Skyler decided to try to intimidate her with as much scientific babble as she could muster.

"You see this formula here?" Skyler pointed to a long and complicated chemical reaction written out in the proper symbols. "This is the basic science of the project. Without this, the rest of the work would be useless." Skyler could say this with a straight face because the very impressive first diagram was the Krebs cycle. The nine step Krebs cycle was a basic component of cellular metabolism and something she had been forced to memorize in her Microbiology class. Skyler was sure her mother would be working on something in her chosen field of Biology and there was nothing more basic in Biology than the Krebs cycle. She could tell Brodie was fascinated with the intricate circular diagram she had drawn. She pressed this advantage.

"Now here is the beginning of the whole thing, the catalyst to the project as it were." Skyler pointed to a string of interconnected letters.

```
    H                    H
    |                    |
  H-C---- XANTHINE --- C-H
    |         |          |
    H         |          H
  H-C-H
    |
    H
```

She could tell Brodie had no clue that the formula was merely the diagram of a molecule of caffeine, a substance that Skyler had used many mornings as a catalyst to get her butt out of bed.

Turning to the final page of her renderings, Skyler showed Brodie a piece of paper filled from top to bottom with chemical formulas and reactions. "The discovery of this process was a particularly sweet victory," Skyler noted, adding a tone of scientific pride to her voice. It should have been sweet, for on that paper was the chemical formulas for every ingredient in a chocolate chip cookie that she could recall.

"This is more like it," Brodie beamed. "I knew you would see the wisdom of cooperation. Cooperation with me will prove to be very beneficial." Her voice lowered, "Cooperation with me will prove to be very pleasurable." The frankly lustful look that showed in Brodie's eyes made Skyler want to squirm in disgust, but she managed to feign approval of the redhead's interest.

"Well you've managed to convince me that it's best that I work with you rather than resist you," Skyler murmured.

A licentious smirk crossed Brodie's features. "Many women have found resistance to me to be futile, but believe me, working with me will be worth it." Without warning Brodie grabbed Skyler's face between her hands in an agonizingly tight grip. "I've always wanted to 'play doctor' for real," she said as she lowered her mouth to crush painfully against the American's. Skyler forced herself not to react violently to the brutish kiss even when Brodie's tongue invaded her mouth and ravaged rather than explored.

The mercenary's hand dropped to Skyler's breast and squeezed hard. The blonde moaned when the squeezing touched an area already bruised by Brodie's previous beating. Agnes smiled as she pulled back from the forced kiss, mistaking Skyler's pain filled groan for passion.

"Too bad I don't have time to play at this moment, but as I said to you earlier, I can't make heads or tails of your work." She lifted from the table the papers Skyler had written. "I do know someone who will understand it though. You will forgive me if I don't trust you, Doctor, but you need to realize something. I don't trust anyone." She chuckled at her own feeble attempt at humor as she straightened and moved with the papers toward the door.

"Don't worry, Professor Tidwell, when I receive faxed confirmation that this is indeed credible work on your behalf, I'll be back and we can resume exploring the pleasurable aspects of a partnership." The Irishwoman rapped sharply on the door and it opened immediately. Stopping just short of leaving the room she turned back to her captive.

"Of course, if you're trying to trick me or have been less than completely honest with me, I'll return also, but in that case we'll be exploring the far less pleasant aspects of your pain threshold." Brodie's smile was cold as she left the room, slamming the door behind her.

At the door's closing Skyler moved as quickly as possible to the small sink where she leaned over and lost the contents of her stomach. Rinsing her mouth and scrubbing her face with a small rough cloth, she removed the last traces of Brodie's assault.

Closing her eyes and taking a deep shaky breath, Skyler realized her last gamble wasn't going to pay off. She had run out of options and it was only a matter of time before Brodie uncovered her ruse.

"Where are you, Agent Black? Where the hell are you?" She moved back to the table and dropped heavily into the chair as despair washed over her again.

****

It was the north and western parts of the mine that had caved in. That, fortunately for Addison, left her with only the southern and eastern areas to search. It was highly unlikely Skyler Tidwell was being held in the lowest level of the mine. That was, at the time, still under construction and was the trigger that had caused the collapse of the north and western caverns.

Pacing down the narrow trench, Addison turned a corner. She stopped suddenly as a cough alerted her to another presence. Addison moved up against the right wall and waited. Another man, wearing the same blue uniform, emerged from a framed doorway ahead to the right and disappeared into the opposite wooden enforced passageway. He was armed yet carried a newspaper in his left hand. Addison followed him into what was clearly a makeshift bathroom. It was cold, dark and the aroma was less than pleasant.

Addison lowered her weapon back to her side and released it. "Excuse me?"

The man spun around to find Addison smiling up at him. His expression was one of confusion.

"You wouldn't be a love and tell me where I could find Marlene Tidwell, would you?"

Outraged, the guard pulled out his gun, aiming it at the soldier's head. "So you must be the Addison Black that Miss Brodie has been speaking of."

Addison shrugged. "Well, I don't like to brag..."

"Oh man, have you just made one huge mistake!" The overly confident man, who Addison had already identified as the one who had been standing guard at the southern entrance, laughed. "She knew you were coming, you know. She has just reinforced the men ten fold." He aimed his pistol lower. "You ain't ever gonna see the light of day again."

Addison pouted. "Does that mean no directions?"

"Only to the afterlife, lady."

"Well thanks," Addison grinned. The friendly gesture didn't reach her eyes. "But I haven't finished in this life yet."

Completely taking the stunned guard by surprise, Addison kicked the gun out of his hand. It skidded along the gravelled ground and hit a makeshift wall. As the man turned back, Addison slipped a hand to her back and drew a pistol on him.

"Want to play round two? Do you think you can remove this from my hand before I pull the trigger?"

For her answer, Addison received a pair of hands held high above the guard's head in surrender.

"That's good." Addison stepped closer. "Now get to your knees."

The guard did as he was told and Addison stood behind him. "One last time. Where is Marlene Tidwell?"

"Why don't you go fuck yourself?" was his only response.

Addison laughed. "Sure, I'd do a much better job than you ever could." And with that Addison sent her pistol slamming down onto the back of the guard's head. He collapsed to the floor.

Addison stood over the limp body. "And just for the record... I never make mistakes."

It didn't take Addison long to hide the body. Slipping uniformed trousers down his legs she deposited the unconscious form upon the toilet, locking the door and climbing over the temporary partition.

Once again finding herself in the narrowly dug tunnel, Addison ventured further into the earth. She thought about the guard's words, wondering whether they were true. She would have considered it a bluff except he knew within an instant just who she was. If they knew of her mission to rescue the presumed Marlene Tidwell, then Brodie's plans may have changed. That could bode dangerously unpredictable for Skyler. Addison was at least glad for the fact that it seemed they were as yet unaware they had the wrong person. Knowing now that she had to act faster, Addison readied herself. Taking the Spas 12 shotgun from her back holster, she increased her pace down the mineshaft.

Very soon the agent came upon a group of Brodie's men. They congregated in a large room, illuminated by several lanterns. In the far corner stood a large generator. Its mechanical hum and churning engine overpowered the men's conversation. Knowing the generator was responsible for the main power within the mine, Addison made a strategic decision. Removing one of Samuel's pens from her arm pocket, she stood by the door and peeked inside. There were eight men scattered around the room. Each was engrossed in conversation, Gaelic of course, and seemed to be preparing an arsenal of high-powered weapons. Addison realised the mineshaft was also being used as a storage facility.

Assured that no eyes were upon the doorway, Addison passed it by, halting on the opposite side. Taking the pen, she lodged it between two planks of wood that stretched out across the top of the doorway. They were obviously there to assist in the reinforcement of the constructed passageway. It was a risk, but one Addison was willing to take. The soldier was confident her plan would work. She wanted to cause a minor cave-in of the mine's tunnel to block off access to the generator, but she didn't want to cut the generator's power – yet. A direct blast to the generator would be highly dangerous. The scent of its fuel was enough of an indication of that. Addison still, for the next few minutes at least, needed light.

Carefully, Addison grasped the protruding pen. "Okay, Addy," she whispered. "Get ready to run." Exhaling slowly, Addison tapped the pen's cap... and ran.

She had just enough time to reach the end of the shaft and turn the corner before a resounding explosion shook the tunnel. Addison continued to run until the force pushed her to the ground. She covered her head, feeling loose rubble hit her body. Several seconds passed before calmness eased into the air and Addison lifted her head. Though the artificial light remained, the room was filled with a cloud of sediment and dust. It momentarily impaired her vision.

"Well if they didn't know I was here before, they sure as hell do now!" Readying the Spas, Addison covered her mouth with the collar of her coat as she rose to her feet. The dust was still floating in the already tainted air as Addison closed in on the eastern shaft.

****

Within a larger cross-section of the mine, groups of men began swiftly rallying into action. They arranged themselves into seven groups of four as an enraged Brodie ran towards them. Holding several sheets of paper, twisted and creased within her hand, she began issuing orders.

"I want you to split up and search every square inch of these tunnels. If that was Addison Black you have my orders to fire at will." Agnes threw the papers to the ground. She had just received word back about the information Skyler had given her and her temper was already sky high. "I don't know how she managed to find us so fast, but it's of no concern. She **will not** leave here... got it?"

The men answered with a chorus of, "Yes, ma'am!"

"And if by any chance you can manage to bring her back alive, do so." Brodie's voice lowered. "I welcome the chance to slit her interfering little throat." She cast a gaze upon her men. "Well, what are you standing around here for? Get to it!"

As the troops ran toward several narrow tunnels, Brodie, red faced and seething with anger, headed towards Skyler's confines.

From a crevice within one of the tunnels, Addison watched Brodie. She noted the passage the Irishwoman took, knowing she

65

would be making her way to Skyler. Fast approaching footsteps closed in on Addison and she knelt close to the wall, hiding from view. She smirked as the men passed her by.

"I hope these aren't your highly trained soldiers, Agnes," she mumbled and ran out into the empty cross-section. Addison ran directly towards the eastern shaft.

****

There was no way Skyler wouldn't have been able to hear or feel the explosion Addison created. It shook her small cell-like room, causing the roof to shake and small particles of rubble to fall from above. Skyler was instantly concerned. The blonde knew she was in some form of underground containment facility and that knowledge scared her greatly. Still... a small hope flickered within Skyler that just maybe she would get out of the room alive. What else did she have to hope for?

Hearing the door unlock, Skyler rose from the rickety wooden chair she had been resting upon. Brodie pushed the wooden barrier open and strode purposefully into the room. Skyler was unprepared and taken completely by surprise as Brodie caught her by the throat and pushed her up against the wall. She slapped her hard across the face. The impact stung greatly, breaking Sky's lip. She felt a warm trickle of blood flow into her mouth, followed by its tangy, metallic flavour.

Brodie held Skyler by the jaw. "I thought you would have learned by now that it isn't wise to fuck with me, Professor Tidwell."

"I..."

"Shut the fuck up," Brodie interrupted and struck her again. Skyler felt her head slam into the wall.

"Chocolate chip cookies? The Krebs cycle? Caffeine? Did you honestly think you could get away with a trick like that? I am beginning to believe you have no idea of just whom you are dealing with. Seems I have to show you once again." The words dripped from Brodie's lips like acid.

Skyler felt panic slice through her veins. "No..."

"I didn't say you could speak," Brodie shouted. She leaned closer. "From now on you will do exactly as I say... every moment of every miserable day of what could possibly be the remains of your life... if you don't co-operate. Got it?"

Skyler's lip throbbed, her head ached and her breathing laboured harshly in fear. She remained quiet, not knowing whether she had been given permission to speak, but instead nodded her head. She was beginning to realise just how dangerous a situation she was in and wished she hadn't played with Brodie.

"Lucky for you, we require the data so we are giving you one last chance… and I warn you, Professor, screw with me again and I'll not only hurt you…" Brodie paused and smiled nefariously. "Don't you have a daughter?"

Sky's eyes widened as she was pulled from the wall.

"Right now we're leaving here and that means you are coming with me." Brodie turned around, Skyler still within her grasp, only to find Addison leaning in the doorway.

The government agent smiled. She paid little attention to Skyler, focusing solely upon Brodie. "Surprise!"

Brodie blinked and looked past Addison. "Stevens!"

Addison looked down at the lifeless body lying several feet away from her. "I don't think yelling will wake him up!" She stepped further into the room. "Do you pay your men for lying down on the job?" Not waiting for a response, Addison took a good look at Skyler for the first time. "Professor Tidwell?" This was not the girl Addison was expecting to find.

Skyler nodded in confusion. She wondered who this woman was.

Addison turned back to Brodie. "Well, if you will excuse us… Agnes," she smirked, knowing full well the redhead despised her first name. "We really need to get going."

Eyes blazing, Brodie pushed Skyler away from her. She pulled a concealed knife from her hip, brandishing the six-inch, silver blade towards Addison. "You will not be leaving this place alive, Black."

"Oh, a challenge!" Making a swift decision the agent dropped her shotgun and H&K. "Well, I only have a minute to play." Addison held out her arms. "Let's make this quick, shall we?"

Brodie flicked the knife in her hand. "It won't take long."

The women lunged towards each other. Brodie swung the knife across Addison's stomach, but the agent twisted out of reach. She backhanded Brodie, impacting her face. Blood sprung from the redhead's nose.

"That one's for the shot I saw you lay upon the doc here."

Skyler backed up against the wall, bewildered by the events unfolding before her. Gut instinct screamed at her to run while she had a chance. However, not knowing exactly what was beyond the door, Skyler stayed put. *This is Addison Black?*

Brodie wiped the blood from her nose. She looked at the bright red substance upon her fingers before licking it off. Then she hit out, striking Addison across the face. "And that one's for my Ferrari that you totalled two years ago."

Addison rolled her eyes, unaffected by the strike. "You really do hold a grudge, don't you?" she taunted.

Growling, Brodie lunged for Addison. The agent, again, blocked her attack, knocking the knife clean out of her hand. It slid across the floor, only stopping when it collided with Skyler's foot. The blonde kicked it under her bed in fear.

The women fought, blows being traded and blocked, but it was Addison who easily gained the upper hand. The recent blow to Brodie's head had left her reflexes rather sluggish. Even Addison could tell that, for some reason, Agnes didn't seem at her peak. Not that she minded. Time was of the essence and her priority was getting Skyler out of the mine as expeditiously as possible.

Two swift blows by Addison, one of which effortlessly knocked Brodie's front tooth out, sent the redhead hurtling back against the wall. She hit her head once again and fell into an unresponsive heap upon the floor. Addison stepped towards her and kicked the bloody tooth lying on the dirty ground.

"Well, there's something else for you to hold a grudge about." Addison turned to Skyler. The doctor still stood against the wall, staring at Brodie's unconscious body. Addison addressed her carefully. "Skyler? Skyler Tidwell?"

Sky blinked, focussing her eyes upon Addison. "Yes."

"My name is Addison Black." While she spoke she inspected Skyler's wounds. "I was sent here to bring you home."

The blonde hissed as Addison touched her lip. She brushed Addison's hand away. "I'm fine. I hurt a little, but nothing is broken, believe me."

"Okay," Addison shrugged. She turned her back on Skyler and picked up her Spas 12, securing it to her back before reclaiming her submachine gun. "We have to move. Brodie's men are still out there. The lift at the other end of this shaft is incapacitated. Remote activated I think, so we need to get back to the main cross-section.

"With all those men around?" Skyler shook her head. "Sounds like a mistake to me."

"I have a plan," Addison replied. "And trust me; I never make mistakes." Readying her H&K, Addison stood by the door. She checked both left and right for any approaching soldiers but found the coast clear. "Okay, let's go." Skyler stood her ground for a moment, bewildered by the sudden change in events. Addison addressed her impatiently. "We don't have time for loitering, Doctor, we need to move… now." The last word was spoken with force, encouraging Skyler to bite her tongue and abide with Addison's wishes.

They moved down the narrow shaft, Skyler close behind Addison. From the distance they could both hear the sound of Brodie's men. Addison switched her weapon to rapid fire as they entered the mine's cross-section of tunnels. The agent crouched down to her knees, indicating that Skyler should do the same. She looked around until she found what she was searching for. High above and fixed to the wall, was a shiny new, metal box. Addison knew it was the junction box and conduit for the mine's lighting. With a sly grin she turned to Sky.

"Okay, Doctor Tidwell, take this." Addison handed the professor her torch.

Skyler frowned. "What are you going to do?"

"Well…" Addison clipped a high-powered light to the sight attachment on her H&K. "I am going to do this…" Lifting the submachine gun to her right eye, Addison took aim at the junction box. She fired a rapid chain of bullets, each precisely making their mark. Sparks flew, followed by a large explosion of electricity. The mine fell into complete darkness.

Chapter 7

"Jesus H. Christ!" Skyler cried as the last spark disappeared and the blackness descended. "What the hell did you do that for?"

"Just evening up the odds, Doctor Tidwell," Addison explained. "They can't hit what they can't see."

"That's fine logic, Agent, but how are *we* supposed to see *them*? Funny thing about darkness, none of us can see in it!"

"Possibly we could if you would hand me back that torch." Addison's voice floated to her in the dark and Skyler extended the flashlight in the direction it came from. She misjudged the distance and her hand brushed across fabric covering a firm and well-developed upper arm.

"Sorry, forgot I had it," Skyler said a little sheepishly. She felt Addison's hand come up and touch her elbow. It traced a path to her hand where its warmth was removed as she relieved the scholar of the flashlight. With a small click a steady beam illuminated the area they were standing in.

"That's better. Now, Doctor Tidwell, let's get the hell out of here, shall we?" Addison turned to head down the corridor but was stopped by the American's voice.

"Agent Black, can you do me a favor? For the last two days I've had to pretend to be my mother and frankly I'm tired of it. I want my own life back. Do you think you could you call me Skyler please, just so I feel like we both know who I am?"

Addison brought the light to bear on the recently liberated prisoner and saw she was still shaken by her recent experiences. "It would be my pleasure, Skyler," Addison said smoothly. "Now can we get the hell out of here?"

Skyler did something she hadn't done in almost forty-eight hours.

She smiled. "What are we waiting for?" Addison found she couldn't help but respond with a smile of her own.

"Not a thing," the agent said and turned again to lead the way. "Stay close. Do what I tell you the instant I tell you to do it and we'll get you out of here and back to your life soon." As Addison picked her way past pieces of the exploded junction box she felt a hand touch her back and grasp lightly to the material of her black jacket. She knew Skyler needed the contact and didn't complain. "If we run into trouble, I'll need that back, but I'll loan it to you for now."

"Thanks," the scholar returned in a quiet voice. Skyler was grateful the agent understood and they moved along at a careful but steady pace. At each juncture of the main hall to connecting corridors, Addison would douse the flashlight and push a button on her wristwatch. The dial changed colors and Addison would wait a few seconds before indicating they should proceed. The first three cross-halls were traversed uneventfully. The fourth hall was different.

Addison slowed as she approached the next passageway and doused the flashlight. Bringing her arm up she pressed the button on her wristwatch. The face changed colors but this time small dots appeared where it had remained blank before.

"Damn. Playmates ahead," Addison whispered. Snapping off the watch, she turned to Skyler. "Stay here and stay down. This won't take long."

"If you think you're leaving me here, Agent, you're crazy. I'll stay down but I'm not staying here." Skyler's voice held determination and Addison would have argued, but she heard movement down the hall she had just scanned.

"It's a moot point now. They're here." Flipping the watch back on, the agent scanned the area again. "Four of them," she said to herself as much as to Skyler. Reaching out she grabbed Skyler and urged her against the wall of the corridor by placing her hands on the American's shoulders then slid her down to the floor. Leaning forward, she spoke to Skyler in a barely audible whisper, "Don't move and don't make a sound; I don't want to confuse you with our friends coming up the hall. It wouldn't be healthy for you." Skyler shivered at Addison's words as well as from the warm breath that blew across her ear. *Good grief,* she thought, *out of the frying pan and into the fire. Brodie or Black, is one better than the other?*

Addison had already moved away and reached to pull her pistol from the holster where it had been housed. If Skyler hadn't known the direction she moved away in, the tiny noises of Addison's preparations wouldn't have been noticeable at all. A sudden light from the crosshall made Skyler squint in the return of stimuli to her starved sense of vision. As soon as the light appeared though, a sharp popping sound immediately preceded its extinguishing.

Four more reports followed, then silence reigned again in the tunnel. Skyler's eyes shifted back and forth in the darkness. She waited nervously for a few minutes then ventured in a low voice, "Agent Black? Addison?"

"I thought I told you not to make a sound," Addison said into Skyler's ear. The American jumped at the sudden noise and swung out blindly. Addison intercepted what should have been an almost perfectly placed blow easily.

"Easy, Skyler. I'm one of the good guys," Addison said.

"I was beginning to wonder about that. What happened just now?"

"There were four guards and they were an obstacle in the corridor we need to head into. I cleared a path." A tiny click and the flashlight was on once again. Skyler noticed the British woman wasn't even breathing hard.

"Look, before I go any further with you, I want to know a few things. You see, trust seems to have become a big issue for me in the last day or so." Addison considered the request then nodded.

"Fine, as long as we move while we do it. I checked those guards and they weren't amateurs. They were professionals right down to their equipment and choice of weapons. We need to get out of here as quickly as possible."

"That's just it," Skyler began as she took her place behind Addison again. "Where is here? I know they wanted my mother, but why? Who are you exactly and though I won't turn down the assistance, why did you help me? Oh, and who the hell is Agnes Brodie?"

Addison glanced back quickly before returning her attention to the route ahead. "When you ask questions you don't go halfway, do you?" She paused here to steer Skyler around the bodies of three men and a woman.

Skyler tightened her grip on the black jacket.

"They were professionals, Skyler. They would have killed us without a second thought."

And you would know all about that, wouldn't you, Agent Black? Skyler thought. She tore her eyes from the grisly sight and kept moving.

"I can only give you the answers to your questions as I know them." Addison tried to take Skyler's mind from the bodies left behind. "You've figured out they were after your mother, but I can't tell you why. The truth is I don't know. I have a few suspicions, but at this point they would be just guesses. Agnes Brodie is a bit difficult to explain as well. Let's just say if there is an unsavory pound to be made, Brodie will be there trying to make it. We know she's been involved in gun running, smuggling and dabbled in the drug trade. We also believe she's been working as an assassin for hire. Don't doubt this, Agnes wouldn't have left you alive at the conclusion of her business with you."

Once again, Addison felt the American's grip tighten. She stopped in mid-stride and turned to Skyler. "She didn't...hurt you, did she?" Skyler knew what Addison was asking. She blushed and looked uncomfortable but didn't turn her eyes from the intense gaze of the British woman.

"She...kissed me. I knew what she wanted and I let her believe I was receptive to the idea, but it was just to buy some time. She beat me once, very skillfully." Skyler did look down then. Addison's jaw clenched and she reached out to touch her companion's arm.

"Skyler, look at me." Reluctantly, the scholar raised her eyes. "You did what you had to do to survive. You lived; you won. It's as simple as that. We have reliable information that quite a few others who crossed her path didn't."

Skyler felt a rush of gratitude for the understanding she was being shown. "Who are you?" She knew that was the least of what she wanted to know about the intriguing woman, but the question was the best she could do at the time.

Addison gave her a cocky grin and a little half bow. "Addison Black, agent of Her Majesty's government at your service. I've been assigned to achieve your liberation so may I suggest we get on with it?" Skyler smiled for the first time in what felt like a very long while and she nodded to the agent. Addison turned and they began to walk again.

"As for where we are," Addison's voice floated back to her, "We're in what used to be a working coal mine in the Scottish highlands. There are only two sections of this mine that are accessible from the surface as the northern and eastern sections were lost in a collapse a long time ago. You were held in the western section and we are going to make our ascent to the surface at the southern entrance. Any more questions?"

Plenty Skyler thought, but out loud she said, "Not at the moment."

"Good," Addison said, "Because we're here and this was far too easy."

"You killed four people and you say it was too easy?" Skyler's voice had dropped to a whisper as she felt Addison still as well. She watched as the agent removed a pair of simple sunglasses from one of the multiple pockets on her jacket. Skyler didn't recognise or understand why Addison would be putting on sunglasses, but she had a fair idea. "Night vision specs," she said, "So that's how you took care of those four."

"Uh huh," Addison confirmed as she slipped the dark glasses into place and edged near the elevator she had entered through, snapping the flashlight off as she went. The doors were ajar just as she had left them, but she had an uneasy feeling about the whole situation. She paid heed to those feelings; they had saved her more than once.

The agent leaned into the elevator, peering up through the car's roof. She then turned quickly to Skyler and asked, "Can you climb?"

"Of course," Skyler answered with more confidence than she felt. She refused to let the British agent see her as weak or a victim. Why that was she couldn't say and didn't have the time to examine.

"Good then," Addison said as she pulled the American into the elevator. She handed the once again illuminated flashlight to Skyler then crouched and sprang upward, grabbing the edges of the hatch with both hands. Skyler watched with amazement at muscles flexing in well-toned arms and legs as Addison tucked her legs and pulled herself up through the hatch at the same time.

She was still marvelling when a black clad arm dropped back through and a hand beckoned her. Snapping back to reality, Skyler grasped the proffered hand and was unceremoniously hauled up and through the hatch. When both of her feet rested on the roof of the elevator, her balance failed her. Two strong hands on her arms arrested her momentary bobbling.

"Thanks," she croaked weakly, losing herself in the intense gaze of the agent. It was a gaze made even more intense and dark by the muted shadows of the flashlight that still dangled limply in one of Skyler's hands.

"Good job I had my vitamins this morning," Addison quipped, with a lopsided grin. She left her hands in place while she scanned the area above them.

"We won't need this anymore," the agent said as she returned her attention to Skyler. The Brit moved her right hand down the American's left upper arm to the hand holding the flashlight. The warmth of Addison's hand on hers as she took the light was in stark contrast to the colder air of the shaft. Addison placed the flashlight on the roof of the car, aiming the beam up the cable.

"Up you go" Addison said as she indicated the elevator cable. "Don't worry, I'll be right behind you." Skyler took a deep breath and grabbed the cable, ready to prove her fitness or be mortified by failure. As she tensed for the climb, there was suddenly noise from the top of the shaft.

"Ladies, I can't believe you want to leave my party so soon," Agnes Brodie's voice drifted down the shaft. Her voice had a slight whistling quality, probably the result of her lost tooth. "Here I was thinking I had been a neglectful hostess, but now I have a second chance to show you both my hospitality!"

Addison grabbed Skyler and pushed her against the wall directly below the open doors. At this angle they couldn't see the doors anymore, but Brodie's words came down clearly.

"As this is my party, I get to fashion the guest list and I've decided to delete you from it...permanently!" Agnes laughed at her own joke. "Don't be concerned though, I'll send you away with a few party favors."

Rapid-fire shots sprayed down the shaft and Addison pressed her body closer against Skyler's, shielding her from any stray bullets.

"Did you enjoy those?" Agnes cackled. "I hope so because there is much more to come. And Addison?"

Skyler felt the British woman tense, but she said nothing.

"Addison!" Brodie screamed and another burst of gunfire rang out. This time the angle was a little better and the walls near them were struck, sending pieces of stone and concrete bouncing painfully off them.

"What do you want, Agnes?" Addison called out.

"That's better," the Irishwoman said. "I just wanted to tell you a few things before I kill you and the professor there." Her voice was almost conversational in tone. "You were really such a fly in my ointment, Addison. Remember Tangiers? Of course you remember Tangiers. That was such a sweet deal you managed to screw up for me. Those six SCUD missiles should have garnered me a net profit in the millions, but you had to come calling. What did I get for my trouble? Destroyed SCUDS and a decimated team. When you were finished I had a mere handful of men left; they were loyal though, they stayed with me. It might interest you to know those survivors are the team currently placed outside the elevator down there. They're very anxious to renew your acquaintance."

On cue, light flooded into the elevator from outside the still open car doors. Even Skyler could tell Brodie wasn't bluffing.

"Shit!" whispered the black-garbed agent.

"I tell you what, Addison," Brodie's voice resumed. "I'm a fair woman, I'll give you the option. Drop down into the elevator and meet the team or come up here and face me. You have ten seconds to decide!"

Skyler watched as Addison hesitated only a moment before fishing in her jacket pocket. She removed the pistol she had taken from the first guard and leaned slightly into the roof opening of the elevator car. Bringing her arm back, she aimed carefully and tossed the pistol through the opening. The projectile apparently hit its intended target because the elevator car gave a slight jerk and slowly started to ascend.

"We're coming up!" Addison yelled. In the next few seconds the agent was a blur of activity. She retrieved her flashlight, rummaged in her jacket pockets and pulled a shotgun from the holster on her back. She then moved closer to the American and whispered, "Skyler..."

"Agent," Skyler quickly interrupted, "It's me Brodie wants and what she thinks I can give her. Use that. There's no sense in both of us dying. Send me to her; you try to get away. Just make sure my mom is okay."

"I can't do that, Doctor," Addison said calmly as the car rose further, now almost halfway up the shaft.

"Why not?" the scholar asked.

"Because this is our stop." With that, Addison, shotgun still in hand, put both arms around Skyler in a bear hug. She picked up the smaller woman effortlessly, took two long strides across the top of the elevator car, twisted and launched them both through the air.

Addison's back bore the brunt of the jolt as they broke through the old boards on the side of the shaft. Landing hard, Addison nonetheless rose quickly to her feet and, setting the flashlight on the shotgun as a guide, pumped several powerful shots toward the bottom of the still moving elevator car. The sound of metal snapping followed the shots and two heavy metal cables whipped by the opening in the shaft wall. The elevator car itself seemed to come to a complete standstill momentarily before following the cables down the shaft. The resounding crash almost, but not quite, drowned out the sound of Agnes Brodie's voice.

"God damn it! You fools! Go get some equipment! I want to get down there **now**!"

"Hey, Agnes!" Addison yelled up at the furious redhead. A silence from above ensued. "How does it feel to get shafted?"

"Fuck you, Addison! I'll kill you, bitch! You and that blonde are dead!"

The Brit chuckled on her way back to where Skyler still lay on the floor.

"You just couldn't resist, could you?" Skyler asked as she shook her head.

"No, I couldn't," the agent said with a grin. "Shall we go, Doctor? Agnes seems to be in a foul mood and it won't take her long to figure out a way in here." She extended her hand and assisted Skyler to her feet. "By the way, thank you for flying Black Airlines."

"Remind me to fire my travel agent," the American shot back, but as she was tugged along deeper into the darkness she thought, *but damn is that pilot cute.*

Several minutes later Addison stopped abruptly ahead of the doctor and dropped the hand she had held onto while guiding Skyler along. They had been moving through what appeared to be part of the long deserted original mine. Thick timbers braced the walls and rusted tracks lined the floor.

"Why have we stopped?" Skyler asked as she came around Addison to be confronted with the same dilemma the Brit faced. They had arrived at a junction in the passageway where three identical tunnels broke off from the larger one they had come through.

Shining the flashlight down each new tunnel, they could ascertain no difference in them except for a rotting sign in each bearing letters and numbers apparently acting as route names.

"Do you have a preference, Doctor?" asked Addison as she indicated the three passageways. Skyler studied them for a moment before turning to Addison and asking, "Do you have a match?" The British agent plucked a small plastic container from one the seemingly multitude of pockets in her jacket.

"Of course you have a match. Why did I doubt that?" Skyler took a match out of the box and struck it against a small piece of sandpaper she found attached to the bottom. Moving into the first tunnel on the left she held the lit match above her head. The action was repeated in the center tunnel and then in the one on the right.

Blowing the last match out she returned to Addison and stated, "I'll take the middle tunnel."

Addison pocketed the remaining matches as she moved forward without hesitation into the passageway the doctor has selected.

"How do you figure?" Addison asked as she felt Skyler move along behind her again.

"Well," Skyler's voice came from the rear, "the match's flame was stationary in the left and right tunnels. It flickered and bent slightly in the center one. It isn't a huge amount, but there's definitely air circulation in that middle tunnel. Old archaeologist's trick."

"Clever girl," Addison complimented as she continued along the chosen route.

"I'm **not** a girl," Skyler muttered, but stumbled along behind Addison anyway. Within a few minutes another two junctions had been reached and the tunnels chosen. By the time they reached the next meeting of passageways, the airflow was so noticeable that matches were unnecessary. With the possibility of escape came a renewed sense of energy and their pace quickened. A final turn led to a slightly wider area that contained no tracks. It was much cooler than previous areas. It was also a dead end.

Shining the light around the area, the beam landed on a square box-like contraption suspended by thin metal wires from the high ceiling of the chamber. Following the line of sight provided by the cables, the pair could just make out a few stars through the top of the room.

"Emergency exit," Addison observed as she moved toward the cage. "Let's go." Skyler looked with suspicion at the rickety contraption.

"Addison, look at this thing. God knows how old it is. I'm not sure it will hold one of us, much less both of us."

"You have a better idea?" Addison asked as she stepped inside the cage and bounced a little, testing the ancient wooden floor. Skyler didn't and joined the agent in the cage. It was close quarters and they were pressed closely together as the lift had obviously been meant for single person use.

"Going up, madam?" Addison asked in a sophisticated tone and pulled hard on the rusty wires. With a protesting squeal the ancient cage lifted from the tunnel floor. Skyler closed her eyes and prayed that the workmanship of years ago would hold up.

Addison grunted with the effort of lifting both of their weight, but in a few minutes the cage reached the top and clicked into place. Skyler moved quickly from the perilous perch. Addison followed and moved past Skyler to lead the way out into the cold Scottish night.

"Free at last!" Skyler exclaimed.

M J Walker and Val Brown

Chapter 8

The rain, which fell so heavily before Addison entered the mines, had now ceased. Clouds hung low in the dark sky. A strong wind pushed them swiftly through the atmosphere. It was cold, below freezing, and the icy winds whipped around the doctor and soldier as Addison gained her bearings.

Skyler shivered and gasped sharply. A biting wind thrashed against her flesh, chilling her to the bone. The temperature had dropped drastically. Addison noted the rain soaked grass had frozen and it crunched under her footsteps. Without the presence of a moon, the land was dark and ominous. Addison's torch provided the only source of light.

The agent turned to Skyler, shining her torch upon the shivering woman. She instantly realised the young doctor's condition as she stood with arms wrapped around herself, trembling.

"Cold?" Addison asked. She released the rucksack and shotgun from her back. They slipped to the ground with a thud, forcing Addison to cast her torch around their vicinity before turning it back upon Skyler.

Teeth chattering against each other, Skyler hugged herself tighter. "C-Cold isn't the word."

Beginning to unload ammunition and random equipment from her pockets, Addison crouched down and placed her torch upon the frozen ground. Once her pockets were empty she shrugged the thick coat from her shoulders. "Here, put this on."

"What about you?" Skyler enquired, as she willingly accepted the black, padded coat.

Addison opened her backpack. "I'll wear this." She pulled out the khaki, camouflage jacket. "It's not as warm as that, but I'm used to this kind of weather... besides, you might be suffering from shock.

You should, if anything, keep warm."

"Shock..." Skyler shivered violently. "It's ... not every day I get kidnapped, held prisoner, beaten, shot at and come on to by the same person."

Addison paused in the middle of putting on the jacket. She felt a flare of anger once again at the thought of Brodie touching Skyler. "She will more than pay for that." The agent grimaced, wondering what Sky had to do in order to 'play along' with Brodie. Her disdain for Brodie deepened and Addison knew that after she had secured Skyler's safety, she would return and put a stop to Agnes Brodie, one way or another, once and for all.

Replacing the shotgun and SMG ammunition in her pockets, Addison sighed. "Listen... we need to get moving. I want to get to the Jeep before they catch up with us. I need to get you out of here."

"Usually I'd insist I can take care of myself, but in this instance I agree with you." Skyler took the torch Addison handed to her. "Lead the way... where exactly are we, by the way?"

Holding her H&K submachine gun, Addison turned on its attached light. "The Grampian Highlands." She took the handheld, electronic display map from her pocket. Switching it on she checked the compass and started moving. "It's about a half an hour walk." The agent strode off, hearing Skyler follow. "I left the Jeep within a group of fir trees."

Skyler sped up her gait and walked along side Addison. The agent could see Skyler periodically watching her from the corner of her eye. "What?" she finally asked.

"Pardon?"

Addison continued scanning the area. "What is it you're thinking, Skyler?"

"Well it's just that... you aren't what I would have expected as my 'knight in shining armour'."

Snorting, Addison smirked. "You expected a bloke?"

"Sort of."

"Sorry to disappoint you." Speaking before Skyler could respond, Addison said, "Your mother thought the same."

Skyler stopped momentarily in surprise. "You spoke to my mother?" She caught up to Addison who hadn't stopped moving.

"She was at the HQ of the government branch I work for."

"And that is?"

"Classified" Addison responded. She didn't miss the grunt and quietly muttered 'of course' from Skyler but chose to ignore it. Instead, Addison picked up her pace. The temperature seemed to drop further and Addison was sure it had reached at least minus six degrees Celsius. By the light on her weapon she could see her breath escape in large puffs of vapour. Apart from the wind and Skyler's presence, the land was gravely silent. They were still unable to see more than fifteen feet ahead. The mix of clouds and fog severely hindered the agent's vision, but her electronic mapping device helped immensely. Addison reactivated her watch's heat and motion sensor. If there were anybody close by they would be detected.

Both women continued to walk in an uneasy silence. Skyler remained close beside Addison and the agent could sense her uneasiness. She could fully understand. It was cold, dark, and there was a contingency of armed soldiers trying to kill them. Although these were times in which Addison excelled, she understood it would be terrifying for anybody who wasn't used to the life she led. To Addison, however, this was plain sailing.

As a distant rumble echoed over the land, Skyler jumped and grabbed Addison's arm.

"You okay?"

Skyler nodded. "Yeah. What on earth was that?"

Addison looked around them. "My bet is Brodie just destroyed the mine. She won't want any clues left behind so she has no doubt turned the place to rubble. Access will be unlikely."

"How will you catch her now?"

"Don't worry. She will get hers." Addison gripped her weapon tighter. *And I am going to enjoy every second of it,* she thought.

They continued on in silence for several minutes before Skyler found the need to speak again. "It's getting colder," she noted and tried vainly to warm the hand holding Addison's torch. "How much further do we have, or is that classified too?"

Addison stopped. She turned to face Sky and shone a light upon her. "Do you have some sort of problem with me? I mean, correct me if I am wrong here, but I do know sarcasm when I hear it."

"That wasn't sarcasm," Skyler responded and strode ahead of Addison.

The agent kept her pace behind Sky. "Could have fooled me." Addison shook her head. "What is your problem?"

"Problem?" Skyler sighed. "I don't have a problem... I just don't much appreciate being treated like a kid." She increased her pace, seemingly unaware as Addison took her elbow and adjusted her direction as they neared the Jeep. "You dive in to that place, shooting people left, right and centre. The information you give me is sketchy at best and you won't even say who you work for. I still have only a

83

rough idea what the Gemini Project really is. I wasn't expecting any of this. A quiet visit with my mom before I started on my next job was all I wanted."

Addison spotted a familiar group of trees. "Oh well, excuse me if I was too busy saving your arse while trying to get mine out alive, to stop and answer all your questions!"

"It's not that I'm not grateful…"

"Uh huh," Addison interrupted.

"I just don't like to feel out of control. I like to know what's going on."

"You want to know what's going on?" Addison shone her light towards the trees and emerging Jeep. "That is our transport. We are going to get inside it and I'm going to take you to a plane where some nice big men will take you to your mother. I am sure you and she will have plenty to talk about then. My job is to save your arse, not bow down to every whim." Addison felt that last remark was a little low; maybe it wasn't deserved but she was getting cold and feeling anger towards Brodie and her antics. No doubt that anger was misplaced, but Addison was occasionally too pigheaded to admit she was wrong.

Both women stopped beside the camouflaged Jeep and Skyler shone her torch into Addison's face. "You're quite rude, you know."

Addison smiled as though being given the greatest of compliments. "Thank you, and believe me…" she pulled the rucksack and shotgun from her back. "It didn't just happen overnight." Addison unhooked her submachine gun and along with the shotgun and rucksack, she opened the back door and tossed them into the vehicle. "It took me a long time to perfect this." Closing the back door, Addison walked to the driver's side where Skyler was still standing. "You driving?"

"You don't think I could?"

Addison shook her head. The tone of 'almost indignant' amused her. "I am sure you could. I never go into any situation with preconceptions." She moved to open the door. "If there's one thing I've learned it's…" as the door opened a high pitched beep echoed from underneath the vehicle.

"Oh FUCK!" Addison grabbed Skyler's hand and began to move. "RUN!" she yelled, still holding Sky's hand as she pulled the shocked woman with her. Skyler ran, trying only to keep up with Addison. They managed to get no more than eight strides away from the Jeep before the entire vehicle exploded into a ball of hot, orange flames. The force of the blast jolted Addison and Skyler into the air for several seconds before they fell onto the cold, hard ground and rolled further away from the fire.

Addison hugged Sky against her body, shielding the doctor from flaming debris falling around them. The heat was palpable, a stark contrast to the intense cold of moments before. She remained still, protecting Skyler, while realising that she was going to have to rethink her plans. Addison looked towards the flames that brightened the dark night. Tiny explosions continued to erupt from the burning wreckage. Skyler jumped every time one rang out into the night air and it alerted Addison to the woman in her arms. She pulled back slightly to look upon Skyler. Shocked green eyes glittered with unshed tears and the fire's orange hues flicked upon her features. Addison had completely wrapped her body around the doctor upon impact to shield her from injury. They lay on their sides, Skyler within the embrace of the soldier's arms and legs.

"Are you okay?" Addison asked.

Skyler's breathing laboured. Her chest rose and fell against Addison. She shuddered and whispered, "I think so." Sky blinked. "How did you know?"

The agent's eyes scanned the tree line. "I heard the activation sequence. It's a..." Addison paused as movement within the trees and warning beep from her watch drew her attention. "Don't move," she whispered.

Beginning to understand Addison's instincts, Skyler froze. "What is it?"

"There's somebody out there." Drawing one hand behind her back, Addison pulled a pistol from its holster. "Keep still and try not to move a muscle." Black watched intently as the figure emerged from the trees and began to close in upon them. She knew instantly Brodie sent this person and was probably out there to make sure Addison failed in her mission. If the blast didn't finished them off then the high-powered weapon with laser sighting would. Addison's eyes ran over Sky's body and she spotted the glowing red dot trained upon the doctor's body, positioned over her heart.

"What's going on?"

"Don't... move," Addison pressed. She watched and waited as the figure drew ever closer. By the firelight she could identify the uniform Brodie's men had worn. "Listen... when I say 'now' I want you to roll out of my arms, but stay on the ground, okay?"

"Okay," Skyler whispered with uncertainty.

Addison breathed shallowly. She held the Beretta pistol with her finger resting lightly on the trigger. Her eyes remained focused upon the cautiously approaching figure. He drew near.

"Ready?"

"Yes."

Addison waited a little longer. As the man reached five paces away from them Addison whispered, "Now!"

In swift succession Skyler rolled from Addison's embrace as the agent aimed and fired two rounds at their assassin's weapon, knocking it clean out of his hands. She jumped to her feet, holstering the Beretta, and as he attempted to regain possession of his Uzi, Addison charged him. They collided with a heavy impact and fell to the ground, Addison on top of him. Astride his back she instantly captured his flailing arms and grabbed a hand full of thick blonde hair with her other hand. He was trapped.

Behind her, Addison heard Skyler scramble to her feet. She remained a distance away from them, but picked up the torch and shone it upon the man underneath Addison's grip.

Yanking his head back harder, the soldier spoke firmly and to the point. "First of all you have five seconds to give me your name."

"Myers," was his strained but rapid reply.

Addison nodded saying, "Good boy." She lessened her grip a measure to show the young man his willingness to answer her questions would be beneficial. "I see you understand it would be wise to comply. Now tell me... who sent you?"

Myers declined to respond, but struggled once again.

A groan escaped from Addison and she released Myers head, punching the side of his face. She then regained possession of Myers' hair and pulled him roughly, ignoring his yelp of pain. "Wrong answer," she seethed. "Try again."

"Okay... Miss Brodie, Agnes Brodie sent me." Myers breathed nervously and rapid puffs of air billowed past his lips. "She ordered me to watch out for you... just in case."

The cogs of Addison's mind began to turn. "One? I find it hard to believe she sent just one of you. How many of you are out there?"

"Two," he answered.

Addison tugged his arms tighter.

"Alright, six. I swear there were just six of us sent out to sweep the area for any sign of you." Myers groaned in relief as Addison loosened her grip upon him. "Our orders were to bring you to her... dead or alive."

"And what of Professor Tidwell?"

Skyler stepped closer on hearing her name. The torchlight shone directly into Myers' eyes, forcing him to squint in the glare. A bloodied nose glimmered red in its beam.

"I don't know… honestly." Addison knew on this he was telling the truth. It was doubtful Brodie would share her plans with her men, men she considered disposable. "All I know is that Miss Brodie is scheduled to report back to some foreign alliances in two days. We were to go with her. If she hadn't obtained the information she wanted by then she was to bring the Professor along."

That confused Addison. "Where was this meeting?"

Myers didn't answer. The only sound to greet Addison's ears was the cracking and popping of her burning Jeep.

Due to her position upon Myers, Addison's foot was closest to her hand. She pulled the Baby Browning pistol from its holster on her boot and thrust it against Myers' head. Skyler gasped, but remained silent. "I held no qualms in killing your comrades back in the mines… want to test whether that has changed?"

"Skye…"

Addison frowned and Skyler jumped upon hearing her name.

"They're meeting on the Isle of Skye. There is a place within the Cuillin Hills; I have never been there so I don't know what it is."

The agent silently processed Myers' information. She knew he was telling the truth. Although there was probably plenty he was neglecting to tell, it was still enough to help the mission. Addison re-holstered the Browning pistol. Then with a rapid thrust she delivered a harsh blow to the back of Myers' neck. His head fell limply.

"What did you do?" Skyler asked, now approaching.

"Don't worry." The agent climbed to her feet. "I just put him to sleep for a while. He will keep nice and warm by the fire." Nudging the inert body with her booted foot, Addison stepped over Myers. She looked at the burning vehicle. Orange flames flicked harshly in the wind, refusing to relent under the strong easterly gusts. Dark grey smoke spiralled into the atmosphere. The aroma was overpowering, but it was a scent Addison was used to. She shook her head as she realised that most of her equipment had been destroyed. "Bollocks," she whispered and turned to Skyler.

Sky looked hopelessly at the burning vehicle. Addison thought she saw a glimmer of emotional despair, but with the darkness and flickering light, she wasn't sure. "Umm… Skyler, are you alright?"

Skyler nodded.

"You didn't receive any injuries, did you?" Addison had tried to shield Skyler's body as they fell, receiving the majority of the impact herself.

She shrugged. Skyler did hurt, especially considering the beating she had also received not long ago. That, together with the explosion, made the doctor feel like she had tussled with a wild animal... and lost. "I'll be okay," Sky insisted. "What are we going to do now?"

Forcing out a weary breath, Addison checked her pockets. All she had now was what was on her person. She took the radio from her pocket and walked closer to the flames. Skyler followed. Addison tried to test the communication device and attempted to turn it on. It failed to respond and she realised it had been destroyed. In her fall Addison had broken the radio. She knew she had felt something give upon impacting the ground.

"No 'COM' with HQ," she said, throwing the radio into the fire. Next she checked her other pocket and pulled out the electronic handheld map. That was still intact. "Well, we have a map." She placed it back in her pocket. "Night vision specs." Addison briefly lifted a pair of regular looking dark sunglasses from her top pocket. "Plenty of ammo, although some useless shotgun cartridges." Running a hand through her shaggy black hair, the soldier folded her arms. "We have plenty of money and cards... what is important is that we get to a phone." Striding back over to Myers' unconscious body, Addison took his weapon and spare magazine. "We must keep moving now. It might not be safe to make camp tonight. We should get to the next town and a phone ASAP. I'm going to head towards Skye though. If Brodie is having a party, I'm going to gatecrash!" Readying Myers' Uzi, Addison jerked her head. "Let's go."

Casting one final glance at the burning Jeep, Skyler followed Addison into the night.

****

The door to General Blithe's office swung open and the statuesque man strode into his secretary's reception. He had been working late, very late indeed. It was a quarter to five in the morning. Though Headquarters never ceased to remain in operation, Miss Bakersfield worked a simple nine to five job. She wouldn't be in for another four hours. Antonia Bakersfield lived with her aging father; she cared for him during the night while a nurse, provided by HQ, cared for him during the day.

The General rubbed his tired eyes. He had been waiting on Addison Black to contact him with confirmation of Skyler Tidwell's liberation. He thought she would have been in contact by now, but he held little worry. His faith rested squarely on the agent. She wouldn't fail in the mission.

Striding over to Miss Bakersfield's desk, Blithe opened the

bottom drawer. There he found a silver keypad. He punched in a code known only to Antonia and himself. From behind came a familiar mechanical 'click', as filing cupboards built into the wall were unlocked. He turned to the middle drawer, slid it open and flipped through the slim black expense folders. After setting up Marlene Tidwell's accommodation he'd filled out the appropriate form for all expenditures needed for the temporary living arrangements. He had then given them to his secretary to file away. Unfortunately, Blithe had been unable to sign the documents until confirmation had been received from the Prime Minister's office. It was simple red tape forcing him to wait, although he knew there would be no problem. Now that confirmation had arrived, he could finalise the documents.

Scratching his signature upon three forms, Mark placed them back into the drawer and closed it. Still sitting at Antonia's desk his eyes slid to the white telephone sitting by a computer screen. Although it was still quite early in the morning, he felt the need to check upon Marlene Tidwell. Regular checks were supposed to be carried out, so he took it upon himself to fulfil the deed.

He picked up the receiver and dialled a secure code to get an outside line. Then he dialled a second secure code and finally Marlene's apartment number. It began to ring and Blithe waited for her to answer... and waited... and waited. Finally, after a minute had passed, Mark disconnected the line and dialled another. This was answered immediately.

"Security."

"This is General Blithe... I want you to check on apartment A2 in section B, right away. I need confirmation that our guest is okay... I'll wait on the line."

"Right away, Sir."

The line fell silent as Mark's orders were carried out. Resting one hand upon the desk he drummed his fingers on the thick wood in rhythmic beats of three.

Moments later the voice returned. "General... the guest in apartment A2 isn't there. I have detected signs of a struggle and the back door was open. We have a situation, Sir."

"What?" Blithe rose from the chair instantly, wondering how this could be possible. "I'm on my way."

Slamming down the telephone, General Blithe dashed out of the office.

****

89

Keeping on the move had been the only way for Addison and Skyler to keep relatively warm. Skyler was exhausted. With the exertion and excitement, if she could call it that, every inch of her body felt weary and in desperate need of rest. Unfortunately for her, Addison had refused any request to slow down, stating it was in their best interest to keep moving. Skyler didn't care at that point; all she wanted was hot food and a warm bed. The blonde doctor was beginning to think she resented Addison greatly.

Leading several paces ahead, Addison reached the summit of a large rocky hill and looked into the valley below. "Well it's about shagging time."

Scowling at the agent's use of language, a sure sign of limited vocabulary in her eyes, Skyler asked, "What is it?"

"Civilisation." Addison swept her hand over the view in an introductory gesture as Skyler reached her. "Or as close to it as possible. There are even a few street lamps out there. I am betting we could get to a phone in no time."

Skyler looked down at the small village within the valley. It wasn't particularly large, she estimated. By the amount of houses and buildings scattered over the area she presumed there was less than a thousand inhabitants. The sight alone, however, was enough to fill her with hope. "Food and a place to rest, here we come."

"Telephone and transportation," Addison countered. "You can do the food and rest once we have that sorted." She began to trek down the rocky hill.

"Don't you ever rest?" Skyler called after her in weary exasperation, and then muttered, "Or is that an Energizer battery you have stuck up your ass?"

"Yep," Addison chuckled for the first time. "And it powers my hearing too!"

Skyler winced as she followed the soldier towards 'civilisation'.

****

A worn wooden signpost proclaimed the town was called Innisbeth. It swung in the cold night breeze on squeaking hinges, a not so silent sentinel at the town's edge. Addison and Skyler moved up the narrow main road, wanting both to race to the nearest shelter and yet remaining necessarily wary of running into more of Brodie's men.

"I wouldn't think Agnes would be so stupid as to show herself in the open. Her ilk seems to prefer the shadows, like most vermin," Addison observed with repugnance.

There were precious few lights on in the small town at such an early hour. Approaching one of the nearest homes with a light on, they were surprised when the door opened just as they were about to knock.

An older gentleman, fully dressed against the Scottish elements and carrying an antique metal lunch pail, jumped in fright. Ascertaining that it was only two women outside his cottage, he relaxed and leaned against the doorframe.

"Jesus, girls! You nearly took my life in surprise." The man's accent was thick and Skyler was glad she had studied dialects as well as languages. "There ain't usually a soul about when I leave for work in the morning." He took a deep breath and brought a steady pair of gray eyes to bear on them. "And who might ye be and what are ya doin' rummaging around at this hour?"

Addison took control of the conversation. "We're sorry to disturb you, sir, but we've run into a bit of car trouble several miles back. We're on official government business and would appreciate the use of your phone."

Skyler could see the gray haired man's mind working as he tried to reconcile "official government business" with the rough and bedraggled look of his visitors. Addison seemed to sense his hesitation also and she removed a small white card from a cargo pocket on her black trousers. Skyler saw it contained only one line of print.

"If you'll just call this number, sir," the agent continued, "and mention the name Addison Black. I'm sure everything will be explained to your satisfaction."

The man took the card, looked at the number and back at the pair. "I'll be late for work."

"We won't keep you but a minute, sir"

"My telephone bill…"

"You'll be generously reimbursed for any expense, Mr…"

"MacSwain," he supplied. "Well…wait here." He closed the door and the sound of a deadbolt being thrown was heard.

"Something you said?" Skyler asked.

"More likely something you wore, killer," Addison replied as she indicated blood stains and burns on her jacket that Skyler still wore.

"What was that number you gave him?"

Addison shrugged. "Well, normally I would have let my rapier-like wits and good looks secure my passage out of a situation like this, but I have you to think about. I merely gave him a contact number that should allow us…"

The rest of Addison's explanation was cut off as Mr. MacSwain opened the door again. "What are ya standing out in the night air for?

91

You'll catch your death. Please, come right in." He moved away from the door, motioning for them to enter. The cottage was small, but homey and blessedly warm. It was all Skyler could do not to let slip an audible sigh as she was shown to a comfortable floral print overstuffed chair.

"There's a man on the phone for you, Miss Black. He says it's urgent. I'll just put on the kettle to make you a nice cup of tea."

Skyler was amazed at the change in MacSwain's attitude and raised her eyebrows at Addison. The agent merely moved to the phone that rested on the top of a small bookcase just inside the main room and said over her shoulder, "My credit card must have been approved."

Snatching up the receiver, Addison said only, "Black." She listened for a few moments, glancing over at Skyler as she did.

"Yes, I understand. That's unfortunate," Addison spoke into the phone. "She's here with me. A little the worse for wear, but basically sound." Skyler felt an irrational sense of pride at the assessment. The agent continued the conversation as Mr. MacSwain returned with a small tray bearing two steaming mugs of tea and a plate of chocolate covered tea biscuits. Skyler took a mug gratefully and wrapped both hands around it as she sipped and made small talk with the gentleman. She assumed Addison was relating the details of her rescue and their current situation as she overheard the phrases "Brodie", "Innisbeth" and "Isle of Skye".

Mr. MacSwain consulted his watch and said to Skyler, "If I don't leave now, they'll be lined up outside waiting for me to unlock the gate to the woollen mill. It's in the next town so I need to be going. I suppose I can rely on Miss Black to lock up, eh?" He chuckled and winked at the American as he moved toward the door.

"Thank you so much for your help, Mr. MacSwain," Skyler said to the departing man.

"No thanks is necessary, lass. It's an honor to be of assistance." He came to attention, saluted Addison crisply and was out the door. The scholar returned her attention to the woman in black.

"No, I'll tell her. Yes, I'm sure. Goodbye, sir." Addison hung up the phone and turned to Skyler. "Ground transportation will be here in an hour. You'll be taken to the closest airport where you will be escorted back to London. Ah, tea. Just what I need and...Jaffa cakes!" Addison took up one of the spongy chocolate covered biscuits with the orange jelly filling and popped the whole thing into her mouth.

"If I did have a weakness, which I don't, Jaffa cakes might be it," the agent proclaimed. She picked up a second treat and it soon followed the first.

"**I'm** going to be taken to the nearest airport? You're not going?" Skyler asked.

Addison took a healthy swallow of her tea. "No, I have other business to attend to." By her tone of voice Skyler knew she was going after Brodie.

"Well, good luck in the hunt, Agent," Skyler said. "Um, Addison, what are you going to tell me? The conversation? You were going to tell me something. No, wait; let me guess. You were going to tell me that there is a big warm room waiting for me at the Ritz in London. Or maybe you were going to tell me you've arranged an hour long soak in a Jacuzzi tub followed by a vigorous massage by a hefty Swedish woman named Inga?"

Addison took another swallow of her tea as she studied Skyler in an appraising manner. "You don't seem to be the type to lose your composure so I'll give it to you straight. Your mother has gone missing. She's apparently been taken." The agent's breath stilled as she waited for a reaction.

The slow and calm manner in which Skyler set her mug back on the tray belied the surge of adrenalin now coursing through her veins in response to Addison's words. The scholar moved from the chair and walked directly up to the Brit, moving within inches of her face. She would have been looking directly into her eyes if Addison hadn't been an inch or two taller than her.

"Missing and apparently taken? You said you talked to her. How could she have been taken? Weren't you people and your super secret organization watching her?" With each sentence Skyler's voice rose.

"You're telling me I endured a kidnapping, imprisonment and beating all for nothing? What the hell is your problem? Is there only one fabulously skilled operative in your whole outfit? If that was the case then they should have left you with her and sent Average Joe Agent after me!" Skyler punctuated her statements by poking her index finger several times squarely onto Addison's breastbone.

The agent narrowed her eyes and her voice became deadly. "Don't poke me. I don't like it." Skyler realized she was jabbing a woman who only hours earlier had killed several people without batting an eye.

"Oh, um...sorry," she mumbled, but was sidetracked only momentarily. "It doesn't change the fact that your people dropped the ball and let somebody..." She stopped there and began to think.

"Somebody, but not Brodie. It couldn't have been, she was busy trying to eliminate us. That guy you interrogated said something about

93

'foreign alliances' and a meeting on the Isle of Skye. That's it, isn't it? There's a bigger plot going on here than just Agnes Brodie and her gang, isn't there?" Addison said nothing.

"That's where you're going on your 'business', isn't it? You're going to the Isle of Skye because you know that's where Brodie is going and where you think they've taken my mom!" Skyler took Addison's silence to mean she was right.

"That's good, Agent. You can just book two tickets to the Isle of Skye. I'm going with you."

Addison did react to that. "There's no way in hell you're going with me so get that thought out of your head. You're going back to London as planned and that's final!"

"Think about it logically here, Addison," Skyler said. "The way I see it there are two options. One, I can go to London and start trumpeting the fact that there is a secret government organization that allowed a well known scientist involved with biological studies to be 'taken' right out from under their noses. Two, you can take me with you and assure yourself of my silence and safety because I'm not safe in London, am I, Agent Black?"

Addison's jaw tightened and she felt herself being backed into a corner. She knew the abduction of Marlene Tidwell had to be facilitated by someone on the inside and discovering who the traitor was would begin on the Isle of Skye. If Addison sent Skyler back to London she couldn't guarantee her safety or that she wouldn't be taken again to use as a bargaining chip to force Marlene's co-operation. Her whole mission had been to prevent such a thing from happening in the first place.

"Field decision, you go," Addison growled. "But only for the two reasons you mentioned. I want your safety and your **silence**."

Skyler was elated as she watched the agent move to the phone again. "I'll be silent as the grave, Agent Black," she said and could only hope her words wouldn't be prophetic."

Chapter 9

Addison sat on an old leather couch, slouched down into the oversized piece of furniture. Her thighs were wide apart; one hand held a cup of strong, yet cool, tea that sat upon her stomach. The other hand rested beside her face, a single finger tapping her chin. Mr. MacSwain's house was silent apart from the echo of a ticking wall clock.

The two-story house was sparsely decorated; obvious signs that Mr. MacSwain lived alone. Piles of newspapers, dating back more than ten years, sat stacked in the back room. An aging record player stood in the corner beside a large selection of long playing records. They were all highly maintained with careful, loving pride. There were no signs of a television so Addison presumed the player was Mr. MacSwain's only source of entertainment.

Casting her eyes around the room, Addison noted the lack of decoration on faded, floral papered walls. Mr. MacSwain lived a simple life. In a certain way the agent could see a similarity between him and herself. Though her life was anything but simple, she saw loneliness in the Scot's living that she shared.

Turning back to Skyler, Addison observed the blonde doctor. Skyler sat in the chair opposite her, eyes closed in a moment of much needed rest. At that moment she looked so peaceful, so innocent. It was a stark contrast to Addison herself, but deep down inside, something she had longed to be. Skyler was innocent, Addison reminded herself. She should never have been exposed to this kind of life and Addison doubted Skyler's decision and understanding of what it meant to go with her.

"That was blackmail," she said offhandedly.

Green eyes blinked open. A second past before understanding dawned on Skyler. "Yeah, I suppose it was."

"Do you have any idea what could and has happened to people who have tried to black mail Her Majesty's government?"

Skyler's self-confidence faltered. "Um... no, but if that's the case, why did you agree I could come along then?"

For a moment, Addison pondered that very fact herself. "Because, like I said, I do feel you'd be safer with me for the time being." The agent had thought long and hard in considering Marlene's abduction and Skyler's safety. She came to only one conclusion, but it was a possibility she wouldn't bring to light at that time. Tidwell, mother and daughter, lives depended on it. Placing down her tea, Addison leaned forward, her elbows resting upon her knees.

"Well?" pressed Skyler.

"I have my reasons." Addison really didn't want to vocalise her suspicions until she obtained a little more proof.

A spark of annoyance flashed through Skyler's eyes. "I don't know why I even bothered. Are you always so cloaked and caged?"

"Only when needs be."

"You see that response?" Skyler pointed out. "What does that mean?"

Addison felt an impish mood take her. "Why do you ask?" Skyler clenched her jaw. The soldier could see her hackles begin to rise.

"Do you even know how to answer a simple question?"

"As opposed to?"

"That!"

"What?"

"I bet it's one of your lessons, isn't it?" Skyler stated. "In British spy school or whatever the hell you are. 'How to answer a question with a question'."

Addison nodded. "Yes, actually it is, right there before 'The art of yanking the proverbial chain to your advantage'."

"What?" Skyler's eyes drifted away from the soldier as her thoughts pondered over Addison's words. A flicker of understanding illuminated the doctor's features. "Okay, that's it. I've known you for less than twenty-four hours and you've proved to be one of the most..." she struggled to find the word which she felt best described the agent. "Infuriating... people I have ever encountered!" She placed down her empty cup and regarded Addison seriously. "Unfortunately for you, this isn't going to change my mind. I'm still going with you to the Isle of Skye."

Okay, Addison thought, *it's crunch time.* Placing down her own cup, Addison took the last Jaffa Cake from its box. "Look, Skyler, I have to be honest with you. Compared to some of my other assignments, what we just went through was a piece of piss. Things can get nasty... very nasty. I am talking blood, pain, violence and death. My job is to deal with people who don't respond to politeness or diplomacy. If you don't put a terminal stop to them, they will keep coming and coming and coming... until one of you is dead. Brodie is a fine example of that." Addison stood slowly. "You're coming with me because I'm concerned for your safety. But you must understand where we are going might well be all I just described. I can protect you, never doubt that, but you must be sure you know what you are getting yourself into and at every moment do exactly what I say." Finishing her speech, Addison sat back down and bit into her treat. She waited for Skyler's response.

Rising from her own seat, Skyler looked towards the adjoining door. "Give me a minute to think, will you?" She wrung her hands together. "I'm just going to wash up a little."

"Okay, but don't take too long." Addison motioned towards the window. "Our transportation will be arriving pretty soon."

With a nod, Skyler left the room.

Tapping her foot upon beige carpeted floor, Addison turned her attention to the old record player. She got up out of the chair and walked over to the pile of records by its side. Tentatively, she lifted a small handful from the pile and flipped through the selection. Many titles were unknown to her, but one particular sleeve caught her eye. It was a Cliff Richards album. Addison recalled how her mother had loved him and his music. Whenever she was playing his songs or watching his films Addison wasn't allowed to speak or make a sound. She remembered once looking through the collection of songs and receiving a beating from her mother for "touching what didn't belong to her". For a brief second, that same fearful emotion passed through her, but she brushed it aside. Addison slipped the pristine vinyl from its sleeve and placed it on the turntable. With an overpowering urge, she turned on the system and placed the needle on the record. Teak effect speakers crackled and hissed before a familiar song filtered into the room.

Addison crouched down, record sleeve in hand. The memorable melody of 'Summer Holiday' filled the room and Addison's reveries. She recalled her mother and the deadly look she would receive as she walked into the room. It was a clear warning that the wisest thing she could do was to keep quiet and leave. Addison always did, resenting

97

her mother a little more every time. Needless to say as she reached her early teens she spent as little time as possible with her parents.

Suddenly, and for the first time in many years, Addison wondered what became of her parents. Were they still alive? When she left for the Marines, much to the disgrace and shock of family and friends, she had bid a last farewell to her old life. None of them could believe or understand why she did it. She never told any of them what happened the night that changed her forever. How could they understand? The only thought that her mother and father seemed interested in was the fact they would have less money coming into the home. She wondered whether they missed her at all.

Hearing movement behind her, Addison turned to see Skyler step back into the room. She graced the agent with a questioning look.

Switching off the player, Addison returned the album to its sleeve and placed it back upon the pile. She made sure it was in the exact position she had originally found it.

"I was just reminiscing," Addison offered. "You don't see many of these around anymore."

"No, you don't." Skyler looked out the window. She saw what appeared to be two cars pull up outside the small house. Momentarily ignoring them, she turned back to Addison, whom she could see was also aware of their presence. "I'm coming with you."

Addison pursed her lips. "Okay." She nodded swiftly. "Then I need to give you something… but let's wait until we're on our way." With those words Addison opened the front door. Standing on the other side, just about to knock, was Quinton Zimmerman. "You took your time," the agent said and stepped out into the street. Skyler followed her but remained by the doorway to Mr. MacSwain's dwelling.

"Well excuse me! I heard you already trashed one of our vehicles." Quinton leaned up against Addison's new 'set of wheels'. "So what do you think?"

The soldier nodded, she was impressed. "Nice."

"Nice?" Quinton gasped. "Addy, this is a Subaru Forester turbo. It has the engine of an Impreza, all wheel drive," He ran his hand over the navy blue paintwork. "The handling is great. I have one of these myself."

"Quinton, you're not trying to sell it to me, you know!"

Quinton carried on regardless. "Plus, a bonus is that it looks like your average Joe Nobody's land cruiser. Perfect for you and this kind of job."

"I get the point." Addison peered through the window. "Looks good." She briefly registered the two uniformed soldiers who stood by a second, more traditional military vehicle. "There's been a change of plan."

Quinton turned from his appraisal of Skyler to Addison. "Change? What kind of change?" Suspicion was clear in his voice.

"Well," Addison paused, knowing Quinton would not like her intentions. "You will no longer be escorting this woman back to London."

Skyler frowned at the term, 'this woman'.

"What? What exactly do you mean, Addison?" Quinton's voice rose. "We are under direct orders to escort the female in your care back to Headquarters."

"I changed my mind."

"You can't do that. The General will blow one!" It was common knowledge that Mark Blithe could, at times, have a very short temper.

Addison merely shrugged. "He'll understand."

"Oh yeah... just like he did when you commandeered a certain yacht last year."

"I was in a rush."

"It was the Queen's."

"She wasn't on it."

"Lucky for you!" Quinton sighed. "Why?"

Rolling her eyes, Addison patted the taller man on his back. "Look, just tell Blithe I will explain it all when we next talk."

"I strongly advise against this." Quinton put his arm on Addison's shoulder and spoke quietly in her ear. "This could be very dangerous. Are you sure you know what you are doing?"

"Always, Quin." She took the Forester keys from his hand and turned to Skyler. "Are you ready?"

"Yes." Skyler walked up to the passenger door of the car.

"You have the envelope?" Addison questioned Quinton.

Quinton Zimmerman took the white envelope out of his inner pocket and handed it to Addison as she handed him Myers' weapon. She took the item back into Mr. MacSwain's house and placed it upon his coffee table. It was a 'special letter' occasionally given to civilians on behalf of Her Majesty Queen Elizabeth II, thanking a member of the public for assisting her government's soldiers in a time of need. It was always highly appreciated and better received than reimbursement for expenses incurred.

Exiting the house, Addison closed the door behind her. Quinton had already climbed into the Jeep behind them. He sat in the passenger seat beside a broad Marine Commando. Addison nodded in thanks.

Her friend just shook his head.

"One last chance?" Addison offered Skyler.

For her answer, the blonde opened her door and got into the vehicle.

"I suppose that's a no." Walking around the Forester, Addison climbed into the driver's seat. She pushed the key into the ignition and started the engine. "No turning back now." Addison pulled out onto the village street and began their perilous journey.

****

By midday, Addison had escaped the rough dirt tracks that passed as roads and found a semi-decent 'B' road. It was still one lane in each direction, but at least the ground was level. That made for a smoother drive. For the most part they were still surrounded by the Highlands. The great hills would recede the closer they drove towards the ocean.

Addison yawned. She looked to her side where Skyler slept beside her. The blonde's head rested upon the window. Addison was thankful, once again, that the rocky terrain had eased, making sleep for Skyler possible. The young doctor looked exhausted. Rest, however much it was, would do her a world of good.

Up ahead, Addison spotted a welcoming sight. It was a mileage sign and logo for the next service station. She would soon require fuel and was sure Skyler was as hungry as she was. Apart from that, her bladder had been screaming for relief for the past half an hour. With added enthusiasm, Addison increased her speed and soon saw the sign for a small roadside café and petrol station. She pulled into the car park.

Needing to wake Skyler, Addison turned to the dozing blonde. Reaching over she tickled Skyler's nose. There was no response. She tried again, only to have her hand brushed away. Smiling, Addison leaned further over to Skyler.

"Hey," she whispered.

Skyler hummed, turning towards Addison's voice.

"Wake up!"

There was no response.

"Skyler?" Addison leaned back slightly. "Skyler, wake up. Break time."

The blonde slept on.

"Don't make me do this the hard way."

Nothing.

100

Addison shrugged. "Fine." Clasping her hands around Skyler's shoulders, the soldier shook her while calling, "Skyler Tidwell, wake the hell up!"

Shocked green eyes flew open. "What are you doing?"

"Well it's about time. Bloody hell woman; how the hell do you wake up in the morning? Does your alarm clock have a built in fog horn?" Addison unbuckled Skyler's seat belt. She held her thumb and index finger close together. "I was this close to checking for a bleeding pulse."

"I'm a heavy sleeper," Skyler replied. She followed Addison as the ebony haired woman exited the Forester.

An early afternoon chill greeted them. Addison looked around the service station. There were two buildings; the largest was to the left. A new, red brick establishment offered cooked foods and a selection of coffee. To the right was a smaller, narrow building. It was the petrol station offering a limited selection of travel snack foods, maps, magazines and only three petrol pumps. The colours were clear, indicating one of each fuel: unleaded, diesel, and four-star. Addison and Skyler headed towards the diner.

"Heavy sleeper?" Addison laughed as they passed a dark green tractor. "The only other person I know who can sleep like that was my uncle Benny and he was in a coma for two years."

"Funny!" Skyler replied in a droll voice. "So, is that the wit you say you rely on in tight situations? If it is then I think any response you get is nothing more than sympathy at your lame sense of humour."

Addison grinned widely. "Believe me... I am quite capable of causing **many** reactions in people!" She pulled open the single swing door. "Ladies first."

Skyler walked into the café, Addison by her side. The fragrant aroma of home cooked foods and fresh coffee was a welcome invasion to the senses. Although the café was quite large, with ten circular tables and several, more private, booths, only six people inhabited the establishment. Two sat at the counter, Addison could tell they were locals. A young couple sat in the middle of the room. By their dress she could easily surmise they were from a larger city. Two heavy goods drivers sat devouring hearty lunches. Addison headed towards the corner booth and sat in a vinyl chair opposite Skyler. A laminated menu stood in the centre of the table beside empty salt and pepper pots. Picking up the menu, Skyler browsed the diner's offerings. "Oh my god, they have black pudding. I know what that stuff is." She grimaced and placed the menu down, sliding it over to Addison.

"No, you order," Addison replied. She brought out her wallet and placed a twenty-pound note upon the table. She had plenty of money. In Addison's ever-constant need to be prepared for any situation, on every mission she carried a certain amount of cash and several credit cards, provided by Special Operations, of course. It was important that each agent had an unlimited expense account on each mission because they could never know if and when they would need the cash... even if it were to be used as a bribe. She slid the note over to Skyler. "Get me a tuna sandwich, four of them, two bottles of mineral water and a black coffee. Get yourself whatever you want as well. I'm just heading to the bathroom. I'll be less than a minute."

"Why do I have to go?" Skyler sat back in her chair. "And what was it you said about wanting to give me something? You never did."

"One, because they love Americans up here... and two, when I get back I will tell you." Saying that, Addison headed off towards a wide blue door.

As promised, Addison returned within a minute to find Skyler still at the counter, ordering their food. She sat back at the booth and waited. Addison watched as Skyler spoke to a very handsome Scotsman. She would have thought there was interplay of serious flirting occurring between them, but on catching a glimpse of Skyler's expression, she could see the interest was only one way. Just as she was about to go over and innocently intervene, Skyler headed back to their table.

"So how long will it take?"

Skyler sat back down. "Conner says about fifteen minutes."

"Fifteen? There is hardly anybody here!" Addison adopted a curious expression. "I bet it wouldn't have taken so long if you hadn't been flirting with chef boy over there." She knew she was goading Skyler, but couldn't seem to help it. There was a fire in her eyes that Addison found both daring and exciting.

"I was not. I was only giving our order."

"Then why is he looking over here like a lovesick school boy?"

Skyler turned and sure enough Connor was looking over in her direction. She smiled innocently, gave him a slight wave and turned back to Addison. "He's just being friendly. I didn't give him any encouragement."

Addison nodded. "Good," then added rather swiftly, "We can do without the attention." She traced her fingers over the table absently. "Listen... what I wanted to give you was this." Cautiously, she pulled an item from her pocket, an item that had previously resided on her boot, and placed it on the table. Addison kept her hand upon the gun and holster, shielding it from prying eyes.

102

"What it is?" Skyler tried to peer under Addison's hand.

"It's a pistol."

"What? Green eyes grew wide. "No way."

"Look," Addison leaned closer, lowering her voice. "I am in a position to give you this and you must take it."

Skyler shook her head. She was adamant. "No... I can't... I could never shoot somebody."

"That's not what I am asking." Addison took a deep breath as she began explaining herself. She kept her hand covering the Browning pistol. "I don't want you to use it on anybody, I would never **ever** ask that of you. Think about this logically... if you were to fire a gun in the vicinity of a flock of birds, what would they do?"

"I guess they would fly away," Skyler answered, still not positive where Addison was heading with her reasoning.

"Exactly." Addison looked down at her hand. "Remember, it's the person holding the weapon that bears the responsibility. All I'm asking is that you take it for insurance. If you are confronted, sometimes just to point one of these things in a person's direction is enough to scare them away. If not then fire a round **near** them as a warning. Just like the birds, it can be enough to scare somebody away."

Skyler appeared to think for a moment. "And what if it isn't?"

Taking Skyler's hand Addison placed the pistol upon her palm. The gun lay between their hands. "Then I would have heard the shot, I would recognise the sound and will be there for you. It's a worst case scenario issue, but I like to be prepared."

With a sigh, Skyler nodded her head. "Okay... but I hope to God I never have to use it." She took the pistol and attached it to the back of her jeans, imitating the way Addison wore both of hers.

"I do too." The agent pulled out two spare clips. "These go with it. Just put them in your pocket."

Skyler took them silently, slipping them into the pocket of Addison's coat, which she still wore.

Just then, Connor appeared at their table holding a fully loaded tray. "Ladies," he said, filling their table.

Addison watched as a large plate was placed in front of Skyler. She frowned at Skyler's choice, but waited for the waiter to leave before she made comment. Eventually he did.

"You turn your nose up at black pudding, yet you are prepared to eat haggis?"

"It's supposed to be the owner's special, secret recipe," Skyler defended as she poked a fork into her meal.

"Yeah? Well so was my aunt's 'broiled pig's head stew' but that didn't appeal to me either."

In the background, soft tones from a radio floated through the air. Addison looked over to where Connor had turned on the small wireless. He twisted the dial to a station playing love songs and looked over at her table.

"Ugh..." Addison groaned in annoyance.

Skyler carried on obliviously. "And you're the one who's supposed to have the adventurous spirit."

Addison picked up her sandwich. "I know my limits."

"Pigs' heads?"

"And sheep stomachs." Addison bit into her sandwich. She chewed thoughtfully. Something had suddenly occurred to Skyler and Addison could tell it seemed to trouble her. She didn't need to guess what Skyler was thinking. "You're worried about your mother."

Skyler placed down her fork. "How can I sit here like this, knowing there's a high probability my mother could be suffering at the hands of the same person I did?" She pushed her plate away, losing her appetite. "I want to keep moving, Addison. I don't want her to suffer a second more than she has to."

"Okay." Addison rose to her feet, swallowing. "We keep moving. I'll fill the car, you grab us some snacks for travel and we'll get on our way."

Skyler smiled. "Thank you."

****

Guided by an onboard satellite navigation system, Addison had agreed for Skyler to take the wheel. It gave the agent time to rest her tired eyes. Though she had gone much longer without sleep, she indulged Skyler's request to drive. She knew the blonde didn't want to feel useless.

Looking out of the passenger's window, Addison watched as they passed tall telephone pylons. Cables stretched out between each thick pole, occasionally connecting to a farmhouse or solitary dwelling scattered over the Scottish highlands. Looking at the lone buildings, Addison was reminded of her own home; her lighthouse, standing alone on the Cornish coastal cliff-tops. Sometimes Addison yearned for that solitude. It was her only escape.

Turning from the view, Addison loosened her jacket. Skyler had increased the car's heating and the agent was beginning to sweat. Unhooking the last button of her jacket, Addison unclipped her seatbelt. She shrugged out of her outer layer, chucking it onto the back seat.

"I wonder what goodies Quinton left for us." She twisted in her seat to where a black backpack, similar to the one destroyed in the explosion, sat behind them. She unbuttoned the carrier and began to root inside. She had left the Uzi she took from Myers with Quinton. They would be able to run a weapons search to assess where Brodie, or the organisation she worked for, obtained their arms. For that reason Addison looked with curiosity for what Quinton would have left for her in return. Finding nothing, Addison made a mental note to check the boot of the Forester later.

Through her rummaging, Addison found a new pair of binoculars. She also found a small device that looked like the handle of a kite. It was a solid metal object with two buttons, one red and one green. On pressing the green button it would shoot out a cable for climbing high walls. The red button would re-coil the cable after use. It was another of Perkins' inventions and one of Addison's favourites. She attached its handy pouch to a free space upon her belt.

"Oh great, a clean shirt." Addison pulled the black garment out of her new backpack. She turned to Skyler. "Do you want it?"

The doctor smiled. "I think on the grimy scale you rank the highest. You should take it."

Addison began to undo her dirt encrusted, slightly torn, shirt. She had no reservation about undressing in front of an audience because she was wearing a tank top under her shirt. Slipping her arms from the garment, Addison threw it onto the back seat beside her jacket. She could see Skyler observe her briefly from the corner of her eye.

"You were in the Marines." Skyler didn't seem at all surprised.

"Pardon?" Addison looked to her arm where the fact was clearly tattooed onto her flesh. "Oh yes, yes I was."

"Must have been rough," Skyler observed. "I bet you saw it as a challenge though, right? I mean… you are obviously the kind of person who thrives on…"

"Hey…" Addison interrupted. "What do you mean, 'kind of person'? Are you psychoanalysing me now?" She slipped into the clean shirt. "I suppose that's another letter or two you have after your name."

"And what does that mean? Is that a dig?"

Fastening her buttons Addison shrugged. "I just noticed you have an awful lot of letters there, Doc. What's your aim, to out-letter the alphabet? I think you are almost there with the Greek one. It is a hobby?"

The question seemed to catch Skyler by surprise. Addison wondered whether she, in fact, knew the answer to that herself. Skyler thought for a moment. "It's what I do. It's what I enjoy."

"I suppose." Addison drummed her fingers in thought. "I am sure there must be more exciting hobbies though? I mean... some people knit, okay not so thrilling to everybody. Others build models out of matchsticks or go bowling. There are even a few crazy folks out there who watch trains or collect watches or coins. I suppose it is a case of whatever floats your boat."

"Precisely," Skyler smiled with a nod. "Everybody finds something interesting. It doesn't have to fit into other people's view of entertainment."

Addison lifted her body slightly and tucked the slim fitting shirt into her combat trousers. She wasn't finished, however. "I just happen to be of the point of view that there are a lot more fun and interesting things you can lock yourself in a room with than a pile of old, musty books."

Skyler pondered Addison's words. Her reply was something Addison never expected. "You never did so well at school, did you? You're obviously better educated now, with the work you do, but at school, you weren't really interested, were you?"

"Touché," was the agent's only reply. "But I do stick to my point. I have logged **many** hours on this subject." The lascivious undertone was anything but.

"Okay." Skyler turned the Forester left towards an approaching harbour. The Atlantic Ocean began to emerge ahead of them. "Maybe that will be my next course of study then."

Addison winked. "Fine, but after you graduate I want you to report back to Professor Black and tell me how right I was!" She held her hand out and Skyler shook it.

"It's a deal, Professor."

They maintained eye contact and grinned slyly.

Addison gave a self-satisfied nod and then looked as a mass of fishing boats appeared before them. "Keep us out of view. We're here."

Chapter 10

"I know I drove, but where is 'here' exactly?" Skyler asked as she manoeuvred the car slowly through the narrow streets.

"This is Kyle of Lochalsh," Addison informed her. "It's just a Scottish coastal village, but it's the place where we're going to meet our contact. Hopefully by now Quinton and his staff have arranged a boat over to the Isle of Skye.

"To find my mom and get her the hell out of danger. I can testify how nasty those bastards can be." The American's voice was strained with tension.

Addison didn't reply to Skyler's comments. She knew the mission and knew the brutality Skyler had suffered. Without looking at the scholar she asked, "You're okay?" Although the question was simple and the agent's demeanor seemed offhand, the tone was sympathetic and it touched Skyler.

"I've been better, but considering what Brodie had in mind, I could have been a lot worse. Addison?"

The agent drew her gaze back into the car from the homes and businesses that they were passing. Like Skyler, she had noticed several closed shops and didn't wonder at the reason locals might cooperate with strangers. Money was a potent motivator.

"Yeah?"

Skyler hesitated a moment, the verbal bantering and occasional butting of heads making her a little embarrassed. "I...well, I guess what I wanted to say was thank you. It just occurred to me that I never did tell you that. So…thanks. I appreciated you getting me out of that mess."

Addison smiled. It was a soft smile and unlike the cocky grin she had sported at other times. "You're entirely welcome, Miss Tidwell. I'm glad to have been of service." Skyler returned the smile and there seemed to be a flash of true camaraderie between the women. It appeared to Skyler that at that point Addison realized she was dropping her guard and she watched with a pang of dismay as the shield of indifference was raised again. "That's what they pay me for. Foil a plot, rescue a Yank…it's all in a day's work." She resumed viewing their surroundings and Skyler thought how beautiful the already attractive agent had looked in that brief interlude. The momentary lapse by the English enigma was precisely that… momentary. Now Skyler could almost see her mask slip back into place.

"Pull in here," Addison directed. The Forester slid smoothly into a place in front of a weather worn grey building, its faded paint and beaten façade a testament to the storms off the North Atlantic that battered the Scottish coast. A carved sign in the window read, "Fairworth Antiques, F. Fairworth, Proprietor".

Skyler turned the key and the engine stilled. "What are we doing here?"

"Fairworth is the name of our contact. There was a note along with an address in the bottom of the bag Quinton gave me. Apparently we'll be able to get a boat from him. I imagine he's a retired fisherman or something like that who lets his boat out on occasion. That would seem likely in a village like this."

Easing from the car, they made their way to the front door. A small white sign beneath the name of the establishment read, "Gone to tea. Haddock's Head Pub, directly behind you."

"He's gone, but not far," Addison observed as she turned to spy the pub across the road from where they stood. "We don't have time to wait, let's go find him." The pair crossed the cobblestone road and entered an equally weather worn building on the opposite side.

The interior of the Haddock's Head was at odds with its exterior. The room was warm and cheerful and the bar was immaculate right down to the polished wood and gleaming brass rail. A plethora of bottles lined the shelves behind it. Cozy tables were set for tea and patrons enjoying a steaming pot of tea or a pint of ale with their afternoon food occupied several of them.

Skyler observed as Addison scanned the customers. Nodding her head, she moved decisively toward a gray bearded gentleman seated alone enjoying a crustless sandwich and a small glass of amber liquid.

A navy colored pea coat hung over the back of the chair next to him and a gnarled cane, resembling a corkscrew more than a walking stick, leaned against the table.

Straight off a fishing boat Skyler thought. *Damn, Addison's good* she admitted to herself. The agent approached the older gentleman and asked, "Fairworth?"

The man seemed to ignore them, but a soft voice behind them said, "Yes?" The women turned to be confronted with a very attractive brunette somewhere in her mid-thirties holding a half-filled pint of lager. "I'm Fiona Fairworth, can I help you?" she asked in a pleasant burr.

"You own Fairworth Antiques?" Skyler questioned and received a look from Addison that said, "I'll do the talking".

"Oh, an American," Fiona gushed, "I love Americans! Come looking for a bargain, have you?"

"Actually," Addison interrupted, "We're here to arrange transportation to the Isle of Skye. I believe my Uncle Tony made the arrangements."

Fiona's face gave away nothing, but her eyes reflected understanding. "Surely now I remember. Transportation for two, correct?" At Addison's nod the brunette smiled. "Won't you come right this way? We can transact our business in the shop." The Scottish woman gave a short wave to the bartender and turned toward the door. She drained her lager and set the glass on a nearby table. Looking at Addison, she winked and said, "Liquid sunshine, most excellent for fighting off this brass monkey weather." Fiona's laugh was as smooth as the whiskey her country was famous for and she led them out the door and back across the street.

"Your Uncle Tony?" Skyler whispered as they moved.

"Blair," Addison explained in a low voice as they entered the shop behind the Scotswoman.

As soon as they were inside, Fiona said to Skyler, "You're the American, so that makes you..." her attention turned to Addison.

"Anxious to be on our way," Addison finished for her.

"Of course," the brunette assured her. "I must say, Agent Black, I wasn't expecting..."

"A woman?" Addison challenged.

"Someone quite so attractive," Fiona countered. Addison was pleased with this reply and opened her mouth to respond to Fiona's flirtations, but caught sight of Skyler out of the corner of her eye and stopped herself.

"About the transportation?" the agent asked, getting back to business.

"Of course," Fiona said. "I've arranged for you to go along with my man Darren. He's waiting for you at the docks and will be ready to go anytime you get there."

"The sooner the better," Skyler interjected. They received directions to the boat docks and moved to exit the shop.

"Come back when you have the time to stay longer," the Scotswoman said to Addison, placing a familiar hand on the agent's arm. "Oh, and you too, miss," she added as almost an afterthought to Skyler.

"I bet," an annoyed scholar said under her breath as an inexplicable pang of jealousy stung her. "I'd like to come back all right. Come back and slap her."

"Slapper?" Addison asked. "I'm sure she is." The agent held out her hand for the keys and, receiving them, slipped behind the wheel of the car. Skyler moved into the passenger seat.

"She is what?" the scholar questioned.

"A slapper" Addison replied.

"God, I forgot that practically bionic hearing of yours," Skyler groaned. "Hey, what's a slapper?"

Addison quirked her cocky grin as she started the vehicle. "I believe you scholarly types would call her a woman of easy virtue."

"Easy virtue is an understatement," Skyler scoffed. "If I hadn't been there she would have been on you like white on rice."

"Probably," the agent confirmed as she guided the car.

"I can see why," Skyler said without thinking. To cover her slip she changed the subject. "By the way, your advanced arsenal must not include psychic powers. I thought Fairworth was going to be a grizzled old fisherman."

"Well," Addison observed dryly, "She was fishing for something alright, just not fish."

"Oh, brother," the American laughed. "We're going to need a damn big boat if we're going to haul that huge ego of yours across to the Isle of Skye."

Addison laughed as well, but further conversation was prevented as they arrived at the boat docks. Several long docks were divided into individual slips and the vessels there ran the gamut of small ships. There were sleek powerboats moored alongside small trawlers and stately sailboats. The Englishwoman guided the Forester into a space adjacent to the waterfront.

"Let's get the gear and find the boat," Addison instructed. They left the vehicle with the backpack given to them by Quinton and while

Skyler scanned the boats for the "Maid of the Atlantic", Addison went to the trunk and opened it. Rummaging inside she made several thoughtful selections that were deposited into a tubular shaped duffel bag and slung over her shoulder. At that moment Skyler rejoined her.

"You're not going to like this," the doctor said.

Addison narrowed her eyes. "Why not?"

"Because **that**," Skyler said, "is the Maid of the Atlantic." She pointed at a decrepit vessel that resembled a miniature tugboat. It was loaded with crates and rode low in the water.

"Bollocking hell!" Addison spat. "That bucket of barnacles will take forever to make the crossing. I'll wager I could swim there faster!" She walked toward the boat, then stopped to survey it with hands on her hips. "I'd say that thing couldn't go much faster than..."

"Fucking bitch!" At Skyler's tone, Addison spun around to find the source of the American's irritation. She didn't have far to look as she followed Skyler's line of sight. On the opposite side of the marina, a sleek powerboat started and revved its considerable engines. A nondescript man sat at the wheel, but there was no mistaking his redheaded passenger.

"Brodie," Skyler muttered as she reached back to the pistol attached to her waist. Pulling it out she moved toward the boat that was backing slowly from its berth. "I'll kill her."

"No you don't," Addison said as she grabbed Skyler from behind and pulled her down, effectively shielding them from the boat Brodie was in. Addison rolled on top of Skyler and used her body weight to hold the American in place.

"Let me go, damn it!" Skyler hissed up at the agent. "I'm going to kill her!"

"And kill your mother in the process!" Addison said as she looked down into green eyes that glittered with hatred. Her words, however, seemed to take hold as Skyler's struggling ceased. "If we take out Agnes now, we lose the greatest chance we have of finding your mother quickly. Let me handle this." Skyler breathed hard and her jaw worked as she clenched her teeth. Addison kept looking the scholar directly in the eye as she said earnestly, "Trust me."

There was nothing in her extensive academic experience to prepare her for this decision. Skyler knew she had to decide quickly so she went with her gut instinct. "Do it," she said.

Addison immediately rolled off the blonde and came to her feet in one fluid motion. She moved in a crouch down the dock, paralleling the movement of the powerboat as it eased through the marina. As she went she pulled her own pistol from her waistband and fished in a pocket with the other hand. Skyler rolled to her stomach in time to see her fit a cylindrical extension on the barrel of the gun and shove something inside. The ebony haired woman then moved to the very end of the dock, a spot that would be the closest the boat would come to their position.

Addison dropped to one knee and brought the gun up. She held the pistol in her right hand and she cupped that hand in her left to steady her aim. As the now loudly throbbing boat passed, Skyler saw Addison's hand jerk a fraction of an inch. Then the agent dropped back to a concealed position as the boat passed and picked up speed as it headed out to sea.

When it was sufficiently out of sight, Addison rose up and walked back to Skyler. She gave her hand to the American and assisted her to her feet. The puzzled expression she sported made Addison know what was coming.

"Ask," the agent said.

Skyler stepped up close to Addison. She stared into calm brown eyes. "You said to trust you. I **did** trust you and you just let her go. How could you do that? You just let her go," Skyler said in a disappointed tone.

Addison leaned forward until her forehead almost touched the American's and smiled. "There's letting someone go and then there's letting them go with a farewell gift." She stepped back and walked over to the duffel bag. She removed a square black box the size of a Walkman. She pulled an antenna from the object and flipped a switch on the face. A slow, steady beep issued from the object.

"Gotcha!" Addison said in triumph. She looked at Skyler. "Tracking system. Works with some of those lovely satellites our countries have spinning overhead. Agnes may get to the Isle of Skye ahead of us, but we are going to know exactly where she lands thanks to this little beauty."

"You shot a transmitter at the boat, didn't you?" Skyler asked, clearly impressed. Addison nodded her head. "Then I'm sorry I doubted you, Agent Black and I'm glad I trusted you. I won't question you again."

Addison laughed at that statement. "Yes, you will, Doctor. It's in your nature to question everything. Now, let's follow that boat." She glanced from Skyler to the Maid of the Atlantic. "Slowly."

****

At that moment a disembodied electronic voice came over the

speakers into the lab where Marlene Tidwell sat. The tone was distorted and it was impossible to determine the true voice it concealed.

"Professor Tidwell, welcome to our facility. I'm truly sorry we had to resort to heavy handed tactics to bring you here." Marlene unconsciously brought her hand up to her cheek where a deep cut had been closed with butterfly sutures. It had stopped bleeding, but it now throbbed with pain. She shifted on the high stool she was perched on.

The voice continued. "You know what we want, Doctor. We want details, all of them. Project Gemini is important to plans that are already underway and we have waited long enough to get this information. There will be no further delay. You may use the paper and pens on the laboratory table in front of you. Begin now."

Marlene was a little in shock by her violent abduction, but it wasn't enough to blindly follow the instructions of her captors. "You must be joking. I'm not going to give you the information about my research."

"On the contrary, Professor, you will. Please direct your attention to the closed circuit monitor on the desk next to you." Marlene glanced over as the screen flickered to life. An image of a young blonde woman being hustled into a building was shown. Even bound, gagged and with hands secured behind her back, the woman was unmistakable.

"Skyler!" Marlene cried and moved from her stool to get closer to the monitor. The image faded as she neared.

"What have you done with her?" the American yelled into the room.

"She is quite unharmed and is our guest. Did you think that Agent Black would free her? I regret to inform you that Addison Black is dead and that your daughter remains our guest. She will be freed, along with yourself, the moment we have verified the information you are going to provide us with."

Marlene did not have the resourcefulness of her daughter. She did not know that the footage of Skyler was over twenty-four hours old and that her daughter was no longer being held. All she had was the heart of a mother and that heart told her to do whatever had to be done to secure the safety of her child.

With a feeling of desperation and no hope left, Marlene returned to the lab table. She picked up a pen and began revealing Project Gemini.

****

As the Maid of the Atlantic chugged her way across the water toward the Isle of Skye, Skyler settled up against a secured stack of crates and closed her eyes. Crossing her arms over her chest to ward off the cold sea breeze, she tried to rest but found her mind drifting time and time again to her mother. She knew Brodie was speeding ahead of them and she worried what a meeting between Agnes and her mother would mean to her mom's well being. She shifted restlessly against the crates.

A warm form moved next to her and she opened her eyes to see Addison who had left her spot at the front of the craft where she had been scanning the sea with binoculars. They sat shoulder to shoulder on the gently pitching deck.

"I estimate an hour for the crossing at this speed," Addison informed her. "The tracking device is working well. We're not going to have a problem finding where they put ashore." Seeing the concerned look on Skyler's face she added, "Don't worry, we'll find her. We'll get her back, find out who's behind this scheme and put a closing note to Agnes Brodie's biography."

"She's got a big head start on us, Addison. You know that a woman like Brodie doesn't need much time when she's determined and my mom doesn't have you around to help her out." Skyler dropped her gaze to the deck.

"Hey," the agent said as she gently lifted the American's chin. Your mum and you are made of the same genetic material, right?" Skyler nodded. "Well you had to get your pluck from somewhere. Remember I met her before I came after you. She didn't strike me as someone who would give in to the likes of Agnes."

"I just hope she's safe," Skyler said as tears misted her vision. She rubbed them from her eyes with the back of her hand. "Damn it! I don't want to start this. Talk to me about something else. Anything as long as I don't have to think about what might be happening to her."

"Okay," Addison agreed. "Why don't you tell me what you know about your mother's work? Maybe if I understand the nature of Project Gemini a little better it may give me a clue why all this is happening."

"To tell you the truth, I don't know everything she had been working on," Skyler began. "I've been out of the country for a while, but I do know she was working with the tuberculosis bacteria. She had been looking at other, more beneficial, applications for it."

"Tell me about that then. Start at the beginning. There has to be something here I don't see yet."

Skyler's superb mind went to work then and she pulled out what she recalled from a class she had taken in Epidemiology. "Tuberculosis has been around for a long time. There are scientists now who have found evidence of tuberculosis in the skull and spinal bones of Egyptian mummies dating back four thousand years, but it wasn't until Hippocrates wrote about a disease he called 'phthisis' about 2,400 years ago in Greece that we have a written record of the problem." Addison listened and marveled at Skyler's recall.

"During the Middle Ages, it was postulated that most Europeans were infected and the disease probably accounted for one in every four deaths. Today the World Health Organization estimates that fully one third of the world's population is infected and three million die from it every year. Even Great Britain and the United States saw a resurgence of the disease in the eighties and nineties, probably because of AIDS, which makes people more susceptible to the disease, and the emergence of multi-drug resistant strains. Basically, wherever there is overpopulation, crowding and poverty, you're going to find tuberculosis."

Skyler paused here and shivered as a gust of wind blew off the ocean and chilled her again.

"Cold?" Addison asked.

"A little," Skyler replied. Addison moved closer and wrapped an arm around Skyler.

The American hummed in happiness. "Man, you're warm. You're like a portable electric blanket."

Addison just chuckled. "I've always been that way. The doctors doing my physical for the Marines thought I was coming down with some sort of illness, but it seems my core temperature runs a little higher than almost everyone else. I don't know why that is, but feeling cold has never been a problem for me. Don't let me interrupt you though. Go ahead with what you were saying."

Skyler returned to her lesson. "Okay, tuberculosis is caused by a micro-organism called a mycobacterium. There are several types of mycobacterium and each one causes a different disease. One can cause tuberculosis; one causes leprosy and so on. They look like strings of link sausages under the microscope and are known as bacilli. Droplets spread the bacilli, usually the kind you find when a person coughs or sneezes. It can affect many body parts, but eighty percent of the time it infects the lungs."

"I know mom had figured out a way to inactivate the disease portion of the mycobacterium. I'm not sure how, but I do know the bacilli is sensitive to heat and UV light. Anyway, she apparently developed a strain that could carry drugs instead of disease. The drugs were going to be used to fight cancer. Can you imagine how much easier it would be to inhale chemotherapy rather than have it injected into your bloodstream? This was only the tip of the iceberg; the medical implications are enormous!"

"I can understand that but what is Project Gemini?" Addison asked.

Skyler shrugged. "I know mom said the Gemini part was her idea. Gemini indicated the twin nature of the bacteria. First it was a deadly disease carrier and now she hoped it would cure disease. What else there is to know about the project is common knowledge. Your government and mine gave her grant money to set up a lab in England and take the technology as far as it could go. Whatever she had been working on recently, I don't have any idea."

Addison was silent a moment. "Okay, let's see what we have... a germ of some kind... highly contagious. Works best in a crowd. Carries disease or possibly drugs now." She stopped suddenly as Skyler drew in a breath sharply. "You're thinking what I'm thinking, aren't you?"

Skyler looked up into the deep brown eyes of the agent. "I think I am. Biological warfare?"

"Uh-huh," confirmed Addison. "Fuck."

Chapter Eleven

Shadowed by an armed guard dressed in navy overalls and a scientist sporting a pristine white lab coat, Agnes Brodie swiped her identification card through an electronic locking system. Immediately a door, by which they were all standing, clicked in several places and its numerous bolts were deactivated. With a confident air, Brodie pushed the door open and stepped inside a wide, illuminated room. Freshly painted white walls increased its brightness. It was a simple space, decorated only with one metallic table in the centre, a camp bed to the right and sink to the left. What appeared to be a closed circuit monitor was built into the room's table. The building they inhabited stood five miles from the sea. It was four stories high and over two hundred years old. Marlene Tidwell was held in a secure room at the top of the structure. Her window had been previously bricked up without plastering; white paint merely covered the masonry. It marked a clear indication where the room's window used to be.

Seated at the table, Marlene Tidwell watched nervously as the fearsome looking threesome entered. They were the first real contact with people she had received since arriving at this unknown destination. First to enter was a tall redhead. She wore her hair down around her shoulders, was dressed in similar attire to the man who entered second, but she held a definite manner of authority. Last to enter the room was a stunted, stocky man with a smooth bald head. His white lab coat was fully buttoned to his neck with nothing more than a light blue bowtie showing under his chin.

Nervously, Marlene waited for one of them to speak.

"Professor Tidwell," Agnes greeted. "So nice to finally meet you... at last. I must say your daughter did try and lead us to believe she was in fact you. Unfortunately for her, we are a little wiser than that."

"What have you done to her? Where is Skyler?" Marlene rose from her chair in panic. "If you've hurt her I'll..."

"Yes?" Brodie asked bluntly. Her eyes glowed with a predatory gleam. "I happen to think you are in the least of positions to be making threats, Professor." Brodie walked over to the table and sat down opposite Marlene. She waited with apparent expectation for the Professor to do the same. She didn't wait long as Marlene sat down rigidly in compliance.

"Good... now let's set out the facts shall we? You have something I want. I have something you want." Brodie grinned humourlessly. "Surly it doesn't take a PHD to realise how this can work to both our advantages." Brodie's eyes scanned the papers beside Marlene. "You give me what I want and I'll give you what you want." She folded her hands together upon the table and waited.

Though Marlene would do anything for her daughter's safe return, she felt physically ill at the mere thought of handing over the secrets of Project Gemini. Not only was it a highly dangerous experiment, it was also her life's work and something she had worked so hard to accomplish. She knew its devastating potential in the wrong hands. Unfortunately, her maternal instincts overrode every warning that besieged her good sense. She was a mother. Images of her daughter, bound and gagged, the nightmarish possibilities ran rampant through her mind.

Marlene picked up and held the papers in front of her. "If I give you Project Gemini, you give me my daughter?"

"Yes."

"What proof do I have that she is still alive?"

Brodie ground her teeth in frustration. "You saw the video, didn't you? That was her coming into the building."

Reluctantly and with a heavy sensation in her stomach, Marlene handed over the breakthrough that was Project Gemini.

Agnes smiled in smug satisfaction. It was a warped motive, but she got so much more pleasure from seeing a captive squirm as they, not so willingly, handed over the information she required. It had a higher element of malevolence than merely taking what she wanted.

"Pickering!"

The hairless scientist to her right took the papers from Agnes and flicked through them eagerly.

118

Brodie's eyes remained upon Marlene. "That contains Gemini's duel nature? Both Jekyll and Hyde?"

"Those are the key elements of Project Gemini," Marlene replied hollowly. "All the research my team and myself carried out on its applications, my creation of the vessels structure and how it is refined and manipulated to accommodate the Jekyll and Hyde."

With little belief in Marlene's words, Brodie looked to Atkins for proof this was what she wanted. She received an excited nod in response.

"Excellent." Brodie rose to her feet. "You have complied well, Professor." Jerking her head, Brodie indicated it was time to leave. The door opened as Marlene leapt from her chair.

"Wait!"

Brodie stopped and turned to Marlene.

"My daughter?"

"Ah yes." Brodie pursed her lips as her eyes scanned the papers in Atkins hands. "Once I have everything I need from you, Skyler will be returned to you."

Marlene strode around the table. "I gave you Project Gemini."

"Yes, you did." Agnes smiled. "And once we have carried out initial tests, which I may consult you on, I will be sure you have given me all I require. That is when you will get what is coming to you. For now... you will wait." Finishing her statement, Brodie left the room. Its door bolted shut behind her.

Marlene stared at the closed barrier. Realisation of what she had done crashed down upon her. She fell to the floor in tears; her sobs echoed around the empty room.

****

Night was falling rapidly. Though the day had been cool and an expanse of powered blue sky had stretched out over the land. The sun had shone high, unable to warm the air, but as the glowing orb bowed gracefully into the horizon, it cast a spectacular tangerine glow into the atmosphere. A warm comfortable glow, reflected by the ocean, cast upon the two women travelling within the Maid of the Atlantic.

With tracking device in hand, Addison guided the small boat through an estuary and along a wide, winding river. Setting down the tracking system, Addison turned to Skyler. The doctor sat upon a wooden, slatted crate, resting her feet upon the deck. Skyler looked out across the river that was bordered by high rolling hills on either side.

Unable to leave the helm, Addison turned back to guide their leased vessel. They were less than a mile from where Brodie's speedboat had docked.

"Would you take over for a moment?" Addison inquired. She looked to Skyler and then indicated the steering.

"Sure," Sky replied, taking over. "I've done this before. It was a much bigger boat though, down the Nile when I was on a dig in…"

"Egypt!" Addison exclaimed. "You've been to Egypt!" Realising she probably seemed a little too enthusiastic she toned down her demeanour. "That… um… must have been interesting."

Skyler didn't reply straight away. She studied Addison for a moment in thought as the agent picked up the duffel bag Quinton had left her and slid open the zipper. Hearing no answer, the agent eventually looked up to Skyler. She noted the doctor's expression and arched her eyebrows in question.

"Oh yes, it was," Skyler admitted. She paused before asking. "So you have never been to Egypt? It is such a beautiful place. Steeped in history."

Addison looked up from her inspection of the duffel bag. "Egypt was a dream of mine as a kid. You know how you get that feeling that if you had lived before it would have been in a certain time and place?"

Skyler nodded.

"Well Egypt was mine." She smiled, pulling a shotgun from the bag and standing it upon the deck so she could lean her weight upon it. "I used to dream of great adventures there when I was a kid. I put posters up on my bedroom wall of the Pyramids and Sphinx. Didn't last long though." Addison set down her new shotgun, internally thankful to Quinton for supplying her with her favourite Spas 12.

Turning away from Addison, Skyler steered the boat around a sharp bend in the river. It began to narrow. Without looking back at the agent, Skyler asked, "Why didn't they last long?"

Addison shrugged. "My parents ripped them off the walls. To put it politely," she smirked, "they called them hopeless aspirations."

Once again it took Skyler several moments to reply. "That must have hurt."

"Hurt me?" Addison laughed. "No… tough as old hobnail boots, me. It takes more than some ripped paper to get me upset!" Wanting to believe her own bluff, Addison turned her attention fully on the carrier. "Okay, so what exactly do we have here?" She began pulling out the items. "Shells for the Spas, torch, leather gloves, handcuffs, strap, two throwing knives and wrist sheath… and oh look at these, five grenades. My favourite toys!" She lined the items up along the deck, discarding the empty duffle and picking up her sturdy backpack.

Pushing up her left sleeve, Addison attached the knives and sheath to her forearm. Slipping out of her jacket she loaded the rucksack and shrugged it onto her back, followed by the shotgun.

"Well I'm ready to rock 'n' roll."

"Good, because look." Skyler nodded towards the speedboat. It was moored beside a marshy bank, tied to a rusty metal pole.

"Okay." Addison switched off the tracking system and slipped it into her backpack. As Skyler guided the boat to the bank, Addison grabbed a rope and jumped onto the marshy shore. She secured the boat, and then turned to Skyler. She held out her hand, assisting the doctor ashore.

"This is the plan. I scope out the outer area and get a feel for the place. Then you wait while I go in there."

"What? No way!" Skyler shook her head adamantly. "There is no way you are leaving me out here... alone!"

With a sigh, Addison ran both hands through her shaggy dark locks. "Listen, Skyler, if you want me to do my job you must trust me and do exactly as I say. I will make sure you are safe." Addison readied her Spas, loading it with shells. "I don't know what I'll find. I never presume, but yours and your mother's safety is of the utmost importance. I will find somewhere safe for you to wait." Addison's expression turned serious. "You don't want to be around when the penny drops, Skyler."

"Okay." Skyler looked up towards the sky where the first stars were making their appearance in the darkening expanse. "I trust you, Addison. I'm just..." Skyler bit her lower lip. "I'm just scared."

Addison internally cursed herself. *Of course she's scared,* she admonished. *You have to be cold and dead on the inside to be able to do this.* Addison ignored the chill her thoughts wrapped around her heart. She placed a comforting hand upon Skyler's shoulder.

"Trust me, Skyler, that's all I ask." The blonde nodded and Addison added a reassuring squeeze. "Thank you." She smiled softly. "Now, let's go."

Taking the lead, the soldier jogged towards Brodie's speedboat. She knelt to the ground, her eyes scanning the earth. Two sets of footprints stretched out from the boat; they headed northwest. Addison rose to her feet.

"Two sets of prints. I recognise Brodie's, but the indentations are deeper, like she was carrying something. She was with a man, short and heavy set." Addison smirked, "By the size of these footprints I'd say this guy is lucky with the ladies!" She chuckled, but her joke didn't seem to lighten Skyler's disposition. Addison pulled out her torch. "The night has all but fallen, Skyler. We need to move." Handing her torch to the blonde doctor, Addison readied her shotgun and they began.

The evening was fair and clear. A subtle aroma of moist earth permeated their surroundings. It was, however, the foreboding sense of approaching danger that kept Addison's senses alert.

"Move the torch over there," Addison indicated, pointing to the right.

Skyler did as requested, highlighting footprints that stretched out towards a valley between the hills. "What do you expect we'll find, Addison?"

"What is the worse you could possibly imagine?"

Confused by the question, but nonetheless considering Addison's words, Skyler searched her imagination. "The worst I could expect is … a whole army of men guarding my mom, surrounded by a twenty foot high fortress. Wild dogs guarding the boundaries; towers with huge guns and a mine field."

Addison nodded. "Okay, well I expect nothing, yet something thirty times as frightening as that."

"I don't understand," Skyler responded with a frown. "What do you know that I don't?"

"Nothing… and that's the point." Hearing a noise to her right, Addison swung around with a speedy reflex. A rabbit hopped frantically away from them. She continued to follow Brodie's tracks. "The point is to never have any preconceptions about what you are going to find… but… at the same time, be prepared for the very worst. I don't know what will happen around the next corner. I won't presume, but I will be ready for anything. It's the only way to stay alive, Skyler." Addison stopped walking. She turned to face the doctor and Skyler stood still. "If you are going to stay one step ahead of your enemies, never underestimate them."

"That's what you were taught?" Skyler shone her light away from Addison. The women gazed intently into each other's shadowed features.

"No," the soldier responded. "That is what I learned the hard way. That lesson was a life changing jolt in my life."

Skyler stepped closer. "What happened?"

Swallowing hard, Addison recalled the night in question, the night that changed her from a common street criminal to a soldier in Her Majesty's Armed Forces. It was a period in her life that she had never before shared with another soul. She never intended to. "Maybe later," the agent relented. "Right now we have a mission to complete." Turning, Addison resumed tracking the sets of prints. She sensed more than heard Skyler's unspoken question and decided to change the subject.

"So, Doctor Skyler Tidwell, tell me something?"

Skyler increased her pace and walked beside Addison. "What's that?"

"In a way I suppose you are an adventurer like me... travelling the world due to our occupations."

"I guess..."

"Do you have a home, a retreat of your own?"

"I have an apartment back in Pennsylvania. You?"

"A place down south." Approaching a hill, Addison noticed the footprints veered around it. She reached out to take the torch from Skyler. Her fingers found the cool digits of the doctor as she slowly slid the object from Skyler's hand. Redirecting its beam, she followed the prints.

"Why?" asked Skyler as she followed Addison.

"Just making conversation."

"Hmm." Skyler looked at Addison intently. "Maybe making conversation or maybe trying to steer the conversation from uncomfortable topics?"

Addison refused to take the bait. "Tell me honestly...you really do have some kind of qualification in psychology, don't you?"

"Yes, I do."

The soldier grinned. "You see... I knew it! You have a very analytical mind, Doctor, it must be highly beneficial."

Skyler shrugged. "You do too."

"Nah," Addison re-clasped her Spas with both hands, holding the torch against its barrel. "I'm a shoot first, ask questions later kind of girl. You on the other hand, your mind... your words... are your weapon."

"What does that mean?"

Addison turned to face Skyler, holding the shotgun diagonally across her chest. "I happen to think that must mean you have pretty good oral skills!" She took a step closer to Skyler. "I just hope you find time, in that busy life of yours, to keep up the practice."

"I..." Skyler's mouth worked silently as she tried to respond to Addison's words. She was unsure whether that remark was flirtatious or simply a compliment on her behalf.

Holding back a grin, Addison stepped away from Skyler. She looked down at the prints then ahead seeing a light in the dusky distance. "I do believe we are here!" She crouched down and motioned for Skyler to do the same. Reaching for her backpack, Addison pulled out the pair of binoculars and switched them to night vision. She zoomed in on the green imaging.

Placing her hand upon Addison's back, Skyler whispered, "What do you see?"

"An old stone building," Addison replied. "Looks pretty derelict and abandoned, but that's Brodie's preference. Four stories high, quite large and strangely medieval in appearance. There are several vehicles around the area that I can see and so far four visible patrolling guards. They're armed." Addison studied further. She zoomed in onto a small door, half built into the ground, and made a mental note to check it out."

"What now?"

The agent handed her binoculars to Skyler. "You stay here a moment." She then handed over her shotgun and pulled out a single pistol and screwed a silencer onto its barrel. "I'll be back in just a second. Wait here."

Skyler watched as Addison moved cautiously toward the fortress and kept watching until the agent melted into the blackness. Emotionally, she was torn. On one hand she was impressed with Addison's courage and willingness to risk her life for Skyler's mother. On the other hand, Skyler resented Addison for leaving her behind after promising to bring her along when they liberated Marlene.

The American didn't think "bringing her along" should only consist of letting her take a ride on The Maid of the Atlantic and then leave her behind at the crucial moment. Besides, she might be able to help the agent in some way. Her clinical experience alone might prove invaluable. The longer Addison was gone, the greater was Skyler's urge to go after her.

The American reached behind her and assured herself the gun she had been given earlier was still in the holster attached to her waistband, then moved forward from her hiding place holding Addison's shotgun in a ready manner. She slipped ahead stealthily, but had only taken a few quiet steps when a hand was clamped over her mouth and a strong arm wrapped around her body. Skyler struggled briefly until Addison's voice spoke low in her ear.

"I thought I asked you to stay put." Skyler's reply was muffled by Addison's hand so she relaxed and grunted to let the agent know she wouldn't move or make any noise. The iron grip loosened and the hand covering her mouth was removed.

"I couldn't help it," Skyler whispered. "You were gone for a long time and I thought you might need my help."

Addison turned to Skyler and peered at her closely with a sceptical look. "One, I was gone possibly five minutes and two, what would you have done if I was in trouble?"

Skyler became annoyed at Addison's superior attitude. "Well, one, it was seven and a half minutes and two, I don't know, but I would have thought of something."

The agent's eyes narrowed and her voice took on a deadly tone. "I brought you along to keep you safe, but God help me, if you don't do as instructed again, you won't need to worry about Agnes because the mayhem will be started by me. Am I making myself clear?"

Skyler's jaw worked and Addison readied herself for an argument. She was surprised when Skyler merely said, "Perfectly. I'm sorry."

The American could see the anger leave the agent at her meek reply. Addison gave her a small grin and a wink. "One, it's okay and two, shut your gob and follow me."

Skyler knew by the teasing tone that she was forgiven and whispered back, "One, right behind you and two, lead on." Addison gave a small snort of laughter at the joking, but sobered immediately.

"I found an old door next to the end of the building. It looks like an old tradesman's entrance. It's chained shut, but I'm sure I can get past that. Quiet now." Addison slid her night vision specs back on and crept toward the fortress walls with Skyler trailing behind her. Only once did she have to motion Skyler to be perfectly still as a guard passed by on a parapet overhead.

They crossed a depression in the turf and slipped up to the door Addison described. It was solid appearing, the ancient timbers thick and sturdy. A new chain hung through an iron hinge and was closed with a large lock. The agent reached over to Skyler and removed a thin strip of metal from the collar of her jacket that the American still wore. The flexible skewer was slipped into the key slot and in seconds an audible click was heard as the lock popped open. Addison removed the lock and slid the chain soundlessly through the iron hinge.

Opening the door slowly, Addison whispered, "We're in."

****

Brodie opened the door to the small lab. She remembered the earlier treachery of Skyler Tidwell and hesitated at the portal assuring herself that no traps had been set by the currently captured Tidwell family member. Confident the way was clear, Agnes entered and walked over to Marlene who had resumed a seat on the lab stool.

"Professor Tidwell, it's nice to see you again. I'm sorry to bother you, but the gentleman who was with me earlier, Dr. Pickering, has a few questions of clarification for you."

"I've given you everything," Marlene said in a dejected manner, not looking up at the Irishwoman. "Isn't that enough?"

Brodie tried for a genuine smile, but failed. "Now, now, Professor, don't be like that. You've done well and to show our appreciation we've made a gesture of good faith. At this very moment, your daughter is being transported to the nearest large city where she will be deposited quite unharmed on a city street. When you have cleared up a few minor details, it is our intention to take you to that same city. I daresay that if you continue to cooperate, you'll be reunited with your daughter within twelve hours."

Marlene did look up then. "Skyler is being set free? And she hasn't been hurt?"

"I swear on my sainted mother's grave, the last time I saw her she was headed for freedom. Now, shall we join Dr. Pickering in the main lab? He seems to be a bright man, but your work is quite advanced apparently and he needs your help." Marlene made no reply, just shrugged and stood up.

Brodie motioned with her head for Marlene to move ahead of her toward the door. As the American passed by her, Agnes said nonchalantly, "I suppose it was like that at the University? You needed to provide the guidance for Project Gemini?"

"I guess so," Marlene agreed, "But it's probably not that the other researchers weren't intelligent. It was just that the difficult part was my discovery and is my area of expertise. Probably until this point when I gave you all the information," the American said as she got to the door, "I've been the only one who has understood everything about the project."

"The only one," Brodie said thoughtfully. "Imagine that." To Agnes's mind, Marlene had just sealed her own fate.

****

Pale light poured from the open door as Addison and Skyler slipped inside and into an empty corridor.

"That was simple," Skyler observed quietly. "You'd think they would have more guards here."

"They did," Addison confirmed as she took the shotgun back from the American. "There were three more patrolling the grounds outside."

Three guards in seven and a half minutes the American thought. Skyler watched as Addison rechecked her weapons and realized once again that she was in the company of a very dangerous woman. That image clashed with the tiny glimpses of humor and humanity Skyler had been allowed to see and the American couldn't decide which aspect was the real Addison Black. Though she knew it was unlikely, Skyler wondered if Addison might be interested in seeing her after they rescued her mother. The scholar was intrigued by the agent and was curious about what Addison might be like in a situation not filled with stress and danger. She was also somehow certain that no matter how formidable Addison was, she would never hurt Skyler. These thoughts flowed through her mind in a matter of seconds and by the time Addison had completed her weapons check, Skyler was focused again on their task.

"Ready," Addison stated. Skyler could feel a palpable change in Addison's presence. It felt a little like a coil being tightened and held in check, waiting for the opportunity to be released into action. If Skyler hadn't hated Agnes Brodie to the core, she might have felt a little sorry for her having Addison Black as an enemy.

"I have a little experience with coastal fortifications," Addison said. "Since the time of the Viking raiders, the most secure place would be the center of the keep. It makes sense that it would still be the same now."

"Agreed," Skyler said. Her amazing recall sent her mind through several relevant courses and classes. "That sunken area outside was probably a moat at one time. We should definitely go up as we work toward the middle." Addison looked at the American, but her "game face", as Skyler thought of it, was firmly in place and her expression unreadable.

"Let's move out." Addison led the way down the corridor they had stepped into. It was apparent they had entered a little used area of the fortress. There were only a handful of doors in the corridor and most of them were empty or mundane storage rooms. Addison was thorough though and searched each one quickly but efficiently. They progressed steadily, finding a second corridor that moved perpendicular to the one in which they entered. It was obvious this passageway led toward the center of the fortress.

It was only a matter of yards before the sound of an agitated voice reached them. Addison raised two fingers to her lips in a gesture of silence. Skyler nodded her head in understanding as Addison moved soundlessly toward the voice. Skyler followed a few paces behind, studying the agent's movements and mimicking them.

The black haired woman moved to the nearest point to the voice where she would still be unobserved. Reaching down into her black combat boot, she removed what appeared to be something like the foil wrapper from a piece of chewing gum. She bent the foil and moved part of it around the corner, studying the image reflected back at her much like a dentist using a mirror in a patient's mouth.

Bringing the foil back, Addison glanced at Skyler. She raised one finger and mouthed the word, "radio". The man in the next corridor raised his voice just then and they could hear his end of the conversation clearly.

"I can't believe it! Damn, who is responsible for this? How did they get past our defences? They've got to be stopped!" Skyler looked at Addison in alarm. She wondered what the agent would do now that their presence had been discovered. She could tell the Brit was processing the information she was hearing and weighing her options. The guard's voice rang out again. "Go, Rangers!"

Addison smiled unexpectedly and, in a swift, decisive movement, slipped around the corner and executed a sharp chop to the base of the man's neck. He crumpled to the floor of the fortress in an ungainly heap. Skyler followed Addison a fraction of a second later, but was only in time to see the agent remove the man's radio from his pocket and pull the earpiece out. Putting the tiny speaker to her own ear, Addison smirked.

"Scottish football. Celtic leads the Rangers one to nil."

Skyler blew out a breath in relief, realizing that the man had been listening to soccer on the radio and that they hadn't been discovered. Addison dropped the radio on the unconscious guard and continued down the corridor the man had been watching.

"As we get closer to your mum, the number of guards will increase. They'll also get better," Addison said as she resumed her methodical checking of rooms. In one they found a communications center. Though shut down at the current time, Skyler could tell Addison was noting the location of the room that held both a satellite telephone as well as a short wave radio.

"This wouldn't be untended unless something of greater importance was happening," Addison observed. "My guess is that something is the presence of the eminent Dr. Marlene Tidwell. We're getting close, I can feel it."

The pair worked their way to the end of the corridor that opened into a wide, open area with a stone staircase heading up to the next level. Faint sounds of activity drifted down from overhead.

"She must be up there," Skyler whispered as she moved to the steps. She had just placed one foot on the first step when her arm was grabbed and she was pulled back against the British woman.

"I think you're right and that's why this is as far as you go," Addison said in a lowered voice as her eyes watched the landing at the top of the steps.

"What are you talking about? That's my mother up there and I want to make sure she's safe!" Skyler's voice was intense, but remained at a whispered level.

"If you want to make sure she's safe, you'll stay here. Skyler, look... I can't keep focused on your mum if I have to worry about you and you know I will," the agent reasoned.

"But..."

"No," Addison interrupted, "No buts. I need to do this alone. Please." The agent's reasonable tone did something that a command could not have done. It gained Skyler's cooperation.

"Okay, I'll stay here. I've got your back." Skyler pulled out the pistol she had received from Addison earlier and assumed an aggressive stance.

"That's kind of you, Calamity Jane, but if its all the same to you, I would prefer you not to get into any gunplay." She took Skyler by the arm and pulled her over to a door situated under the staircase. Peering quickly inside, Addison pronounced it "perfect". She ushered Skyler through the door. There wasn't a room inside the door; rather it was the landing to another set of stairs, this one leading downward into an inky blackness. It was damp and musty smelling.

"Old portal to the moat level I'll wager," Addison stated. As they moved onto the landing, Addison's boot caught a small stone and sent it over the edge. A moment later a small splash was heard.

"It's flooded, Addison! God knows what kinds of creepy-crawly things are down there. Let me go with you! I won't get in the way." Skyler clung to Addison's shirt as the agent moved to leave.

Gently, Addison disengaged Skyler's hand. "Come now, Doctor. You're a woman of science! You've probably dissected worse things that are down there."

Skyler looked uncertain. "You won't forget I'm here, will you?"

"Not a chance," the agent assured her. With that, Addison slipped out the door leaving Skyler on a darkened landing, alone with her imagination.

"Damn, why didn't I ask her for those night vision glasses? Okay, I'll be fine. No problem. Mom always said there's nothing in the dark that isn't there in the light." Skyler was comforted by that thought until a distinct splash echoed from below. "And that's what I'm afraid of." Briefly, Skyler's mind weighed the options of dealing with an irritated British spy and the possibility that the splash was caused by a snake.

Skyler hated snakes. *Really* hated them. A second splash sounded, slightly closer than before. As the sick feeling of fear increased, Skyler made her decision.

She was going after Addison.

Chapter Twelve

Addison ran one hand along a rough stone wall behind her. The size of bricks used to build such buildings surprised her. She estimated they were approximately twelve times the size of modern day construction bricks and far superior in quality. When she was younger, Addison had dreamed about living in a home of such magnificence. It reminded her of the stones used in ancient pyramid constructions. As a youngster of five or six, she dreamed of living in a great pyramid, miles away from her parents.

Standing at the foot of large, stone stairs, Addison kicked the first step. Readying her Spas, she held the barrel in her left hand with her right finger poised over the trigger. She looked up the flight of steps. Although the building had been updated and electrical lighting illuminated the dark passages, the stairs curved to the left obstructing her view of the next level. There was a strong, dank aroma in the air. It reminded her of an underground dungeon she had visited at a Bastille in France. However, there was the subtle scent of something else that Addison was yet to identify.

Standing tall, her back aligned with the wall, Addison began her ascent. She took the stone steps slowly, her senses on full alert.

"There was an Englishman, an Irishman and a Scotsman," Addison began in a low voice. "They were climbing a tall mountain in an effort to reach its peak. They'd heard a genie lived at the top who would grant every good man one wish." It was an occasional habit of Addison's. Although she loved her work and thrived in precarious situations, Addison despised the tense atmosphere. She often tried to diffuse it by making up jokes, however lame they might be.

Senses attuned to any oncoming figures from above or below, Addison continued. "So they reached the top of the mystical mountain and found a beautiful, jewel encrusted lamp. The Irishman picked it up eagerly and rubbed it with his sleeve."

Addison paused as she heard a noise from above. She listened carefully, but on hearing nothing more, resumed her trek. "With a puff of smoke the stereotypical genie appeared before them. In a deep voice he said, 'For granting me temporary respite I allow you all one wish… if… you take a leap of faith.' The men looked at each other. 'What does that mean?' asked the Irishman. 'Who cares,' said the Englishman, 'we can have anything we want!' Now being a typical Genie, there was a catch. 'To obtain your wish, all you have to do is jump off the mountain, call out your desire and it shall be yours.' Well obviously this was a fearsome notion, but the Scotsman, believing to be the bravest, went first. Standing at the edge of the mountain he took a deep breath and yelled 'Money!' as he jumped. Sure enough he landed in a gigantic bundle of cash. As the Englishman moved to go next, the Irishman pushed past him and approached the ledge. With a triumphant call of 'Women!', he jumped and landed within an endless group of women, all willing to do his bidding. Now as for the Englishman, he thought himself smarter!"

Addison was beginning to reach the last few steps. She looked both ways once more and continued. "The Englishman thought 'to have the best of both worlds, why not wish for rich women!' It was an excellent plan. Stepping forwards he approached the edge of the mountain, but tripped on a stray rock. 'Buggering Hell' he shouted as he fell from the ledge!"

Reaching the top step, Addison froze as cold steel was pressed into her side. From behind a male, Scottish voice said, "I don't get it."

Addison's smirk remained. "I guess it's English humour!"

The guard stepped closer. "Drop your weapon."

"How about this," she replied, unfazed. "A dyslexic man walks into a bra!" Not waiting for his response, Addison thrust her head back. She connected solidly with the unknown man's face and felt his nose crunch under her impact. Addison spun around, swinging the side of her hand into his throat. As the bloody faced man gasped for air, she kicked him down the stairs.

Addison watched him fall, her mind replaying the last expression upon his face. He would have died before he hit the bottom step. Another ghost to fill her subconscious. Pushing those thoughts to the back of her mind, Addison pressed on. She had to find Marlene before Brodie could find a way to extract the information from her. Addison was beginning to realize the terrible possibilities Project Gemini held.

Unlike the ground level, the first floor had a different aroma. It was the scent Addison had subtly detected, an almost clinical smell, similar to that of an indoor swimming pool. The agent walked down the passageway, but stopped by a small room to her right. She looked inside and spied many unmarked boxes. Curiously, Addison stepped closer. She lifted the top lid and peered inside. There she found dozens of Petrie dishes. She opened another and found carefully contained test tubes. A further box contained hardware for a highly powered microscope.

"Bugger me," the agent exclaimed. "This is more than just a holding facility, it's a fucking laboratory!" Addison rubbed her forehead. "Okay, Addy, think. They have Marlene here and they obviously think they have the technology to replicate Project Gemini." The agent nodded to herself, she knew she might well have to totally destroy the building.

Suddenly, approaching footsteps alerted Addison to unwanted company. She turned, standing by the door, her back against the wall. The pattern of footsteps suggested four people. Addison decided to wait until they passed. Their conversation was in Gaelic. Three of the four were in conversation. When the fourth voice finally spoke, the others fell silent. They were no more than two feet away from Addison.

The soldier stilled her breathing. Her body pressed up against the wall, she gripped the Spas with both hands and waited. Addison's senses detected somebody approaching the room. A hand reached inside to the handle, ready to re-close the door. Hopes that the guard wouldn't look her way, however, were short lived. As the young man turned and spotted her, Addison knew her cover had been blown. It was time to let everybody know who had crashed the party.

Addison swung the hilt of her Spas into the guard. It connected with his chest and he stumbled backwards. She leapt through the doorway, finding three more surprised guards awaiting her. Aiming her shotgun at the nearest man, Addison pulled the trigger.

Nothing

She pulled again and again, her eyes growing wide as the remaining men reached for their weapons.

"Shit!" Addison cursed.

Throwing her shotgun to the side, the agent's eyes registered three weapons aimed straight for her. As her nerves sparked a flash of alarm, she dived back into the storage room, crashing into the piles of boxes. Hundreds of glass test tubes and scientific implements smashed under her weight. Luckily for Addison her thick clothing shielded her skin from most of the splintering glass. Her hands, however, were not so lucky. Multiple shards pierced her flesh causing the agent to grimace in annoyance. She was unable to remove the splinters due to the fast approach of guards closing in upon her.

Rolling towards the right, Addison took shelter by a wall, effectively evading a burst of ammunition. Her palms temporarily out of action, she leapt to her feet. The first man appeared in the doorway and, using all her might, Addison delivered a strong kick, knocking him backwards and into the remaining men. Taking advantage of the extra seconds she charged out into the narrow passageway, intent on an expeditious victory. Using the strength of only her legs and feet, Addison dispatched a series of powerful kicks. It was a flurry of action. The woman, smaller than her opponents, thrust her booted feet and knees into vital bodily organs and joints. One by one, each guard was incapacitated and rendered unconscious until only Addison was left standing.

Watching the last man slump down the wall with a resounding thud, Addison blew out a relieved breath. There was no point in hiding the bodies. Her time was limited. Addison looked down at her hands. Slender shards of glass stuck out through her flesh as bright red blood seeped around the wounds. She sighed and began pulling the glass from her palms. Fresh blood began to flow but she paid little heed. Finding Marlene Tidwell was her primary concern. She started down the corridor, but stopped as a sharp gasp alerted her to another's presence. Addison turned to see a middle aged man standing down at the other end of the passageway. He had greying brown hair and wore a white lab coat. The expression he held was that of an informant ready to run for help. She couldn't allow that.

As the man drew in a deep breath, Addison pulled both Beretta pistols from her back and shot him with her left gun. The blast ricocheted around the narrow walls and Addison knew she had to act fast.

Pistol within each grasp, the agent ran towards a slim archway. Passing under the stone crest she was confronted by another three men. They charged her, firing at will. Addison ducked, lunging into a forward roll before coming to her feet and taking out each threat with a single shot. She continued to run, her heavy footsteps pounding the cold, hard floor.

Into view came another set of stairs. She took them two at a time, speedily approaching the building's third of four floors.

****

Marlene Tidwell stood between two abnormally large, fully armed, ruffians. In front of her sat Brodie's scientist, while to her left stood the woman herself. Brodie overlooked their conversation as a reluctant Marlene explained vital details to Pickering.

Suddenly, loud shouts from the outer passages filtered through to Brodie's ears. Her head whipped around sharply, eyes open in question.

"What was that?" she asked, looking around the room rapidly. "We have intruders? That can't be possible." Brodie turned to the closest guard beside Marlene. "Go and check it out," she ordered.

"Ma'am," he replied and carried out Brodie's bidding.

Approaching the door to the laboratory, he didn't even have time to touch the handle before the barrier was thrust open. Moving with such force, the wooden door flew from its hinges, colliding with his heavy set form and depositing him upon the ground. The door landed on top of him and the guard Addison had used as a battering ram, on top of that.

Brodie stared with bewilderment at the sight. She managed to bring herself around in time to see Addison stride through the doorway. Already the agent was firing at those who attempted to stop her progress.

"Brodie!" Addison yelled. She aimed her right hand forwards and shot another thug approaching her. Addison's left arm sprang to the side, firing at a woman carrying a Colt 45.

Scientists and technicians ran for their lives, screaming and diving under tables and behind cupboards.

"Don't fuck with me, Brodie. Just hand over the Professor."

Agnes' decision was swift. Pulling a hip holstered revolver from Marlene's remaining guard, she pushed him towards a side door. "Take her to the boat," she barked harshly and then turned back to Addison. "There is nothing I enjoy more than fucking with you, Black."

Brodie fired her gun repeatedly causing Addison to dive for cover. As she fell to the floor, the guard holding Marlene escaped through the side door while Brodie ran through the passageway in which Addison had arrived.

Springing to her feet, Addison's eyes switched between the two separate doorways. It wasn't a tough decision. However much she wanted Brodie, the soldier ran for Marlene.

Holstering the left Beretta, Addison felt her congealed, bloody hand pull away from the pistol's rubber grip. There was no time to assess the potential damage caused to her hands. She could not allow Marlene to disappear once again. If not for her country and US, UK relations, then she had to do it for Skyler.

Jumping over a wide desk, Addison sprinted after Marlene and her temporary captor. She slammed into the door, pushing it open with a tremendous clatter. Ahead of her, Addison discovered a long, narrow hallway. The cold, brick walls offered no exit but a single doorway, twenty-five meters ahead of her. It was swung halfway open and in the process of closing; an obvious sign Marlene was not too far ahead of her. The agent could just hear Marlene's voice pleading to her captor for release.

****

Relieved to be away from the darkness of the unknown, Skyler stepped cautiously through the ground floor entrance hall. She jumped as several shots echoed through the building. With a trembling hand, Skyler reached for the Browning pistol Addison had given to her, but paused.

If she had to, would she actually use it? More importantly, Skyler considered, would wielding a weapon instantly label her a threat for elimination? She drew her hand away from the Browning. Like Addison had said, unless she found herself in immediate danger and in a situation that called for desperate measures, it was not recommended she brandish the pistol at all. Addison wanted her to use it as a call for help. Still, Skyler hoped she would never have to make that call.

From above, the sound of gunshots increased. Skyler paused, realizing the danger that lay ahead. Her green eyes caught sight of a lifeless body lying at the bottom of the stairs. Its face was unrecognisable due to the amount of dark red blood obscuring the battered features. Whoever he was, he had died a quick but painful death. Skyler held little doubt it was Addison who had caused that death.

Deciding to press on, if at least to find her mother, Skyler approached the stairs. *Don't look,* she told herself, and stepped over the dead body blindly.

The stairs curved to the left. Skyler looked up the stone mounts as her confidence faltered. "What am I doing?" she asked herself. "There's a potential war zone up there and I'm running to it?" Trepidation trickled through her veins. Skyler leaned back against the wall, hearing raised voices followed by more gunshots. She wanted to close her eyes, click her heels and wish herself, and her mother, a thousand miles away from this place. But what about Addison? Skyler's mind moved to the woman who was up those stairs, alone, and single-handedly fighting Brodie's men. Realizing the courage it must take for Addison to carry out her job, Skyler bolstered her own confidence. If Addison could do it, so could she.

Turning to continue her path up the steps, Skyler froze as she found herself confronted with one incredibly angry redhead. Brodie's eyes took on an almost joyful expression.

"We meet again," said the Irishwoman as she pointed her revolver at Skyler. "Interesting," she continued. "Now I'm perplexed. Why would Addison Black bring you along, I wonder?" Brodie descended the steps, forcing Skyler to back away. She walked backwards, only just managing to miss the body on the ground floor.

"Correct me if I'm wrong, but anybody would think Agent Black cared about what happened to you." Brodie prodded her bottom lip with her left fingernail. "But that would beg the question, why would she leave you here, roaming around this place in such a dangerous situation?"

Skyler refused to speak. Suddenly finding herself face to face with Brodie brought to mind the malevolent capabilities of this woman and her fear increased tenfold.

"Miss Tidwell," Brodie suddenly adopted the expression of a scolding mother. "Have you been acting wilfully again?"

"Where's my mom?" Skyler asked. "Where's Addison?"

Brodie smiled maliciously. "They are the least of your concerns now, Miss Tidwell. I'd say I wouldn't be wrong in presuming Agent Black has a soft spot for you. If there's one thing I love it's spoiling anything that woman values."

The cold smile fell from Brodie's lips as she advanced upon Skyler.

****

Eating up the distance between herself and the door, Addison ran through the passageway. She burst through the barrier and came to an abrupt halt, narrowly avoiding a collision with a waist high, wrought iron railing. Standing in the cool open air, Addison looked to her right. She was presented with a recently installed, spiral-staircase. The thuds of descending feet sounded beneath her. The agent looked over the railing to see Marlene being pushed down the steps by one of Brodie's henchmen. She took after them, keeping her focus on the pair's progress. As soon as they reached the bottom step and touched solid ground, Addison leaped over the railings. She fell eleven feet to the ground, barely landing upon her feet as the soldier tucked her body into a forward roll. Momentum pushing her back to a sturdy stance, Addison found herself several feet away from Marlene and her retreating captor.

There was little thought, only a basic instinct, as Addison fired two rounds into the guard's back. Her aim was precise, swift and fatal. Marlene shrieked, terrified by the explosions. Brodie's man fell to the ground, but the professor kept on running, fear and confusion clouding her mind and sparking a simple impulse for survival.

"Professor Tidwell," Addison shouted.

She continued to run.

Addison started after her. "Marlene, it's okay. It's me, Addison... wait!" She easily caught up with the fleeing woman, clasping her arm and pulling her to a halt. Marlene shrieked again, but Addison clasped her with both hands, pistol still within her right, as she calmed her. "It's okay, it's me."

"Agent Black." Her relief was evident.

"Yes. You're okay, Professor Tidwell." Addison paused and looked around suddenly. She heard a group of rapidly approaching footsteps.

Taking Marlene by the arm, she led her swiftly over to the spiral staircase, situating her between the iron and the building's wall. "Wait here and keep down."

Running back into the open, Addison holstered her Beretta and swiped an MP5 machine gun from the dead guard. She turned in time to see five of Brodie's men appear from the side. Addison fired instantly, releasing a stream of bullets upon the men. To keep moving was essential; it was the only way to dodge the weapon's fire aimed upon her. She ran to the right, feeling vibrations from the weapon aggravate her wounded palms. Cries of pain, as her would-be assassins were hit, filled the air. Addison didn't stop firing. Her finger squeezing the trigger, she ran forwards, ready for more of Brodie's men. When the MP5 ran out of ammunition, Addison dropped it. She picked up another weapon from the scattering of fallen men and looked about. The atmosphere had stilled and the strong metallic aroma of fresh blood flooded her senses.

Breathing rapidly, Addison scanned her surroundings. Feeling assured that the present danger had eased, she headed back to where Marlene remained huddled behind the iron staircase.

The professor jumped as she felt a light touch upon her arm. She looked up, instinctively knowing the gentle contact would only come from a friendly presence.

"Are you alright?"

Shell-shocked eyes gazed upon Addison. "Is it over?"

The soldier looked around her once again. "I hope so. No doubt Mark Blithe has been monitoring the situation so I am sure company will arrive very soon." Addison helped Marlene to her feet as her thoughts turned to Skyler. "But right now we need to go and get..." her words silenced as the distant hum of a helicopter approached them. She turned to see the large, black aircraft swiftly approach.

Addison frowned; something about the helicopter didn't seem right. It appeared to be a standard military aircraft, but its approach pattern was almost erratic. It began to land quite a distance away from them and Addison continued to aim the MP5 in its direction.

"ADDISON!"

Black's head whipped to the left, instantly recognising the voice. Her heart leapt into her chest and Marlene cried out an anguished "No!" as Skyler, held at gunpoint by Brodie, was dragged into view. The Irishwoman pulled her towards the helicopter.

"Brodie!" Addison bellowed, aiming her weapon. "Release her."

"Forget it, Black." Brodie pushed the steel barrel of her Colt revolver harder against Skyler's head. She pulled her roughly, causing Skyler to stumble in her effort to remain upright.

Addison moved closer, feeling the aircraft's propeller draft thrust against her face. Black hair danced furiously around her head. Her palms began to sweat, stinging the open cuts. Addison knew she had never felt this anxious before. She tried to take aim at Brodie, but the redhead shielded the majority of her body behind Skyler. One miss-shot could hit Skyler and, for the first time, Addison couldn't bring herself to take that chance.

"Do something," Marlene begged Addison. She called out her daughter's name helplessly.

"What use is she to you now?" shouted Addison, hoping to reason with Brodie before she boarded the helicopter.

"What use is she to you?" Brodie asked, almost cryptically. Was she able to see the underlying apprehension in Addison's eyes from such a distance? "You know me, Black." Brodie slid into the helicopter, a terrified Skyler followed. "I do like my toys. This one is definitely something to play with. And the more it angers you... the more enjoyment I'll get."

"NO!" Addison ran forwards as the helicopter began to rise, a sobbing Marlene behind her, but it was no good. Their voices were drowned out in the wake of the tremendous hum of the aircraft. She looked around her, frantically searching for something, anything she could use to stop Brodie. It was too late. The helicopter moved further and further into the distance and all Addison could do was stand her ground, helplessly. She threw the MP5 to the ground in anger.

"God fucking damn it." Addison kicked her weapon across the grass.

As the helicopter disappeared into the horizon all that remained was Addison's shallow, seething breath and Marlene's quiet sobs. The soldier turned away, facing the medieval building and carnage of bodies upon the ground. *Focus,* she said to herself. Her shoulders rose and fell noticeably as she breathed deep, calming breaths. Running both hands through her hair, the agent's eyes scanned the bodies. She had an idea.

Starting a search through the deceased men, Addison hunted out and found a radio. "Excellent." She turned it on, adjusting its digital readout to a specific frequency. Before speaking, Addison cast a gaze upon Marlene. The silent professor looked around their surroundings in shock. Tears of anguish, of a mother's fear for her child, trailed glistening streams down her cheeks.

"Marlene?" Addison placed her hand upon the professor's back. "I know you may see this as futile at the moment, but try not to worry. I will get her back."

"How?" The expression of fear was as clear in Marlene's voice as it was upon her face. "Do you know where that woman has taken my daughter?"

Twisting the volume dial upon the radio, Addison shook her head. "Not yet, but I will." She kept her hand upon Marlene's back and ushered her into movement. "We have to get back into the building."

"No!" Marlene stopped. "I can't go back in there."

"Yes you can. Everybody inside has more than likely scattered. If I am to find out any clues as to where Brodie has gone, I have to dig around." Addison gently eased Marlene into moving. "It might very well be safer in there than out here."

"Why?"

"Because I'll be in there," Addison replied.

Marlene didn't respond, but silently followed Addison.

The soldier readjusted the radio volume. "Come in HQ, this is Black." Reaching the bottom of the spiral stairs, Addison ascended the steps with Marlene behind her.

"Roger, Black, this is HQ. A team was dispatched to your

location and is currently en-route."

"E.T.A.?"

"Fifteen minutes."

"Roger that," Addison replied. "Black out." The soldier switched off the radio and threw it over the staircase railings in anger; the realisation that she had made a mistake weighed down upon her. She thought she could keep Skyler from harm. She thought the place she had chosen for her would be safe. She was wrong. Because of that, Skyler was once again in the merciless hands of Agnes Brodie. Addison knew how deep Brodie's interest in Skyler had been and the notion troubled her. She hated to think what Brodie's nefarious mind had planned.

Reaching the top step, Addison led Marlene back inside. They crossed a narrow passageway and entered the laboratory. Bodies of slain soldiers remained upon the floor. The splintering of glass and scattered instruments crunched underfoot.

"Were you aware of an off-room or office that might have belonged to Brodie?"

Marlene tried to focus her thoughts. All she could think about was her daughter, but she had to trust that Agent Black would be the person to bring her home safely. The soldier had rescued her already. "I was held in a room above this floor. Apparently it was the top one. I did notice several other rooms. One door was open and it contained a filing cabinet."

"Up it is then."

They took the stairs to the top floor. Addison began searching the rooms. Most were empty, but one did appear to be a temporary office that she presumed belonged to Brodie. It was a perfectly square room. In the far-left corner sat an old wooden desk. Its light wood showed signs of distress and age by faded cup rings and a multitude of chips and dents. Upon the desk sat a laptop computer. A wire ran from its side, indicating it had been connected to a cellular phone for Internet access. Addison booted the computer as she continued to survey the room.

The walls were bare stone, adorned by nothing but the decay of time. Opposite the desk stood a filing cabinet and beside that, a small, brown cardboard box and plug-less paper shredder.

"What now?" Marlene asked.

"We search." Addison sat in front of the laptop. She flexed her sore hands, feeling the wounds split open and fresh blood trickle to the surface. "Check out the filing cabinet and that box. I'm going to have a look through this baby." She patted the compact computer.

Once ready, Addison gained access to the computer's hard drive. Her fingers flew over the keyboard as she searched out prospective evidence. Behind her, Marlene began opening the first of four drawers. It was empty. She opened the remaining three to find them in the same condition. Pushing the last drawer closed, the professor opened the cardboard box. Inside she found numerous manila folders containing sheets of paper. She began searching through them avidly.

Meanwhile, Addison scrolled through the computer's hard drive. She didn't know what she expected to find, but knew it wouldn't be a nice accessible folder labeled 'Brodie's secret files'. What she wanted was any scrap of evidence, dates, incoming notifications, flight plans; anything that would give her some form of clue as to where Brodie might have taken Skyler.

She wasn't having much luck. Brodie obviously kept all files on disk and if there was anything to be found, the redhead kept it on her. In frustration, she slammed down the laptop screen. Though she did know a lot about computers, how to access deleted files wasn't top of her capabilities without specialised military hardware and that was something she hadn't been given.

Spinning around in her chair, she turned to Marlene. "Find anything?"

Marlene shuffled through the papers. "A list of names. Some documents written in Gaelic by the look of them."

"Let me have a look at those names."

Marlene passed over several sheets of paper. "There are a lot of what I think are printed maps, road maps, blue prints, underground sewage systems and even building designs. The trouble is they all have a red cross going through them, almost like they were rejected. Maybe this was a box of garbage?"

"Maybe," Addison answered. "That would explain the shredder nearby. It doesn't have a plug so maybe these were slated to be destroyed, but they ran out of time." Her eyes slid down the paper. "These names aren't crossed out though." She read each name, one by one, hoping to seek out something familiar. She was unsuccessful.

Placing them to the side, Addison moved to the floor and knelt beside Marlene. "There has to be something." Picking up the scattered sheets she looked through them. Her eyes stopped over a familiar stretch of land.

"I recognise this one. It's almost like I know it because I've been there." Addison studied it closely then searched through more maps and blue prints. "This one looks very familiar too." She held out the detailed, sketched area of land. "I feel I have been here, for sure." She held two sheets of paper side by side. "They are all of the same scale. I bet that if they were sorted we'd have a huge mapping system here. They must fit together like a jigsaw, but we don't have time to play around now." There were no other details upon the sheets of paper but a single, seven-digit Alfa-numeric code.

"If only I could get access to that computer's recently deleted files right now."

Marlene's eyes twinkled in acknowledgement. With out a word she rose to her feet and strode over to the laptop. "Give me a minute," she said.

Addison placed the sheets of paper upon the ground, her head twisting from left to right as she tried to recall from memory why she recognised certain parts of the maps.

Rapid tapping came from Marlene before she said, "Give me one of those codes."

Addison picked up a sheet of paper. "I324H57."

"Okay." Marlene was silent for several moments. "I don't believe it," she finally proclaimed. "I've got it."

"What?" Addison strode over to Marlene. "How did you do that?"

"I've worked with computers for as long as I can remember. I've designed and built programs myself. I know as much about them as I do myself. All I had to do was search out the files flag-marked to be overwritten." Marlene read through the list upon the screen. "That map reference refers to a section of land and buildings in Haifa in…"

"Israel," Addison finished. "That's why I recognise them. I was there almost two years ago."

Marlene picked up the list of names. "There are quite a few obviously Jewish names on this list, Agent Black."

A feeling of dread slithered through Addison's spine. She had originally thought Brodie's operation would end upon Isle of Skye. If her suspicions were now correct, the hierarchy of this organization was larger and a lot more dangerous than she and Special Operations had originally anticipated.

Hearing the approaching sound of military helicopters looming overhead, Addison's fear for Skyler intensified.

M J Walker and Val Brown

Chapter 13

"What in hell could you have been thinking?" General Mark Blithe stood behind his desk and continued the tirade he had started over an hour ago. The Special Operations Headquarters in London was teeming with people trying to fly low under the radar of Blithe's ire.

"I sent an experienced agent on a mission and I got a novice's mistakes in return! I can't believe you took a civilian into that situation!" The general looked at her intently, his eyes searching for an explanation.

Addison had stood silently up until that point knowing there was nothing Mark could say to her that she hadn't already said to herself on the trip back from the Isle of Skye. Now, however, she had thought about it and decided to defend her actions.

"It seemed the right thing to do at the time. It was a judgment call," she said.

Mark was silent for a moment. "I've given you your head on missions, Addison, and you've given me no reason to question your judgment... until now. I'm going to need an explanation of your actions or you'll leave me no choice but to remove you from the field and place you on desk duty until an inquiry is concluded in this matter."

Addison knew there was no way she could allow herself to be removed from the mission. Her fists clenched at her sides with the very thought of it. It was going to be a calculated risk. She knew that somewhere in Special Ops there was a traitor. Someone had been feeding Agnes Brodie information; she had been too well prepared for Addison's arrival. Addison suspected everyone, but the question was: could she trust anyone? She decided to take the risk.

"Look, Mark, I'm going to be honest with you here. The reason I took Sky...Miss Tidwell with me was my hunch that we've got a leak here at HQ. I don't know that for sure, but it is a strong enough idea that I wasn't sure she'd be safe here."

Whatever reaction the general might have to her statement, she wasn't prepared for the one she got. Mark blew out a breath and slumped down into his large leather chair. "Thank God."

"Thank God for what?" Addison was perplexed.

"Depending on what you said, I bloody well **would** have pulled you from the field. I suspected the same thing as you ever since Marlene Tidwell disappeared from a supposedly secure area. I admit I even doubted you, but it seems to me you'd try to turn me from that thinking if you were the traitor."

Addison relaxed a little and felt better being able to confide in someone. "There's too many coincidences, too many unexplained happenings."

"Any ideas who it might be?" the general asked.

"There are a few people who are more likely than others, but at this point it's all conjecture. I've got nothing concrete right now."

"Well, I'll work on it from this end and see if I can come up with something. Meanwhile, what happened on the Isle of Skye, Addison?"

The agent frowned. "It was a cluster fuck. We got in just fine and I got to the professor, but after that it was as if we had no luck at all. Brodie slipped away from me by sending Marlene in the opposite direction. Then Brodie runs into Skyler who I had left in hiding and to top it all off, my shotgun jams at a crucial moment."

"Jams? What do you mean by 'jams'?"

Addison elaborated. "Just that. I pulled the trigger and nothing happened."

"That's odd. You're usually so thorough with your weapons check."

"Always, but this was a replacement weapon I got in Scotland."

"Hmm. One of those things I suppose. How are the hands?" Addison looked at her bandaged palms. The shards of glass had done damage and there was a shadowing of blood under the top layer of gauze from when she had clenched her fists.

"They're not bad," she said almost off-handedly.

"I'll bet," Mark scoffed. "Your leg would need to be nearly severed by a rusty chainsaw with an artery spurting litres of blood for you to even say the situation 'might' be serious." Addison knew the statement was close to the truth. She had grown up in a tough area and to admit a weakness was a little like letting sharks smell blood. There could be no confessing that you were in pain, that you cared or that you might need another person.

"I'll be fine," Addison commented in a slightly irritated tone. "I'm not bothered."

"You never are," the general observed. "Nonetheless, you will see Samuel for some protection for those hands. My father was a carpenter you know. His first rule was that you must take care of your tools so don't argue with me. It's futile."

Addison grumbled, but was able to acknowledge to herself that some type of cover would be advantageous. She healed remarkably fast, but while that was happening she couldn't afford to have her hands become slick with blood. "Fine," she acquiesced, "I'll see Samuel when we're done here."

"Right. Now, where are you in the process of finding and retrieving Skyler Tidwell?"

"The papers we found in the office on the Isle of Skye showed an area I believed to be in Israel. I've had Logistics check my conclusions against satellite mapping and rechecked those with terrain charts. There's no doubt about it, the territory shown is in Israel. It's basically in the same area I worked in two years ago. You remember that mission?" Addison asked.

"Very well. Your performance was exemplary and there has been no further trouble from those individuals, from those who survived at least. Do you have any contacts in that area?"

"A few," Addison shrugged, "but I'm not sure they can help me in this instance. I won't count on any outside assistance."

"So what you are saying is that we are back to where we were at the start of this entire episode. We have Marlene Tidwell, but Agnes Brodie has her daughter," the general summarized.

"I would say that's accurate, Mark," Addison admitted.

"It would be accurate except for one small detail." Marlene Tidwell spoke as she entered the office. She was dressed in dark sweats that Addison recognized as Special Operations standard issue. "Please forgive me, Miss Bakersfield said you were expecting me and that I could come in."

Leaping to his feet, Mark Blithe moved around his desk and over to the American. "How are you feeling? Please, sit down." He escorted Marlene to a chair placed opposite his desk. He made no move to return behind his desk, opting to perch on the corner of the desk near her.

"The doctor in the Infirmary says I'm fine. Thank you for insisting he examine me though, it was very kind of you. Thank you also for my two escorts, they never left my side."

The general waved her off. "It was nothing, the least we could do. I just wanted to be positive you were safe."

Addison watched the interplay between her superior and the American. She knew Mark Blithe had been a self-proclaimed confirmed bachelor and his obvious interest in the attractive woman amused her. She knew better than to let that amusement show externally though. Instead she returned the conversation to Marlene's first comment.

"Professor Tidwell, you said we were back to the beginning except for 'one small detail'. Would you care to share that detail?"

Marlene looked uncomfortable. To her credit though, she brought her gaze up and looked them in the eye. "Project Gemini has been compromised."

****

Skyler blinked her eyes open. Her brain felt fuzzy and her tongue felt thick. It was taking her some time to get her bearings. Only two things were clear to her foggy mind. It was clear she was on a plane to a destination that was anybody's guess. It was also apparent that though she still wore her jacket, the gun Addison had given her was gone.

Damn, Brodie, she thought. *Just say 'no' to drugs.* She remembered Agnes coming at her with a syringe as two muscular thugs held her. It was easy to predict the coming period of unconsciousness. She wasn't wrong.

Squeezing her eyes shut against a brief wave of nausea, Skyler's thoughts flew back and forth between her own situation and concern for her mother. She was able to take some comfort from the fact that when she saw her mother last, she was in the company of Addison Black.

Addison. The last look she saw on the agent's face as she was whisked away in the helicopter was a mixture of rage and concern. The rage was under control, like everything about the agent, but it was the concern that occupied Skyler's thoughts. Skyler couldn't forget locking eyes with the agent as the helicopter lifted off. Maybe it was wishful thinking, but she could have sworn she saw something like an apology there.

Addison had nothing to apologize for though. She has kept her

148

promise and liberated Skyler's mother. Skyler's current predicament was her own fault and she was well aware of it. If duct tape hadn't been binding her ankles together, Skyler would have kicked herself.

Snakes? I was worried about snakes? I run from imaginary serpents and run right into the deadliest viper there is. As if on cue, the door to the cockpit of the small jet opened and Brodie walked into the main cabin.

"Welcome back, Skyler. I'm sorry for the need to use the drugs on you again, but I couldn't have you alerting the authorities at the airport. Well-placed bribes can buy silence, but not even well paid allies can cover up a woman screaming for help," Agnes explained. "Airport security doesn't look at private aircraft as close as public ones, but I didn't have time to deal with it. Thanks to your friend, Addison Black, I needed to make a hasty exit from that part of the world."

Skyler picked up on Brodie's implication that their destination was a long way from where they started. She decided to try to reason with the mercenary.

"Look, Brodie, first of all Addison Black isn't my friend. I never met her before she showed up in Scotland. Second, you know now that I'm not my mother. I can't help you and you got away cleanly. There's no need to make this any worse for either of us. When we land, why don't you just let me go? I'm no threat to you."

Brodie laughed. "Of course you aren't, but Addison is. A very big threat and despite your protestations to the contrary, I have an idea that keeping you will give me a distinct advantage in dealing with the beautiful but lethal Agent Black. I also have an idea that the relationship between you and Addison is more than you're willing to say right now. Addison doesn't hesitate to take attractive women to her bed. Make no mistake; we will see Addison again. She will not take this setback lightly."

"I don't know why we would see her again. I'm not anybody. I'm certainly not worth some big British agent's time," Skyler tried.

Brodie continued to be amused by Skyler's attempts to talk her way out of the situation. "Well, one thing is a certainty. You didn't lie when you said you hadn't known Addison Black long. Addison is an agent for Special Operations, a highly secret division of MI-5, and only the best of the best work for Special Ops. These agents are deadly and determined. Addison won't let this go. I took you right from under her nose and that's going to piss her off. Add that to the fact that she's attracted to you and we have the makings of an agent soon to be hot on our trail. That's good."

"You think she's attracted to me?" Skyler couldn't keep the

pleased note from her voice and she would have preened a little had her forearms not been duct taped to the arms of the seat she was in. "I mean, if she did come after us and she is so skilled, why would that be a good thing?"

Brodie turned to return to the cockpit. "Because, my sweet Skyler, caring about someone gives you a weakness. Addison has never had a weakness before and it's going to lead to her long overdue destruction." Agnes pulled open the door to the cockpit, but was stopped when Skyler called out to her.

"Brodie! I can't do anything to stop it, so will you satisfy my curiosity? Where are we going?"

Agnes studied her immobilized captive and decided she could be generous. "Ever been to the Holy Land, Skyler?" She laughed and disappeared into the cockpit.

Shit, the American thought. *We're going to the Middle East.*

****

"So I told them everything about Project Gemini. I didn't want to, but they convinced me that they still had Skyler and I couldn't stand the thought of what they would do to her. After I met Brodie I knew Skyler's life would mean nothing to that woman," Marlene concluded. She had just spent the last several minutes describing her abduction and captivity to Addison and Mark Blithe.

"I didn't think anyone knew where I was and I had no choice when Brodie threatened Skyler. She's my daughter and my only family. There's nothing I wouldn't do to keep her safe." Her voice broke then and tears appeared in her eyes.

"That's perfectly understandable, Marlene," the general soothed. "No one could expect you to be able to withstand that kind of pressure." During her account, Mark had moved to a chair next to her and had placed a comforting hand on her shoulder. The American looked up at him in gratitude.

Addison had remained standing during this time, but now she moved to sit on the spot on the desk that the general had vacated. "I know you're tired and upset, Professor, but I need to know about Project Gemini. It wasn't so important before, but if I'm to get your daughter back I need to have all the information that Agnes Brodie has."

Marlene nodded. "I understand and I'll be more than glad to do anything I can to help."

"Just put it in layman's terms, if you will," Addison requested.

"Not all of us are as smart as Skyler."

Marlene smiled. "Not many people are, it can be a little daunting."

"Just a little," Addison agreed. "Now, about Project Gemini?"

"Yes, well I suppose you know some of the basics. My work was using the tuberculosis bacterium as a vehicle to deliver chemotherapy to cancer victims. We found that by removing the virulent part of the cell that we could replace it with something beneficial. We turned something deadly into something potentially lifesaving. That was the two sided nature of the work." Marlene looked down and wrung her hands together. Taking a deep breath, she continued.

"One day I was visited at the college by a representative from the federal government. He said they were impressed with my work, but did I realize that the research could be used for purposes other than which it was intended? The very aspect that made the bacilli so useful, its high transmissibility, was what could make it potentially the greatest delivery agent for all kinds of chemical or biological weapons. Just imagine a new type of suicide bomber. He allows himself to be infected or carries the bacilli that have been loaded with some kind of bacterial agent. Anthrax, Ebola, smallpox…the list is potentially endless. The tuberculosis bacillus is highly transmissible, especially effective in a crowded area. That's the reason you see so much tuberculosis in prisons and slums. So let's say this guy walks into a subway or a sporting event or a meeting of Congress. One pass and he infects dozens who infect dozens more. It's a catastrophe of unimaginable proportions in no time. I couldn't let that happen to my work."

"How did you come to England to work?" Addison questioned. "It seems like the United States would want you where they could supervise you in this work."

"That's just it, it wasn't only the US that was interested. Britain and the US both wanted to make sure that the research wouldn't fall into the wrong hands and wanted us to come up with a way to deactivate the bacilli should that very thing happen. We wanted to turn what might be a deadly bacillus into a benign one again. That was the Dr. Jekyll and Mr. Hyde work we were involved in and that's why the project was called Gemini, after the Greek twins. I was offered complete use of the facilities at the University here to pursue my work and I took it."

"And now Agnes Brodie and whoever she is working for or with has it too." Addison's voice was grim.

"I'm afraid so," Marlene said apologetically. "The only bright spot is that the technology is very advanced. Even with the information I gave them, it will take weeks to get to the point where they will be able to extract the tuberculosis from the bacillus. The process can't be shortened or the risk of not neutralizing the bacillus is too great. They might just end up causing their own demise."

Mark Blithe interjected, "So, you're saying we have some time, just not a great deal of it."

"Right," Marlene agreed. "Even with the most modern laboratory facilities I would say they would need three weeks at a minimum."

Addison stood. "I'll prepare to leave right away. I have several things to take care of, but I should be on my way by morning. Professor, I… I think your daughter and I became friends of a sort during our brief time together. As determined as I was before to get her back, I am even more determined to bring her back now." Addison said no more, but her expression spoke volumes to the other two people in the room. She nodded at them and left the office.

In the next office, Antonia Bakersfield was busy working at her computer's keyboard. Addison sauntered over to her and flashed the same saucy grin she always used to charm the general's secretary. "How's the woman with the best fingers in HQ?"

Antonia blushed. "And how would you know? You've never given me the chance to show you."

"I'm pretty sure I couldn't handle you, Antonia. Besides, I'm just a humble public servant. I'm not allowed to provide you with fringe benefits."

Antonia laughed at Addison's harmless flirting. "Well, if you ever change your mind, I'll be happy to provide you with excellent service."

"I'll keep that in mind, Miss Bakersfield. In the meantime, can you book me a flight? Tomorrow, commercial or military, it doesn't matter. Final destination is Tel Aviv."

"No problem, Agent Black. Any special needs?" She used the Special Ops code for weapons.

"No thanks, I can handle the rest of the details. When you have the arrangements completed, could you contact me down in Samuel's lab? I need to see him and have some quality time with Spike before I leave."

"No problem, Addison. I'll call you when everything is set."

"You're a dream, Miss Bakersfield," the agent said as she headed out the door.

****

"Spike, I missed your furry little arse!" Addison whispered as the scruffy little dog bathed her face with short licks from a pink tongue. The dog was finally calming down after greeting Addison with unabashed excitement.

Samuel walked into the lab then with a flat box. "The size should be about right."

Addison tucked Spike under one arm as she approached the scientist. "Leather, right?"

"Would you wear anything else?" Samuel asked as he opened the box to reveal exquisitely crafted black leather driving gloves.

"Nice," Addison commented. She set Spike onto a nearby table and pulled the gloves from the box. "They're strong enough to protect the palms but not heavy enough to get in my way. Hmm, they just need a minor adjustment." She pulled open a drawer on Samuel's desks and extracted a large pair of scissors.

"Oh, Addison, you wouldn't! I worked hard on making these special gloves and there's no..." Samuel trailed off in dismay as the agent neatly snipped off all the fingers. Setting the scissors down, she slipped the gloves on and flexed her hands.

"Perfect, I'll take them. Come on, Spike, there's sausages with our names on them. Then we have to talk about how badly you've treated Samuel while I was gone and how I'm sure you won't act like that again while I'm out of the country...starting tomorrow." She heard a wail of pain from Samuel as she closed the door to the lab. "Gee, Spike, you'd think Uncle Samuel isn't looking forward to being your roommate again."

The agent bent over and scooped up the little dog in her gloved hands. "Maybe later we can talk about an unusual woman I met recently. I think you'd like her." Spike tilted her head, hearing a tone of voice from her mistress that she hadn't heard before. It was going to be an interesting evening.

Chapter 14

Addison had to hand it to Miss Bakersfield. If there was one thing she could rely upon it was her ability to deliver. The flight to Tel-Aviv had been a smooth, luxurious crossing. First class was the only way to travel and at the government's expense just sweetened the deal. She made a mental note to thank the general's secretary, not, however, in the way she had often insinuated in the past.

Although Addison came to meet Antonia Bakersfield when they were drafted into Special Operations, Addison had been aware of her, in name, almost a year before. Antonia had served in the armed forces herself. She was injured in an incident of friendly fire and had lost the hearing in her right ear. Miss Bakersfield had never wanted to leave the military and when General Mark Blithe approached her with a job proposition, she readily accepted. She and Addison were some of the first to arrive at Special Operations HQ. They connected immediately as friends, though their flirtatious banter remained.

Winters in Israel pretty much resembled a British summer. As Addison stepped out into the Middle Eastern sun, she pushed a pair of dark shades over her eyes. The atmosphere was warm and the scent of recent rainfall clung to the air. A clear blue sky stretched above the land. Addison felt warm solar rays bathe her skin, the heat enhanced by her dark attire. Black combat boots and trousers were hardly summer wear. Her white tank top would have been moderately acceptable if not for the black shirt hanging loose and undone over it. That was unavoidable though and the only way to conceal the weapons attached to the back of her belt. Although Addison held identification and credentials to carry such weapons, to the average civilian they would appear suspicious, especially on an international aircraft.

Slinging a small rucksack over her shoulder, Addison stepped further into the sunshine. People busied themselves about, anxious to get from point A to point B. She heard both Hebrew and English spoken around her. Across the road, Addison saw a rugged black cat, one of many feral felines she would expect to encounter in Israel.

Turning to her right, Addison left Sde Dev airport. She scanned the road ahead, searching for available transportation. Finding a taxi wasn't difficult, as public transportation was always readily obtainable by the airport. Spotting a white car, Addison adjusted her shades and jogged over to the vehicle. She leaned into the passenger side window finding an aging gentleman with a white beard behind the wheel. He looked to her, anxious for a fare.

"Where can I take you?"

"My Place," Addison said and slid into the passenger seat.

Her driver nodded wordlessly and pulled out onto the road. Though Tel-Aviv itself was a hub of modernization, Addison's required destination was just outside the main city, near the beautiful and historical port called Jaffa. My Place was a bar situated in a lesser-populated part of the city. It wasn't an area visited by tourists or holidaymakers. In fact, if you hadn't have been previously introduced, you probably wouldn't even know it existed. Its name had confused Addison on first encounter, but she soon discovered that many bars in Israel had English names.

Addison gazed silently out the cab window. Coming to Israel was a leap, some would say a guess, but to Addison it was an educated guess. Not only did she consider the evidence she found on the Isle of Skye, but also it was known that Brodie had contacts in Israel. That and the fact that she had spent several years living in Bethlehem and her activity during that time had been little known. Addison was confident in her beliefs and a planned meeting with an old friend would help secure those points.

Her drive took almost half an hour, but as the cab pulled up outside My Place, Addison handed over only thirty-five shekels and stepped out into the narrow street. She stood to the side as several people on bicycles rode past her. Addison approached a set of stone steps and descended down to a small door. She pulled it open and stepped inside.

My Place was large and dimly lit. It had no windows so natural lighting wasn't available. Low powered lighting illuminated the bar and several tables held candles wedged into liquor bottles. Conversation was limited to a low hum; men at small tables discussed work or played card games for small amounts of money. The aroma of years of stale cigarette smoke hung in the atmosphere. It clung to furniture and walls like it was part of the establishment's character. Fresh filtering smoke left a steamy glaze in the room, distorting vision like the misty grip of an early morning fog.

Approaching the bar, Addison sat on an empty stool. A young man with slicked back brown hair and holding a towel while drying a shot glass leaned against the counter. He smiled as his eyes gave her a brief inspection.

"Vema ani yachol la'ashot bishvilech?"

"Jack Daniels, toda," then added, "kafull," as an after thought. If she was going for the good stuff, she might as well get her money's worth.

The bartender nodded and disappeared momentarily, returning with a double shot of whiskey. He placed it on the bar-top. "Fifty-five shekels."

Addison slid payment across the counter, leaving a tip as she took her drink. She strolled over to a vacant table in the corner of the bar and sat down. Placing down the glass, Addison pulled a candle towards her and ran her fingers through the orange flame. The flesh of her fingertips turned black as the warmth increased.

"You ought to be more careful," a strong accented voice said. "You could get burned in a lot of ways."

Holding back a smirk, Addison pulled her hand away and looked up and to her left. A familiar face stood above her, his expression neutral. Brown eyes gazed upon her with caution. Rising to her feet, the agent stood eye level with her old acquaintance. The pair studied each other silently. An air of tension expanded between them, but it was Addison who made the first move. Holding out her hand she supplied a small smile.

"Alon, it's been a while." Alon hadn't changed, Addison noted. His hair was still cropped in a short, convenient style. It was the kind of look that needed no maintenance when he rose from a night's sleep. A deep scar around his left eye looked a little more faded in colour, but was still highly noticeable.

Her hand was accepted and Alon shook the appendage firmly. "Addison Black, I was surprised to know it was you I would meet."

"You should know never to underestimate me, Alon." Addison offered a chair to Alon as she sat. He followed suit, taking a chair opposite her. Addison picked up her Jack Daniels.

"I learned that lesson after you slept with my sister, Agent Black."

The agent sighed, placing down her glass. "It was two years ago... Agent Yamburg... and I told you back then I didn't know Shiri was your sister. I thought we went over this." Addison took a drink of whiskey. "I'm not here to dredge up the past, Alon. I have important business."

As much as Addison would have argued her point, she didn't have the time. Every second that passed was added time Skyler spent alone and in the hands of Agnes Brodie. Arguing events that transpired over two years ago were of no consequence or interest to her.

The brief night Addison spent with Alon's sister was nothing more than the result of too much drink and the rush of a winner's high. She had been playing poker with Alon and three of his friends in this very bar. It had been going for a while and the drinks had been constant. Thinking he had a good hand, and not having enough money to back him, a drunken Alon had placed Shiri, who was serving behind the bar, in the pot. He lost. Fortunately, he acknowledged in relief, Addison had won the hand and his sister. He didn't think there could be a poor outcome. It didn't turn out to be the best way to discover his sister's sexual preference.

Alon leaned back in his chair. "Right... well I understand you are tracking down a known criminal who you believe has entered this country." Alon placed a black briefcase upon the table separating them. He pulled out several sheets of paper. "We ran a check on everybody who entered the country in the time span you gave us." He pushed the papers over to Addison. "We didn't find the name Agnes Brodie listed anywhere. In fact, apart from basic evidence detailing her living in Bethlehem, we have nothing on her at all."

The agent frowned and scanned the documents. There had to be something. "What about monitored activity you guys have been running?"

Alon Yamburg was an agent for the Mossad, Israel's CIA and otherwise known as the Institute for Intelligence and Special Tasks. Addison knew with their help she would be able to find Brodie if she were in this country. Like the United States' CIA, the Mossad was responsible for all human intelligence collection, covert action and counter-terrorism. They had eyes and ears everywhere.

Nodding, Alon opened a black folder. "We have many organisations under surveillance. I ran data links and found something that could be useful to you."

The agent's interest was piqued. Drinking down the remainder of her Jack Daniels, Addison dragged her chair around to sit beside Alon. "Tell me."

Alon opened a map. "There is a research plant here." Alon pointed to an area of desert in the southern area of Israel, close to Eilat. "It is owned by a Dr. Kleein; this is a name we have no information on."

"Okay?" Addison asked in confusion.

"But it is run by a woman called Sadie Bregon." Agent Yamburg took the top sheet of names of people who had entered the country in the past twenty-four hours. His finger tapped the fourteenth name upon the sheet. "She touched down in Eilat early this morning."

"Sadie Bregon?" Addison read the name over and again. Her fingers drummed upon the table as she studied Alon's information.

"She entered the country with fifteen assistants and cargo. The laboratory she runs is said to test cosmetics made by minerals obtained from the Dead Sea."

Addison pulled a pen from Agent Yamburg's case. She twirled it around her fingers in thought.

"What is it?" Alon asked as Addison began striking a line through the letters of Sadie Bregon's name.

"It's just occurred to me that if you rearrange the letters of Sadie Bregon…"

"Yes?" Alon asked.

Addison grinned. "You get Agnes Brodie!"

"You do?" Alon rechecked the letters. "This is a very interesting development. But we still don't know about Dr. Kleein or who he is."

"Hmm." Addison rechecked the map. "But at least I have a destination." She rose from her chair. "I know where I'm heading."

"Where we are heading!" Alon piled the documents back in his case and stood beside Addison. "You know I have to accompany you on this, Addison. Besides, I can get us on a flight to Eilat within the hour."

Addison folded her arms. She knew the Mossad would demand one of their agents work with her, but she had one condition. "Fine, but I call the shots. This is my mission and I have much riding on this, Alon. I know Brodie. We have to do this my way."

"You know the guidelines I have to follow, Addison, but we can work together. We did once before, remember? This time though, we will stay away from celebrating a successful mission."

Addison smirked and shook Alon's hand. "You have a deal, Agent Yamburg."

****

Deep breath, keep your eyes open. Skyler repeated those words like a mantra and slowly she started to feel better. She didn't know if it was the sound advice she remembered from her first aid class or the fact that it had been several hours since Brodie had given her the vile tasting liquid.

Skyler wasn't sure of exactly what comprised the noxious cocktail, but she knew for certain it contained Ipecac elixir. She knew that by the almost immediate vomiting she'd done. The fact that she was given the liquid on the way into the airport from the plane gave her an idea of what Brodie had planned. The cramping, nausea and dizziness that accompanied the frank vomiting were as unpleasant a side effect as Skyler ever hoped to suffer from.

Two "associates" of Brodie's helped her walk into the airport while Brodie took charge of getting her past Immigration and Passport Control. She handed over a British passport to the waiting Israeli official.

"I warned her not to eat the steak and kidney pie at that pub, but would she listen to me? I'm afraid Dr. Simpson is an independent woman with a mind of her own. Of course, it might have been the several pints of Guinness that she consumed along with the pie, eh?" Agnes winked at the official as she handed over her own passport as well. Skyler could see Brodie was traveling under an Israeli passport and wished she had the strength to yell out to the official or alert airport security.

The official was solicitous of her condition and offered to summon an ambulance, but Brodie assured him that it would not be necessary and that she would be taken to her private doctor as soon as they entered Eilat. If there was one thing Skyler understood about Brodie, it was that they would be nowhere near Eilat. Unfortunately for Skyler's stomach, she had been correct.

Skyler, Brodie, several helpers and a small mountain of packing crates had been loaded into waiting trucks and they had headed out into the countryside. Though Skyler was wedged between a large henchman at the wheel of a truck and Brodie on the passenger side, the fresh air blowing in the window was very welcome. It was warm but not oppressively hot and they went through several checkpoints without incident. A gun to Skyler's ribs assured her continued silence. For the time they were on the paved highway the journey wasn't so bad, but the moment they turned off onto a dirt and gravel track, Skyler knew her tenuous control over the residual nausea was lost.

The sour taste of stomach acid in her mouth was a small price to pay for the outraged look on Brodie's face when Skyler expelled the liquid remnants of her gut directly on the Irishwoman's shoes. The convoy of trucks ground to a momentary halt as Brodie leaped out and cleaned her shoes on the sparse vegetation in the area they were passing through.

The group of trucks continued on its trek in a southerly direction and headed into a bleak area, mountainous and unwelcoming. The road deteriorated to a wide, winding trail and steep hills shot up on either side. *The perfect place for an ambush* Skyler thought as there would be little cover for anyone foolish enough to follow Brodie's trail through there.

After what seemed like a lifetime, the convoy broke free of the mountainous terrain and emerged into a relatively flat valley. Being in the lead truck afforded Skyler a view of what lay ahead. A group of obviously new buildings was situated in the middle of the valley, well away from the steep slopes present on all sides. *It's like a box canyon in the western States* Skyler thought, *very secure, very safe and virtually impregnable.* It was not a comforting thought.

As they moved nearer the compound, Skyler noted that they were headed for the largest building. She wondered at how such a large base had been built so far from the general populace. That question was answered when she spied a helipad to the side of the group of buildings. A wall circled the compound and at regular intervals there were elevated guard towers manned by serious looking men and women with automatic weapons. Patrolling the grounds were teams with dogs. Skyler had been to two previous establishments that Brodie had been connected with, but this third one was obviously the most heavily fortified of them all.

The American's spirits sank as she viewed the compound. The possibilities for escape would be very slim. *Slim, hell... face it, Skyler, they're nonexistent.*

Their truck pulled to a stop in front of the largest building. It was boxlike and painted a tan color that would make it difficult to pick out individual edifices from the sky. They disembarked and Agnes pulled Skyler along by the sleeve of Addison's jacket that she still wore. Weakness from the episode of vomiting and a sense of futility prevented her from putting up any resistance as she stumbled along behind the redhead.

They entered the building and Skyler was roughly directed into an office and onto a plush sofa. Her relief at sitting and not being jostled was a balm for her unsettled stomach and spirit. Her head lolled

161

to the side and she drifted in and out of sleep as Brodie worked over various maps and papers. They had been at the compound possibly thirty minutes by Skyler's estimation when the phone in the office rang.

"Bregon," the redhead said into the phone. "Yes, one moment." Brodie picked up an electronic device and attached it to the mouthpiece of the telephone. She flipped a switch on the device and a small button glowed red.

Scrambler, thought Skyler, now more awake.

"Secure here," Agnes spoke into the phone. "We arrived about half an hour ago. No, no incidents." Agnes looked down at her shoes and grimaced slightly as she listened to the person on the other end of the phone. "Yes, I still have her. Look, you just pay me the money as promised and I'll take care of the 'how'. I know what I'm doing here. Doctor Tidwell will be my insurance policy against any further problems from our troublesome friend, not that I expect any. God, it was sweet! The expression on her face as we took off was priceless! Why is there never a camera when you need one?" Agnes chuckled while reliving the moment.

Her laughter was suddenly cut short and she sat straight up in her chair. "What? You're bloody well joking! When?" Brodie consulted her watch. "Probably in the country by now. You're sure of the information? Yes, of course it is. I'm sorry; your information has always been good. No, there will be no mistakes this time. I understand. Will you be joining us here?" Agnes listened again. "Very well then, I'll deal with any problems that may arise from that quarter. Thank you for calling, Dr. Kleein." The redhead flipped the switch on the scrambler and hung the phone up.

"Well, Doctor, it appears I may have a little more entertainment than this remote location usually allows. I must give Addison Black credit; she somehow manages to always make her presence felt. It appears she has headed for Israel also. Well, being in the same country and having you freed are two very different things."

"Brodie, I can understand why you kept me when you thought I was my mother. I can even understand why you needed me for your escape from the Isle of Skye, but why did you bring me here? You must know I can give you no information on my mother's project."

Agnes snorted. "I don't need you for anything like that now, Doctor. Your mother was quite cooperative in that matter. It should only be a matter of time before we will be ready to use that information to our advantage. No, your passage has been bought for less financial and more personal reasons. Tell me, are you and Addison lovers yet?"

Skyler opened her mouth to deny it, but common sense prevailed

162

and she surmised her usefulness to Brodie would be enhanced if the Irishwoman thought that she and the British agent were involved.

"Well, uh, she's a difficult woman to resist, don't you find?" Skyler said diplomatically.

Brodie's face darkened. "No, I've never had the pleasure."

But you wanted to, didn't you? Skyler thought, knowing she had just gotten an insight into Brodie's motivation for bringing her along. *Maybe I can use that.* "Well, that's a shame because Addison is a fantastic lover. The things she can do with her hands and mouth are incredible." Skyler didn't have to feign the blush that crossed her features. "The only thing is, Addison tends to be a little possessive. I mean... we weren't together that long, but she said she would kill anyone who touched me."

Brodie brightened at that thought. "Oh, she did, did she? Well I think that maybe I have a way to just ruin her whole day then. I was going to have your body at my leisure very soon, but I think Addison may be about to pay us a little visit and she's going to walk right into my trap if she does. I'm going to save you for that time. She's going to hate seeing me enjoy you and I will enjoy that! It's almost a pity that I'll have to put a bullet in both your heads afterwards. I might have really loved a threesome with you both."

Skyler's settled stomach threatened to revolt again at the picture in her mind of what Brodie was suggesting. She pushed those thoughts aside to more positive ones. Addison Black was on their trail and Skyler had been a firsthand witness to the British agent's determination. She knew she would see Addison again; she felt it and never questioned it. Skyler only had to stay alive long enough to make that meeting possible.

M J Walker and Val Brown

Chapter 15

Dust from two blue and red quad bikes rose from Israel's desert plains. The growl of high-powered engines echoed over the barren land Following Alon, Addison steered her bike skillfully, trailing her friend as they rode over the sandy, desert ground. They had flown to Eilat and had arrived early evening, but to be sure of enough light Alon suggested they leave early in the morning. It had been a tough decision. Addison wanted to leave as soon as possible, not wanting Skyler alone with Brodie any longer than necessary, but she trusted Alon and she trusted his knowledge of the desert.

Leaving at first light though had one drawback. It was still relatively cold. Addison had not dressed for the cool weather. She knew it wasn't worth it and she did have a higher than normal internal body temperature, but zooming across the desert on the 170CC bike caused cool air to thrust against her skin. Addison released one hand from the handlebar and adjusted the red bandanna covering her nose and mouth. She didn't want to breathe in any grains of sand. Getting those into awkward places was the last thing she wanted bothering her. For that reason she wore her dark sunglasses, keeping her vision safe from wheel-generated dust.

Before they had left, Alon and Addison went over the supplies they would need for their mission. Addison had a plan, but she was keeping it to herself. She already knew Alon would protest and he would have less ground to stand on when they were at the laboratory site. Alon had packed his backpack with necessary aids; Addison hadn't bothered. For what she had in mind she knew it would be futile. All she packed was a bottle of water and two grenades. Apart from her Berettas, extra clips and boot knife, the soldier was lightly armed.

Addison realised Alon was beginning to slow down so she followed suit until they came to a complete stop. Pulling the bandanna from her face and placing the glasses upon her head, Addison dismounted her bike. She looked at Alon with questioning eyes.

"Why have we stopped?"

Shrugging off his backpack, Alon leaned against his bike. "I need a drink." He unzipped the black carrier and pulled out a clear bottle of mineral water. "We still have a way to go, Addison, but we should be there between ten and eleven o'clock." Taking a long drink, Alon sat on the sand in front of Addison. "So tell me. We both know it's not good to make a case personal, but I feel that is what is happening with you right now. What have you not told me?"

Addison sat down beside Alon. "Agnes Brodie is a long time pain in my arse. She has crossed the line one too many times, Alon, but this time she went too far. I am putting a stop to her once and for all."

"But you are not telling me what she has done. It is something. I can tell."

Picking up a stone from the sand, Addison drew lines in the grainy surface. "She took the woman I was protecting out from under my nose. I don't know how she did it. I thought I had kept her safe. I had only just rescued her from Brodie. I know that woman enough to know she is not going to make life easy for Skyler. This is a highly organised situation and Sky is nothing more than a fly in the ointment."

Alon seemed perplexed. "A fly in what?"

The agent smiled. "An annoyance that can be easily exterminated, especially once she has served her purpose. I just fear what that purpose will be."

Pulling one leg up, Alon balanced his arm over his knee. "You like this woman, this Skyler?"

Addison smirked as her thoughts turned to her brief time spent with the American. "She isn't like any woman I've met before. She has a lot of strength and intelligence, but at the same time she seems so naïve, like she has substituted a lot of the more exciting parts of life for study and further education. But... she has spunk!"

Alon blinked in bewilderment. In his knowledge of the English language he knew of only one meaning for the word spunk. "She has..." he motioned his hand in a questioning manner that pointed to his manhood.

Releasing a laugh, Addison shook her head. "She has a spark, an inner fire, je ne se qoi, a... she has a life loving attitude that takes no crap."

166

He smiled, his eyes shining with boyish mischief. "So you do like this Skyler!"

Addison shrugged, but remained silent. It didn't matter whether she liked Skyler or not. She knew better than to let personal feelings interfere with a mission. She had to rise above them if she was to succeed. Not only Skyler, but the lives of many people depended on her. Addison wouldn't fail; she would not fail them. Rule one, and the most important rule for completion of a successful mission, was to never allow your own feelings to interfere with said mission. Every life taken, heart broken or bridge burned...it was all for the bigger picture, the greater purpose.

Closing her eyes, Addison pulled her glasses back down and directed her face towards the sun. Its heat was rapidly increasing and already Addison could feel beads of sweat form upon her back and brow. She wiped the moisture away from her hairline and turned to Alon. The Israeli Mossad agent was busy checking their communication equipment. He rifled through his backpack checking and re-checking their supplies. Addison's gaze wandered to the area around his eye and above his eyebrow. Scaring was evident, the result of a bomb blast that had showered him with shards of shrapnel as he patrolled Israeli borders while in the army. He was only eighteen at the time. Fifteen years later and those scars were as noticeable as ever.

Alon rose to his feet. "I need a pee, back in a moment."

The English agent grimaced. "Thanks for the details, Alon!" She waited as Alon disappeared behind a rock and stood, shouldering her backpack. With very little inside, it was unusually light. She wandered back to her quad bike and waited. As Alon returned, Addison mounted the vehicle and pulled the red bandanna back over her nose and mouth.

"You ready?" he asked

Addison replied by offering a thumbs up.

Alon gave a swift nod. "Then let's get going."

****

Marlene Tidwell stood beside General Mark Blithe in the very nerve centre of MI-5, Special Operations. It was a high tech, state of the art monitoring compound, half a mile below the surface of Headquarters. Marlene noted that it looked very much like a smaller version of Flight Control at NASA in Houston. Large screens covered the far and side wall. Each one displayed different information from satellite positions, world breaking news, operative whereabouts, weapons activity, communications and links to world organisations. Lights flashed, equipment beeped and over thirty voices conversed on classified information.

"This is the heart of the operation!" Marlene commented. "I understand that my being with you allowed the access, but should I be **in** here?"

Blithe surveyed the room. "You already have a high security clearance with your work and I can act at my own discretion. I have no doubts about your trustworthiness. Besides, I want you safe and there is no safer a place to be than here. In fact, if a war were to break out, this would be the safest and most secure place around."

"For us yes... but we aren't the ones in danger." Marlene's lip quivered and she attempted to take hold of her emotions. "I saw that woman drag my daughter off at gun point. I saw how scared Skyler was. I can't get that image out of my mind, Mark."

"I do understand." Blithe placed his hand upon Marlene's shoulder. "But I do still insist I have the best agent on the job. Whatever Agent Black does, I guarantee she will move heaven and earth to secure Skyler's release and safe journey home."

Folding her arms, Marlene leaned back against a desk. "I don't question that at all. What I don't understand is why you don't send an army in there. Why use just one operative? Surely a group would be better?"

"You would think so, and in some instances that is the case. However, there are times, we have discovered, when sending a single, skilled operative into combat can actually be a lot more beneficial. Our operatives are the best, Marlene, and we deal with these one-man missions. That is what Special Operations is about. If you need a task force of highly trained men you send in the Special Air Services; if you plan a one man mission, we are the team you contact." The General leaned upon the desk beside Marlene. "Exact knowledge of our operative's whereabouts can be monitored." He pointed to a small screen on a long table of ten visual display units. "The screen that reads SO2 in the corner, that is Agent Black. Although we've had no communication we know she flew from Tel-Aviv to Eilat yesterday afternoon and at this moment is travelling northwest across the desert in Biqa'at Timna."

Marlene squinted. She leaned forwards to gain a clearer view of the screen. A green dot moved slowly across an electronic, touch screen map. "How are you able to keep such an accurate positioning?"

"As you can understand, we work in highly precarious situations. Knowledge of your operative's whereabouts and well-being is sometimes essential, especially if they are out of the country and unable to make voice contact. Each agent has an implant in their shoulder, their left shoulder. It keeps constant track during operations and supervises vital signs. This isn't something we use all the time though, mainly when an agent is undercover, working internationally or in any situation where they are unable to keep vocal contact." Mark picked up a small, narrow object that looked almost like a television remote control. "We activate the implant with one of these. The agent must be present at the time." Mark demonstrated by holding the gadget up to his shoulder. "And you simply switch it on with this green button." He pressed the button and instantly another screen was activated within the nerve centre. The code name SO0 blinked at the bottom of its screen and his position flashed into the display. "And that is how it works." He turned it off and the screen went black.

"Marlene took the remote from Mark's hand. "An ingenious device."

"Well, not really," Mark replied. "Samuel got the idea after Agent Black got Spike, her dog, electronically tagged. Addison wasn't too happy about being tagged like Spike. I told her that at least if either of them got lost it would be easier to find or identify them."

Marlene smiled. "And what was her reply?"

"My dear, Marlene." Mark placed his hand upon the professor's back as they began to leave the busy room. "Obscene finger gestures and foul language must never be repeated in the presence of a lady!"

****

It took another hour and a half for Addison and Alon to near 'Sadie Bregon's' 'cosmetic laboratory'. They abandoned their bikes and travelled the remaining distance by foot so as not to alert anybody to unwelcome engine sounds. The sun was now high in the sky. It shone down upon the agents with a searing heat. Addison walked beside Alon, her eyes scanning the terrain. Rocks and sand was all there appeared to be; it was all there had been for miles.

Alon stopped. He looked around and then pointed to the mountainous rise to the right. "Over there," he said. "There is a valley."

They approached the rise together, crouching as they neared its peak and eventually crawling onto their stomachs. Addison looked down into the valley below.

"Fuck me!" Her eyes scanned the area. There were several new buildings, the middle of which was the largest. What surprised

Addison was the armed manpower guarding the site. She approximated thirty men and woman. There were two watchtowers, patrolling guards and dogs.

Accepting the binoculars Alon offered her, Addison took a closer look at the situation. "Oh yeah," she mumbled as she zoomed in on the highly secured compound. A high wall topped with electric wire bordered the area. "These guys definitely look like they're protecting the secrets of the 'all day' lipstick!"

"My thoughts exactly... sort of." Alon turned to Addison. "Now that we have a visual, I think we are going to need back up, right?"

"No," replied Addison. "I have a plan to infiltrate the place. I know you are not going to like it, but you must trust me, Alon. It may sound risky, but it will work. I know Brodie well enough to know that."

"Why did I have a bad feeling you would pull something like this?" Alon sighed and readied himself for Addison's 'plan'.

****

Skyler winced as Brodie jerked her up hard by her arm.

"Let's move, Blondie. I have work to do and you need to be put in a place for safekeeping before I do it." The American fought down the urge to struggle with Agnes. Remembering the beating she had taken in Scotland made her cautious about pushing the mercenary too far.

Be careful walking this line, Skyler. She needs to be angry, but not out of control. If she is, maybe she won't stop to consider what an exciting woman like Addison Black would want with me. That might keep me alive. The American flashed a charming smile in Agnes' direction.

"So, Addison is on her way. Somehow that doesn't surprise me. She tends to be a bit focused. So have you and Addison done much...uh...business together?" Brodie directed her out of the office and down a long pristine white hallway. As they passed several doors with glass windows, Skyler could see people in full laboratory gear. Dressed in blue cover gowns, masks and face shields, the personnel appeared to be busy setting up equipment being removed from boxes that Skyler recognized as being part of the ones they had brought with them in the convoy.

"We've had our encounters in the past," Brodie sneered. "Even more than Addison knows! Oh, she's tried to take me out, but she could never quite make that happen. I've got nine lives, Doctor, and

170

Addison Black hasn't come close to running me through them all!"

Skyler thought back to the conversation she was privy to in the office. "As long as you're going to kill me anyway, do you mind if I ask you something?"

Brodie cut her eyes at the scientist. "You can ask," she said in a tone that clearly implied there might not be an answer.

"It's just that I've wondered how you managed to do it. Addison is one of most lethal people I've run across and yet you've come through unscathed. I would think there's not many people who have gotten the best of her and it's rather impressive that you've managed it."

Agnes puffed up a little at Skyler's words. "Not many is right!" The mercenary appeared thoughtful. "Let's see, there's been me...and me!" She chuckled at her own joke. "I am the thorn in Addison Black's side, I am the fish that got away. I am also going to be the one to end the career of SO2."

"But how did you do it? I'm sure there are a lot of people in your profession who would be envious of the success you've had in matching wits with the Special Operations agent."

Brodie stopped before a thick metal door. She fished a key from the pocket of the khaki trousers she wore and inserted it into the lock. Turning the key she pulled the door open to reveal an even more Spartan cell than Skyler had inhabited in Scotland. It appeared to be a converted lab. There were mattresses on the floor next to metal cabinets and a deep sink in the corner of the room.

"Sorry for the poor accommodations, Doctor," Brodie said with feigned solicitousness as she guided Skyler inside. "We never really expected unwelcome guests at this rather remote location. I'm sure you'll be able to make do though. There is a bathroom through there." She indicated a small door in one wall. "No lock though, I'm sure you understand. You are something of a resourceful woman in your own right and I won't underestimate you again." Agnes unconsciously brought her hand up to her head, touching the area injured by Skyler's booby trap in Scotland.

"No hard feelings on that one, right?" Skyler asked.

"Of course not. I would have done the same thing you did except for one detail. I would have been ready to terminate you as soon as you were vulnerable. You were soft, Doctor. Softness gets you nowhere. Ask Addison. Up until now I never found the tiniest shred of softness or weakness in her." Agnes reached out and ran the back of her hand along Skyler's cheek. "How does it feel to know you are going to be the cause of the demise of the infamous Addison Black?"

171

Skyler jerked her head away from Agnes' touch. "She isn't dead yet, Brodie!"

Instead of becoming angry as the scientist expected, the Irishwoman just laughed. "Oh, yes, I can certainly see what attracts Addison. You have a very interesting spark. It's going to be a shame when I have to extinguish it."

A cold chill passed down Skyler's spine. Though they were tinged with amusement, Brodie's words were deadly serious.

"Oh, by the way. Just so you don't get lonely, I've assigned you a guard all of your own." From the hallway behind her a huge man loomed over Brodie. He was less a man than a small mountain of humanity. Standing at least six and a half feet tall and weighing what Skyler estimated to be well over three hundred pounds, the man stared at her with what was almost disinterest. A shock of short, spiky brown hair topped a ruddy complexion.

"Skyler, this is Shamus. He's been with me a long time and has remained a good and faithful employee throughout. She reached up and patted the huge man's cheek as if he were little more than a pet pit bull. "Shamus, meet Doctor Skyler Tidwell. You will be interested to know she is a particularly good friend of Addison Black. You remember Addison, don't you?"

The man's eyes narrowed and he literally snarled, revealing a gap where his front two teeth should have been. "Addithun!" he said with a heavy lisp. The disinterest in his eyes was replaced by open and frank hatred.

Brodie smiled with sympathy at the large man then turned back to address Skyler. "As you can tell, Shamus has an unfortunate history with Addison Black. About three years ago he was assisting me with a project in Portugal. We were providing necessary supplies to a group in Eastern Europe that MI-5 didn't like. Addison Black of Special Operations was dispatched to interfere with our business. Somewhere along the way Shamus and Addison crossed paths. Show Skyler what her girlfriend can do when she doesn't like you, Shamus." The huge man raised a meaty hand up to show Skyler four thick fingers and a tiny stump where his right thumb would have been.

"Didn't know Addison took trophies, did you? Shamus hasn't been happy with the loss of his thumb; he had been quite attached to it. Since that time he has vowed that one day he would have his revenge on your friend. I think if I were you I would try not to upset Shamus. Addison or Addison's friend...I'm fairly certain it's all the same to him."

Skyler looked at the menacing hulk and decided that at this point, cooperation would be her best option. She raised her hands in a gesture of surrender. "You'll have no problems with me." She turned and moved further into the room muttering, "For now" under her breath.

"Good," Brodie said to her back. "It wouldn't do for Addison to find her lover already dead when we finally get her in our hands." The Irishwoman turned to leave, but stopped as Skyler called out to her.

"Brodie! You never answered my question. How did you manage to get the best of Addison all this time?"

Agnes paused only momentarily on her way out of the room. "I've beaten her so far by using something you as a Yank can understand. Let's just call it 'insider trading'!" Brodie chuckled and passed through the door. Shamus glared at her, almost daring Skyler to become a problem. Then he pulled the door closed, leaving Skyler alone in the room.

The American expelled a breath she hadn't realized she was holding. She dropped to one of the mattresses haphazardly thrown on the floor. She lay back on the mattress and looked up toward the ceiling, her eyes on an iron bar covered skylight.

Okay, you're alive. That's what counts right now. All you have to do now is wait for that one woman wrecking crew named Addison Black to get here. Skyler knew she was trying to keep her own spirits up and turned her mind to more productive matters.

Insider trading? What did Brodie mean by that? A traitor? God, please just let this be Agnes spouting off. Mom, where are you? Are they keeping you safe? Addison, I hope you left her in good hands. Worrying about her mother took Skyler's mind off her own desperate circumstances, but not by much.

Chapter 16

"ARE YOU," Alon lowered his voice, conscious of their surroundings. "Crazy?"

Addison moved backwards, assuring she was out of view. "No. I know exactly what I am doing. This may well be the best way I can gain access into that place."

"No!"

"Alon," Addison reached out and pulled the man down and away from the ledge of the valley. "Don't you think I have thought about this? I asked you to trust me, now please do so."

Shaking his head, Alon rose to his knees. "What you are planning is…"

"The best way to infiltrate that place. Brodie is going to know I am on my way. She will expect me to make a mistake." Addison moved to her knees, mirroring Alon's position. "She thinks taking Skyler is going to have an effect on me, force me to panic or drop my guard. I know her, I wrote her psychological profile for God's sake. I'm going to give her exactly what she is expecting. She'll be too busy congratulating herself to even realise."

"And you expect me to stand by while this takes place?" Alon shook his head. "You **are** crazy."

"If you want to live you will keep out of sight. Don't watch if that is the case. I need you as my man on the outside. You will be able to contact General Blithe back in London and assure him all will be okay."

"You cannot be sure of that."

"Blithe trusts me, Alon. In his own words he gives me my head on missions because he knows my judgement is always a sound calling.

175

I understand you may not think this is an intelligent move... I might even have to agree with you, but the fact is that I have given this much consideration. If I have to let her think she has won in order to allow her caution to lower, then so be it. I know the way Brodie thinks and what's more, I know the arrogance which lies behind that mind." Addison pulled the backpack from her back. Alon opened his mouth to speak, but the raising of a hand silenced him. "Look, Alon, this is not a suicide mission. This is not a case of me finally losing my marbles or going off the deep end with some dodgy, half-cocked idea. I mean... fuck... grant me with some presence of sense. I sure as hell am not going to like it, that I can guarantee, but I endured worse while training with the Special Forces." *Maybe,* Addison added to herself in thought.

When the agent finally paused for breath, Alon jumped into the momentary silence. "But she could kill you and then where will Skyler Tidwell be?" This was his last hope for an argument. Although the Mossad could easily stop her from taking such a risk in a country that was their 'jurisdiction', Alon knew he was powerless against Addison alone. She had a will of iron and no amount of pulling rank would work with her once her mind was set. Alon had learned that lesson the hard way.

"I doubt very much she would kill me, but if she did HQ would be aware and a counter plan would be brought into play. Opening her backpack, Addison pulled out the half empty bottle of mineral water. She drank down the remainder of the container. "Believe me, Alon, I have thought this through."

The Mossad agent looked on helplessly as Addison took the Colt survival knife from her boot and strapped it inside her footwear, hidden from view. He realised Addison had intended this the whole time. She really had given this plan serious consideration. With a sigh of resignation, Alon asked, "What do you want me to do?"

Fastening her bootlace, Addison smiled sincerely. "Just get in contact with General Blithe. Tell him what is going on. Assure him of my motives and confidence in this. Placate him when he blows an artery basically." Addison reached inside her carrier and pulled out the two grenades. She looked over at Alon, registering his sombre expression.

"I don't like this, Addison."

"I know."

"It's very dangerous."

"It will work." Addison looked around the desert grounds. "Listen, Alon, you don't have to watch when this goes down. In fact, it's probably best you don't."

"I'll watch," Alon said adamantly. "I'll need to make sure you get inside there alive. I will watch and I promise not to intervene."

Addison nodded. "No matter what happens."

"No matter what happens," Alon echoed.

"Thank you." Taking a deep breath, Addison held a grenade in both hands. "Let's get this started, shall we?"

Alon looked away. He couldn't believe he was actually allowing this to happen. Granted, when faced with the stubborn will of Addison Black it was hard to win, but that didn't lessen the fact that what she was doing was so terribly dangerous. He believed many other ways of infiltrating the compound could be determined, but at such short notice and with Addison adamant on her plan, he knew he was out of time and outnumbered. With Addison plus her determination that was practically two against one.

"I'll need you to keep monitoring their movements from this position." Addison patted down her body. "Do you have a pen?"

Alon produced a black ballpoint. He handed it to Addison and the British Agent took his hand, holding it palm down. She began scrawling a set of numbers upon his skin.

"This is a secured frequency you can use to contact HQ. It goes straight to the General so only he will answer."

"Right." Agent Yamburg studied the frequency, memorising each digit and then proceeded to remove the ink from his hand. "I'll remember."

"Okay." Pushing a grenade into each pocket, Addison held out her hand and Alon shook it firmly. "See you later, mate."

"Try to remain in one piece, Agent Black."

"Will do." Addison took a deep breath. She turned back to the valley and crawled towards the ledge. She looked back down to the buildings below. Addison knew her best point of entrance would be by the front, steel gates and not by breeching the site's defences. Three armed guards stood by the gate, one beside an electric lock and holding a dog, the other two patrolling the vicinity of the barrier as they conversed quietly.

"It's now or never, Addy," the agent mumbled and rose to her feet. She was suddenly in clear view of the guards below. Addison estimated the ledge down into the valley was a thirty-foot slant of sand and rubble. She braced herself for what she was about to do.

Strolling slowly across the peak of the ledge, Addison waited to be spotted. When she was certain at least one pair of eyes had registered her presence she stopped walking and looked towards them. "Here we go," she said and raised her hand, waving as she began to move down the slope.

"Hello?" she called and purposely tripped on a stray rock. The agent braced herself as she went down. She hit the ground with a thud, careful not to cause any undue harm as her body began a dramatic fall of which any Hollywood stunt man would be envious.

Rolling down with the appropriate and well-placed yelps and curses, Addison travelled into the valley with a swift descent. She came to a halt eight feet away from the guards, landing on her back with a thud and scattering of sand and dust. Groaning, Addison stood and looked at the men, two of whom trained guns upon her, the other restraining a large Alsatian.

Addison held out her hands. "Hey! I'm sorry, but I just fell down that hill and you are aiming a gun at me? Look, I'm lost and was hoping you could help me. I'm not sure where I am." Addison noted these guards were dressed differently than Brodie's other men had been dressed. They wore lighter weight clothes, a colour similar to military desert stripe in a light sand camouflage.

"This is a highly sensitive government site, Ma'am," a guard lied. "I suggest you turn around and head the other way."

"Okay... I can do that, but I'm lost. You couldn't just tell me where to go... you know, kind of point me in the right direction?" Addison delivered her most innocent expression. "Please? I don't want to be lost in the desert. You hear so many stories of people disappearing in the desert and never being found."

The guards looked between each other and lowered their weapons with a nod. "Where is it you want to go?" the first guard asked.

"It's called ... um... damn it, I can't remember... they have such peculiar names!" Addison patted her breast pockets. "I have it written down somewhere" She continued to search her body, pushing her hands in each front trouser pocket. Addison clasped a hand around each grenade tightly, making sure her thumbs held the pins at the ready. She pulled them out of her pocket, keeping the backs of her hands concealing the explosives as she chattered away.

"I can't remember how to pronounce it but I know it begins with a 'Y'." As calmly as placing a piece of gum in her mouth, Addison grasped both pins in-between her teeth and pulled. They disengaged from the explosives. Grinning with pins still between white teeth, Addison turned her hands around to display the grenades to the guards.

Shock registered on the men's faces and they dived to the ground for cover. As they did so, Addison threw both grenades over the wall and into the middle of the compound's courtyard. Before the

178

explosives even had time to erupt, Addison spat out the pins and pulled both pistols from behind her back. She fired instantly, taking out each guard before a combined blast echoed over the wall and shook the very foundations on which she stood. Addison ducked, allowing rocks and sand to fall around her.

Not even waiting for the dust to settle, Addison took a run up, lunging towards the gate. She jumped high, placing her feet upon the steel rods of the gate and swiftly climbing up to boost herself over the barrier. She jumped down, landing on the other side of the wall and surveyed her surroundings. People were still rising from the ground in bewilderment. She took a mental calculation of only seven guards severely hurt by the explosion and figured she still had around twenty to brace herself for.

Berettas ready, Addison began running, firing at the people around her. Several bullets hit their target before her shots were answered by enemy fire. The agent dodged the fire, but cursed at the painful burn of a bullet slicing across her side. She stumbled, dropping one gun and clasping her waist. Suddenly the sting of sharp teeth around her leg made Addison trip and fall. The remaining pistol fell from her right hand as she struggled to free herself from the growling hound clamped around her leg.

Swinging out her left foot, Addison kicked the dog hard. It whimpered and released her. Addison quickly rolled to her feet. She turned to find her weapons only to be confronted by five guards. The agent blocked the first couple of punches, but allowed the rest to hit their mark, barraging her stomach, chest and chin with a series of hard knocks. Each one felt more painful than the last. She accepted each blow attempting only to remain upright and throw out the odd punch to at least make a show of trying to fight back. In fact, this was her intention from the very beginning.

Not wanting to appear too easy, Addison increased her attack, releasing a few more punches and series of kicks for good measure. Suddenly and completely unexpected, Addison's eyes were exposed to an assault of mace. Then she did cry out, thrusting both hands over her eyes as she fell to her knees. Violent kicks and the odd punch continued until Addison lay upon the ground, willingly showing defeat. She was smart enough to know when she had put up enough of a fight, but knew it had to look convincing. Every part of her body protested at the pain of each assault. She felt searing jolts of agony rock her frame. Blood pooled in several places on her body including her lip, gum and eyebrow.

Without warning the attack stopped and an eerie silence fell over the courtyard. Addison panted heavily, her hands still clutched over her watering eyes. The sound of approaching footsteps forced Addison to move to her knees. Unable to see through eyes blinded by tears, Addison waited. She knew who it was.

"Addison Black... forever a pain in my backside."

"Agnes," Addison seethed with contempt.

Brodie remained two feet away from the British Agent. She stood, arms folded, glaring down with a superior air. The Irishwoman's men remained silent, holding their weapons directed towards Addison. The soldier was surrounded, temporarily blinded and physically injured and yet so far everything had gone to plan.

"I knew you would fuck up, Agent Black, but I never thought it would feel so good to have you on your knees before me like this."

Ignoring Brodie's obvious taunting, Addison remained calm. "Where's Skyler Tidwell?"

"Ah... the girl. Well, she's alive if that's what you're asking. Currently enjoying my hospitality."

"If you've hurt her I'll..."

"What?" Agnes laughed. "I hardly think you are in any position to make threats, Black." Stepping closer, Agnes Brodie knelt upon one knee in front of Addison. She lowered her voice, leaning closer to speak into the agent's ear. "You're mine, Black, and you know what they say... 'Revenge is sweet'."

A flash of anger prickled Addison's spine and she lashed out, delivering a blind punch at Brodie. A honed sense of distance and judgement connected her fist solidly with the redhead's chin and she fell backwards as Addison felt the butt of a pistol hit the back of her head. She too went down, landing face first on the sandy ground. Addison spat bloody grains of sand from her mouth, but remained upon the ground as Brodie stood back up.

"Bind her hands together," she said and wiped the droplet of blood from her lip. She sucked the metallic tasting essence from her skin.

Addison felt her hands clasped from behind as she was hauled to her feet. Her wrists were tied together with a strong nylon rope. The fibres dug tight into her flesh, chafing and sore. Her eyes stung and tears blurred her vision. Addison kept her head lowered. This may have been her plan, but she was beginning to feel vulnerable. The British agent tried to remain focussed upon her objectives. Find Skyler and destroy Project Gemini.

Brodie began issuing orders. "Clear the bodies. Post new guards by the gate." She turned to Addison and two large women standing on either side of her, armed and waiting for orders. "As for Miss Black, bring her with me."

Addison felt a hand on either shoulder as Brodie began to walk towards the main building. She was pushed behind her. They walked in silence, Brodie leading the way as they entered a clinically scented hallway and walked down towards a room at the end of the passage. Addison tried to look around her, attempting to gain some insight as to the lay out of the facility, but her blurred vision made that impossible.

Guided into a room, Addison was pulled to a halt. Her vision had begun to clear slightly and she was able to make out dull edges. The urge to protect her eyes and ease the irritation was strong, but with her hands bound together from behind, that was impossible. Addison stood silently, allowing her senses to assess the situation. She heard movement behind and suddenly found herself being pushed backwards and down. Addison landed upon an uncomfortable wooden chair. She felt her ankles bound to the chair's front legs by more nylon rope.

"Okay, you can leave us for the moment."

Nodding, both women complied as they left the room, closing the door behind them.

Unable to contain her smile of delight, Agnes turned to the British secret agent and perched herself on the edge of her desk. She folded her arms, her eyes wondering over Addison's bound form. "I have to say, Black... this is a moment I have waited for."

"I bet," Addison replied.

"Oh please, let's not get bitter now, you have to admit my time would come."

Addison remained poised upon the chair although she was very uncomfortable. "Oh believe me, Agnes, your time will come soon. That I guarantee."

Brodie shook her head. "Always like to have the last word, don't you? No matter..." Rising from the desk, Brodie stepped towards Addison. "Now excuse my hands for a moment, but I do have to check you for any concealed weapons, you understand." The redhead didn't wait for an answer as she began sliding her hands up Addison's right leg.

Addison fought against the shiver of repulsion she felt when Brodie's hands slid along her inner thighs. "Why would I conceal weapons? You have more than enough for me right here."

Laughing at Addison's frankness, Brodie continued her search. She pulled many pistol clips from the side leg pockets of Addison's combat trousers. "I'm sure you were thinking of getting in here and using my arsenal against me." Agnes stepped behind Addison, continuing her search. She ran her hands up Addison's arms. "Unfortunately your stupidity finally showed up through a weakness for the good doctor." Brodie's hand found the bullet wound on the agents side and she pressed her fingers into the injury.

Addison grimaced but kept her emotions under check, ignoring the pain. "Fuck you, Agnes."

Stepping around Addison, Brodie leaned into her. "Was that an offer?"

The agent snorted. "The only way that would happen was if you favoured necrophilia."

Brodie seethed. Moving away, she backhanded Addison. "You are so arrogant that you would actually think I would be interested in you!" She stepped backwards, moving around her desk and sitting upon a large, comfortable leather chair. Agnes placed her fingertips together under her nose. She smiled maliciously. "Now that blonde doctor, however, is a delight I have had the pleasure of sampling." Brodie hummed in a low brassy tone. "Sweet," she whispered.

It was hard not to rise to the bait when Brodie used Skyler. The agent felt physically repulsed by the mere thought of Skyler being harmed in any way whatsoever. If Brodie had so much as touched her improperly, Addison quietly pledged to make the woman suffer tenfold.

Attempting to adopt an indifferent air, Addison sighed. "If you are planning on a slow torture and death then can we get on with it as this is getting tedious… **Agnes**."

"GUARDS!" Brodie bellowed. Instantly the two women who had escorted Addison into the room re-appeared inside the doorway.

Brodie walked around her desk. "Yes that is my plan, Black, but all good things come to those who wait. I have business to attend to first and I am afraid that must come first. As for yourself… well you won't be going anywhere for a while. First however…" Brodie pulled a knife from her hip. She twirled the sharp object in the light. With her vision clearing slowly but surely, Addison was just able to identify the shining knife for the threat it could be.

"Hold her," Brodie ordered and Addison felt her shoulders restrained firmly to the chair.

Cold steal from the sharp blade moved slowly down Addison's face and smeared the blood that had collected around the wound on her brow. The British agent held her breath, ready for Brodie's next move… whatever that would be.

"Tell me," Brodie cooed. "How does it feel to experience fear both of the unknown and of the inevitable?"

"Wouldn't know."

Agnes smiled. "Oh... you will." She handed her knife to one of the guards and ordered the binds around Addison's feet be severed. The order was carried out swiftly and the agent was hauled to her feet.

"Let's go, shall we?" Brodie led the way out of her office and down another corridor.

Though her vision was still fuzzy, Addison was able to make out a lot more around her. She made mental notes of the building and its layout, locations of guard placement and apparent room usage. She would need the information later.

They came to a halt beside a door guarded by one very tall man. He seemed familiar to Addison, yet his features were still unfocussed.

"Shamus," Agnes addressed. "You remember Agent Black."

"Addithun," Shamus mumbled and recognition dawned upon the agent.

She sensed its arrival before it even made contact and braced her stomach muscles as a solid punch hit her square in the abdomen. Addison doubled over, feeling the very breath leave her body. She gasped through her teeth and blew out a calming breath.

"Now, now, Shamus." Agnes patted the burly man's arm. "I promise you can have as much fun as you want with her later. For now let's just stick her in containment shall we?"

Addison righted her position as Shamus unlocked and opened the door. Her eyes searched for Skyler and the gasp of shock told her the blonde doctor was indeed in the room.

"Addison!" Skyler cried and made to move, but stopped as Shamus turned his weapon upon her.

"A gift," Brodie said and pushed Addison with force into the room. The agent stumbled through the doorway and fell to the ground. "Maybe you should take advantage of these last few days you have left... although looking at her... she is in no condition to do anything!"

Finishing her statement, Brodie gave the nod and Shamus slammed the door shut.

Knowing it was now safe, Skyler leapt to her feet and ran to where Addison was climbing to her knees with a bloody grin.

"What did she do to you? **How** did she do this to you?" Skyler assessed Addison's injuries visually. "Oh god!"

"Just untie my hands," Addison said. "And don't sweat it. I am fine. This was the plan."

Skyler pulled at the rope holding the agents wrists together. "It was your plan to get the crap beat out of you?" She held Addison's face and looked at the redness around her unfocussed eyes.

"Yes." Addison flexed her arms, glad to be free from the

restraint. She rubbed the chafing around her wrists. "Let Brodie think she has us beat because soon… the last thing that bitch is ever going to see… is me… right before I send her straight to hell."

Chapter 17

Skyler reached around Addison and drew her up by the shoulders, assisting the battered agent to one of the mattresses on the floor. The Brit dropped heavily and groaned as she landed even though she did her best not to make a sound. Skyler took the opportunity to survey the damage done to the agent.

"Jesus, did they put you in a meat grinder or what?" the American said as she reviewed the various cuts, bruises and wounds.

"No," the agent replied, "It was just Agnes' little welcoming party."

"If that's how she says hello, let's hope we don't have to find out how she says good-bye. Holy shit, what is this?" Skyler found the large bloodstain on Addison's side.

"It's nothing, just a scratch. The bullet grazed me really. The damn thing wouldn't probably even be bleeding now if Agnes hadn't taken great joy in searching me for weapons."

"Did she find any?" the American inquired.

"What I let her find," the agent replied in a cagey tone of voice.

Skyler was already tearing up a threadbare sheet that had been left on the mattress to create makeshift dressings. "Well, I'm going to take a close look at all these wounds. We don't have much, but there is clean running water and some powdered hand soap in the bathroom. I can at least try to stop the bleeding."

"I appreciate it, Skyler. I've been trained to do it myself of course, but something tells me you probably know as much about tending to these things as I do." Addison winked at Skyler to let her know her words were only to be taken as gentle teasing.

The blonde blushed. "Yeah, I guess you know me well enough

by now. I did have a few classes when I thought I might like to become a doctor. A little pre-med looks like it might come in handy right about now."

She opened Addison's shirt and took a look at the damage done by the bullet. "It's only a flesh wound Addison, but I think it needs stitches to hold the entrance and exit wounds closed. There's not a damn thing around here to use to do it though." She rose from the mattress and moved to the sink to dampen the scraps of the fabric she had torn.

Addison appeared thoughtful. She looked Skyler up and down with an appraising eye. "How are you, Skyler? How has Agnes treated you?" The words were unspoken, but Skyler knew what Addison was referring to.

"She didn't touch me, Addison. I'm fine. I guess being your girlfriend had its positive aspects." The scientist returned to the woman on the mattress, settling next to her.

The agent frowned in confusion. "My girlfriend?"

Skyler averted her eyes from Addison's questioning ones and began gently cleaning her facial cuts. "Um, yeah. I sort of realized that Brodie has a thing for you and I thought if she believed I was your girlfriend, she would wait for you to show up before she…before she touched me. I guess she thought it would torture you to see her use me like that."

Addison's jaw clenched briefly before she spoke softly, "That was good thinking. You've got the instinct for survival. I'm glad you told me because now I can make a better show for Agnes while the rest of my plan takes place."

For the first time in many hours, Skyler felt a sense of hope. "What is the plan? Please tell me it has something to do with Agnes Brodie getting a can of whoop ass opened on her!"

Addison chuckled at Skyler's words, and then grimaced as the split lip moved painfully. "I'll tell you what, you will be the first to know about the plan after I think it up."

The words sunk in slowly, but they finally made it into Skyler's mind. "You came here without a plan? You don't know how we're going to get out, do you? Why did you do that?" she asked incredulously.

This time it was Addison who dropped her eyes. She shrugged and said, "It's my job. There was something here I wanted out and nothing was going to stop me. Granted, I could only pre-plan my entrance because I didn't know what I would find once I was inside, but make no mistake, I will get us out of here. After I settle a score

186

with one pain in the arse Irishwoman that is."

Skyler accepted Addison's word. She had no choice but to trust the agent who had tracked her down against what Skyler had assumed to be enormous odds. Something about the agent's mere presence made her think Addison could actually pull it off. She went back to work on the wounds.

"How was I anyway?" the British woman asked.

Skyler thought Addison referred to her physical condition. "Well, except for the bullet wound to your side, the injuries are relatively minor. I thought your ribs might have been broken by the look of the darkening skin there, but I think now that they are probably just bruised. Did you know you actually have a boot tread mark on your skin?"

Addison raised her head. "No, I mean how was I as a lover? Certainly you had to convince Agnes that was the case."

Skyler blushed again. She was beginning to believe Addison was doing it on purpose. "You were okay."

Addison raised an eyebrow. "Just okay? Damn, I must be slipping. I've really only had rave reviews before this." She raised the uninjured side of her mouth in a gentle smile.

Skyler rolled her eyes. Even injured, the woman before her could engage in banter. Skyler could at least play back as that's what Addison seemed to want, rather than serious concern over her well being. She took a fresh cloth and began to gingerly work her way around the slightly oozing bullet wound in Addison's side.

"Oh, you were good, damn good if the way I described it to Brodie was the truth. I was a well-satisfied woman and you were an attentive and possessive lover. It was short, but our affair was very exciting and very hot."

"That's more like it. I was about to think my reputation would suffer!" Addison watched as Skyler frowned at the wound in her side. "It's that bad, is it?"

"Hard to say, but I'd feel much better if I could get it closed properly," Skyler replied.

Addison considered this a moment. "You look good in my jacket," she said as her eyes roamed Skyler's body. "Then again I suppose after what you told Agnes, that you would be used to being inside my clothes." She waited as Skyler laughed lightly at her jest. "I don't suppose she left you un-searched?"

"No, she took the pistol you gave me right away and she had a lot of fun looking for other weapons too." She shuddered as she remembered how revolting she founded Brodie's barely disguised groping. The redhead had not hidden the fact that she knew there would be nothing concealed in Skyler's crotch, yet she took great delight in exploring that area thoroughly. Agnes might have found her ministrations exciting in some way, Skyler found them repugnant.

Addison reached out and placed her hand on Skyler's upper arm. "I see you had the pleasure of Agnes' attentions. I'm sorry that happened to you, Skyler. She will pay for it, I swear that to you." Addison let her eyes show the truth of that statement.

As Skyler looked into those eyes, she noticed for the first time how red-rimmed they were. The whites were irritated and bloodshot. "What happened to your eyes?"

"Smelled like mace at the time, but it might have been a combination of mace and pepper spray. It will be all right, my vision has cleared up almost completely now," the agent said off-handedly.

"Almost! As soon as I get these cuts cleaned up and figure out something to do with those holes in your side, I'm going to help you over to that lab sink and flush your eyes for a while. You never know what long term problems might occur if you don't get all of that stuff out of your eyes now." Addison was amused at Skyler's tone, but didn't show it. She knew this was how the American needed to feel helpful and, in her present state, Addison wasn't going to be protesting too much.

"Yes, Doctor," the agent said with mock meekness.

"Good, I wouldn't want to have to get tough with you," Skyler said with a smile. She felt responsible for every blow that Addison had suffered. If she'd only done as the agent asked back on the Isle of Skye, the Brit wouldn't be in agony now. Skyler felt her own eyes sting, but it was from tears and not the noxious substance that had assaulted Addison.

The black-haired woman moved her hand up from Skyler's arm and reached to touch her face briefly. Skyler felt a shiver pass through her at the very gentle touch, a reaction so unlike the one she had to Brodie's hand. She closed her eyes as Addison's hand left her face and slipped down to the collar of the black jacket.

"Skyler, I need to ask you a question," the agent said in a voice barely above a whisper. Skyler opened her eyes and met the warm brown ones of the woman in front of her. Skyler felt a tug on the collar of the jacket and she was pulled slowly forward.

Skyler went with the urging and leaned toward Addison. As she came nearer she swallowed thickly and replied, "Yes?" Addison pulled the scientist a few more inches closer to her and moved her hand around to the back of Skyler's neck. Skyler's eyes closed again and she tilted her head ever so slightly as her lips parted. At this range she could feel the warmth radiating from Addison's body.

In a flash, Addison's hand left Skyler's neck where it had rested and moved in between them. Held between her thumb and index finger was a gleaming silver needle.

"Can you sew?"

****

Several corridors away, Brodie sat behind her desk in the office. In front of her stood two trembling men. The pair were the lone survivors among the guards at the front gate and they were held at gunpoint by more of Brodie's soldiers.

"I realize you are fairly new to the organization, gentlemen, but incompetence simply cannot be tolerated."

The bolder of the two dared to offer an excuse. "But ma'am, you said we should let her get past us into the compound where you would be waiting."

Brodie slammed a fist down to the desk. "I know what I said! Do you think I'm a fucking idiot? When I showed you her picture, didn't I say she was extremely dangerous?"

The men nodded quietly.

"And yet you let her practically destroy the area inside the gate and cost me the lives of eight very good men. Well, seven very good men and that useless fuck-up that was with you outside."

Brodie extracted the large knife that she had menaced Addison with earlier. "Your guilt is not in question, only your punishment is. What to do, what to do?" Agnes tapped the knife on her chin as she thought. "You know, you're lucky I'm shorthanded right now until the replacements for my dead men arrive. Maybe I'll let you live after all."

The men slumped a little in relief; they knew they had been fortunate.

"No," Agnes reconsidered. "I guess I just need one of you and I don't give a good god damn which one it is." She tossed the knife up, handle first, between the men.

They grappled for it and the chance to live. Finally, the smaller of the two men planted his boot in the crotch of the larger man. As the second man doubled over, he lost his grip on the knife. The smaller man wasted no time in cutting the throat of his vulnerable foe.

"Very nice work," Agnes complimented. "You are forgiven and may return to your duties after you remove this eyesore from my presence. Have it done by the time I get back." She indicated the body

189

on the floor.

"Yes ma'am, thank you, ma'am! I won't fail you again," the victorious guard groveled.

"I know you won't," Brodie said as she rose and walked past him, heading for the door. Moving behind him, she pulled her pistol out and calmly fired a single shot into the base of his brain. He died instantly and crumpled to the ground without a word.

"Clean this shit up," she barked at her men. "I have more important fish to fry."

****

Skyler sat on the mattress, legs crossed as she began poking the black thread through Addison's needle. The agent looked on, fairly amused by the comical expression Skyler held. Deep in concentration, the tip of her tongue poised above her bottom lip, eyes focused upon her task. Getting thread to stitch up Addison's wound hadn't been a problem; Skyler had simply removed some of the stitching from the inner lining of the soldier's jacket.

Sitting to the side, with one hand bracing her weight, Addison looked around the room. It was basic and obviously intended as a work room. The walls were a sterile white and above them, diffused light illuminated the space perfectly. There was a sink in the corner. Its white porcelain and gleaming pipes proved this room had never been used.

Addison closed her eyes. The stinging in them was getting stronger yet she resisted the urge to rub them. As soon as Skyler stitched up her side, she intended on bathing the irritated area.

"Got it," Skyler declared triumphantly as she pulled the thread through the needle. She looked up at Addison. "It's probably going to be best if you take your shirt and top off. The less obstruction I have the better. Plus I'll be able to check the rest of your torso too."

"Okay, Doc, but you may have to give me a hand. I'm not sure it's a good idea to lift my arm so much." Addison shrugged her shoulders out of the black shirt as Skyler assisted her on the opposite side. Addison then un-tucked her dirty, bloodstained tank top and the blonde helped her in slipping it over her head. Once free of the hindrance her clothing provided, the British agent lay down on her uninjured side.

"Is this where you offer me a shot of whiskey or a piece of wood to bite upon?"

Skyler smiled as she shuffled into position. "Sorry... but you

190

were a tough Marine Commando type, this is one of those times when you have to act all butch and impassive. I wish I could help you more, but we don't have anything." Skyler positioned the needle. "Are you ready?"

"Go for it." Addison kept her body relaxed. Eyes upon Skyler, she watched as the blonde attempted to close the first wound. "Have you ever done anything like this before?" she asked, just as the blonde was about to make her first pierce through the skin.

Skyler jumped. Her eyes slid to Addison in a glare of accusation. "Does my jumpiness give you an answer?" She sighed, calming her nervousness. "I know how, but let's just say my practice is a little limited." She turned back to Addison's wound and proceeded to pierce her flesh with the needle. She worked precisely, attempting to make the joins as neat as possible.

With each pass of steel though her flesh, Addison winced. She could feel every action, from the prick of the needlepoint, the slide as it moved through her skin and the tug as the cotton was pulled through and tied. She had to admit... although it wasn't the first time she had been injured in the field, it was the first time she was without even the basics of medical supplies. Addison knew asking Brodie would be pointless. The redhead would take great pleasure in refusing. She planned on killing them anyway; this would do nothing more than provide her with added sport.

While attempting to close the bullet's exit wound, Skyler pushed the needle into Addison's flesh a little too far. The soldier closed her eyes and released a grunt of pain.

"Fucking, bloody, bugger, bollocks, bastard, balls!"

"Oh I'm sorry," Skyler gushed. "With the oozing it's difficult to judge the position of the needle. I keep having to wipe the blood away." Skyler stopped for a moment to give Addison time to calm.

The soldier took a breath, blowing out through pursed lips. "No, don't stop. The sooner this is over the better. I sure would kill for a bottle of J.D. right about now though."

Skyler smiled. "Oh I don't know... going through the list of swear words you know is quite an amusing education." She paused in thought for several seconds. "Well it would be if it wasn't for what I'm doing and why I have to do it."

Opening her eyes, Addison laid her arm out straight and placed her head upon the extended limb. "Sorry. I know it's a bad habit, but some things you just don't grow out of. It's kind of like my favouring towards Jaffa Cakes!" Addison turned her vision back towards Skyler and watched as the doctor leaned forwards and bit the cotton, severing it from the stitching. She felt the warmth of Skyler's breath upon her skin. The pleasant sensation made her smile.

"And your parents didn't wash your mouth out?" Skyler grinned as she checked over the wound. "I only swore once when I was a kid. My dad heard me and said if he ever heard me use language like that again he would wash my mouth out with soap!"

Overlooking Skyler's question, Addison asked, "What did you say?"

The American snorted. "I said, 'ass'! I'd heard my dad's partner say it once when he was talking about some guy they captured and 'sent his ass to jail'!"

"Oh yes, your dad was a police officer!"

"Uh huh." Skyler moved away from Addison's stitches and began inspecting her other wounds. She rolled Addison gently onto her back. "What about your parents, what did they do?"

"Ah... well..." Addison paused, finding herself in a curious predicament. She had always avoided questions about her parents. However... Addison found she didn't want to lie to Skyler, it felt easier to ignore the question or divert the conversation. As she battled between conflicting thoughts her attention was captured when she felt a tug on her black combat trousers. She looked down at Skyler curiously. "I don't think I was injured down there!"

Skyler looked up into the agent's eyes, surprise and embarrassment clouding her expression. She blushed and looked away. "Sorry... I um... I saw this tattoo on your stomach and I guess I just forgot myself as I tried to get a better look at it."

Addison lifted her head and looked down at the line of Chinese characters that went from beneath her belly button and disappeared under her trousers. They ended just above her pubic bone. The small words were written in red and outlined in black.

"What does it say?"

"Do you want to know what it really says or what I tell people it says?" Addison smirked, careful of her cut and bruised lip.

"Both," Skyler said with intrigue. "What do you tell people it says?"

The soldier tried not to smile too wide for fear of breaking the cut that had begun to knit on her lip. She had given every woman she had bedded the same explanation for what the quote said. "This way to heaven," Addison stated simply.

Skyler blinked, then snorted, lowering her head as she chuckled quietly. "You didn't!"

Addison shrugged and nodded.

Shaking her head, Skyler asked, "And what does it really say?"

Sobering quickly, Addison licked her upper lip. What it really said was a far more personal quote and came from Psalm 126:5. "Tears may linger at nightfall, but joy comes in the morning."

The smile on Skyler's lips broadened. "That's beautiful," she said sounding almost surprised, yet her brow crinkled in a frown. "Not what I would have expected though. It's from the Bible, right?"

With a nod, Addison attempted to rise, not wanting to venture further into explanations of the reasons behind such a quote. She rolled onto her side, Skyler helping her. "Yeah well, that's why I stick to the more common explanation!" Addison rose to her feet and Skyler handed over her black shirt. It seemed natural for them to assume the white, bloodstained tank top was no longer an option for wear.

Fastening the buttons, Addison watched Skyler fill the corner sink with water. There was no hot running water so they had to make do with cold.

Skyler dipped her fingers into the water. "Time to soothe your eyes." She scowled at the chilly temperature. "I guess the best thing to do would be to cup handfuls and hold them against your eyes."

"Hmm," Addison said and leaned forwards. She held open her right eye and took out the single brown contact lens. Instantly her vision cleared completely and she blinked a couple of times, looking down at the lens that had obviously been damaged by the assault spray. Throwing the useless eyepiece to the floor, Addison righted her position and looked to Skyler. The blonde had been watching her movements curiously and now looked at her in confusion.

"You wear contacts?" she asked.

"Contact," Addison replied. "Just the one." She stood awkwardly under Skyler's open stare.

The American stepped forward and placed her hands on Addison's shoulders, looking into her eyes. For the first time it became apparent that the dark eye was indeed very dark. Her other eye was a deep blue. "I don't..."

"Just one of those things," Addison stated off-handedly and moved past Skyler to the sink. "An accident caused a paralysed pupil."

"So why the contact?"

Addison dipped her hands into the water. "It's a distinguishing feature, the contact hides that. I could have gone blue as usual, but I think the darker eyes add to my character!" She chuckled throatily. Cupping pockets of water in each hand, Addison placed them over her eyes. She felt an instant relief as the cool water soothed her skin. Skyler remained behind her and the ex-S.A.S. soldier could practically sense the unspoken questions flying around inside her mind.

Cupping more water, Addison splashed it over the rest of her face. The stitched wound on her side felt warm and she resisted the urge to splash the cool water on the throbbing bullet hole. Skyler had done all that could be done and she just had to wait it out. Addison was sure it would heal rapidly. She always had in the past.

Shaking the remaining water from her hands, Addison turned back to Skyler. The blonde handed her a torn piece of the sheet she had used to dress the soldier's wounds and Addison patted her face dry. It felt a little better to wash some of the grime off her flesh. Dropping the sheet upon the side on the sink, Addison looked up at her 'cellmate'. She was surprised to find the blonde still gazing at her.

"What, did I miss a spot?" she joked.

Skyler smiled. "No...it's just going to take me a while to get used to looking at you again."

"Hmm." Addison supplied her limited smile. "That will wear off pretty quickly I am sure," she joked.

For a moment they stood in silence, staring at each other as the reality of their situation began to sink in. They were trapped together in this room for an indefinite amount of time. Addison had been formulating plans and ideas in her head, but it would take her a while longer to learn all she need to about Brodie's facility and Addison hoped she had enough time to accomplish that before Brodie decided she was ready to play.

Walking over to the mattress, Addison sat down and patted the space beside her. She looked up at Skyler in expectation and the blonde got the message, taking a seat next to her.

"So tell me," Addison began. "What have you been able to determine from our hostess since she captured you?"

"Apart from the fact that I don't like her? I really, really don't like her!"

Addison smiled. "Uh huh!"

Sighing, Skyler laid her head back against the wall and thought. "There are two things that come to mind. First, the fact that she called herself by a different name..."

"Was it Sadie Bregon?" Addison interrupted. "Did you meet anybody called Kleein or Dr. Kleein?"

Skyler shook her head against the wall. "I never met a Dr. Kleein, but she did talk to one on the phone and during that conversation she called herself Bregon, yes. Also, I managed to get out of her the reason she has been able to remain one step ahead of you for so long and she called it 'insider trading'."

Addison sighed heavily. "We kind of figured that."

"What?"

"That she has a contact within the organisation, which means we have a double agent working in my branch."

"Special Operations," Skyler said. "She told me you worked for MI-5."

"She seems to know a lot about me."

The blonde nodded. "I was confused though. You called yourself Agent Black yet you are in the Military. What exactly is your job title, if you don't mind me asking?"

"Not at all." Addison bumped her shoulder against Skyler. "That I can answer. Yes, I am an agent working for Special Operations and within that I do have a ranking, but I am also a soldier in the British Military and my ranking as such is Captain."

"Captain Black!" Skyler appeared impressed. "You look too young to be a Captain. Can I ask how old you are?"

Addison grinned. "Older than you," she replied, forcing Skyler to bump a shoulder back against her.

"I figured that!"

"I'm thirty-four," the soldier answered. "Any more questions?"

"I was just asking," Skyler defended. "You seem to know so much about me after all."

"Well believe me, I haven't lived the kind of life that makes for interesting dinner conversation. In fact, it's more likely to put people off their dinner."

The blonde didn't seem convinced. "I doubt it's that bad. What about your childhood? We all have crazy stories about what we got up to when we were younger!"

"What about yours?" Addison diverted.

"Mine!" Skyler shook her head. "Mine is the exception. The craziest thing I did as a kid was doodle in a library book when I was daydreaming."

"So it was you!" Addison took Skyler by the wrist. "For years there has been an outstanding warrant for the person who did that! I can't believe it. I caught the phantom library book doodler!"

Both women laughed, but their amusement was short lived as a loud voice shouted from outside their room. It was followed by several more voices and then the sound of footsteps leading away from the door echoed into the distance. Skyler felt their imprisoning walls begin to close in around her.

"She's going to kill us, isn't she?" Her hopeless tone was clearly evident.

"She wants to... she may think she is going to... but she isn't."

"How can you be so confident, Addison?" Skyler looked at her, pleading with the soldier to give her hope. Fear was beginning to take hold and it was down to Addison to release that. "It's God knows how many people against the two of us and I'm not exactly the soldier type."

Addison placed her arm around Skyler. "Hey, I promise you will get out of here."

"And you too!" Skyler stated adamantly.

"I'll be right there with you, that I guarantee."

Sighing, Skyler slumped into Addison's embrace. She rested her head upon the British woman's shoulder. "I hope so."

Addison let her own head fall back against the wall. She closed her eyes, allowing her body a moment of complete rest. She released the aches and pains of the last few days and felt her muscles ease into submission. With Skyler in her arms, she felt good. *Too good*, her mind cried out in warning, but she chose to ignore it. She knew the rules... No agent was allowed 'to engage in any form of improper conduct with or referring to a sexual nature or form an emotional bond with the mission's focussed protection.' *No matter how good it felt to hold them,* Addison's mind added.

Pushing those thoughts away for the time being, Addison closed her eyes and laid her cheek upon Skyler's head. Both women slipped into a light but much needed rest.

Chapter 18

Skyler woke slowly. She couldn't tell how long she'd been asleep, but the area visible through the skylight was dark. Even with the obstruction of the bars, a multitude of stars showed themselves and for a little while she just looked up at them in silent awe. The stars appeared like benevolent eyes, watching down and over them.

It made Skyler think back to the revelation that Addison had two different colored eyes. Well, an injury that made it appear so anyway. On another person it might have been unattractive, but it only gave the British agent a more intriguing look. The American couldn't stop wondering what it would be like to see those eyes darken with passion, the kind of passion she had led Brodie to believe she had already experienced with Addison.

The scientist's head was still against Addison's shoulder. They had slid down a little in their sleep, but Addison's arm had stayed around her. Skyler felt safe and very warm... too warm. Even accounting for the agent's higher than normal body temperature, Skyler could tell she was running a fever.

As surreptitiously as possible, Skyler brought her hand up to Addison's abdomen. The agent's shirt was open and the flesh exposed. The American made the move as natural as she could in order not to wake the slumbering soldier. When her hand reached its intended target, Skyler knew she was right about the temperature.

"I've got a fever, haven't I?" The agent's voice startled the American and she jumped a little in Addison's arms. The brunette winced as her side was jostled.

"God, I'm sorry," Skyler said. "I didn't know you were awake."

"I've been awake for a little while now. I didn't move because you looked so comfortable. You also looked like you needed the rest." Addison purposely omitted the fact that she was comfortable too and had rested well with the blonde next to her.

"I did," Skyler agreed. "What I need more is some food. It's been a long time since I nibbled on the things you bought me in Scotland and what little Brodie did provide, she caused me to throw back up with her never-ending supply of drugs." With no food between them, Skyler felt she should change the subject and keep their minds off of it. "How are you feeling? Is there much pain?"

"A little," Addison admitted. "It's nothing I can't handle though. The good news is your stitching seems to be holding up. I can't detect any bleeding."

Ever the student, Skyler had to know the truth of Addison's words for herself. She moved her hand across the agent's belly until it reached her side and she felt the dry bandages under her fingertips. A trail of gooseflesh on Addison's skin was left in the wake of her wandering touch.

"You're right, the stitches seem fine. Now if you don't succumb from a fever, we only have Brodie's little plans to deal with. She said she's going to put a bullet in both of our heads after she 'enjoys me' in front of you." Skyler shook her head. "She must not have had enough love as a child."

"There's a lot of that going around," Addison said and nearly bit her lip as she let the information slip.

"So what happened when..." The rest of Skyler's question was cut short as they both heard a key in the door's lock. The door opened and light flooded in from the hallway. Both women squinted as their eyes worked to become accustomed to the brightness. The shapes of Brodie and Shamus were clearly outlined in the backlight. The AK-47 Shamus held was also clearly outlined.

"Oh Shamus, isn't this precious?" Brodie asked sarcastically. "Look at the lovebirds all nestled together. It's so sweet."

"Thweet," Shamus agreed. He gave what could have been a laugh, but sounded more like the low-pitched rumbling of a volcano.

"Let's get something straight here and now," Brodie said, the usual menace returning to her voice. "I don't give a fuck whether you starve or not, but my superior requests I keep you alive and unharmed for a bit longer. Just in case we need to contact Doctor Tidwell for assistance while we are setting up our own version of our work, we're going to keep you alive, Skyler. The reason for you continuing to draw breath is less clear, Addison, but I have my instructions and therefore you eat." She crouched down and slid a paper tray over to the mattress. Sandwiches were piled on the tray along with two paper cups.

"It's simple fare I realize, but you'll have to forgive that. You can get water from the sink. Now, if you don't want to have your cause of death listed as lead poisoning, you'll not move until the door is closed and locked." She stood and moved back through the doorway.

"Agnes, I just hate to dine in the dark. How about a little light in here? Or maybe just a candle to set the mood for my woman and I?" Addison asked as she tightened her hold around Skyler's shoulders and leaned over to place a soft kiss on Skyler's head.

Brodie's features darkened and it was all Skyler could do not to break out into laughter. She held herself in check; she was afraid Brodie would take the food she so recently delivered.

"Most certainly," the Irishwoman said unexpectedly. "I can afford to be generous now. I have a thick steak waiting for me in my quarters and a willing companion waiting for me in my bed."

"A steak and a companion?" Addison asked. "That's two unfortunate cows then!" This time Skyler did let loose a small laugh.

"You have half an hour," Brodie said sourly. She reached over to an unseen panel outside the door and light flooded the room. "Enjoy it." The door slammed shut and the key could be heard turning in the lock. Skyler wasted no time in sitting up and moving toward the sandwiches. Taking one, she passed a second to Addison and they each hungrily took a large bite.

"Holy Christ, it's peanut butter!" Addison said as she forced herself to swallow.

Skyler was having the same reaction to her sandwich. "At least you can identify what's on yours. I've got no idea what the heck this stuff is." Addison took the sandwich from her an inspected the contents.

"Marmite!" she said delightedly. "It's been forever since I had Marmite!"

"Trade?" offered Skyler.

"Deal," Addison replied. They swapped sandwiches and began eating again. After two more bites each they stopped and looked at one another.

"Water!" they said in unison.

"I'll get it," Skyler said as she moved to the sink with the paper cups. Returning, she handed one to Addison and set about finishing her first sandwich. As she did she surveyed Addison's physical damage again. The various cuts and bruises looked slightly improved. She was halted in her inspection as her gaze reached Addison's face and the unique eyes of the agent held her.

"How do I look?" Addison inquired.

Stunning? Beautiful? Delectable? Skyler ran the gamut of words through her mind. "Better," she chose. She passed Addison one of the two remaining sandwiches and started in on the other.

"No television, no music and no books," Addison observed. "What will we do for entertainment?"

Skyler had a comeback on the tip of her tongue, but left it unsaid. "Um, talk?"

Addison did a quick survey of Skyler's body, but agreed. "Talking is good. So, I've met your mum and I know your dad was a police officer. Do you have any other family?" The agent decided that asking the questions was highly preferable to answering them.

"Not really," Skyler began. "It's just us. Listen Addison, before we talk about anything else, I want to apologize to you."

The agent was puzzled. "What for?"

Skyler looked down, unable to meet Addison's eyes. "For what happened on the Isle of Skye. I…I didn't listen to you. I left the room under the stairs and decided to come look for you. That's when I ran into Brodie and made it possible for her to get away. Because of that she is free, we're in here and you've been shot. I'm so sorry."

"That's water under the bridge," Addison said generously. "Let's just try and concentrate on the here and now. She reached out and lifted Skyler's chin with two fingers. "I hadn't had a holiday out of the country in quite a while and I heard Israel was lovely this time of the year so you actually did me a favor."

Skyler gave a small smile. "You're crazy, you know."

The agent shrugged her shoulders. "So I've been told." The two women felt the bond between them forming again. Addison seemed to be about to say something more when the lights went out.

"Fifteen minutes. Agnes couldn't even tell the truth about that," Addison commented.

They sat quietly a few moments as once again their eyes adjusted to the change in light. When Addison could see clearly, she saw Skyler sitting cross-legged at the place on the mattress where she had last seen her. "What's wrong?" the agent asked.

"Nothing," Skyler replied.

"Your mum is safe, Skyler," Addison commented, guessing at the reason for Skyler's change in mood. "My boss, General Blithe, is personally seeing to her safety. When I say personally, I mean exactly that. I think there's a little spark there between them."

"Really? That's nice to hear. I've wanted her to find someone for a long time. Sometimes I felt like she gave up a lot of her own life trying to be both parents to me."

"Do you want to tell me about it?" Addison asked. She felt Skyler wanted to talk, but was reluctant to do so. The American stood then.

"I need to..." she indicated the bathroom. "Do you want to go? I can help you over there if you like."

Addison nodded. "Maybe just some help up to my feet." Skyler moved to Addison's uninjured side and used her body for leverage as the agent pulled herself to her feet.

After the agent visited the bathroom, she waited for Skyler to return. As the scientist emerged she said, "I never realized that going to the bathroom was such a visual experience. Some things just don't need to be done by feel."

"And some things do," Addison quipped. She couldn't see it, but she knew Skyler was blushing. What she could see was Skyler shiver a little.

"Cold?" Addison asked.

"It's gotten a little cool in here now. All my blood must be in my gut digesting Brodie's feast," Skyler said wryly.

"Come over here and help me down. If I'm going to run a fever I might as well share the warmth at least," Addison offered. Skyler assisted the Brit back to the mattress and moved next to, but not quite touching, her. "Skyler, I'm warm, but I'm not radiant. Move closer, I swear you're safe. I'm too injured to try any funny business." Skyler scooted closer and the warmth from Addison's skin enveloped her with the same safe and comfortable feeling she'd had on waking. Almost reflexively, Addison bent her arm around Skyler's shoulders.

"So you were going to tell me about you and your mum," the agent prompted.

Skyler gave Addison a brief synopsis of the day her father had been killed. "It was a long time before I could stand to see a police officer's uniform. It always reminded me of my dad being taken from me. I think when I was really young I wanted to be a cop like my dad, but after he died and I saw how losing him broke my mom's heart, I swore I'd never get involved with anyone in that field. The uncertainty would be too much. I'd never know if the person I loved would be coming back home everyday."

Addison had listened to the tale in silence. Her heart went out to the young woman who had lost a man she so idolized at such an early age. "Skyler, did you ever ask your mother if she regretted marrying your father?" she asked gently.

"No, but I can tell you what her answer would be. She never regretted marrying him. No matter how short their time together, she loved him and cherished every moment."

"There's your answer then Skyler. It's love, don't you see? Love is what makes the difference. Your mother knew everything you just said about the uncertainty of the future of a person in law enforcement, but she took the risk because she was in love. You say you never want to be involved with someone in that profession, but I think love might just change your mind."

"Maybe," Skyler said quietly, her voice thick with tears. "It hurt though, Addison, it hurt so much to lose him. It changed my life forever." She said no more as the tears came then. Skyler wept for her father and for the situation she was in now. Through it all Addison held her and gently stroked her back, whispering soothing words to the smaller woman. Eventually Skyler's tears subsided, her breathing evened out and she fell into an exhausted sleep. Addison stared up through the skylight for a long time before succumbing to the need for sleep herself.

****

When Addison opened her eyes again a new day was well underway. That fact was clearly evident by the bright Israeli sun shining down through the skylight, hot and unrepentant. Its glare stung her eyes and she turned away from the intrusion. Addison had been aware, on waking, that Skyler was no longer beside her. She didn't have to worry about her whereabouts, however, as the closed door to the bathroom gave that away.

Before Addison fell asleep, she had pondered on Skyler and their conversation. The blonde had spoken so freely about her father and her feelings about his death. It was an unknown concept to Addison, talking about her past in such an open manner. Not only had she never thought it the kind of information you would share with another, but also she'd never thought anybody would be interested in hearing it. She felt ashamed and what was more, she didn't want anybody to think she was looking for sympathy. Addison's view though had changed drastically. When it came to Skyler, Addison found she was very willing to listen to her. She wanted to know more about her. That was a startling revelation to somebody who before had only been interested in learning a person's responses in the bedroom. When it came to Skyler, Addison wanted to know everything. *Strange*, she thought.

Feeling a numbness settle into her legs, Addison decided it was time to stretch her limbs. She certainly didn't want to rely on Skyler to help her stand. It was important to Addison that she recover to a point where she would be able to carry out her rapidly building plan to destroy Project Gemini while getting Skyler and herself out alive.

Bringing up both legs, Addison braced herself on one hand. She pushed herself to her feet, surprised at how strong she really did feel. The sleep she'd had over the past hours had helped immensely in aiding her body to heal. If anything, only her side still concerned her. Addison feared she might have an infection.

As she walked a circuit of the room in an effort to stretch her legs, the door to the bathroom opened and Skyler stepped out. She could tell the blonde had used their limited facilities to freshen up a little.

"You're feeling better?" Skyler asked.

Addison nodded. "For the most part I feel a lot better." She pulled her leg back, grabbing hold of her foot and stretching out her thigh. "How are you?" Addison asked. She referred to Skyler's mental as well as her physical state.

Pushing both hands through her hair, Skyler sat down upon the mattress. She looked up to Addison and offered a lopsided, weary smile. "I'm pretty much scared, tired and confused." Skyler watched Addison as the soldier continued to warm up her limbs. "I feel like there are millions of thoughts whirling around in my mind and I can't make sense of any of them. The only thing keeping me grounded is the knowledge that you're here and I know you'll do everything in your power to get us both out of here."

Addison stopped her movements. She bent down in front of Skyler and tucked a lock of blonde hair behind her left ear. "You have my word, Sky." Turning, Addison sat back against the wall beside Skyler. Her side still hurt and she could feel it throbbing with persistence. Addison looked to where Skyler sat beside her. The doctor smiled softly. "What?"

Skyler shrugged. "Nothing, I just like you calling me Sky is all."

The British agent grinned in return. The way Skyler's eyes sparkled when she smiled was enough to warm her heart. Addison looked away feeling suddenly self-conscious. Skyler was an extraordinary woman, she acknowledged. She was so willing to open up and express what was in her heart and mind. Was it really so simple?

Aware that Skyler's focus had moved from herself, Addison looked back to her. The blonde seemed lost in her thoughts. Addison wondered what was going on behind those expressive features. She nudged Skyler with her shoulder, pulling her from contemplation.

"What are you thinking about?"

Stretching out her arms, Skyler turned to face the wall and lay down upon her back. Facing Addison she lifted both knees and placed her feet upon the floor. Skyler folded her arms across her chest and addressed the soldier. "I was thinking this morning and one thing stayed in my mind. I was wondering... I mean... how do you do it? How can you find it so easy to pull that trigger, to deliver that final blow of death?"

Addison looked down at Skyler. She swallowed, suddenly finding difficulty in the subconscious act. The agent was more than surprised by Skyler's question; it scared her. Did people really see her as a cold-hearted killer, able to take a life as easily as she could snap her fingers? Addison had to accept that was probably the assumption many people would initially take.

"Easy?" she asked. "You think it's easy to do it?" Addison looked down at her hands resting in her lap. She pressed her fingertips together. "It's not easy, Sky, but it's my job. I do it because I believe what I am doing is right. You know... the first time I ever came up against Brodie I almost killed her then and there. I stopped myself, believing she would learn from her mistakes and become a better person." Addison shook her head. "Because of my foolishness and idealistic beliefs, many hundreds of people have died. Innocent lives that should never have been in the line of fire but were because I let Brodie live to see another day."

"You can't believe that is your fault, Addison."

"It doesn't matter whether it is or not," Addison insisted. "As far as I am concerned it is all my fault. I work within the law doing a job we all believe is right. All we are trying to do is protect the innocent and stop the villains... whatever it takes. It isn't easy, Skyler, but I am prepared to face the consequences when I stand in front of the big chief."

"General Blithe?" Skyler asked in confusion.

Addison smiled. "No... God." She brought up one leg and balanced her wrist on her kneecap.

Silence fell between them. Skyler slid one arm under her head and stared up at the ceiling. She drifted deep into thought yet Addison could see a question was forming in the blonde doctor's mind. The agent waited, wondering what was going on inside Skyler's head. Addison sighed and let her head fall back against the wall. She closed her eyes and prodded her bottom lip, noting that the swelling had lessened.

"When did... how old were... no, it doesn't matter."

With a frown, Addison opened her eyes and looked down at Skyler. "You know you have to ask me now!"

Skyler shook her head. "No, I really shouldn't ask. It probably isn't an appropriate question."

"Oh no, those are the ones I love the most." Addison smiled. She turned around onto her side, lying in a similar position as Skyler. "What?"

"You don't have to answer."

"Out with it."

"Well... I was thinking about how it must feel to take a life and I wondered how old were you when you first took a life. The first time you killed."

Addison remained silent. She rolled onto her back, looked up at the lighting. "The very first life?" she asked quietly.

Skyler nodded, then not thinking Addison could see she said, "Uh huh."

Lying beside Skyler, Addison's thoughts drifted to that very incident. She remembered the precise moment she felt the splash of blood upon her face. The way her heart had drummed in fear and the cold sinking feeling as the words, "You are a killer" echoed in her mind. She had never spoken of this incident before, but the desire to tell Skyler was as strong as a screaming ball of frustration, coiled and ready to explode. Something inside assured Addison it was okay to speak of this with Skyler. She felt honoured Skyler had trusted her enough to speak of her father and wanted that to be returned.

Continuing to stare up at the lights above them, Addison said, "When I was a kid, summers really were summers. You could play out in the streets day after day through the summer holidays and generally make a nuisance of yourself." Addison smiled to herself, remembering those times. "In 1976 we had this great heat wave in England. We are talking so hot that we would only venture out in the evenings when the temperature began to cool. Well apart from that one day a water pipe burst in the neighbourhood and it was like an invitation to a kid's street party!"

"I remember it was late one summer afternoon. I was in my bedroom feeling too hot to even move, when my dad came into the room." Addison saw Skyler's head turn to look at her. She knew it was the first time she had mentioned her parents and it seemed Skyler realised that fact as well.

"He came in holding a rifle in each hand, telling me how he had won them in a card game. Naturally I thought it was pretty cool. I saw them as new fodder for my games of Cops and Robbers or Cowboys and Indians... except these were no toys. My dad told me we were going out into the woods for some target practice. He said it was time I made him proud by honouring the family name! I knew he had been drinking, but I only thought we were going to shoot at his empty lager cans." Addison felt like laughing at her own stupidity. Even then she knew her father better than that.

"So, armed with a pocket full of shells, he took me out into the large wooded area of trees. It was a place my friends and I would play in, but it was just too hot so nobody was around. Most of them were probably at home, camped out by the refrigerators. Like I said, we only ventured out in the evening when the temperature dropped that year."

Skyler remained silent, listening intently to Addison's words.

"I remember I was standing in the middle of this large wood, loaded shot gun almost two thirds my size firmly within my grip. The sun was still high in the sky, casting shadows and causing shafts of light to shine through the treetops. I could feel sweat trickle down my brow and my tee-shirt clung to my back with the moisture."

Addison folded her arms over her chest. However warm she was painting this picture for Skyler, a cold chill passed through her spine. "I had been told not to talk. My dad said we had to remain quiet, so I did as he said. I knew better than to ignore or question his words! So there we waited in the middle of this small forest that was only there because the council wasn't allowed to cut it down and build more high rises."

"It was a protected area?" Skyler asked.

"It had been there a long time... hundreds of years, I was told." Addison spoke softly, answering Skyler's question though she never made eye contact. "Anyway... we had been there for about half an hour when we heard this rustle. My dad was the first to see it and he pointed it out to me. It was a fox... a female one, he said because of her size. As soon as he aimed that shot gun... I remember begging him not to do it. I loved foxes." Addison smiled. "I was a major Basil Brush fan."

"Who?"

The soldiers smiled. "Basil Brush was a hand puppet on children's television. He was this hilarious little aristocratic fox who wore a Sherlock Holmes type jacket and told really lame jokes. I remember his laugh the most. It had me in stitches all the time." Addison paused and she brought her mind back to the story. "I couldn't believe he was going to shoot that beautiful fox. She had such a deep red coat, a thick bushy tail. So innocently foraging around, looking for food. I pleaded with Dad not to shoot the fox, but he said they were nothing more than a pest and it would be good for me to watch what happened to pests!"

"How on earth would that be good for you?" Skyler exploded. "How old were you?"

"I was eight." Addison returned to her memory. The more she thought about it the more it began to feel like it happened only yesterday. "He fired," she said. "He pulled the trigger and this almighty bang exploded around us. Then I heard a gut-wrenching scream as that fox was hit."

"Jesus!" Skyler moved to reach out and touch Addison, but something made her stop. "He killed it!"

The soldier shook her head. "I thought he had, but I followed him over to the body and he'd caught it in the stomach. She was still alive... whimpering in pain." Addison brushed both hands over her face and sighed heavily. "Blood... it was everywhere."

"My dad just sneered at the sight and told me to leave her, that she would die soon enough. I felt this overwhelming urge to protest, but I feared him too much to dare. Luckily he thought he spotted a rabbit and went off after it, leaving me alone with the fox." Swallowing, Addison finally turned to look at Skyler. She feared the blonde's reaction, but Skyler showed nothing but compassion and understanding.

"I'll never forget her expression, the look of absolute fear... fear of me. Her body trembling and blood soaking into the ground around us... this beautiful animal... she was dying a slow and painful death." Addison bit her bottom lip hard. She felt the recently knitted wound re-open. "I remember I started to cry. I honestly tried to stop myself because if my dad caught me I would be in so much trouble for being weak." The agent looked back to the ceiling. "I couldn't help it though. The fox was whimpering... crying in pain... it was the most awful sound. I fell to my knees trying to calm her. I didn't know what else to do. She was dying, terrified and alone. I tried stroking her, it didn't matter that I was getting blood all over me too. I just wanted to ease her suffering. To try and make her understand that it did hurt to get hit, but the pain never lasted." Addison felt her eyes cloud with tears and tried valiantly to will them away. "But that look in her eyes. I could almost feel her terror, Skyler. Her whimpers of pain... the smell of blood. I kept telling her, 'don't cry, I'll make it better... please don't cry'."

Sniffing, Addison closed her eyes. Her brow dipped into a frown. "She was so beautiful Skyler. I wanted to take her home and nurse her better. I briefly wondered whether I would get away with hiding her under my bed. It was stupid, I know, but really I was just trying to push from my mind the acknowledgement of what I had to do."

"You had to kill her," Skyler said softly and Addison nodded.

"Well anyway," Addison said quickly, trying to move her tale along. "I got to my feet and took that shotgun. I placed the barrel right up to her head. I was crying so much I could hardly see her through my tears. Taking a deep breath I placed my finger on the trigger, whispering 'I'm sorry, I'm sorry'. My whole body shook." Addison felt a single tear stray from her eye and roll down the side of her face. "I looked down at her one last time, seeing that same trembling expression gazing back up at me. She knew what I was going to do and I hated that fact... then I think I counted to three, closed my eyes and fired. My shot rang out through the forest as her blood splattered my face and body. My ears rang with the noise, but I dare not open my eyes, afraid of what I would find. Next thing I knew, however, was my dad standing beside me." Addison turned and looked back at Skyler. The blonde's eyes glittered with emotion. "He patted me roughly on my back making me stumble forwards into the remains of the dead vixen. The sound of his voice was one of fucking pride as he told me I'd done him proud... that I was a killer and had that killer instinct. I didn't want to believe him, you know? But wiping a hand over the moisture on my face and seeing the smears of blood... I thought maybe he was right."

A long silence stretched out between them. Addison began to feel self conscious in her confession, but then Skyler reached out and removed a tear from her cheek.

"He was wrong," she said softly. "Compassion made you do that, Addison, not a desire to kill." Skyler reached out once again to remove another tear that had slipped from Addison's eye, but the agent stopped her. She caught her hand in a swift movement and held the appendage between them.

"Can I ask you something, Sky?"

The blonde nodded silently.

"Do you think I am a cold blooded killer?" Addison felt the doctor's answer would be very important to her. When Skyler looked away, Addison thought she had received it and a sinking feeling plummeted within her stomach... but then Skyler spoke.

"No, I don't. I will admit when I first met you I didn't see a difference between either you or Brodie, but now I see you at opposite ends of the spectrum. Addison... you don't kill because you enjoy it...

you do it because you're prepared to take whatever means necessary to uphold the law and protect the innocent. It takes a lot of strength to do that. Brodie kills because she gets a kick out of it. She enjoys the power."

Addison smiled softly. She felt a rush of... something... towards Skyler, but unsure of how to express herself she simply lifted the hand still within hers and kissed Skyler's knuckles reverently. "Thank you," she whispered.

The moment was broken instantly as Addison heard approaching footsteps from beyond the door. Simultaneously, both women righted their positions and waited for their visitor to enter. The huge metal door unlocked and in walked Shamus, followed by Brodie. The redhead held another tray upon which were two plastic bowls.

"Morning," Brodie greeted insincerely. "I brought you breakfast. You may want to make it last, however, as this is all you get today." Brodie placed down the tray. "I won't apologise for the food. It's porridge and of course being the last to eat you get what no one else wanted. Naturally it's cold... oh and the black bits are just pan scrapings. That's what you get for eating the last dregs." Brodie pushed her hand into a pocket. "If you don't like the taste, try these." She dropped a handful of small paper containers around the tray, one of which fell into the bowl of cold, burnt porridge.

The Irish woman waited, her eyes moved from Addison to Skyler and back to Addison again. When nothing was said, Brodie spun on her heels and left the room. The door locked behind her.

"I think she was expecting you to say something," Skyler said as she shuffled over to the meal Brodie left them.

Addison shrugged. "Just letting her think she has us a touch demoralised."

Skyler dipped her finger with great caution into a bowl and tasted the contents. Her face contorted in disgust. "God, that's vile. At least we have sugar!" Skyler tore open one of the sachets.

"Hold on." Addison picked up another sachet and inspected the paper containers. Its name and contents were written in Hebrew. "Well I got some good and bad news."

"Huh?" Skyler looked down at the packet of white grains. "What is it?"

Shaking the sachet, Addison ripped open one corner. "The bad news is this isn't sugar. The good news on the other hand, is that it's salt!"

Chapter 19

Skyler didn't say anything for a moment. "Okay, I'm stumped. Why are you so excited about the salt? Are you planning on experiencing sodium depletion or is this some mysterious British porridge ritual I haven't heard of?"

"Salt, you dozy bugger!" Addison said playfully. "We can use it to treat my wound infection. I would have thought a well educated woman such as you would have known that."

"Right, salt to treat the infection. Did you learn that technique in spy school?" Skyler asked.

"Well, no, but everybody knows it's a fact. I even saw it in a movie once."

The American nodded. "This movie, did it have John Wayne in it?"

"It might have," Addison admitted sheepishly.

"I thought so. Look, Addison, salt is a great thing. I wish we had some yesterday when I was sewing your wound up. I would have preferred to clean the wound with saline instead of water before I stitched it, but it's a closed wound now. Saline can clean nicely, but it's not a treatment for an infection. I'm sorry, it's just a myth."

"Damn Hollywood!" Addison growled in mock annoyance. "First I find out there really isn't a Wonder Woman and now this!"

"Reality kind of sucks, doesn't it?" Skyler asked, looking around at her place of confinement. Her countenance fell a little.

"Oh, I don't know. This reality isn't too difficult to take." Addison's sweet comment had Skyler feeling better again.

"Oh, hell, I almost forgot! I do have some good news."

"Give it to me, we could use a little about now," Addison instructed.

"Well, I've done a little more rummaging around here and it's not quite as bare as I thought at first."

"Really? Did Brodie leave a traditional English breakfast with all the trimmings lying around by any chance?" the Brit asked.

"I wish! No, but there was something I couldn't figure out and it was bothering me. I thought about it when we were rinsing your eyes yesterday, but forgot about it because other things interested me more then." Skyler indicated Addison's unusual eye color. "In every lab there is a sink or some area that is designated for decontamination in case of a spill or accident. Brodie wouldn't give a damn about it, but the scientists working in an area like this would and I found it!"

"You did? Where?"

"Well the hose was curled up behind the toilet tank where it is connected to the water supply. Add that to the fact that you've got a small drain in one corner of the bathroom and you've got a decontamination room!" Skyler exclaimed.

"That's terribly interesting, Skyler, but I'm not quite able to see why you're so excited."

"Because, Super Stinky Spy, yesterday you were sweaty and dirty and dashing, but you've had overnight to ripen. This morning you just need a shower."

As much as Addison enjoyed the thought of rinsing the residual perspiration and filth from her body, she homed in on the other aspect of Skyler's comment first. "So, you think I'm dashing, eh?"

Skyler rolled her eyes. "Oh God, I forgot that monumental ego of yours." Skyler fluttered her eyelashes coquettishly. "Oh yes, Agent Black, I think you're dashing and brave and dangerously sexy. Does that make you happy?" she asked sarcastically.

Addison puffed up just a bit. "I have heard it before, but it's nice to know I still have it! Now, if you'll excuse me, I am off to the bath. Have this place spotless by the time I return if you please and by the way, I won't be breakfasting." She glanced down in disdain at the bowls Brodie had brought. "I'm afraid I've started on a low crap diet!" With that, she disappeared into the bathroom.

Skyler laughed, but had to agree with the sentiment about the porridge that was now looking more and more like concrete.

Addison's head popped out from the bathroom door. "You know, it's too bad we don't have a bar soap in here instead of the powdered stuff. We could use it to soap the floor by the door and when

Agnes came in here next time, she might just 'slip up' and let us catch her off guard."

Skyler almost laughed. "Nah, that will never work. She's way too clever for that."

Addison looked thoughtful a moment. "You're probably right," she said and ducked back inside.

Skyler saw Addison in her mind's eye, slowly stripping off her garments. A big part of her wanted to go into the bathroom, catch the agent removing her clothing and look at the revealed form. Addison's body was firm and strong and Skyler wanted to know what it would be like to feel that body respond to her with ardor. To see those amazing eyes darken with passion. To…

Skyler's lustful daydream was interrupted by a shriek from the bathroom. The American tossed the images from her mind and raced to Addison's assistance. As she pulled open the bathroom door, Skyler saw that her daydreams were a pale comparison to the actual sight of a very naked British agent.

Addison stood there with the water spraying away from her. She was obviously at ease with her completely exposed body. Skyler ran through her extensive list of adjectives again to describe the solid, beautiful and slightly battle-worn body. She settled on the word "devastating".

"Oh my God, that was bleeding cold! Why couldn't they decontaminate with warm water?" the agent asked as she shivered a little. Noticing Skyler staring at her, she grew concerned. "Are you okay, Skyler? I didn't scare you, did I?"

"No, no," Skyler said hastily as she backed slowly from the bathroom. "Don't worry about it. You're good. You're very good." She blushed as she closed the door. Dropping her forehead to the door, she drew in a shaky breath. She could hear Addison humming in the shower and knew she would need a cold one next.

****

"God-damn it, I'm in charge here and I say how they are treated!" Agnes screamed into the phone. She had been annoyed by the unexpected phone call from her superior. 'Dr. Kleein' had spies everywhere and it seemed had received reports on Brodie's handling of her two prisoners.

The Irishwoman listened to the voice on the other end of the line and then spoke. "Well, maybe if you shared a little of your plan with me I'd understand. Why do I have to keep Addison Black alive?" She sat down behind the desk as she heard what she had previously only guessed at. She let out a whistle between her teeth.

"Okay, I see your plan and I have to admit I like it. The destruction, in any form, of Addison Black is more than welcome."

Instructions were received and acknowledged. "And what about Skyler Tidwell? I should inform you that I think she's the weak link in Addison's armor. They're lovers, I'm sure of it. We can use that to our advantage and to Addison's great dismay." The redhead smiled as her observations were welcomed by her contact.

"Oh, one last thing," Brodie said into the phone. "Our work here is proceeding at a remarkable pace. Our scientists report that we are well ahead of schedule and I believe we will be able to put the plan into action very soon. Completing this project and the downfall of Addison Black, has there ever been a sweeter combination?"

The voice on the phone effectively ended the conversation and the connection was broken. Brodie sat a moment as she formulated her plans. A decision being made, she picked up the phone again and tapped in an extension. "Infirmary? Send Dr. Richardson to see our guests in Lab Three. I want them checked over carefully. Oh, tell him to arrange some food for them as well." There was a brief pause. "Of course with the usual precautions, stupid! If Addison Black so much as gets a toothpick to use against me, I will use your skin to wallpaper my office." She smiled, knowing the threat was not an idle one. "Good, get it done."

Brodie hung up the phone and thought about her two prisoners. *Well, Addison, I guess for you there are a few things worse than death.*

****

General Blithe and Marlene Tidwell returned to his office. Miss Bakersfield was sorting reports and files in the outer office as they entered.

"Oh, General, I've completed arrangements for Professor Tidwell to have accommodations in the most secure wing of our facility and have arranged around the clock protection," Miss Bakersfield informed him.

"Right on top of the situation as always, Antonia, but this time it isn't necessary. Professor Tidwell will be staying at my home. Please arrange for surveillance outside my house, but I will be seeing to her safety personally this time."

Marlene looked surprised, but Antonia merely took the change of plans in stride. "Certainly, General, I will take care of it immediately.

What time would you like your car to arrive, sir?"

"Half an hour should do it. I would like to have Marlene get some rest as soon as possible. She's had quite the time of it recently."

Miss Bakersfield nodded. "I understand, sir. Everything will be ready when you are prepared to leave."

Marlene spoke then. "General, I appreciate your offer, but it isn't necessary for you to go out of your way like this. I don't want to impose on you."

"It's no imposition, it's a pleasure. My guest room hasn't had such a lovely occupant in a long time. We will have a secure line there and I will be kept up to date on the situation with Skyler. Please say you'll accept my hospitality," the General said in his most persuasive manner.

Marlene smiled at the man. "You're very kind and I accept with gratitude." Marlene turned to the assistant. "Thank you also, Miss Bakersfield. I know you arranged for the medical check-up and the change of clothes and so much more."

Antonia blushed a little. "I'm just doing my job, ma'am. If I may say something to you?"

Marlene nodded.

"I know you're worried about your daughter," Antonia said, her voice softened with sympathy. "I daresay I would be also if I were in your position, but if there is one thing I know…no, one thing we **all** know here… is that Addison Black is the very best there is. She can do things that would seem nearly impossible for another agent to accomplish. Around here, that skill is known as 'Black's Magic' so try to keep your hopes up and believe in that."

"Magician or miracle worker, I have no choice but to believe in her," Marlene said. The General took the American's arm and guided her into his private office as the phone rang at Miss Bakersfield's desk.

The phone in the inner office buzzed and the crisply efficient voice of Miss Bakersfield was back. "Line three, General. Secure line, routed through the satellite and the Tel Aviv office. Agent Yamburg of Mossad calling and will speak with only you."

"Very well, Antonia," the general replied. He looked at Marlene and picked up the phone.

****

Opening slowly, Addison peeked around the door from their makeshift bathroom. Locating Skyler she grinned and emerged from the partitioned room, fully dressed. Standing to attention, Addison

215

saluted the doctor.

"Decontamination complete, ma'am. Sweaty odours neutralised." She lifted her arm above her head and sniffed her armpit. Addison frowned. "Almost completely!" Allowing her arm to fall back to her side, the soldier swooned as a feeling of dizziness overtook her senses. She lowered her head, and adjusted her position to lean against the wall. Addison knew the bullet wound on her side had become infected and was beginning to affect her body. She wasn't going to let Skyler know how ill she was beginning to feel. Addison needed to keep her sprits high for the blonde. Although the soldier was formulating a plan, the notion of how well she would feel when that plan was put into action crossed her mind several times.

Looking back to Skyler, Addison smirked as she cleared her senses. "I didn't think I would smell that bad **after** a shower!"

Skyler narrowed her eyes in suspicion, but then she shrugged. "Imagine what it was like for me **before** you were decontaminated!"

"So that was why you came into the room while I was naked. You wanted to see whether I really was getting clean. And here was I thinking you were out to catch an eyeful!"

Her jaw dropping, Skyler shook her head. "I heard a shriek. Not that I would have expected such a sound to come from a tough ex-marine!" She placed her hands on her hips.

"Pure exaggeration." Addison shook her head. "Besides, that sure as hell wasn't concern I saw in your eyes!" Her own eyes scanned the ceiling in thought. "In fact, if I remember correctly, your eyes did linger in certain areas lower than my face for a couple of moments."

"You are incorrigible!"

"I try my best." Addison's 'Cheshire cat' grin gave away her playful banter.

Skyler scowled and folded her arms. A witty comeback died on her lips as the door to their room was unlocked. She moved a step backwards and Addison turned, standing two steps in front of Skyler in a protective stance. She waited silently, their humour of moments before all but gone as the door opened.

Three people stood in the doorway: Brodie, Shamus and a second man neither woman was previously familiar with. By the way he was dressed, Addison was correct in her assumption that he was a medical doctor. The traditional gentleman's suit and semi-circular glasses, from which he peered over, reminded Addison of her own childhood G.P.

"Two visits in as many hours," the agent remarked. "Why, aren't we the lucky ones? I never realised how much you cared, Agnes."

Brodie ignored Addison's comment and stepped into the room.

"If she so much as takes one step towards me, Shamus, shoot out her knee cap. In fact... shoot both of them... We might as well take advantage of Doctor Richardson's presence while here, eh?"

Aiming his AK-47 lower, Shamus grinned and Skyler gasped. Addison held up her hands in a gesture of compliance. Now was not the time to anger Brodie and if Addison was to admit it to herself, she really had no inclination to at that point. Her plan wasn't ready, plus the infection caused by the gunshot wound was taking its toll on her body. The soldier just hoped her body would be able to fight it quickly.

"Now, if I were you, Agent Black, I would behave. I don't bring my own personal doctor to treat all my... guests."

Though remaining outwardly cool, Addison was surprised by that comment. A number of questions rose in her mind. Not only why would Brodie enlist the aid of a doctor to check up on her, but also, what was the point considering her intention was to kill them both. What was Brodie's plan now? What had changed and what was possibly more important... if the 'Dr Kleein' was Brodie's superior, what did he want? Externally, however, Addison's questions were a little different.

"Personal Doctor!" She turned to Dr. Richardson. "So when did you lose your licence to practice?"

"Shamus!" Brodie called. "Warm up that trigger finger."

Addison carried on regardless. "Unless... hold it... I refuse to be treated by a Veterinarian. That may be adequate for Agnes, but I..."

"One more word, Black, and it's bye-bye kneecap!"

The soldier remained silent. She folded her arms across her chest and looked back at the doctor, her brow arched in expectation.

Realising that was his cue, Dr. Richardson adjusted the spectacles on the tip of his nose and ran a hand through his receding, grey hair and stepped forward.

"I was told you were shot in the side. How severe was that? I would like to take a look at it, please."

Addison considered Dr. Richardson's request for just a moment. "Sure," she said and began unfastening the buttons on her shirt. "We... well Skyler, did the best she could in stitching it together. There does seem to be an infection forming though." Releasing her last button, Addison slipped the shirt from her shoulders. "I do have a fever rising in me." The soldier looked over to see Brodie smiling haughtily.

Dr. Richardson removed the covering Skyler had placed over Addison's wound. The area was extremely red and angry. He placed his fingers around her wound and felt the heat. Remarking only in a string of hums, Dr. Richardson placed his hand upon Addison's

217

forehead. He took a thermometer out of his breast pocket, and shook it.
Addison opened her mouth and the doctor placed it under her tongue.
He then commenced a general inspection of the soldier's remaining
injuries.

Sighing, Addison gazed around the room. Her eyes landed on
Brodie and she noticed the redhead's stare... or more importantly, what
that stare was fixed upon. Feeling somewhat amused, Addison looked
down at her breasts and back to Brodie. She waited for the
Irishwoman's sight to move higher and when it did, Addison winked,
wiggled her eyebrows and smiled broadly around the thermometer
sticking out of her mouth.

Brodie flushed, appearing momentarily flustered. She turned
away, gained her composure and looked back at Addison. "So," she
asked. "What is the verdict, Doctor?"

Dr. Richardson took the thermometer from Addison's mouth.
"She has a fever, just like I suspected when you informed me of her
injuries." He reached into his pocket and pulled out a small, brown
plastic container. "These are a strong antibiotic; I would like you to
take one three times a day, preferably with food." He handed the bottle
to Addison who inspected its label cautiously.

"With all intents of offence, Agnes, why should I trust you with
this? You want me dead, not that you will ever succeed, but you really
think I will willingly take pills offered to me by an employee of yours?
The guy's probably as bent as you are." Addison began to put her shirt
back on, but Brodie snatched it from her hands.

"I would adore more than anything to see you endure a long and
painful death, Black. I have many pleasant daydreams of ways in
which I could take your life. The only reason you are alive right now is
because my superior has better plans for you. Don't push me, Black.
However much I am looking forward to your demise, your head on a
platter would be just as satisfying and worth it." Brodie looked to
Skyler who had been standing silently behind Addison. "She on the
other hand is expendable. When I am sure I will have no more need of
her, you may watch her die!"

Addison looked to Skyler. She saw the alarm and fear in her
eyes and tried to offer her a silent message of reassurance. She
wouldn't rile Brodie just yet. She decided to continue with her
compliance.

"So has your **doctor** finished yet? I do so despise this tedious
talk."

Brodie smiled with an air of self-righteousness. She looked back
to Dr. Richardson. "Will she live?" she asked, inclining her head

towards Addison.

Dr. Richardson swallowed. He seemed uncomfortable by the threatening speech being tossed back and forth. Adjusting his spectacles once again and peering over the golden frames he looked Addison up and down. "Yes, but I was curious as to the gloves you are wearing, Agent Black. It seems you're using them as a protective covering. I can see several cuts upon your fingers."

"Oh that's okay, Doc." Addison slipped off the finger-less, leather gloves and showed her palms to the Doctor. "They are healing fine."

"Hmm." Doctor Richardson took the soldiers hands to closer inspect her palms. "Yes they are healing nicely. Clean cuts," he remarked. "Are you up to date with your tetanus injection?"

"Yep."

"Were these cuts the result of glass shards?"

"Sure were."

"Well they don't seem to show any signs of infection." He dropped her hands and as Addison replaced her gloves Dr. Richardson looked towards Skyler. "And what about you, Miss?"

"Skyler," the blonde supplied, speaking for the first time.

"Her well-being is of no concern, Doctor."

"But..."

"Excuse me?" Brodie asked. "Are you questioning me, Dr. Richardson?"

The greying man shook his head. "Of course not, ma'am, but I am a doctor. It is my natural inclination to..."

"Your natural inclination is to follow my orders. There are plenty of other doctors I can put on my payroll. Do you understand me?"

"Yes, Miss Brodie."

Addison cast her gaze around the occupants of the room. "Well this is nice. I almost feel like one of the family. All we need now is for one of us to throw the first punch!"

"Shut the fuck up, Black," Brodie snapped. "Were finished in here. Let's go... I have many more important things to be doing." Walking towards the door, Brodie stopped when Addison called her. "What is it, Black?"

"My shirt," the agent replied.

Looking down to the black garment in her hand, Brodie shook her head. "No... I'll keep it. A little memento to tide me over until I really do have your head on a platter."

"It gets cold in here at night," Skyler said.

"This isn't the Hilton, Miss Tidwell. Why would cold desert nights be of any interest to me?" Delivering one final, malicious smile, Brodie closed and locked the door.

Addison turned to Skyler in silence. She smiled. "Believe it or not I actually knew somebody worse than her!"

Releasing an anguished sigh, Skyler slumped against the wall. She pursed her lips, holding back a trembling lip. "I've never had anybody want to kill me before, Addison. It scares me. What if she..."

"She won't."

"But you can't..."

"Yes... I can."

Skyler gazed at Addison. However much she wanted to believe her, fear overrode her instincts. Not only did Brodie intend to kill her, but also she was looking forward to it and taunted that fact in front of them both. That certainty didn't fill the American with ease.

Skyler was pulled from her thoughts by a warm palm cupping the side of her face. Addison gazed deep into her eyes. Her other hand brushed stray locks from her brow. The agent licked her lips as she wondered how to ease Skyler's fears. She could see Skyler was waiting for her to do or say something, but not knowing how best to convey her assurance, Addison pulled Skyler into a hug. She closed her eyes as she felt Skyler's arms wrap around her back. Warm hands seeped soothing warmth into her flesh and it was only then that the soldier realised she was still topless. She took a deep breath before speaking.

"There probably isn't anything I can do or say that will stop these fears from surfacing... but every time they do... just remember that I swear with everything I am I will get you out of here alive." Addison paused as she considered her plan. "No matter what I do or say when Brodie is around... it is important that you remember that, Sky." The agent felt Skyler nod against her. Pulling back, Addison looked at her. "You okay?"

"I will be," Skyler said. "As soon as we get out of this place."

Addison forced a pout, dropping her bottom lip. "What, you are not happy with my company?" She smiled playfully. "Anything I can do to..." Addison wiggled her eyebrows, "lighten your mood?"

Skyler looked down at Addison's unclothed torso. "Well... this is quite an experience."

Casting her eyes in Skyler's direction, Addison tried to hold back her smile. She pursed her lips together, but the sides of her mouth still managed to quirk into a tiny grin. She looked back at Skyler. "That doesn't sound like a complaint!" Addison's smile turned into one of

220

bemusement as Skyler's eyes remained upon her chest. Placing two fingers under the blonde's chin she said, "I've never had to tell a woman that my eyes are a little higher than that!"

Skyler blushed but laughed. "Well, it is the most decent view in the place!"

"What?" Addison asked. "Did you find my third nipple?"

"Where?" Skyler looked back to Addison's chest and searched the area in question. Several bruises and old scars marred her flesh. "I don't..." Skyler frowned. "You just tricked me. Admit it... you actually like me... um..."

Addison chuckled and ran a hand through Skyler's hair. "Checking me out?" She shook her head in amusement. "Are you feeling okay?"

"Better."

Both women took a step away from each other and Addison looked around the room for her discarded white tank top. Apart from the bloodstained tear and dust covering it, it was still moderately wearable. Addison slipped it over her head and tucked it into her trousers.

"What do you think?" The agent gave a mini twirl. "Bruce Willis, Die Hard, or what?"

"Very macho!" Skyler responded. Shaking her head she sat down upon the mattress and bolstered her back against the wall.

Addison sat down beside her as a feeling of comfort eased over them. Skyler sighed and closed her eyes. "You know... we are very close to Egypt now. Do you think we could go for a visit when we get out of here?"

"You and me?"

Skyler shrugged. "I could be your official tour guide."

"As tempting as that sounds... especially being able to fulfil a childhood dream, I doubt General Blithe would be happy if you and I scampered off to the land of the Pharaoh's when I am supposed to bring you home safe and sound."

Opening her eyes, Skyler peered over at Addison. "Some other time?"

Addison arched her eyebrows. "Seriously?"

"Why not?"

The soldier nodded with a genuine smile. "I might take you up on that!" Addison crossed her legs and leaned back against the wall. She looked up through the skylight to the clear blue sky. The black outline of a soaring bird glided overhead. Addison watched it disappear out of view and then looked away. Sliding her tongue over her front teeth, she began to wonder what the situation was like outside of Brodie's compound. She wondered what Alon had told General Blithe and more importantly, what his reaction had been. After his explosion over Skyler's second abduction, the soldier hoped he would remain confident in her judgement.

"Can I ask you something?" Skyler inquired out of the blue.

"Sure." Addison turned to face the Doctor.

"Earlier, when Brodie was here, you mentioned something about it being like a family experience and you were waiting for somebody to throw the first punch." Skyler's head fell to the side as she studied Addison closely. "What did you mean by that? I pretty much understand that you were afraid of your dad when you were younger, but..." The blonde paused as she wondered how to phrase her words. "Did he raise a hand to you on a regular basis?"

The room fell silent. Addison looked down to the mattress they were seated on. She traced her fingers around the ugly floral design.

"I suppose you could say that."

"And what about your mom, what did she do or say about it?"

"Join in if she felt so inclined." Addison chuckled, but she wasn't joking.

"Are you saying...?"

"Look..." The agent interrupted. "It is no big deal. It was a long time ago; those things don't upset me anymore." Addison looked back at Skyler. "Really. As they say, 'it's water under the bridge'. Besides, I wasn't an epitome of the model daughter myself."

Silence stretched out between the women again. Skyler twisted her position to face Addison. "Was it your mom or dad?"

"What?"

Skyler pointed to Addison's injured eye. "Which one of them did it?"

Addison couldn't help but smile. "Did anybody ever tell you you're quite an astute woman?"

"Sometimes." The blonde seemed nervous as she asked, "So, what happened? If you don't mind talking about it."

The truth was that Addison had always avoided talking about it. For a long time, the memory of how it had happened had been more painful than anything she had experienced since. As a child, spiteful acts of cruelty are often a lot harder to understand. Though it was a sore point in Addison's life, she didn't harbour any doubts about telling Skyler.

"I don't mind," the soldier said softly. "There really isn't much to say. I was six years old. It was Christmas Eve. Being a typical kid I was excited. I couldn't wait until morning and so a little after midnight I went out to see whether Santa Claus had been."

Skyler frowned, completely unsure at that point of where Addison was heading. "Uh huh?"

"Anyway... My bedroom was opposite the living room so I snuck out of my door and crossed the hallway. There was a street lamp directly outside our front room window so it was always brightly lit in there whether it was day or night. The living room was small and symmetrically square. My dad had painted the walls a ghastly mauve colour. It was faded with age and stained with years of cigarette smoke. There was never really much in the room furniture-wise, two sofas, a glass coffee table, television and fake Umbrella plant in the corner. At Christmas my dad would put our imitation tree in the other corner of the room. So basically it was opposite the door and I could see it from my bedroom. Glass ornaments and stringy tinsel on the tree glittered in the lamplight. I remember walking into the living room and looking under the artificial branches. There was a small pile of gifts there and two of them were for me." Addison rolled her eyes. "I was so excited. I couldn't resist peeking... you know... give it a little shake and feel around the edges."

"I did the same," Skyler admitted. "Most children do I expect."

Smiling ironically, Addison sighed. "Yeah... but unluckily for me, I got caught. Both my mum and dad came into the room. My mum went crazy. She started yelling at me, going on about being a sneak and untrustworthy. She said she was going to show me exactly what happens to people who are caught peeking."

Skyler's expression paled. "What did she do?"

"Well..." Addison pictured the event in her mind as clear as it was yesterday. "Mum told my dad to lift me up. She came over to me with a darning needle and told me that people who were caught peeking had their eyes gouged out with hot needles."

"She didn't!"

"She didn't mean to," Addison said. "I know she didn't mean to really, but the combination of her yelling, my struggling to get away from my father's grasp... Well let's just say I was stabbed in the eye. My mum's face was the picture of shock. I think she had just wanted to scare me, but it went too far. I was taken to the hospital and they made up some bullshit story about me falling into a Christmas decoration. Anyway..." Addison pointed to her darkened eye. "The damage was a paralysed pupil."

"My god," Skyler muttered. "That's just... how did... why... I can't..."

223

"It's no big deal."

Skyler was incredulous. "No big deal?"

"My parents were kids when they had me. I was the only reason they got accommodation, through a government housing project. I grew up in a dodgy estate. Don't get me wrong; I'm not making excuses for them... not at all. They were two very selfish individuals who spent all their money on cigarettes and alcohol. Neither of them worked; they lived on handouts from the government. They weren't bothered about what I did, so by the time I was thirteen I was well into my life of crime." Addison looked away from Skyler for a brief moment. When she looked back she smiled sheepishly. "At one time I was quite the 'bad egg'."

"How bad?"

Addison pondered her answer. "Well... I started off with petty theft... shops, things like that. Moved on to stealing from cars and then I was stealing cars and using them to ram raid shops. I sold what I stole and made more money than I ever would have being on the dole or in some minimal wage job." Addison would have had the decency to appear regretful for her actions, but the comical expression of surprise upon Skyler's face amused her.

"But you're... how... you were never caught?"

Shaking her head the soldier brought one leg up and placed her chin upon her knee. She began to open the antibiotics Dr. Richardson had given her. "I was never caught. I loved the thrill of the chase, but I always escaped capture. It was a talent." Addison popped the tablet into her mouth and swallowed it whole.

"Well if you don't mind me asking..." Skyler readjusted her own position and sat back against the wall. "What changed? How did you turn from rebelling against the law to actually being part of it?"

"Well that is a long story but I'll tell you if you're interested?"

The blonde doctor nodded. "I'm interested."

"Okay." Addison's mind drifted as she remembered the night in question.

****

It was Halloween night, a celebration that brought children out onto the streets and teenagers to party in outrageous costumes. For Addison and her friends it was a prime opportunity to case vacant households, find an abundance of cars and basically make money. Armed with nothing more than a list of items she had been asked to obtain, Addison took to the streets. Night had already fallen, turning out to be a beautifully clear yet cold evening. Stars twinkled in the sky above and a chilling wind blustered through the streets. Lightened by rows of orange street lamps, small groups of children dashed about from house to house dressed in homemade costumes.

Dressed in her trademark black jeans, jacket, gloves and baseball cap, Addison and two friends began stalking the streets. Being of the fairly average stature of five foot six Addison had often been mistaken for a teenager herself. Her slight build gave her the agility of movement and that in turn gave her great body strength. To many acquaintances, Addison was known as 'The Magician' due to her ability to get in and out of awkward spaces, enter places unseen and continually escape capture from the police. Still, on this typical night Addison was unsuspecting of the events that would change her forever.

With two friends, Will and Robbie, by her side, Addison walked the outskirts of Saffron City. They were heading into the city centre and to do this they had to pass by a small estate of bungalows, single story dwellings for the elderly. Neither Will nor Robbie was taking much notice of their surroundings, but Addison was. Something in the corner of her eye caught her attention. A dark figure moving around the side of one of the bungalows sparked her interest. Curious as to what it was, Addison informed her two friends that she would catch up with them later and they shrugged an offhanded acknowledgement. Rolling her eyes, Addison turned in the direction of the bungalows.

Walking through the centre of the road to avoid the direct beam of street lamps she approached the small dwelling. Addison turned her black baseball cap backwards and then pushed gloved hands into her pockets. The air began to turn even colder and her breath billowed past her lips in thick vapours. Her footsteps were the only sound that echoed down the lonely road. It was a cul-de-sac, meaning there was no traffic using the road at that time of the evening. Approaching the bungalow, Addison stepped up on the curb and onto a grassy verge. The uncut blades of grass whispered silently over her boots as she quietly walked around to the back of the small home. Walking down a narrow side entry, darkness surrounded her; Addison brushed her gloved hand along the wall as she neared the back door. She found the glass panel smashed and the door open. A dull light reached out through the blackness of the house and a harsh voice alerted Addison to an unwanted presence.

Never having entered such a building before, Addison relied on basic sense alone to guide her into the dull living space. She walked into the kitchen, the scent of cooked food and hum of a fridge freezer being an easy give away to her destination. Concentrating on the shaft of light, Addison crept silently into a small living room and over to a white door standing ajar. It was the bedroom and through a gap between the door and its frame Addison was able to see into the lamp lit room and the frightening scene ahead of her. A youth of no more than twenty years and dressed in colours similar to her own stood over a cowering elderly woman who sat helplessly in her bed. He held her short white hair in one hand while holding a wooden handled kitchen knife to her throat with the other. The knife's silver blade shone in the lamplight causing a flicker of reflection to glint over Addison's face, yet she remained unseen.

Completely unexpected, Addison was overwhelmed by conflicting emotions. Anger, regret, an overwhelming feeling of disgust although not towards the young man holding the knife to the woman's throat, but towards herself. Looking into the woman's eyes and seeing the fear and helplessness within gave her an insight into what those who she had stolen from must have felt. It didn't matter that she had never harmed a living being; the fact remained that the feeling of violation would still have been there. The expression on the elderly lady's face immediately forged an unforgettable imprint into her mind and she felt sick to her stomach.

Addison's self-berating was brought to a halt when she was jostled back to reality by a harsh voice.

"Tell me where your cash is or I swear I will stick this in your neck."

Feeling anger, towards herself as much as the youth, Addison charged into the bedroom, surprising the unsuspecting teen as she shoved his body against the wall. Rapidly she drove her knee into his stomach, forcing him to double over in pain. He howled as the wind was driven from his body. Addison then held onto the back of his head by his hair and thrust her knee again only this time into the youth's face. A loud crunch rose from the impact as his nose crushed against his face and he fell unconscious to the floor. Blood poured freely onto the frightened woman's carpet. Addison found herself apologising repeatedly; not for the mess she had created, but for every act she had ever committed. The image of horror and violation brought home how she must have made her own victims feel. Guilt landed squarely upon her shoulders. Realising she needed to take action, Addison called the appropriate emergency services and waited with the woman, whom she learned was called Betty, for them to arrive. When the first sound of sirens filtered to her ears Addison quietly slipped away never to be seen again.

Addison ran the entire way home, her vision blurred by tears.

The disgust she felt towards herself caused her heart to ache for all those whom she had hurt. Years of stealing, of becoming everything that she hated about the neighbourhood in which she lived flooded her mind. By the time she returned home, Addison fell against the wall of her block of flats and cried. She felt as worthless as both her mother and father stated she was. It took a long time for her tears to cease and it was only when her father appeared outside and kicked her thigh roughly that she managed to be torn from her self-loathing.

Scratching a stubble covered chin, the scrawny man looked down upon his daughter. Overgrown brown hair fell into his glazed eyes and the scent of cigarette smoke clung to his clothes. "We have been waiting for you to get back to go shop for us," Martin Black said. "Get me forty fags and a bottle of gin or vodka, whatever is the cheapest."

Addison nodded silently as she rose to her feet and headed back into the darkness towards the all-night store.

"And bring me back all my change," he shouted before disappearing into the housing block.

The day after, news stories covered the local papers and television stations about an unknown hero who had rescued a woman from being burgled, and possibly more, in her own home. Pledges for this unknown woman to come forward ensued as high gratitude was promised. Addison barely acknowledged it, knowing she deserved no such accolade. She shut herself away from the rest of the world around her as she contemplated her life and her worth in this world. After much consideration Addison came to one decision. As repayment she would serve her country and its people by joining a branch of its armed forces.

On her twenty first birthday, as Addison's father handed her a half drunk bottle of Jack Daniels, she made her announcement that she intended to join the Royal Marines. It was initially met with little interest, but for the first time in her life, Addison felt she was about to do something worthwhile. Little did she know it was a decision that would change her life in the most unexpected of ways.

****

"And that was that," Addison said. "My family and friends saw my joining the Marines as selling out. I was disowned after that."

"Have you seen or spoken to any of them since?"

Addison shook her head. "Nope. I could find out whether they are still alive. Sometimes I feel the urge to do it… but I don't. I can't really see the point."

"Maybe for your own peace of mind?"

"Maybe."

Skyler thought over the soldier's words. "I'm sorry, Addison."

"Sorry? I'm not. Look, this is the way I see it. I don't regret one moment of my life or what happened. Doing that would only leave me wallowing in self-pity and self-disgust. Everything that happened led me to where I am today. We choose what we want out of life, Sky. I'm doing my best to make my life worth living and if everything led to this moment, right here, stuck in this room with you... well then it isn't so bad."

Skyler smiled and looked away coyly.

"Besides, I find the way you talk in your sleep quite amusing."

"What?" Skyler's head snapped back up. "I don't talk in my sleep!"

"Oh yes you do and I must say, I never knew you were into that type of thing!"

"What type of thing?" Now Skyler was confused.

"You know," Addison leaned closer and lowered her voice. "The old whips and chains." She tried not to laugh, but she could already see Skyler knew she was jesting.

"I'm not into that, you..." The blonde leaned forwards and tickled Addison's uninjured side.

"Hey, injured soldier here!"

"Take that back," Skyler said. "Take back what you said or I'll... I'll... I'll tell everybody what a big softie you really are!"

Addison laughed. "Nobody would believe you."

"Yeah? Well I'll tell them how you slept with your arm around me. You hugged me and comforted me when I was upset and how wonderfully sensitive you are! That ought to blow the 'big bad' reputation!"

"Oh okay," Addison conceded. "You are not into 'S and M' and you don't talk in your sleep."

"Thank you." Skyler smiled.

"You're welcome." Addison was silent for several seconds. "But you do snore!"

"Right, that's it." Skyler pounced on the snickering soldier. "Your ass is mine!"

Chapter 20

General Mark Blithe studied the files on the desk before him. His brow furrowed in concentration as he tried to put together the pieces of the puzzle that would lead him to the traitor. Unfortunately, he didn't have many pieces with which to work.

Across the room, on the plush leather couch, Marlene sat and read a large, leather-bound journal with her Project Gemini notes. MI-5 agents, to allow her to put her considerable intellect to work instead of worry, had retrieved it from her apartment.

It had been five days since Addison had allowed herself to be captured in Israel, only one day less than Skyler had been gone, and the silence from the missing women was wearing on them all. Mark glanced over to Marlene who chose that moment to look up from her reading. Their eyes met in mutual compassion then returned to their respective activities.

Mark Blithe was a traditional British gentleman. Although he felt a powerful attraction to the American woman in his office, he would never act on it while Marlene was in distress.

When Addison brings Skyler back, perhaps then I will speak to her about pursuing a more personal relationship, he thought. He let a fantasy of what that relationship might entail pass through his mind. Mark didn't realize a smile had formed on his face until Marlene spoke.

"Penny for your thoughts, Mark," she said. The general uncharacteristically blushed and was momentarily flustered at having been caught woolgathering. He stammered out a reply.

"I suppose I was just thinking that if this were a different time and different circumstances, maybe we…" He was unable to finish the sentence.

Marlene looked at him sympathetically. "I know what you mean. I think if it hadn't been for you, I might not have survived the last few days. You've been a tower of strength for me, never letting me despair or give up hope. I've felt so comfortable with you and so appreciative of all the kindness you've shown me." Mark raised his hand to deny any special treatment, but Marlene stopped him.

"No, don't. You'll never be able to convince me that the way you've treated me is just routine or some international protocol. Face it, you're a good man, Mark Blithe, and I was hoping that once this whole thing is behind us, maybe you'd like to see me in a setting where we wouldn't need armed guards nearby." She smiled at him in an encouraging way.

"I'd like that very much," he said simply.

"Good then. Well, I better get back to work." Marlene indicated the journal in her lap.

"Of course, of course," Mark said quickly and attempted to mask his pleasure as the American returned to her notes. The pair worked in companionable silence for a while until Marlene released a sharp cry.

"Damn it! I can't believe I made such a stupid mistake!" She looked over to the general who rose from his desk in concern. "Oh Mark, I can only blame it on my exhaustion and worry about Skyler!"

General Blithe moved to sit beside her and placed an arm around the shoulders of the obviously distraught woman. "What is it, Marlene? What's the matter?"

She closed her eyes briefly as she composed her reply. Re-opening her eyes, she drew in a deep breath. "When I said it would take three weeks or so for someone to duplicate our work, I was calculating that at the same rate of speed we were going, but Mark, that was an error. As we progressed with the harmful side of the project, we worked on the remedy if you will, at the same time. If an enemy has no interest in working on stopping the bio-terror aspects of the bacilli and only wanted to produce the harmful agents, it wouldn't take nearly that much time." The anguish in her voice matched the look on her face.

Reality dawned on Mark Blithe. "How much time would they need for the synthesis of just the destructive bacilli?" he asked.

Marlene's face became grim. "A week, maybe less."

Mark nodded, but said nothing. *Whatever you're going to do Addison, do it soon.*

****

"You're looking very well, Antonia. It's been a long time," Quinton said as he perched on her desk in General Blithe's outer office.

"Too long, Agent Zimmerman. You really need to get down to London more often. We've missed you since your posting to Scotland."

"Well, I had a few days holiday coming and I thought I would come back down here to see all my old friends, including you," the blonde agent replied. "We had some good times in the old days before you were wounded, didn't we? You cut a wide swath in the service as I recall."

Miss Bakersfield blushed. "Well, that was a long time ago. Things change and now I'm happy right here. I don't see as much action now, of any kind, but it feels like I'm in the center of things here."

Quinton nodded and flashed a grin. "You can't get more in the center of things than working for General Blithe I suppose, and that's really why I'm here."

"What do you mean?" Antonia asked as she leaned back in her chair, revealing a shapely pair of legs.

"To tell you the truth, I've been concerned about a mutual acquaintance of ours."

"Addison Black?" she inquired.

"Of course," he responded. "There are a lot of rumors about her. MI-5 isn't that big an operation that we don't hear things, even up north. I heard she was off to the Middle East and still on the mission that brought her to Scotland."

"Quinton, you know I can't discuss another agent's activities," Antonia said, glancing at the door to the general's office.

"Oh, come on, Antonia, for old time's sake. I'm worried about our girl."

"Maybe you should be. I heard there were a few problems up on the Isle of Skye," she said pointedly.

Quinton shook his head sadly. "I received a report about the problems with the weapon I issued to her. I've got no idea what went wrong there, the equipment checked out fine when I had it. Just one of those damned unlucky things," Zimmerman observed. "That's why I came here now. I desperately want to keep tabs on her and make sure she comes through this assignment in one piece." His boyish grin was made even more earnest now.

Antonia vacillated a moment, then in a lowered voice she said, "Israel."

Quinton's eyes opened wide. "It's true then. Has there been any communication from her?"

Antonia bit her lip. "Just a signal from the bio-chip, but we know a few things more than that. We've had a report from someone on the scene."

"What kind of report? Who?" he asked with barely disguised interest.

"All I know is a Mossad agent notified General Blithe about Addison's whereabouts four days ago. You know about Skyler Tidwell?" He nodded. "Well, she's been taken inside the compound where they think Miss Tidwell is being held."

"Taken, eh?" Quinton said, rubbing his chin. "That's very unusual for Addison; she's not an easy woman to defeat. I wonder what her game is?"

"She's the best, Quinton, we all know that, but what can she possibly do? She's just one woman. She may be good, but the word was that she is unarmed and probably injured. What can she do if she's in that type of situation? I'm very frightened for her!" Miss Bakersfield's voice broke and she appeared to have difficulty maintaining her composure.

Agent Zimmerman appeared thoughtful and placed a solicitous hand on her shoulder. "Addison is very resourceful. Don't count her out. Even I could think of a few things I might do in her place."

"You could?" A note of hope returned to Miss Bakersfield's voice. "What would you do? What will she do?" she asked anxiously.

Quinton held out his hand. "Come on, I'll buy you lunch and we'll talk more about this."

Antonia regarded the hand. "All right, you're on." She took her purse from the bottom drawer in her desk and the pair left together.

****

Addison stretched her muscles and felt satisfaction that, for almost the first time, it seemed she had no pain with full movement. The bullet wound in her side, the gashes on her hands and the various abrasions and lacerations were all healing well. As she prepared for a run through of a few basic calisthenics, she glanced over at Skyler. It appeared Skyler was also feeling the effects of the confinement as she was working on a series of movements.

"What are you doing there?" Addison asked.

"Yoga, nothing really advanced," the blonde replied. It's just a few simple poses I learned as a Physical Education elective course."

232

The agent laughed. "Right, a few simple positions. You look like a bloody pretzel!"

The American laughed and shifted into a fluid series of sun salutes. "Are you calling me twisted?"

"If the shoe fits, wear it," Addison bantered back. "I'll take a few rounds of kickboxing over that stuff anytime." With perfect precision she executed several lightening quick jabs into the air in front of her, followed by a roundhouse kick.

"No doubt about it, you're getting better really quickly." Skyler felt the truth of the words, as Addison had needed her assistance less and less each day. Not noticing the scientist's dismay, Addison continued her vigorous workout. Skyler made slow sweeping movements that left her facing the door of their room. That reminded her of a question she had wanted to ask the agent for some time.

"Addison, I think I've gotten to know you pretty well over the last few days, but something has been bugging me and well, I'm just going to ask you straight out." The agent raised her eyebrows in question.

"What happened to Shamus' thumb?"

Addison regarded her seriously for such a long time that Skyler was convinced she had offended the woman. Just at that moment though, the agent moved to the sink and splashed cold water onto her face.

Turning to the blonde, Addison asked, "What brought this on?" Before the American could respond, Addison raised her hand. "No, wait, let me hazard a guess. Brodie told you something?"

Skyler shrugged. "Well, yeah. She said you took it as a trophy."

"She would!" Addison scoffed. "As you've probably noted, Shamus isn't the sharpest knife in the drawer. He's useful to Brodie's operation the way that 'muscle' is to all illicit organizations."

The blonde nodded as she glanced at the door. "I can see that."

"I think I could forgive the simpleton for that, but it's his annoying personal habits that caused the loss of that thumb."

Skyler leaned against the wall opposite from the sink and waited for the story.

"Shamus wasn't always Brodie's hired help. Before she scraped him off the bottom of the barrel he was a security guard at a very exclusive girl's school. MI-5 had been tracking a particularly nasty international child pornography ring and had discovered, via a very secret computer program, that much of the source material was arising from that school. Because of the international aspects to the case, I was dispatched to end that problem. I went in undercover as a gymnastics

233

teacher and it wasn't difficult to find the source of all the problems."

The agent used the hem of her shirt to mop her brow and face before she continued. "Shamus was using his pass keys to get into the girl's dormitory rooms, showers and any other place he could think of to install cameras that would catch the girls in a state of undress. I disabled one of his cameras in the girl's showers and then scheduled an extra gymnastics practice for that same day. I knew he would rise to my bait and I wasn't disappointed."

Skyler felt her flesh begin to crawl at the thought of the hulking Shamus spying on the young girls and selling their pictures for profit. "What happened?" she asked.

Addison shrugged. "I found his shower camera in a ventilation register and loosened it enough to block the view of the camera. I knew when the culprit showed up to repair the apparatus that I would have him. Shamus was just pulling the register back into place from the boiler room next door when I gave it a kick from the other side. It crushed his thumb and lacerated the artery in it. The doctors had to amputate, as it wasn't salvageable. The only sore point in the whole thing for me was that it wasn't the bastard's todger that needed amputating!"

Skyler was curious about one point. "Why isn't he in jail if you caught him red-handed? No pun intended, of course."

The agent smiled a little at that. "That's where I left him, but the posh school decided they didn't want the bad publicity and agreed not to press charges against him if he purged the Internet of the material and agreed never to speak of it to anybody. Through some bollocking red tape procedures the case against him fell and he was freed. I never did find out who put him up to that job, he certainly couldn't have carried it off alone."

Addison returned to her physical activities, now moving into a series of chops and kicks. Her body responded efficiently as she practiced her martial arts manoeuvres. "Shamus is a pervert and not the main problem, but I know who is and soon I'll be able to do what's needed doing for some time. I'm going to see Agnes Brodie dead." A flurry of kicks, punches and chops followed that statement and when she was finished, Addison stood panting with a grim look on her face.

"God, this thing with Brodie is really personal, isn't it? This goes way beyond her kidnapping me and my mother, doesn't it?" Addison said nothing, but dropped to the mattress that Skyler had moved to while watching Addison move like an apocalyptic dervish.

"You might as well tell me, you know," the American prompted. "I'll just keep bugging you until you talk." Addison had learned firsthand how persistent Skyler could be in prying secrets from the normally taciturn agent, although if the agent were to admit it, she felt a sense of relief having someone to share things with.

"Fine, before you give me a headache by whining about it, I'll tell you." Addison looked away from the blonde as she spoke. "My designation in Special Operations is SO2. I was one of the first agents recruited, but there was one before me. James Easton was a mate of mine. We ran together in the Royal Marines and the Special Air Service as well. He was like a brother to me, concerned and protective even though I could probably kick his arse half the time." She gave a wry smile and continued. "When he was recruited to Special Ops, he recommended me. General Blithe was interested in recruiting me, but Jimmy confirmed what the general thought."

"About three years ago, Jimmy was sent on a mission to Marrakech. There was a rumor of Turkish opium being funnelled through there and the profits being used to finance terrorist groups. This was the first time the name 'Agnes Brodie' had popped up on the Special Ops radar. It should have been a routine infiltrate and sabotage mission, but something went very wrong. We had no word from Jimmy for over two weeks and then his body was discovered in the desert. He'd been tortured in unimaginable ways and shot in the back of the head execution-style. It wasn't until sometime later we found out Brodie did it. By then she and I had tangled and I had let her off easy. I should have killed her the first time we met," Addison bitterly spat out.

Skyler had listened to the gruesome tale in silence, but could keep quiet no longer.

"Addison, that's horrible, but I'm thinking in your trade it would be one of the hazards. I'm sure Jimmy understood the risks and..."

"No!" Addison interrupted. "You don't understand. Just before that mission I came down with a case of chickenpox. Just imagine, a big, bad agent of Her Majesty's government being felled by a childhood illness. Don't you see? The assignment to Marrakech was supposed to be mine. Jimmy went in my place!"

Skyler realized the horrible guilt and anger Addison had been forced to deal with for years and her heart went out to her. She looked into the agent's eyes, now misted with unshed tears.

"You weren't responsible for that, do you hear me? That wasn't your fault. Don't you realize the entire world isn't on your shoulders? You can't save everybody." She pulled the agent to her in a comforting hug. Addison initially resisted the intimacy, but then gave into it and allowed herself to be held.

Not looking into Skyler's eyes, the Brit was able to say, "Jimmy even visited me in hospital before he left. He laughed at my spots and brought me the ugliest puppy from his dog's litter as a get well present. He was the best friend you could ask for and all I could do for him was stand by his wife and daughter as they buried him." She squeezed her eyes shut tightly and used every bit of her considerable will to rein in her emotions. The agent pulled back from Skyler's embrace.

"What Agnes did to Jimmy is not what signed her death warrant though."

Her statement confused the American. "What was then?"

Addison looked directly at Skyler. "She took you." The dark haired woman brought her hand up to Skyler's cheek.

Any reply Skyler might have made to that statement was curtailed by the sound of the door being pulled open from the outside. Shamus' bulk filled the doorway and his tiny eyes darted back and forth looking for any perceived signs of danger as he leveled his AK-47 at the two women on the mattress. A moment passed before he stepped aside and allowed Brodie to enter the room.

"I hate to break up this little party, but I thought I'd personally bring you your lunch today. The soup is cream of asparagus, Addison. I hear asparagus is supposed to be an aphrodisiac," she said as she leered at the agent.

Addison rolled her eyes. "You know, seeing you bring me lunch is enough to put me off forever!"

"From eating?" Skyler asked, unknowingly playing the straight man.

"From women!" Addison replied. Skyler chuckled as Brodie fumed.

"I should thrash you for that, but it would be a pity to have to waste my valuable time on it…for now," the Irishwoman menaced.

The agent just laughed. "Just like you thrashed me in Scotland, right? Don't try to impress me, Agnes; I go for the brainy types like Skyler here." She turned to the American. "Agnes fell out of her pram and onto her head as a mere child. I think that's what has led to her lower than average intelligence and subsequent life of crime." She regarded Brodie again. "Isn't that how you started? Were you a not so bright child smuggling sweets in her nappy?"

Skyler knew she shouldn't irritate Brodie, but she couldn't help but laugh at Addison's needling of the redhead.

Brodie's jaw worked and her complexion darkened. "Fuck you, Addison! Your little blonde bitch isn't the only smart one here, not by a long shot. You think the doctor and her mother are so smart? I've done something neither one could do. I've completed Project Gemini."

Addison and Skyler weren't laughing now as they gave their complete attention to what Brodie was saying.

"I drove them around the clock and the people in the lab completed the job I gave them. Late last night they synthesized the bacillus. I actually held a sample in my own hands this morning." The American and Brit remained silent, as they understood the gravity of the situation.

"No comeback for that little bit of news, Addison? I'm so shocked!" Brodie laughed as she swept out of the room. Shamus glared at them before slamming the door shut.

Skyler looked to the agent. "My God, Addison. What are we going to do now? Project Gemini in Brodie's hands? This has catastrophe written all over it."

Addison glared at the closed door. "It's much earlier than I anticipated, but I have no choice." She turned to look at Skyler. "I'll have to put my plan into action now."

Chapter 21

Beginning a thoughtful pacing around the room, Addison clenched her fists. This had happened quicker than she had anticipated. The soldier had never once underestimated Brodie, or her team, but she had expected her to make a move against Skyler beforehand. Addison acknowledged she couldn't predict Brodie's next move. What she could do, however, was slightly manipulate it. Why should she wait for Brodie to come to them? Taking her off guard before she was ready and prepared to carry out whatever diabolical acts she had devised against Skyler was a more productive course of action. Although the Irish woman never realized it, Addison had been in control of the situation right from the start.

Coming to a halt as she reached a wall, Addison placed her hand upon the cool concrete surface. She took a deep breath and turned to Skyler. The American doctor had been watching her cautiously, not wanting to interrupt Addison's deliberation.

"I hope you are ready for this, Sky, because I'm about to create one hell of a war zone."

Skyler swallowed visibly. "What are you going to do?" She watched curiously as Addison loosened the laces on one of her boots. She had a feeling whatever Addison's plan was, she was to play a focal part in it. When Skyler didn't receive an answer she said, "Addison, please, what are you going to do? I'm not sure I am going to be of any use in a war zone. Apart from the fact that this isn't the most exciting news I've heard!"

Abandoning her boot, Addison looked back to Skyler. She pondered her words carefully, not wanting to alarm Skyler, but to make her understand what she had planned and how the young doctor would fit into it.

"Listen, Sky, we both know what Brodie intends to do, right?"

The blonde paled and nodded. Brodie's intentions had been in the forefront of her mind since she arrived in Israel. "She plans on killing me, slowly and painfully while you watch, in order to make you suffer."

"And I would," Addison admitted. "But I'm about to push her into acting."

"What?" asked Skyler, feeling suddenly very alarmed.

"The tables are about to turn," Addison stated and approached the door. She held her ear to the doorframe and listened carefully. She could hear a pace of heavyset footsteps walking by the door and knew it was Shamus. Addison walked away and stood in front of Skyler. She placed both hands on the American's shoulders. "You trust me, right?"

"I trust you, Addison."

"Good, because we're about to piss Brodie off."

"We're about to... WHAT? Why? I don't understand."

Addison stared deep into Skyler's eyes. "Look, whatever Brodie is going to do, she is planning it right now. That's what her self-righteous bragging was all about. She wanted to scare us. Now, I for one am not going to sit around here and wait for her to make a move. She was never in control of this situation, Skyler, I was... right from the start." The soldier stopped speaking, her head turning to the door at the sound of looming footsteps. They passed swiftly and Addison sighed, looking back at Skyler. "First of all we are going to cause a little bit of a ruckus. Then when Brodie is summoned to sort out what's going on, we will royally piss her off. This should hopefully be enough to jolt her into action. She decides to carry out her twisted little games and I have her."

"How?"

"Well..." Addison paused. "That part is subject to change...or in other words... I am keeping my options open. It depends on how the situation evolves. I do have an advantage over her she is not aware of. But for the present time, the only fact I can be sure on is that all hell is about to break loose. Are you ready for this, Sky?"

Skyler took a deep breath. "Do I really have a choice? As much as I'm not looking forward to it, if this is our only method of escape then I am willing to take it. The sooner the better and I am sure you know what you are doing... right?"

"Absolutely," replied Addison. "But you must do exactly as I say... got it?"

"Yes."

Taking a step away from Skyler, Addison looked at the door then back at the American. "I don't want you FUCKING UP AGAIN!"

Skyler jumped at Addison's suddenly raised voice. "What...?"

Addison looked to Skyler earnestly. "OF ALL THE DUMB, STUPID THINGS A PERSON COULD DO!"

"Addison I..."

The soldier grinned. "Are you meaning to tell me that the reason we are here is because you DIDN'T DO AS I SAID?"

Understanding settled in Skyler's mind. She paused warily before saying, "It wasn't my fault."

With a nod and smile, Addison replied. "WASN'T YOUR FAULT? WE WOULDN'T BE IN THIS MESS IF IT WASN'T FOR YOU!"

"I'M SORRY."

"SORRY? SORRY IS NO FUCKING GOOD NOW." Addison began pacing the room once again. She walked past Skyler whispering, "Oscar winning performance... you watch this!" Still grinning Addison continued. "GOD DAMN STUPID SON OF A ... BY ALL RIGHTS I SHOULD HAVE LEFT YOU HERE. YOU ARE THE DAMN GENIUS! GET YOUR OWN WAY OUT OF THIS PLACE!"

Both women moved a step closer to the door. "What kind of WOMAN, let alone a highly trained government agent, would LEAVE A PROTECTEE ALONE ANYWAY?"

Addison nodded, suitably impressed. "DON'T YOU DARE BLAME THIS ON ME! I CAME HERE TO RESCUE YOU FOR PETE'S SAKE!"

Laughing out aloud, Skyler raised her voice even higher as she said, "AND A DAMN FINE JOB YOU DID OF IT! TELL ME, AGENT BLACK, ARE YOU USUALLY IN CHARGE OF MAKING SURE NOBODY STEALS PAPERCLIPS BACK AT HQ?"

It was at this point that Shamus decided to see what all the commotion was about. Unlocking and opening the steel door, his bulky mass filled the frame. Eyebrows drawn together in consternation he looked between the two feuding women. Addison carried on regardless of her audience.

"IT WAS I WHO SAVED YOUR ARSE THE LAST TIME!"

"I WAS PROBABLY SAFER THERE THAN WHERE WE ARE NOW!"

"YEAH, WELL I SHOULD HAVE LEFT YOU THERE! HIGH I.Q. MY ARSE; A TYPICAL BLONDE AIR HEAD MORE LIKE!"

"Hey!" Shamus shouted in his thick, gruff voice.

Addison knew it was coming, but the impact still slightly stung as Skyler slapped her across the face.

"HOW DARE YOU!" the American yelled.

Bewildered and unsure of how to handle the escalating situation, Shamus re-closed and locked the door in a hurry.

"DO THAT AGAIN AND..." Addison listened and heard Shamus trundle off down the corridor. "I'll damn well..." The soldier sniggered. "Wow!"

Skyler winced. "I'm sorry. I didn't mean to hit you. It seemed appropriate at the time, but..."

"No, it's okay," Addison interrupted. "You did good." She jogged over to the door and listened. So far there was no sound of the oncoming presence of Agnes Brodie. "Phase one complete," she said optimistically. "Only phase two and three to go."

"What's two and three?"

"Piss off Brodie and get the hell out of here. Knowing Alon he will have a few tricks up his sleeve for when the party starts."

"Hmm..." Skyler bit her bottom lip. "And how are you planning on goading Brodie?"

Placing one hand upon the door, Addison closed her eyes and placed her ear upon the steel barrier. She was listening for oncoming footsteps. "Well..." Still not hearing anything Addison approached Skyler and backed her up against the wall. "I do have one idea."

Noting Addison's close proximity Skyler asked, "What's that?"

"Well... do you trust me?"

"I thought we already established that."

"I know but this is important." Pushing one hand up Skyler's arm, Addison cupped her cheek. She stepped closer still until their bodies were touching.

Was this a good idea? Addison didn't pause to consider. In her job it was vital she worked on an instinct bourn from many years of training and experience in the field. It just so happened that Addison's idea of the best way to goad Brodie was for them to be caught in a heated clinch. She didn't, at least to herself, deny the fact that kissing Skyler was a highly desirable thought. Addison knew her actions would be considered a breech of S.O. guidelines but something deeper told her this was right; in more ways than one.

The soldier swallowed. "Tell me to stop and I will."

"I..." Skyler's heartbeat increased as Addison's lips came within mere millimetres of her own. She could feel the agent's warm breath upon her skin and the sensation caused her body to respond with a pleasant quiver. She closed her eyes and closed the distance between them.

Though her senses were still in-tuned to the arrival of Brodie, Addison felt a stirring within the deep recesses of her emotions. Closing her eyes she ran her fingers through Skyler's hair and held her in place. If she weren't able to keep such a tight rein on her reactions, due to Brodie's impending presence, Addison would have relinquished her control completely. The lush sensation of soft lips against her own aroused her senses as she parted her lips and met Skyler's tongue with her own. Addison felt Skyler's groan rumble through her chest. Her breathing increased and Skyler's breasts rose and fell against her own.

As Skyler's hands began a trail up Addison's back the agent heard the definite sound of Agnes Brodie. Hearing Brodie's voice outside the door, Addison knew she had to make this look good. Fortunately that wasn't going to be difficult. In any other situation the agent would have been alarmed by the intense feelings running through her, for the moment, however, she had a dangerous terrorist to deal with.

Hearing the steel door unlock, Addison made a swift decision. Still within the depth of a breathtaking kiss, the agent ran one hand across Skyler's ribs to her left breast. She took Skyler's nipple between her thumb and index finger and stimulated her with a firm but pleasurable pressure.

"Oh!" Skyler released Addison's lips long enough to groan out her pleasure. She thrust herself into Addison as the soldier reclaimed her lips in a deeper kiss and pulled one of Skyler's legs around her hips. Addison heard the door open and felt Brodie's presence enter the room.

Taking Skyler's thigh, Addison held her tight against the wall and thrust back into Skyler. She deeply regretted the fact they were not alone. It felt good, Addison acknowledged, and if she would get a chance to make love... Addison paused, surprised by her thoughts. *Make love,* she asked herself, momentarily losing control of the situation. It was, unfortunately, enough time for Brodie to make her move.

Addison was jolted back to reality by the intense agony of the butt of a gun ramming into her injured side. Reeling in pain Addison was knocked to the ground.

"Fuck," she seethed, rolling onto her back. Looking up she found a feral grinning Shamus staring down at her from the barrel of his gun. To her left stood Brodie. The redhead held Skyler against the wall with one hand, the other holding a revolver pressed against her temple.

"Sorry to break up your good time." Brodie's face was anything but apologetic. "Seems things have got a bit lax around here these past few days."

Addison's eyes switched from Brodie to Shamus and back to Brodie.

"If I remember... you are still my prisoners... and this one..." Brodie pressed her revolver harder against Skyler's head making her wince in pain. "Is no longer of any use to me."

Addison took a deep breath. She placed a hand over her side feeling the warm stickiness she expected to find. Her wound had re-opened and was bleeding once again. Shamus' attack had torn the stitches from her skin. "Screw you, Agnes."

Brodie cackled. "Oh no, that's what I intend on doing." She looked at Skyler and practically snarled. "What about you? Up for some fun? You might as well take advantage; it will be your last time."

Panting, Skyler ground her teeth together. She placed her faith upon Addison as she said, "You heard her, Brodie, screw you," and spat in the terrorists face.

Brodie trembled as an uncontrollable rage ignited and surged through her veins. Backhanding Skyler, she grabbed her by her collar and flung her across the room. Skyler hit the wall and fell to the ground.

"No!" Addison yelled. Her attempt to move was hindered as Shamus pushed her back to the ground with his weapon.

"No more games," Brodie said, wiping her cheek. She left the room for several seconds and returned with a length of rope. Handing the thick twine to Shamus she strode over to Skyler and pointed her revolver down at the blonde's dazed form. "Tie Black up, Shamus. If she makes one move the bitch gets it here and now."

Addison remained calm, keeping her mind in control of the situation. As Shamus stepped towards her she placed her arms behind her back and waited. When her hands were securely bound, Shamus pulled her to her feet.

"You too," Brodie said nudging Skyler with her foot. "Get up."

Skyler did as ordered, still dazed from her assault. When both women were standing, Brodie led them out of their room of confinement and along the narrow corridor. Addison walked slowly beside Skyler, Shamus and Brodie behind them. They were led down the passageway Addison recalled being brought through when she left Brodie's office. Before they reached that room, however, they were veered off to the right to a single door that stood at the end of another long, tiled corridor. Two armed guards stood either side of the entrance. They opened the door for the group to enter and as Addison and Skyler stepped into the room the sight before them sent a bolt of shock through Addison's system.

"What the hell is this?" Addison turned to Brodie who stood behind her hostages with an expression of uncontained excitement.

"You don't like it?"

Addison turned to Skyler, seeing the undisguised fear in her eyes. She tried to assure her with a look that she still had control of the situation. Stepping further into the room, Brodie turned to face her hostages. She kept her weapon trained upon the women.

"The Dark Ages, Middle Ages, Medieval times... nobody did it better than they did. Torture nowadays is so... it's so clinical... so unfeeling. It lacks the personal touch. Know what I mean?" Brodie carried on regardless of her question. "I like to get in there and get my hands dirty, so to speak." She smiled. "What is the point in doing something if you aren't going to have fun?"

The agent's wrists burned as she tested the strength of the rope binding her hands together. Shamus had done a sturdy job but Addison had yet to reveal her trump card. "You are one sick bitch, Agnes."

"Why thank you." Brodie smiled sweetly. It was a smile that never reached her eyes. "Shut the door, Shamus."

Shamus kicked it shut with the heel of his foot.

"Now these are the rules. My boy Shamus has Addison. I have Skyler. If either of you two makes one stupid move the other will... reap... the consequences. A bullet here or there... a cut or two." Brodie glared at Addison. "It all depends on how much you want your little girlfriend to suffer."

"You do realise I am going to make **you** suffer for all of this, Agnes. Hell is going to be a cosy eternity in comparison to..."

"Shut it, Black," Brodie spat. With her gun aimed directly upon Skyler, Brodie stepped backwards. She stood by the apparatus that had shocked Addison when they entered the room.

Brodie's contraption resembled something she might have stolen from a medieval museum. A wooden platform standing waist high, its shape was that of the human form, but with both arms and legs stretched out wide. Lengths of rope were attached to the ends of each platform limb and a table of assorted instruments stood by the wall. Addison could make out several of the objects from her position. One that alarmed her the most was a particularly shoddy looking, rusty knife.

"Well... I don't know about you, but I'm anxious to get started." Brodie swept her free arm towards the table of torture. "Miss Tidwell, if you please."

"Addison?" Skyler whispered in shear desperation.

The soldier ignored her. "I'm going to kill you, Agnes."

Brodie simply scowled and redirected her revolver. "Come here now, Miss Tidwell... or I shoot her," she pointed to Addison, "Where she stands."

Skyler's instincts told her to run, scream and cry; yet fear iced her limbs. She trembled in apprehension.

Lowering her head, Addison whispered, "Just do as she says. Trust me."

Skyler's breath laboured, but with a trembling lip she stepped towards Brodie. She felt a chill slither across her flesh as her heart rate increased further.

The Irish woman nodded in satisfaction. "Good. No need to get undressed. I can take care of that," Brodie addressed Addison. "Black, get into the corner of the room and kneel. I want you as far away as possible, but with a clear view of my entertainment. Shamus..." she turned to the bulky man. "Keep your weapon upon her. If she makes one swift movement... you know what to do."

Internally pleased with Brodie's plan, Addison strode over to the corner and stood with her back to the joins. She dropped to her knees and searched for her loosened boot blindly.

"I'm telling you, Shamus. I haven't had this much fun since that Special Operations Agent I played with in Marrakech."

Addison paused and delivered a steely look towards Brodie. Though the Irish woman might not have realized she was being manipulated, Addison did and as such she kept her reactions in check.

Narrowing her eyes, Brodie used her revolver to prod Skyler. She dug the barrel into her chest. "Climb aboard."

Skyler gingerly placed her hand upon the table and looked over at Addison. The soldier sat, hands bound behind her back, in a semi-uncomfortable looking position. She appeared to be on her knees yet one foot was twisted to the side. Brodie broke a silence that had enveloped the room as she pulled back the hammer on her revolver. Addison nodded to Skyler, indicating she do as Brodie demanded. So with hesitation and much awkwardness Skyler climbed upon the high cross-shaped platform. Heart pounding, she spread her limbs out across the surfaces. Skyler wanted to close her eyes and shut out everything around her, but fear of what would come next kept her senses alert and attuned to her surroundings. She watched as Brodie pushed the revolver into the waist of her trousers and began securing the ropes around her feet.

"It's a pity you won't be here to see my newest toy... a rack. It hasn't arrived yet... unfortunately." Brodie secured Skyler's first hand. "Imagine being strapped to a table like this, but with a difference... it moves and stretches at the turn of a handle." She secured Skyler's second hand. "Could you imagine? Your bones being pulled out of their joints and your flesh hanging on and on until it reaches the limit of its elasticity. Then it begins to rip and tear. I wonder how that would feel. I imagine like a blunt knife pushing and cutting into your skin." Brodie picked up the knife upon her table of implements and turned it to Skyler's line of sight. "Maybe we'll find out."

Skyler whimpered and turned away, a tear running down the side of her face.

"That's enough, Agnes."

Brodie looked over to Addison. "Excuse me? You are addressing me? I hardly think you are in any position to be dishing out orders. Besides, from now on, for every word that passes from your lips, Madam Tidwell here gets twice as much pain." Brodie addressed Shamus. "One move and you can shoot her. Make it a good one, Shamus, in the leg or shoulder. I want her to fully experience the pain."

"Pain," Shamus mumbled and unconsciously looked down to his missing thumb.

"Okay." Brodie peered down at her table of implements. "What first I wonder."

To keep calm was Addison's primary concern. Limiting her movements as much as possible the soldier attempted to remove the knife from her boot. Due to her uncomfortable position, movement was difficult and Addison knew there was only one way she would be able to achieve her goal. It was going to hurt, but it was the only way.

Relaxing her body, Addison focussed on her left shoulder. An injury received many years ago while serving in the marines had made this possible. Concentrating on her shoulder, Addison held her breath as she jolted the bone out of joint. The agent took a sharp, shallow breath, but otherwise remained outwardly calm. With her left arm now released Addison was able to reach further around her body to her boot. She felt the dense rubber grip of the knife's handle and started to slide it from her boot.

Looking back at Brodie, the agent watched her pick up a gleaming silver instrument. It was a surgical scalpel. Addison sped up the retrieval of her knife.

"Don't," Skyler begged. "Please don't."

"I haven't even started yet!"

247

"Skyler," Addison called in a calm voice.

Brodie swung around to the agent. "That's one, Black. Want to inflict any more pain on her?"

Addison remained quiet. Anger seethed through her veins.

With a nod of satisfaction, Brodie looked back at Skyler. "Relax. Simple precision garment removal, that's all." She placed the sharp blade at the neckline of Skyler's top and began an agonisingly slow slice through the material. "I don't know about you, Skyler, but something about this is getting me hot already."

Opening her eyes, Skyler found the courage to snarl, "Go to hell, Brodie."

"Oops," the redhead exclaimed as the scalpel sliced momentarily into Skyler's flesh causing the young doctor to jump. "Better be careful what you say in the future, hmm?" Brodie's eyes glared into Skyler's for brief seconds. She then turned back to slicing through her top.

Her breathing increased. Addison felt a spark of accomplishment as she pulled the knife from her boot. Twisting it around, she placed the handle between her boots and started slicing through the rope's fibres. She acted swiftly, but with caution, careful not to cut into her wrists. One accidental slip in that area would have dire consequences. The agent didn't particularly want to have to deal with a ruptured artery at that moment in time.

Whatever room Brodie had taken them to, it was hot. The sun shone down through a small skylight similar to the one in their room of imprisonment and a direct beam seeped through Addison's skin. She could feel droplets of sweat trickle down her back and forehead. The soldier worked rigidly, trying to move only her wrists and forearms in an effort to slice through the ropes. If she moved her shoulder, the more noticeable her actions would be. This was Addison's only opportunity to set about her plan and she didn't intend on wasting it. She looked back to Brodie and Skyler. The terrorist had just finished slicing through Skyler's top and was beginning to slide open the material.

Shit, Addison cursed internally. If Brodie harmed so much as one more millimetre of Skyler's being, Addison would make her suffer an eternity of pain. The soldier turned back to Shamus. The beefy henchman switched his focus from Addison to Skyler. Every time he looked back to watch Brodie, Addison pressed a little harder, cutting through her bindings faster. She could rapidly feel the blade reaching the end of the fibres and braced herself. Addison's body jerked as the ropes were finally severed. She felt her wrists sag apart and relief flooded her system. Taking the knife in her right hand, Addison positioned the blade in her grasp.

Brodie dropped her scalpel on to the table beside her. "Decisions, decisions," she said, scanning her instruments. Apart from the scalpel, a pair of pliers, an assortment of semi-blunt knives, an ice pick, knuckle-dusters, manual hand drill, surgical saw and hot iron were at her disposal. To Brodie, it was a veritable assortment of highly entertaining toys.

Seeing the blonde's eyes turn to her, Addison gauged Skyler's state of mind. Although she did appear visibly frightened, the soldier could see the underlying confidence shining in her eyes. Skyler still had faith in Addison. It was that which enabled her to withstand Brodie's terrorising, as she knew Addison wouldn't give her that chance.

Her left shoulder incapacitated and throbbing in pain, Addison turned to Shamus. He grinned at her, quirking half his upper lip in a beastly sneer. Addison gripped her knife a little tighter. The beat of her heart echoed in her ears, her focus solely upon Shamus.

"You may not like this," Addison heard Brodie say.

Shamus peeked very quickly to see Brodie pick up a hot iron.

"But I definitely will."

Addison blinked slowly. In her peripheral vision she could see Brodie handle a large instrument, but she didn't turn away from Shamus to see what it was.

"No!" Skyler pleaded emotionally as Brodie moved in on her.

Addison didn't move her eyesight from Shamus.

"Please don't," Skyler said in a higher voice, full of desperation.

Addison waited. Every second felt like an hour as she stared into Shamus' eyes. She adjusted her grip on the knife.

Brodie leaned over Skyler.

"Please no," the blonde pleaded.

Unable to refrain any longer, Shamus turned to watch Brodie.

In a moment of lightening reflex, Addison brought the knife around from her back and hurtled it with deadly precision towards Shamus. The fatally sharp projectile slid solidly into the centre of his throat.

Brodie looked up as Shamus gasped for air. His jaw dropped, eyes wide in shocked horror. The weapon fell from his hands.

Before anybody had a remote chance of comprehending what had just happened, Addison jumped to her feet. She charged at the wall, slamming her left shoulder back into its socket. The pain was sharp and intense, but not enough to overwhelm her.

Shamus fell back against the wall behind him. Blood poured from the fatal wound and gurgled from his mouth as he slid to the ground.

"NO," Brodie shouted. "GUARDS!"

Instantly the two armed men standing outside the door burst into Brodie's room of torture. Still reeling from the pain, Addison charged the men. Jumping into the air she spun into a kick, knocking the first man out cold. As she landed, Addison found herself confronted by the second guard aiming his AK-47 level with her face. The threat didn't stop her as Addison kicked the weapon from his hands. They collided, trading a series of petty blows. It was a match Addison soon tired of and as she blocked his last punch she aimed her fist towards his Adam's apple and delivered an almost instantaneous deathblow.

Turning, ready for another attack, Addison found Brodie surprisingly absent. She had escaped while Addison fought the last man.

"Sky," Addison said, approaching the blonde. "Are you okay?"

Skyler nodded. "Just get us out of here, Addison."

With a nod Addison pulled her knife from Shamus. She sliced swiftly through Skyler's bonds, freeing the relieved blonde. As soon as her legs were released, Skyler jumped down from the table and wrapped her arms around Addison.

"I knew you would do it."

"It's not over yet," the agent replied.

Skyler jumped as a loud siren echoed around Brodie's complex.

Addison stepped towards the door. "I still have a few scores to settle."

Chapter 22

The alarm, which sounded very much like an air raid siren, was accompanied by sharply raised voices. Commanders of Brodie's militia who informed her soldiers of the situation harshly barked out orders. Section heads began rallying groups of men, their objective was clear, to eliminate both Addison Black and Skyler Tidwell. Brodie had ordered her men to use whatever means necessary in order to stop them. She knew her superior still wanted Addison alive but if one of her men were to fatally wound the agent in an attempt to locate and capture her, then so be it. The purpose of her own mission was complete and she'd already received payment. Addison Black was hers.

Agnes Brodie stormed through the compound and out into the open air. It was almost mid-day and the desert sun shone down like a relentless inferno. Armed with a semi-automatic she addressed her soldiers. "If Black leaves this place alive you shall all forfeit your lives. The man... or woman to bring down that bitch will be highly rewarded."

Fuelled with added motivation, Brodie's soldiers readied themselves for Agent Black.

****

Skyler's hand within her own, Addison ran down the narrow corridor towards Brodie's office. Just before they reached her door, two guards appeared in front of them. A man and woman both armed with high-powered submachine guns. Addison dispatched them easily,

251

incapacitating and taking the female guard's weapon before she could blink. Two swift kicks to the face and chest left her lifeless on the ground. Then using the SMG, Addison thrust it into the male soldier's face before kicking him to the floor. Retaking Skyler's hand she led her swiftly into Brodie's office and closed the door behind them.

"What are you doing?" Skyler asked, recognising where they were. If they were to escape, what on earth were they doing in the 'wolf's lair'?

Brodie's office was large. The floor was a buff grey tile and the walls were sparse white and disturbingly bare. In the near right corner stood a large wooden cabinet and it was this that Addison focussed on.

"I'm not leaving here until this building is razed to the ground. But first…" Addison took the submachine gun once again and thrust it against the cabinet's lock. "There are a few things I want back and I am hoping…"

After her third strike, the lock broke. Addison pulled both doors open and scanned the three shelves revealed to her. Although the bottom shelf was empty the remaining two were not. "Bingo! Brodie sure is into her keepsakes, huh?" Addison reached into the very top shelf and pulled her shirt out. She handed it to Skyler. "Put this on." She indicated her top that was shredded open.

"Thanks." Skyler replied and slipped into the garment speedily.

Turning her attention back to the cabinet, Addison reached into the middle shelf. "I'll take these back, thank you very much!" She took her Beretta pistols and after checking each was loaded, she placed them into the empty holsters at her back. Next she took the extra clips of ammunition Brodie had taken from her and dropped them into the side leg pockets of her combat trousers. Lastly Addison grabbed the baby Browning Brodie had confiscated from Skyler and held it out for her. "Take this."

"Addison I…"

"Now is not the time to argue, Sky. Same rules apply, okay?"

The young doctor nodded. "Okay, but the way I am feeling right now, Brodie might not be safe around me anyway!"

Addison gave a short smile. "You and me both." She re-closed the cabinet doors and strode over to Brodie's table. "But let me take care of her… I owe her plenty."

Multiple sets of footsteps ran past Brodie's office and both Skyler and Addison ducked behind the large desk, out of sight. Leaning against the desk drawers, Addison took the magazine from the fallen guard's gun. She checked its capacity, finding it fully loaded. With a satisfied nod, Addison locked it back into place. She held the weapon against her torso and turned to Skyler. The blonde crouched beside her, pistol trembling in her hand as she hid in silence.

"Sky, did you see where the main laboratory was?" Addison whispered.

Skyler shook her head. "No, but when Brodie fist brought me here I did see a couple of guys in isolation suits come up on a lift. I noticed the lift had only one floor... down to a single lower level."

"Right." Addison twisted her body around and took a blue pen and sheet of ruled writing paper from Brodie's desk. She placed the sheet upon the floor and began jotting down a series of seemingly random letters and numbers. "I have a job for you, Sky. While I take care of destroying the physical evidence of Project Gemini, I want you to access the main computer. Can you do that?"

"Well yes, but what do you want me to do?"

Addison handed Skyler the paper. "I want you to get into the computer and open up the network. There has to be a link to the whole system, maybe even a mainframe somewhere. Get in there and direct the main computer to this site address. It is a super virus. As soon as the site is accessed the virus will automatically load into the system and spread through the entire network. Don't worry about getting there. I will be with you."

Skyler studied the obscure address Addison had given her. Her practically photographic memory easily recorded Samuel Perkins' Alpha Numeric super virus; once done she folded the paper and slipped it into Addison's shirt pocket. "It's pretty tough numbers out there, Addison."

"I've had worse."

"You plan on destroying this place and everything in it, don't you?"

Addison shrugged. "Well you did say extreme heat would destroy the Bacilli, and besides, I do love a good bang," she winked.

From outside more footsteps ran past the door. Addison's senses prickled as she heard a presence pause outside the entrance to Brodie's office. She placed a finger over her lips in a gesture of silence. Her breathing softened. The door opened and Addison gripped her weapon, placing her finger lightly upon the trigger. She sensed the single figure step further into the room and looked under the desk surface. A large pair of black booted feet came into view. There was only one move to make. Addison knew making too much noise would instantly alert people to their presence. She didn't want that just yet.

Addison waited for the guard to approach their place of hiding. She held her finger over her lips one more time and winked at Skyler.

The American nodded, her nerves almost gone as she gripped her Browning pistol and remained as silent as possible. From the opposite side of the desk, their threat moved ever closer. Making a swift decision Addison set down the weapon she was holding and then with surprising reflexes she jumped up from behind the desk.

Face to face with a shaven headed man Addison said, "Hi," in a cocky manner as she leaned over the surface of the desk, grabbed a hold of his collar and pulled him over and onto the floor. He landed with a thud; Addison not giving a moment's thought as she delivered two fatal jabs and rendered him lifeless.

Skyler pointed to a black device attached to his hip. "Is that what I think it is?"

"Excellent!" Addison pulled it from his belt. "A stun gun. Do you think you would feel better if you had to use this on somebody?"

Nodding, Skyler slipped the Browning pistol into the waist of her jeans. She took the stun gun after Addison adjusted it to a higher setting.

"Keep behind me; do as I say." Addison peered over the desk. "I'll get you to their main computer. While you are doing that I'll ready the building for a major fireworks party." The soldier turned back to Skyler, feeling a need to reassure her that everything would be fine. "Just stick by me, Sky. Are you okay?"

Skyler took a deep breath. "I have to be."

The apprehension in Skyler's eyes bolstered Addison's need to assure her that she would be all right. It wasn't hard to see that in numbers, the odds were stacked against them, but Addison had come up against larger quantities of foes in the past.

"Sky," Addison whispered. "I promise you we'll get out of here." She unconsciously licked her lips, desperately wanting to reassure her with a kiss. Unfortunately, it seemed inappropriate to do such a thing with a body lying only inches away. Instead, Addison cupped her cheek and ran a thumb over her lips. The memory of how wonderful it felt to kiss those soft, inviting lips passed through her mind. "How about when we get out of here we make plans to go to Egypt. We can go skinny dipping in the Nile!" Addison wiggled her eyebrows causing Skyler to smile. "Ready?"

"Ready."

"Okay, let's go."

Twisting to her feet Addison held out one hand, indicating that Skyler should stay on the ground. She jogged silently over to the open doorway and looked out. Checking the area Addison assessed that the coast was clear. "Okay," she called and Skyler emerged from behind the desk. Stun gun in hand she stood slightly behind Addison.

"Keep behind you, right?"

"Right."

"I can do that."

Holding the weapon in front of her, finger poised upon its trigger, Addison led the way out of Brodie's office. Close by they could hear sounds of commotion from all around them. Reaching a corner the women stopped. With her back pressed against the wall Addison peered around to the next passageway. One armed soldier was swiftly approaching. Addison waited until he was close before she stepped out in front of him.

"Catch," Addison shouted and threw her weapon at the guy. Instincts taking over, the man reached up to catch the machine gun. Addison took advantage of his exposed position by delivering a solid kick to his stomach, just as he caught the weapon. When he doubled over in bewildered pain, the agent regained possession of her weapon, slamming it down into the back of his neck. He crumpled to the ground. "Which way to the lift?"

Skyler looked around them. "Down there." She pointed down the corridor from where the guard had just emerged. "Less than fifty feet away."

"Right." Addison took off again. She could see a set of doors to the elevator and quickened her pace. Suddenly, numerous sets of rapid footsteps began to approach from both directions. "Come on!" she ordered and ran towards the lift. "Get it open!"

To their right, five soldiers began running towards them. Addison opened fire, showering the approaching men with bullets as she backed Skyler into the lift. Then to their left more men appeared. Addison switched to the new threat, firing rapidly as they in turn answered her attack with one of their own.

Safely inside the elevator, Skyler pressed the appropriate button. The doors began to shut so she placed her hand onto one of its mechanical shutters, halting its progress. "Addison!"

"Yeah!" Addison yelled. She continued firing as she backed up towards the lift. Men and women came from both directions and she switched aim constantly, hitting any target that came into view. Once she was inside the lift, Skyler removed her hand and the doors slid shut. Rapid fire was still heard from above as the elevator car descended to the basement level of the complex.

"You did good," Addison commented as she checked her weapon. There was a single bullet remaining.

"I did nothing."

The agent disagreed, saying, "You remained calm and kept your head."

"I suppose," Skyler replied. "I don't feel scared anymore. I feel... energized!"

Addison quirked her eyebrow, but her reply died as the elevator came to a halt. She dropped her useless machine gun and took out both pistols. There was still a painful ache in her shoulder, but Addison had no time to dwell on the fact at that moment in time.

The lift doors slid open, revealing a long narrow passageway. Half way down there were two doors, one to the left and the other to the right, facing each other. At the end of the walkway stood another door and six armed guards. Rapid fire commenced immediately forcing Addison to take a hold of Skyler and thrust them both against the side of the elevator.

"Bollocks," the agent growled. She attempted to look back out, but the firing continued. "I have an idea." Addison placed her hand upon Skyler's stomach, keeping her still. "Don't come out until I call, okay?"

"What are you going to do?"

Addison assessed the size of the elevator car. It was wide enough for what she intended. "I'm gonna do this," she said and ran three steps closer to the back of the lift. Jumping, Addison ran up the back wall until she was centre of the doorway. She then propelled her body through the lift's exit, twisting mid air to face the ground as she began to fire at the six guards. Three men had fallen before Addison hit the ground. She slid along the floor on her stomach, shooting down the last men before her body slowed to a halt.

"Okay," Addison shouted.

Skyler emerged from the elevator. "How on earth did you...?"

"I did gymnastics as a kid." Addison rubbed her chest. "Of course that was B.B."

"B.B.?"

"Before Breasts."

"Ouch."

"Yep." Addison peered through the door to her left as Skyler looked through the glass of the door to their right.

"Storage," Addison stated.

"Bingo!" said the American. Inside she saw several active computers.

"Perfect." Addison opened the door and they both stepped inside. Although the room was small and no lights were active, they could see three working terminals. The upper part of the far wall was half glazed and provided an ample view into the laboratory. Beside it was a door that led into the sterile room. Addison noted an isolation chamber at the right corner of the lab and three suited bodies worked cautiously inside. There was also a larger computer beside the chamber.

Being sure to keep out of view, Addison said, "You know what to do? I need you to access their entire network... worldwide. Bring the bastards down."

Skyler surveyed what she presumed to be the main computer in the laboratory. "Leave it to me."

"Great." Addison turned as Skyler stepped towards the door leading into the laboratory, but before she left she said, "I'll be back for you, Sky."

The young doctor smiled. "I know you will."

Addison nodded. "See you in a while," she replied and slipped soundlessly from the room.

Skyler watched as the agent's form disappeared out the door. She recognized the taut yet somehow fluid way Addison held her body. The expert killing machine was in full evidence.

Skyler marvelled for a brief moment at the paradox the dark haired woman presented. On one hand was the efficient agent, skilled in the arts of espionage and death, but on the other was the loyal friend and vulnerable woman. Skyler was sure Addison would object to the word "vulnerable" if she heard it, but it was definitely true.

And then there was the kiss.

The act that was supposedly just for Brodie's benefit set off a firestorm of wanting within Skyler and she admitted to herself that had circumstances been different, she would have never have stopped with that single kiss. Though she knew Addison was far more experienced than herself in sexual matters, a voice born of pure instinct told the scientist that the agent felt the intensity between them too.

These thoughts took no more than a few seconds before Skyler decided to file them away for later action. That there **would** be action on those thoughts was not a matter even up for debate.

Skyler turned to scan the lab. This was familiar territory for her as her course of study took her across many disciplines from the practical to the arcane. As she searched the lab she kept an eye on the isolation room where the technicians were working. It had to be where the bacillus was being synthesized; it made no sense otherwise.

The technicians were blissfully unaware of the mayhem happening outside the lab. Skyler knew that happy state had to be because of the safety parameters of the room. It would have to be isolated and insulated, temperature controlled and with a negative air flow system. No chance could be taken that a virulent organism could escape and contaminate the facility. Adding those facts to the decontamination suits and respirators the technicians wore and Skyler felt she had a good chance of completing her mission unobserved. Even the alarm, so piercing in the hall, was nearly inaudible in the lab.

She moved cautiously through an amazing variety of sophisticated technology. An electron microscope, cell separator, incubators and every bit of equipment needed to conduct bioresearch and experimentation was present. None of it was what she was looking for though.

She moved closer to the isolation room, keeping track of the movements of the techs as she hunted for the computer system she knew had to be there. There was too much technology not to have it tied together somehow.

She crouched down and was within a few feet of the isolation room before she spotted the terminal and monitor. It was a larger system than she anticipated and was connected to a block of machines on the wall nearest the room with the techs. Scanning the set-up, Skyler realized the computer system was not only connecting the various pieces of lab apparatus, but it was also connecting the lab system with a larger system off-site. *Could be anywhere in the world* she thought. *No telling who's gotten the Project Gemini information if Agnes was telling the truth about their success.*

The American knew Agnes was telling the truth though; Skyler becoming expendable was evidence of that.

Skyler moved back to the main monitor and watched the display a moment. A mass of data was rearranging itself in a linear fashion. The information seemed familiar to her somehow and she searched her memory for the answer. *They're DNA sequencing!* Skyler realized, but she had no idea what was being sequenced. *You can bet your ass it's nothing for mankind's benefit* she thought.

With a last glance at the three techs, Skyler focused on the monitor. While not disturbing the running program, she brought up the control panel and found the modem. Studying the properties screen, she discovered what needed to be done to contact the outside world. Entering the appropriate characters on the keyboard, she reached an open line and quickly tapped out the coded sequence Addison had given her earlier. A connection seemed to be made as a low tone, similar to connecting to a fax machine, sounded from the terminal.

Suddenly the screen before her went black except for a small row of white dots that moved across from right to left. It was her fascination with what was happening on the screen that made Skyler miss the fact that one of the technicians had left the isolation room and moved into the small antechamber between the lab and isolation room where he began to remove his protective suit.

The small dots continued across the screen when one broke away from the line and began moving around the screen as it enlarged. Skyler watched as the dot's circular shape morphed into a figure, still white but definitely with arms, legs and head. Transfixed, she could only marvel as Casper the Friendly Ghost appeared on the monitor.

YOU HAVE INVITED CASPER TO PLAY was the message that appeared on the screen. **ARE YOU SURE?** Skyler hesitated before tapping the "Y" key followed by the "Enter" key.

Casper smiled and the words **SO BE IT** appeared on the screen. The letters faded and a house appeared in its place. The Friendly Ghost flew toward the house and passed right through the front door. The animation ceased there and the screen filled with computer data that literally appeared to disintegrate.

The door to the antechamber opened with a whoosh that let Skyler know it was an air lock and it was a toss up as to who was more surprised, Skyler or the technician. Skyler was more prepared though and reacted swiftly, bringing the Baby Browning to bear on the startled man.

His eyes darted between Skyler, the gun and an intercom located to the American's left. Skyler saw the technician weighing his options. He could now hear the muted alarm and her presence with a gun made it obvious what the commotion was about.

"What's your name?" Skyler asked.

"Joseph," the technician replied nervously.

"Well, Joseph, I've had a really bad day. Please don't do anything to make it worse. Get over here and sit on the floor. You do what I say and we'll all be happy." Skyler moved her head to indicate where she wanted the man to go. The American felt more than saw the technician's intention and she was prepared as he lunged for the intercom as he moved passed her. Bringing up the stun gun in her other hand she delivered a sharp blast of electricity to the man's flank. He dropped to the ground, immobilized in agony.

"Blame that one on Agnes Brodie, she's the one who pissed me off," Skyler told the man as she moved back to the computer screen. She looked up quickly, but the remaining technicians seemed not to have noticed the brief interplay between Skyler and their colleague.

The image on the monitor was changing yet again. The data continued to disintegrate, but now the picture started to swirl. Soon it looked like a vortex.

A black hole virus! Skyler thought. *I've heard of them in theory, but never thought I'd actually see one in action.* A black hole virus was theoretically so strong that it could not only crash computers, but servers, networks and anything connected to the affected computer. Like a black hole in space with a gravitational pull so strong that even light could not escape, the force of the black hole virus was irresistible. Skyler watched as the vortex became smaller and smaller until it disappeared from the screen completely.

Blood red letters appeared on the screen. **NETWORK TERMINATED.** This was replaced by the phrase **CASPER SAYS THANK YOU FOR A LOVELY TIME.** Those words faded from the screen and silence reigned in the lab.

Skyler was slack-jawed in amazement when she realized every piece of lab equipment connected to the main computer was shut down. The laboratory was nothing more than a scientific junkyard.

Unfortunately, the equipment in the isolation room was shut down as well and the technicians were already making their way into the air lock to ascertain the problem. Skyler was spotted easily and she readied the Baby Browning. She took a deep breath and hoped that if she needed to, she would be able to pull the trigger in her own defense.

She didn't need to worry. As the remaining technicians entered the connecting room, the lab was plunged into darkness.

Skyler counted to five slowly and, as she anticipated, low level lighting and a faint airflow began. *Emergency generator for basic life support*, she thought. Glancing at the two techs in the airlock, she realized they were trapped completely in the small room. *Fail-safe mechanism! Can't have the whole lab contaminated in case of a systems failure, right Brodie? You'd rather let your guys die than risk your own skin.* She lifted the hand holding the gun and waved it at the men. They ceased their attempts to make their way out of the antechamber immediately. Skyler nodded at them in approval. She glanced at the technician on the floor who seemed to have passed out.

"Sorry about this boys, but don't worry, I'll stay with you at least until Addison comes back."

And you better get back here, Agent Black she thought. *You and I have unfinished business.*

Chapter 23

Using the butt of one of the fallen guard's machine guns, Addison attempted to open the elevator doors. With the power now gone, usual means of access had been rendered useless. Even with the low hum of emergency power, the lift still didn't seem to be working. It would have perplexed Addison, but she had no time to figure out why it wasn't in operation. The agent's sole purpose now was to find Brodie and nothing was going to keep her from that task. The Irish woman had to be somewhere within the complex. She wanted her dead and that was hardly reason to leave. Besides, Addison knew they would both hold Project Gemini in high consideration. Whatever diabolical intentions Brodie's superior had for the breakthrough biological weapon could not come to completion. It had to be destroyed. The possible lives of millions depended on Addison's obliteration of the bacilli. Fortunately, Addison had already figured out how she intended on doing this.

With a final thrust, Addison grunted as the metal elevator doors slid open. Once fully retracted, the soldier wedged the submachine gun barrel into the gap between door and ground. It was enough to keep the car accessible and Addison stepped inside.

From above her, on the main ground floor of the compound, Addison heard many rushed footsteps and raised voices. It seemed that Brodie's soldiers were concerned on how to get down into the laboratory. Addison looked up and saw the reason why. The roof of the elevator car was solid. There was no emergency access or exit shaft at all. It was an inconvenience for sure, but more so confusing. Why would they design this form of transportation with such a safety flaw? Did Brodie fear the possible contamination of Project Gemini to such an extent that she would do anything to assure the bacilli never moved beyond this underground chamber? It posed a serious question to Addison. What was contained within the bacilli? What, presumably, lethal agents were they working with? That notion sent a twin spasm of alarm and fear through the soldier's spine.

Spinning around on her heels, Addison paused mid-stride in exiting the lift when she found herself face to face with Agnes Brodie. Addison was surprised as Brodie held out her revolver in a gesture of surrender, but the agent retained her neutral expression.

"I've had it," Brodie proclaimed. "I want you, Black. I'm ready for you. Let's end this in style. No weapons... just you and me. When I kill you I want to feel your life drain away under my bare hands."

"You aren't one for subtleties, are you, Agnes?" Brodie's presence suddenly made Addison realise one important fact. The power shut off for the elevator had to be down in the basement level of the compound. Brodie had to have shut it off with her intention to confront the agent once and for all. It was a foolish mistake on the Irish Woman's part, but it did urge Addison to wonder why she would take such a risk. That cold feeling of dread returned once again.

"Okay, fine." Unclipping her pistols, the soldier held them out and together, very slowly; the women placed their weapons upon the ground. "You want hand to hand, you've got it."

There was barely time to react as Brodie pulled a concealed knife from her sleeve and threw it at Addison. The soldier caught it mere centimetres away from her face with her right hand. "Okay... now I am mad." Throwing Agnes' knife to the floor, Addison zeroed in on the terrorist. They collided together with rapid force and it was Brodie who threw the first punch, a move Addison found easy to deflect. She countered the punch with one of her own, but as Brodie blocked her Addison followed through with a solid kick to her stomach that sent Brodie skidding backwards across the floor and towards the main door of the laboratory. She didn't waste any time in getting to her feet.

"Hey, Black," Brodie taunted. "I have to say that woman of yours has some balls!" Addison wondered what it was Brodie was hinting at, but she knew she wouldn't have to wait long to find out. The woman took pleasure in taunting her. "She has no qualms in firing a gun, does she?" The redheaded terrorist took a step closer towards the laboratory door. "It's a pity she is such a lousy aim." Saying that, Brodie disappeared into the lab and Addison followed her. The solider soon discovered what it was Brodie was talking about. Sitting submissively and gagged behind a table was Skyler. The technician she had earlier disabled held her loaded Browning to her head.

262

"It's like we go round and around and around in circles, don't you think?" Brodie traced her fingers upon the desktop as she stood beside Skyler. "The bad guy gets the girl, the hero rescues her, but then does something dumb and so... the bad guy gets the girl, the hero rescues her, but that dumb act happens again and the bad guy gets the girl. I can't help thinking this vicious circle has to come to an end somehow."

Addison sighed, bored with Brodie's speech. She looked around gaining a bearing of their surroundings. "It seems to me I have to eradicate part of the equation." Addison held out three fingers on her left hand. She touched the first finger. "Now I know damn well it isn't going to be me." The solider began to check off her two remaining fingers. "That then leaves either the bad guy or the girl."

"Not to ignore your delusion, but I hardly think you intend on eradicating the girl."

"To rid myself of a headache? I might. You really don't know me as well as you think, Agnes... but then again... you are the eternal burr under my saddle. The point is... what do I want to rid myself of more? The girl who might hang on thinking there is something more between us, or you... insert numerous reasons for that one." Addison's voice was cold and detached.

Brodie closed her eyes shaking her head. "You're bluffing. How stupid do you think I am, Black?"

"You tell me." Addison folded her arms. "I mean, you 'claim' to know so much more about me than she does." The agent didn't dare to glance over at Skyler. "She was a good fuck and I am never one to turn down an easy lay. That's who I am." Addison recognised the sceptical expression in Brodie's eyes and realised she was thinking of the time she had been turned down by the agent herself. Addison was quick to add, "But I don't scrape the bottom of the barrel. It leaves a nasty taste in the mouth." It was at this point that Addison did risk a glace at Skyler. As she expected the blonde looked confused and slightly hurt by Addison's words.

Finding herself once again in the position of Brodie holding Skyler hostage with a loaded weapon, Addison knew why Brodie was so confident in their confrontation. *Think, think, think,* the agent chanted mentally.

"What's the matter?" Brodie asked with spiteful contempt. "Not so confident anymore?"

Addison turned from Brodie to the man holding Skyler. Something about him struck her. Yes, he may be one of Brodie's men, but where as the others she had dealt with were trained soldiers, this man was a mere scientist. He appeared as uncomfortable holding her gun as he would a hot poker. Addison knew this man wouldn't be able to kill on Brodie's orders. She could see the hesitation and awkwardness in his eyes.

Movement diverted Addison's attention and she looked back to Brodie as the Irishwoman walked around the desk and approached her. She stopped when there was less than five feet between them. It didn't surprise Addison when Brodie pulled another knife from her opposite sleeve. She twirled the handle in her hand and assumed a ready combat position.

"Prepare to finally meet your match, Agent Black."

"I'm getting bored with clichés, Agnes." Addison jumped backwards as Brodie lunged at her with the knife. *Deja Vu* the agent thought as she kicked Agnes' hand away from a second strike.

Brodie came at her again, seeing the blade as a further advantage over Addison. She thrust forward, aiming directly for the soldier's stomach, but Addison stopped her, knocking her hand away with a rapid block from her left hand. She countered the attack by punching Brodie in the jaw, followed by an elbow to the side of her face. The Irish woman reeled and stepped backwards, giving her precious seconds to gain her equilibrium. When she did, it was with a solid kick to Addison's stomach. The agent was knocked backwards; she rolled over the surface of a metallic table and landed back upon her feet. Addison didn't wait to react from the pain or for Brodie to advance. Stepping up on a nearby stool she jumped onto the table and lunged herself in a roundhouse kick, knocking Brodie to the floor. Landing above her, Addison dropped to her knees. She stopped Brodie's hand before the blade could make impact with her neck and then thrust the woman's hand to the ground. It took five hits before Brodie released the weapon. As the blade scattered across the floor Brodie swung around trapping Addison beneath her body. Wrapping one hand around the agent's throat, Brodie was only able to connect one punch. As her fist thrust down for a second hit Addison caught Brodie's hand, pushed her fist back and punched her in return. A splatter of blood flew from Brodie's nose and she released Addison's throat in pain. She grabbed the agent's hands and held them above her head.

"You're going to die, Black." Blood dripped from Brodie's nose onto Addison's neck.

"Maybe." Addison rolled backwards and kicked Brodie away. "But not today and not by your hands."

Agnes collided with a side unit and a plastic container of test tubes smashed upon the floor.

Jumping to her feet, Addison stepped towards Brodie. "Careful, those buggers cut deep!"

Skyler had ceased trying to struggle from the man who held her. As Brodie and Addison's fight continued the blonde felt the scientists grip on her lessen. Skyler realised with the right moves she would easily be able to escape from his grasp. Wincing as she saw Brodie pack a punch square across Addison's jaw, Skyler had an idea. *Sing?* She thought, wondering why that word seemed to hold such relevance. Then suddenly it hit her. The beat of her heart increased as Skyler held her breath. *I can do this!* Counting to three Skyler unleashed her attack. Thrusting her elbow backwards she hit the scientist in his solar plexus followed by a harsh kick to his instep. Next she punched backwards at his nose and finished off her attack with a solid jab to his groin. The gun fell from his hand and slid across the floor. Skyler was released instantly and the scientist fell to the ground with a painful groan.

Stepping back in surprise she looked down in bewilderment and pulled the tape from her lips. "Damn, this self defence stuff really works! I was just like Sandra Bullock in Miss Congeniality, except I'm not that clumsy in heels."

Noticing the man was attempting to move, Skyler looked around and found the abandoned stun gun. She retrieved it hastily and attacked her captor with electrifying volts to his side. A cry of pain rose from his lips as he fell back to the floor.

Hearing the peculiar yelp, Addison looked to the source of the sound and found Skyler free from her captor. She stood over him, stun gun in hand. Addison grinned and turned back to Brodie as the Irish woman threw a hefty punch. She allowed the fist to painfully hit its mark and fell backwards over a desk and towards Skyler.

"Addison!"

"I'm okay." The soldier climbed to her feet and rubbed her cheekbone. "Listen, I need you to find the power switch for the elevator and turn it back on." Brodie advanced on the women and Addison kicked her away with a powerful thrust. "It's in one of those two side rooms. Quick... you have to do it now."

"Okay..." Skyler backed up towards the doorway of the lab. "Okay." Turning, she ran through the door.

"Oh Addison," Brodie sang.

Addison turned to Brodie and froze. The terrorist stood in the centre of the room, Browning pistol in hand aimed directly at the soldier.

"This could all end right here, Black."

"It could..." Addison was confidant Brodie wouldn't shoot while the agent was standing in front of the isolation chamber. It was too high a risk. "But I..." Addison paused in her speech seeing the deadly glint shimmer in Brodie's eyes. As her finger applied pressure to the trigger, Addison dived onto the floor.

A single shot rang out and ricocheted around the laboratory. Addison rolled onto her back and looked up in horror. Terror hammered with rapid thumps through her heart. Silence stretched out for several seconds before the room was bathed in a flashing red light. A female voice followed...

"Warning; Isolation Chamber Compromised. Pressure Breach will occur in T-Minus Five Minutes and Counting. Four Minutes Fifty-Nine... Fifty-Eight... Fifty Seven..."

"Oh this is not good!" Jumping to her feet, Addison looked back at Brodie. The Irish woman appeared alarmed by what was happening.

"Let's finish this." Addison vaulted over a counter and struck Brodie before she had time to fully comprehend what had taken place.

"This is all your fault," Brodie seethed.

Addison laughed. "Yeah? So sue me!" Again the agent struck at Brodie followed by a kick that knocked the Browning from her hand. Brodie hit back and a round of savage blows ensued.

"Six... Five... Four... Three... Two... One... Four Minutes. Three Minutes Fifty-Nine... Fifty-Eight..."

The time for fooling around was over. Time was of the essence and they had less than four minutes before the isolation chamber would breech and the deadly Project Gemini seeped into the air.

"What is it?" Addison demanded as she struck Brodie. "What did you use?"

"Screw you, Black." Brodie attempted to strike Addison, but the agent easily blocked her jab. Feeling her annoyance rise she took Brodie by the collar and drove her into the wall.

"Seven... Six... Five..."

Addison thrust her knee into Brodie's stomach followed by a punch square across her jaw. "What's in Gemini? What's the Hyde Application? Tell me."

Brodie laughed. They both knew she wouldn't talk. Instead the redhead spat a mouthful of blood towards Addison... but missed.

Growling, Addison pulled Brodie from the wall and threw her over a stainless steel workbench. More glass vials scattered in the impact and smashed around Brodie as she landed upon the floor.

"Sixteen... fifteen... Fourteen..."

Walking over in rapid strides, Addison spotted her Browning

pistol and swiped it from among the shards of glass. She held it to Brodie's head. "Tell me." Brodie smiled wickedly and Addison struck her again. "Tell me." Her punch pushed Brodie closer to unconsciousness.

"Two minutes... One minute Fifty-Nine... Fifty-Eight... Fifty-Seven..."

"Tell me where it is," Addison ordered. She took Brodie's hair, pulled her head from the floor and pushed the barrel of the pistol hard into her forehead. "So help me, Agnes, you don't deserve a single chance, but this is all you get." Addison looked up as the red warning light started to flash faster.

"One minute Thirty seconds... Twenty-Nine... Twenty-Eight..."

"Addison!"

The agent looked to the doorway where a frantic Skyler burst through the doors.

"It's back on."

"Good... get my pistols and get an Uzi from one of the fallen guards," Addison ordered. "Now... quickly."

Skyler ran to fulfill Addison's request.

"Last chance, Agnes. Tell me what it is."

"Why bother." Blood gurgled from Brodie's lips and she coughed violently. "There's no cure for the poison. You'll die. You will all die." She began to laugh deliriously, but having had enough, Addison delivered one final punch that knocked Brodie out cold.

"I'll just have to make sure I destroy it then."

"Twelve... Eleven... Ten..."

Addison ran over to several large canisters in the corner of the room. She recognised the green colour of the containers and disengaged each valve. Turning a tap with both hands she allowed a flow of pure oxygen to seep into the laboratory.

"Five... Four... Three..."

Next she ran over to a table of four taps. Disconnecting the hoses from each valve she turned them on and the scent of gas filled her senses.

"Addison... we have to get out of here." Skyler re-appeared in the doorway.

"Two... One... Warning Isolation Chamber Breech in Sixty Seconds... Fifty-Nine... Fifty-Eight..."

Knowing there wasn't much time remaining and desperately needing to make sure she and, more importantly, Skyler were as far away from the compound as possible, Addison ran for the doctor.

"Come on," she yelled. "We have to get out of here."

"Like I'm gonna disagree," Skyler said as she handed the pistols to Addison and they ran for the elevator.

"Forty-Eight... Forty-Seven... Forty-Six..."

Once inside, Addison kicked away the submachine gun that was jamming the doors open and they slid shut. She slammed her fingers on the button for the ground floor. Nothing happened.

"Forty-Two... Forty-One..."

"No! Come on." Addison struck it repeatedly and after her third strike the elevator car began to ascend. A sigh escaped her lips and she looked to Skyler. "Almost there."

Skyler nodded nervously and released the submachine gun when Addison took it from her hands. She jumped in surprise, turning her head away as Addison began firing at the elevator's floor. The bullets passed through the metal ground with colourful blue sparks and Skyler hoped the gas Addison released into the room, didn't automatically ignite too soon. Thankfully it seemed the vapours hadn't reached that far yet.

"Thirty-Two... Thirty-One... Warning; Isolation Chamber Breech in Thirty Seconds..."

As the car doors slid open Addison thrust her foot through the littering of bullet holes and a hole seven inches in diameter was formed. Dropping the machine gun Addison took Skyler's hand. "Come on. Let's get out of here."

"Twenty-Six... Twenty-Five..."

Hands firmly entwined, the women fled from the elevator and down two corridors before reaching the entrance of the complex. As they stepped out into the blinding Israeli sun they caught a first glimpse of Alon's attack on the compound. Many Mossad agents were in the process of taking down the remainder of Brodie's soldiers.

Spotting her friend, Addison called him frantically. "Alon"

The man looked up from handcuffing a kneeling soldier. "Addison."

"Give me a grenade."

"A what?"

"A grenade," Addison repeated impatiently.

Alon didn't waste time in retrieving one from his shoulder pack and threw it to Addison. The agent caught it swiftly.

"Now everyone get out of here. RUN! This place is gonna BLOW!"

As soon as her words were spoken people began to turn and run. Skyler did so, as well, but stopped as she sensed Addison run back into the compound.

"Addison?"

"Trust me, Sky. I'll be back. Just run."

The hesitation and concern was clear upon Skyler's face.

"Do it. Run! I'll follow. I promise."

Nodding, Skyler could only do as Addison asked and she turned, running from the compound to the safety of the hills.

Addison turned and ran back into the building.

"Fifteen... Fourteen... Thirteen..."

The agent ran back to the elevator and reopened the shaft doors. Lighting in the building dimmed further to a rapid succession flashing red.

"Ten... Nine... Eight..."

Addison took the pin in her fingers and waited.

"Six... Five..."

Knowing it was time; Addison pulled the pin from the grenade and dropped it through the hole in the elevator car's floor. She didn't wait to see it fall down into the shaft but turned and ran as fast as she was physically able. The elevator doors closed as Addison took one corner and ran towards the exit.

"Two... One..."

Addison made it back out into the open and continued to run. Behind her she heard... "Warning; Isolation Chamber Breech has occurred," before the grenade exploded. Addison continued to run knowing that it was only the beginning because as the initial explosion met with the gas and oxygen the entire compound erupted like a savage volcano.

Its noise was ear splitting. The ground shook and trembled weekly underfoot as pockets of fire opened through the sand. Flames shot into the air like a smouldering inferno. Not even the complex structure could stand over the face of the blast. Its bricks burst apart and scattered across the sand.

Addison ran until the sheer force pushed her to the ground and she landed face first in the sand, arms covering her head. Around her plumes of smoke, shattered brick and savage flames exploded around what was left of the complex, shooting hot debris into the air. Sand briefly filled the atmosphere. Many handfuls of grains solidified to glass through the sheer heat of the blast. The scent was overwhelming and the temperature combined with the sun scalded the land. For many seconds, hot rubble fell like rain upon the ground.

As soon as she felt it was safe, Addison climbed back to her feet. She continued to run towards the safety of the hill where she knew Skyler, Alon and the rest of the team were taking cover. Once far enough away, Addison turned and looked back at the carnage. The inferno of heat had turned the flames, rubble and smoke into a flicking blur. The agent squinted through the haze.

"Addison!" Skyler jumped over the hill and ran into the agent's arms. "Are you insane?"

"Oh I'm okay, thank you for asking."

Skyler ignored the agent's sarcasm. "We destroyed Project Gemini, right?"

Addison ran her hand through Skyler's dusty hair. She hugged the blonde closer and looked over her shoulder at the flickering remains. "Yes, it's destroyed." Addison remembered Brodie's unconscious body lying in the middle of the laboratory. "Everything is destroyed." She hugged Skyler harder as a weighty shadow of foreboding lifted from their shoulders.

Chapter 24

"So, it's the consensus that Project Gemini, at least as far as what was stolen, has been destroyed?" General Blithe asked his agent.

"Yes, sir," Addison replied, shifting on the leather couch in the General's office. She had received medical attention to the wound in her side and it was only occasionally that a twinge of discomfort reminded her of the bullet that had passed through her flesh. "Both our best scientists and the Israeli experts agree that the temperatures reached in the explosion were more than enough to eradicate the bacillus. Both the beneficial Jekyll side and the noxious Hyde application would have been destroyed. They will keep the area under quarantine of course until final culture results of the site return, but confidence is high."

"That's good then," her boss replied.

"I'll be honest though, Mark, I'm still concerned. Brodie practically crowed that they had replicated Project Gemini and had perfected the Hyde application, but she never told us what they inserted into the bacillus or who she was working for. That's information we'll never get from her now."

Mark rubbed his hand over his chin in thought. "Any chance Brodie was bluffing?"

Addison considered this. "I suppose it's always a possibility. Agnes was a liar as well as a kidnapper, thief and murderer. I wouldn't put it past her, but I still want to know who Dr. Kleein is."

Mark nodded his agreement. "Would have been advantageous if she had survived I agree, but if Agnes Brodie and her team were willing to work on anything for money, maybe it's better they were terminated."

Addison frowned. "I suppose so, Mark. Due to the explosion

271

and heat there wasn't much left in the way of human remains. Some of those people had families and they will never know what happened to them. That's not a good feeling, but I wanted to send Agnes to hell. If you had seen that inferno in Israel you would know I more than accomplished that."

"I realize it is cold comfort, Addison, but you've avenged James Easton's death at Brodie's hands and you've rid the world of something vile. It was good work."

Addison reached down and stroked the soft black fur of Spike who was laying contentedly along side the agent on the couch. The tiny dog turned her head to swipe a pink tongue across Addison's hand before settling back in to enjoy her mistress' attention.

"And you got Skyler Tidwell back in good shape as well by what I observed," Mark noted as he moved from the chair behind his desk and began to pace his office. "It was certainly touching when Marlene...Professor Tidwell...was reunited with Skyler." Mark remembered the meeting of mother and daughter on the tarmac as Skyler descended from the transport. The obviously deep and abiding love between them had touched the soldier's heart in a way he no longer had thought possible. Addison, following Skyler down the stairway, was diplomatic in pretending not to notice the errant tear that had appeared in her superior's eye.

General Blithe greeted Addison with the restraint typical of the British in public. "Well done, Black," he said as he clapped her on the shoulder. "Spot on." Addison shrugged, uncomfortable with the attention.

Marlene left her daughter briefly to take the few steps to Addison. Green eyes, so like her daughter's, looked at the operative.

"Agent Black, you made a promise to me and you kept it. You brought my daughter back home safely. I can never repay you for that." She leaned over and kissed Addison on the cheek.

Mark chuckled at the memory of the very lethal Addison Black standing between the Tidwell women blushing to her roots.

"Something amusing?" Addison asked, bringing the general back to the present.

"Um, not at all. I was just thinking about the festivities we have planned for your homecoming and smashing success. Even though the public will never know how close they came to disaster, we know and appreciate your work. I think this gala is just what we need. Confidently, I heard it's possible the Prime Minister may attend. There might be a medal in this for you. Unpublicised, of course."

Addison stuck out her tongue and made a rude noise, indicating what she thought of the prospect of the decoration. Spike lifted her head and added a growl before being soothed again by her best friend.

"Not interested, Mark," Addison said. "You know I never cared for those fancy dress parties with everybody congratulating each other on a job well done that half of them never participated in. It's political and I hate politics."

"Normally so do I but this time I'll be going with Doctor Tidwell on my arm." Seeing Addison's body tense, he immediately clarified his statement. "The older Doctor Tidwell that is." Addison said nothing, but her body relaxed back against the leather cushions. Spike took the opportunity to work her muzzle under Addison's hand, blatantly seeking affection.

"Of course that leaves the younger Doctor Tidwell without an escort."

The agent opened her mouth to issue a sharp retort, but she stopped as the memory of Skyler in Israel assaulted her. In her mind's eye she saw Skyler suturing her after she was wounded, Skyler's wide eyes when she saw her body in the makeshift shower and Skyler responding to her kiss in front of Brodie. She was reminded of the way Skyler ran into her arms after the explosion, uncaring of who saw them together. She remembered the way Skyler reached to drape Addison's arm around her as they sat side-by-side on the transport home from Israel and how right and contented she felt when the American did that.

"You could be right. Maybe I should attend this time," the agent admitted. "Who do I see about an invitation?"

"Just check with Miss Bakersfield on the way out; she's handling most of the arrangements."

"Right then, if you're done with me I'm leaving for the day. C'mon Spike, let's get out of here and get some fresh air. I'll speak to you tomorrow, Mark."

"Give my regards to Skyler," the general said off-handily.

Addison quirked an eyebrow, "Not before I give her my own," she said as she left the office.

At her desk outside, Antonia Bakersfield looked up and gave her best smile to the agent. "It's good to see you again, Agent Black. And looking so fit." The secretary's gaze ran the length of Addison's body. Another time and Addison might have entered into the sexy banter that usually marked their interaction, but this time she was in a hurry to see Skyler.

"Mark said you would be making arrangements for the gala. Put me down to attend."

"Really?" Antonia asked. "You usually never go to these things.

I think you'll enjoy it though; many of your old friends will be there. Agent Zimmerman just contacted me; he seemed quite anxious to attend.

"Quinton, eh? That's good, I've been wanting to speak to him anyway about that weapons problem we had on Skye," Addison noted. "So, put me down for a party of two, Antonia. "Two?" she asked hopefully.

Addison reached down to pick up the scruffy black dog. "Yes, myself and Miss Skyler Tidwell. See you later, Antonia."

The agent strolled from the office, completely missing the crestfallen look on the secretary's face.

****

At that moment, Skyler and Marlene were seated in two very comfortable wingback chairs in the library in General Blithe's home. They had spent every moment of the previous hectic two days together, the reality only settling in now that they were both safe and unharmed. Skyler was prepared for the talk she knew she needed to have with her mother.

"It's been really busy since you got back," Marlene said as she settled back in the chair. She crossed her legs and waited. She and Skyler were closer than most other mothers and daughters and she knew by the way Skyler tucked one leg under herself as she sat that there was something on her mind. Her unique daughter would tell her when she was ready.

"Yeah, they practically grabbed us off the runway," Skyler agreed. She had been met by representatives from the American Embassy as well as their British counterparts and seen doctors, psychologists, security people, counter terrorism experts and a litany of others all of whom had an interest in the foiling of an international biological threat.

Despite all the people included, not a word had leaked to the press. *It's a world in itself,* Skyler marvelled. *I had no idea it even existed.* She found her quick mind absorbing the experience and enjoying it. As many people as she met, the one person she really wanted to see was nowhere to be found. *Where are you, Addison?* She thought over and over again. The last time she saw the beautiful agent, she was being hustled into an ambulance as Skyler was being pushed into a limousine. Their eyes had met briefly and the American could physically feel the reassurance in the look. Then Addison had winked as she stepped into the vehicle.

Thinking of Addison reminded Skyler why she wanted to speak to her mother in the first place. "Mom, it's been great being here with you and it was so generous of General Blithe to give over his house for our use, but..."

"But you'd like a little more space to yourself now that you know I'm fine," her mother finished for her. "You've always had an independent nature," Marlene said as she smiled at her daughter fondly.

"It's not you, Mom, really it's not. It's just that...well, when I was in Israel...Addison and I..." The woman whose life had been scholarly pursuits now found herself at a loss for words.

"Skyler, are you trying to tell me you have feelings for Agent Black?"

Skyler blushed, but met her mother's gaze directly. "I might, would that be a problem?"

"Not for me, honey, but maybe for you. I'm fine with whoever you want in your life. Don't you think I know there is no rhyme or reason in who attracts us? The human heart is a tough thing to understand and the chemistry between two people is just plain baffling. Look at your Dad and I. I don't think there were two more different people, but I loved him with my whole heart and I know he loved me. How something like that happens is just something we haven't been able to unravel. Frankly, I hope we never do. But Skyler, you aren't in this alone; what does Addison think about it?"

Skyler ran a hand through her blonde locks. "God, I'm not sure. I mean...when we were in Israel, and maybe before that, I felt like we had some kind of connection. She's a wonderful woman, Mom, so much more than she lets people see. She's warm and caring and funny and..."

Marlene raised her hands in mock surrender. "You don't have to convince me, I believe you. I saw the look in her eyes when she told me she was going to bring you back. That is one determined woman. So, you need your own place to explore the possibilities. Am I right?"

"Something like that," Skyler agreed. She rose and walked slowly in front of the large fireplace that was a feature of the room. "I'd like to explore the possibilities, but first I have to locate the elusive Addison Black. I don't know where she is or what's happened to her. I haven't heard a word since we've been back and I'm worried sick. My makeshift patchwork on her wound might have caused problems that I don't even know about!"

"She's fine, Skyler," Marlene said in a soothing tone. "She's with Mark."

Skyler stopped mid-stride. "How do you know?"

It was Marlene's turn to blush. "Well, Mark called earlier while you were still asleep. He mentioned Agent Black would be working with him today. Apparently it's standard procedure following a mission of this kind."

Marlene's blush did not go un-noticed by her daughter. "What exactly has been going on here while I was gone?"

"Wait a minute," Marlene objected in a light-hearted fashion. "We weren't talking about me."

"But we could be," Skyler replied. "So what did the general want?"

The older Tidwell attempted to appear nonchalant. "He just wanted me to know you have an apartment available for your use if you want it. I told him yesterday you might want that. It's something of a 'safe house' he said."

"So you and General Blithe are getting pretty chummy, huh?" Skyler was happy her mother was taking an interest in having a social life again.

"I don't know," Marlene said honestly, "but I know I like him. I like him a great deal and he's asked me to accompany him to a formal affair that Special Operations is hosting."

"Are you going?" Skyler asked.

"I wouldn't miss it for all the tea in...Britain!" They laughed at the easy conversation.

Skyler sat back down and leaned forward, elbows on knees, and addressed her mother. "This is all new to me, Mom, and it scares me a little. Books, classes and the university were my whole world for such a long time that it's hard for me to believe this might actually be happening. I might be...falling in love with someone. It's like I'm just starting to have a life now."

Marlene nodded. "Maybe it's time we both started to live."

Chapter 25

The Sheridan complex was a small yet prestigious residence. It stood less than ten miles from Head Quarters and had become a temporary home for Skyler Tidwell. Only four floors high, its white-brick stature gleamed with the vision of recently constructed architecture. To local city inhabitants it was deemed a must-see landmark with its arched windows, moulded brickwork and domed roof. To Addison, it was an eyesore and if it wasn't for Skyler's presence Addison would have preferred to stay away. Stepping into the building, Addison headed for the stairs.

A young woman standing behind a white, Macintosh style, front desk called out to her. "Can I help you, Miss?"

"No thanks," Addison replied. "I'm here to see Miss Skyler Tidwell; she is staying in flat seven."

"Is she expecting you?"

"Oh, of course," Addison fibbed. She pulled a mobile phone from her jeans pocket. "I just spoke to her. She is waiting on me right now. If you wish you can call through and let her know that Agent Addison Black is here to see her." The agent had an inner feeling her offer would only be taken to determine Addison was who she said she was. With a polite smile Addison ascended the stairs to the third floor of the hotel. She chuckled as she pulled Spike out from underneath her black leather jacket.

"Good girl for not moving, Spiky." Addison wasn't sure whether animals other than resident's pets were allowed into the building. Spiky waggled her stunted tail and struggled to get down. "Hold on midget." When she reached the third floor, Addison placed Spike upon the carpeted ground. "Stay beside me, girl." The tiny mongrel trotted happily beside her mistress.

Stopping when she reached door number seven, Addison looked down at Spike. A fluttering of apprehension flickered in her stomach. Though it had only been five days since she and Skyler parted, Addison wondered how the doctor would react to her appearance. From the outset of their meeting they had been put into a position where they had no choice but to tolerate each other's company and although they had seemed to bond as time passed, Addison wondered what Skyler really thought of her. Yes she seemed to like her; Addison was never usually wrong when reading signals. The trouble was; was their presumably budding friendship all there was to it?

Addison flexed her fingers as she stared at the white door. Its brass number seven shone with obvious tender upkeep. Placing a hand upon the door Addison listened to the soft music coming from inside the flat. Another two day's had passed since the meeting Addison had in Mark Blithe's office. She had delayed her visit with Skyler after hearing the young doctor was to move into a temporary residence of her own and Addison decided to give her some time to settle into the flat.

The music coming from Skyler's flat was unrecognisable, at least to Addison. Although she had a varied taste in tunes and styles, this was something she was unfamiliar with. Feeling a scuffle around her ankles Addison looked down to find Spike standing between her feet, waiting patiently.

"I suppose I should knock, huh girl?" Spike walked around her left foot and stood in between her legs again. "Impatient? Okay." Addison knocked on the door with a rhythmic tap.

From the opposite side of the door Addison heard, "Hold on... I'm coming, let me just..." The door swung open and Skyler Tidwell stood before the agent.

"Addison!" The surprise was clear in Skyler's voice.

"Hi." Addison smiled. "Not expecting me, huh?"

Skyler flushed. "Well no. I wondered what happened to you. How are you?" She looked down at Addison's side.

"Oh, you know, healing. A few black and blue marks... a few stitches... they are annoying more than anything." Addison paused. "How are you?" She had been concerned about how the events in Scotland and Israel had affected Skyler. This was a world the doctor was unused to. A world built around secrecy, and great danger. For Addison she had lived many years with the acts that eventuated through her job. Skyler, although she had travelled, never had to deal with the violent underbelly that existed within the shadows of everyday life.

The doctor shrugged. "I seem to be dealing with things in my dreams. I can't really remember them too well so I guess that's good."

Addison nodded and bit her bottom lip. She rolled up onto her toes and back again, trying to think of something to say. She wasn't prepared to leave so soon. The agent felt there was a certain amount of unfinished business they needed to address. The incessant movement of a stunted tail wagging relentlessly against her ankles diverted her thoughts.

"I'd like to introduce you to a friend."

"Oh?" Skyler looked out past Addison to the hallway.

Addison smiled and pointed to her feet. Looking down, Skyler was instantly taken by the tiny black dog looking up at her earnestly. "Go on then, Spike".

"Oh my goodness," Skyler crouched and exclaimed as the little bundle of fur charged her and dove into her arms. "Aren't you just the cutest little thing I've ever seen?" The doctor scooped Spike up and ruffled her head as she attempted to lap at any available portion of Skyler's flesh. "This is your dog?"

Looking on bemused, Addison could only laugh. "Yes she is... and I have to say, I think she likes you!" The agent smirked. "A little too much by her behaviour. Spiky, stop it," Addison ordered as Spike tried to latch her paws around Skyler's neck. The blonde continued to fuss with the excitable mongrel in her arms. Addison could only look on in amusement. She began to wonder whether Spike actually saw **her** as a 'chick magnet'; she certainly seemed to be enjoying Skyler's attention.

Eventually, Skyler looked back at Addison. She blushed once again. "Will you come in?"

"Sure," Addison replied a little too eagerly.

Skyler stepped to the side, Spike still in her arms, and Addison walked into the flat. The dwelling, to Addison's surprise, was actually smaller than she anticipated. She stepped straight into what was obviously a tastefully decorated living room. The colour schemes were cream and beige and black-framed landscapes adorned the walls. Addison noticed, as she ventured further into the room, that it was actually split in half. To her left was the living room and right, was a kitchenette. A door to the far right led into a blue and white bathroom. Addison assumed the door to the left must have been the bedroom. *Small,* she thought, *but efficient.*

Looking back at Skyler, Addison rolled her eyes. "Alright, Spiky, that's enough. Leave the poor woman alone for crying out loud."

Skyler chuckled and placed Spike back down upon the floor. "I think I would have expected you to have a Rotweiller or some other mean looking dog like that."

"I'm not sure whether that was an insult."

"Insult?"

"Well they do say a dog kind of represents his owner. Are you saying I am more of an ugly mean Rotweiller than a cute little flea bitten mongrel?" Addison was quick to add, "I am kidding about the fleas by the way."

Skyler smiled. She looked around her small flat as a moment of awkwardness settled between them. Even Spike seemed to feel the tension as she sat between the two women; ears swept back as she looked between Addison and Skyler. The doctor was the first to speak.

"So... can I get you a drink?"

"Orange juice?" asked Addison.

Skyler nodded and headed towards the open plan kitchen. "I can do that." She opened a small chest high fridge-freezer. Want anything in the juice? Vodka?"

Addison was ready to decline but changed her mind. The way she was feeling, something strong might be a good idea. "Go on then."

As Skyler began preparing the drinks, Addison looked around for Spike. The tiny canine was suspiciously absent from the spot she had previously been sitting. Narrowing her eyes, Addison looked around. Her search didn't take her too far. Spike sat in the kitchen by Skyler's feet, watching her pour two glasses of juice. The agent gave her dog a reprimanding look and pointed to the floor beside her. Spike delayed her obedience by walking between Skyler's feet and wagging her tail. She looked beseechingly at Addison to Skyler and back to Addison.

Oh it's like that, the agent thought with amusement. Shaking her head Addison shoved her hands into her pockets. Her eyes travelled up Skyler's body. Bare feet led to three quarter length black trousers and a simple white t-shirt. Addison couldn't help but notice there was no bra under the white top. She closed her eyes and swallowed. Warmth spread through her veins and coloured her cheeks.

"Are you okay?"

Addison opened her eyes. "Yeah, just a little warm."

"I know!" Skyler motioned to her bare minimum of clothing. "In the US we have air conditioning. Here in England you have radiators. It's almost zero degrees outside yet in here it's practically tropical." Skyler handed Addison her glass and the agent accepted it with a smile. She placed it upon a kitchen work surface and pulled off her jacket. Placing it on the back of the nearest couch, Addison reclaimed her drink. Again, that awkwardness of silence passed between then. Both women gazed at each other, beginning to feel more than they were able to say.

Addison studied Skyler. She gazed upon subtle differences, which was the young doctor at ease. No longer feeling the stress of their last week, the tension had slipped from her features. There was little doubt to the agent that she found Skyler attractive, but suddenly the phrase 'beautiful' came to mind. Her heart increased its beat.

Finding herself under the obvious scrutiny of Addison's gaze, Skyler blushed. Embarrassed by the warm glow upon her cheeks, she lowered her head and stepped past Addison. "Want to sit?"

"Sure." Addison and Spike followed Skyler to two beige couches. The comfortable two-piece suite stood opposite each other with an oak wood coffee table between them. Addison sat down, facing Skyler. Spike settled by the doctor's feet.

"I was surprised to see you," Skyler commented. "I'm glad you're okay."

Addison brushed off her remark. "Nah... it takes more than a crazy Irish woman to keep me down. I'm fine."

Skyler smiled. "I see you have a new contact in," she said, referring to Addison's brown eyes.

"I keep plenty of stock at home." The agent smiled. Taking a drink she happily swallowed down the strong taste of vodka tainted orange juice and placed her glass upon the table. Still feeling strangely anxious, words eluded Addison. Searching her mind, she recalled her conversation with General Blithe.

"I um... I heard your mum was accompanying Mark Blithe to the Gala this weekend."

"Oh yes, she is." Skyler chuckled. "I think mom is looking forward to it. She called me this morning to ask whether I would help her shop for a new dress."

Nodding silently, Addison appeared thoughtful. "I was wondering... You see... I have to attend this Gala myself and thought maybe you'd consider going with me?" The initial surprise upon Skyler's face forced Addison to think she may have read their situation wrong. Her expression, however, changed. The agent wasn't sure whether she was seeing confusion or intrigue.

"Are you asking me because my moms going?"

With a frown, Addison shook her head. "No... it's more like..."

"A date?" The corner of Skyler's lips quirked in a small grin.

Addison pursed her lips to refrain from smiling herself. "Do you want it to be a date?"

"Is that what you are asking?"

A smiled graced the agent's feature. "It is, yes. If you are willing, I would like you to accompany me."

"Why?" asked Skyler

"Why?"

"Addison?" Skyler placed down her own drink and sat back into the couch. She struggled to find the words she wanted to say for several moments. "What happened between us in Israel, Addison?"

What happened in Israel? That was a question Addison had asked herself many times since. There was no doubt both Skyler and her mission started off as just that... a mission. What changed was something Addison hadn't expected. Yes, Addison would be the first to admit Skyler wasn't the first person she had been attracted to while on assignment. The difference with Skyler was the simple fact that Addison felt a never before experienced bond with the doctor. When thinking of Skyler, every fibre of Addison felt drawn to her. It was a powerful need to hold her happiness in the highest priority. Seeing Skyler smile was like seeing the sunrise on the darkest of days and wondering what it was that made her wax lyrical in such ways perplexed her greatly. Holding Skyler had felt good. It was a feeling that went way beyond physical desire and it was this that caused Addison such consternation. Was this really what she thought it to be?

Sucking her front teeth, Addison rose and walked around the coffee table. Pushing Skyler's glass out of the way she sat down in front of the blonde. The table's solid frame supported Addison's muscular physique easily.

"What happened between us in Israel was..." Addison took Skyler's hands within her own. "It was something I want to explore. I know you feel it too." Taking a chance Addison released Skyler's left hand and placed her own under Skyler's breast, feeling the rapid beat of the blonde's heart. Skyler's breathing increased and she closed her eyes.

"Addison?"

The agent gazed at Skyler. Although her lids were lowered, her flushed skin and the way she bit her lower lip told Addison that Skyler did indeed feel what she was feeling. "Yes?" Addison slid off the table and knelt in front of Skyler.

The blonde opened her eyes when she felt Addison move closer. She instinctively opened her legs wider to allow Addison further room. "What are we doing, Addison?"

Addison repeated Skyler's question under her breath. Making an internal decision, Addison rose to her feet and pulled Skyler up in front of her. "I'm not going to deny there's something between us, Sky. Can you?"

Skyler placed her hands upon Addison's hips. "Not anymore."

"Good because..." Addison moved closer. "I want to..." she cupped Skyler's chin. "I need to try something." Slipping her fingers thought silken blonde hair, Addison pulled Skyler willingly towards her. Their lips connected softly. Addison closed her eyes. The feeling of guarded tension, which had accompanied their last kiss, was no longer present. As such Addison let go of the tight rein she kept on her control and allowed herself to sink into Skyler. The softness of her lips was delightful; the velvety caress of Skyler's tongue wrapped sensually around her own. Addison felt her knees weaken and her heart explode within her chest. Slowly, she pulled away.

Opening her eyes Skyler licked her lips. She had to clear her throat before asking, "Did it work?"

"Did what work?" Addison took a breath to calm her fevered pulse.

"You said you wanted to try something." Skyler moved her hands across Addison's back. She felt taught muscles tremble under her touch.

"Well..." There was little doubt in Addison's mind of what she was feeling or what she wanted. "That depends on one thing."

"Which is?"

"Whether you mirror the need I feel to make love with you right now."

Skyler's mouth fell open as her cheeks flushed. She seemed to momentarily search her mind for something to say. Addison waited for her response, but was pleasantly shocked as Skyler wrapped both hands around her head and pulled her into a devastatingly intense kiss. The agent felt herself being pushed backwards until her back was against the wall. The Berettas Addison kept strapped to her belt dug into her back, but she paid them little heed. Instead she pulled Skyler closer, cupping her behind and holding her body firmly. Their tongues wrapped around each other frantically, almost desperate to taste and feel as much of the other as possible. Addison's eyes closed, her other senses taking over her need for Skyler. The soft sweet scent of her, lavender and musk; her delicate encouraging sounds aroused Addison further.

Taking Addison's hands, Skyler held them above the agent's head. Leaving her lips she peppered wanton kisses down her throat. Moaning, Addison said, "I take it this is a yes?"

In response Skyler took both of Addison's hands with one of her own and began massaging Addison's breast through her forest green button down shirt. The manipulations sent bolts of desire down the agent's body. Addison revelled in the sensations, thrilled by Skyler's bold actions. The events, she knew, affected Skyler as much as herself by the way the blonde ground against her thigh.

Panting heavily, Addison pulled her hands away from Skyler's light grip and took her again in a deep, hot kiss. She started backing her up and in the direction of what she presumed was the bedroom.

"Addison," Skyler whispered between kisses. "It's a real mess in there."

Addison pushed the door open, focussed only upon Skyler. "Like I have eyes for anything but you," she said as they passed through the doorway. Addison kicked it shut with the back of her foot. She spun Skyler around and pinned her against the door. From the opposite side they heard Spike whimper for entrance.

"Should we let her in?" Skyler asked as Addison latched onto her neck and pushed both hands up her t-shirt.

"Are you kidding?" Addison chuckled. She caressed Skyler's back feeling muscles quiver under her touch. "Spiky is a joiner and there are some things I refuse to let her be a part of."

"Good idea." Skyler hissed as Addison's hands swept around to the front of her torso and cupped her breasts. "God…Addison." The agent pulled Skyler's white t-shirt over her head revealing an ample chest. Their lips came together again in a kiss hungry and wanting. Groans of escalating passion filled the air.

Addison looked around long enough to locate Skyler's bed and began moving backwards in its direction. She never released Skyler from their kiss that rose in heat and intensity. Stepping over discarded clothing that lay strewn upon the floor, Addison felt the back of her legs hit the unmade bed. She stopped and spun Skyler around.

"God I want you." Soft lips attached to Skyler's neck. Addison sucked gently.

Panting, Skyler held Addison close. "I'm yours." With a grown she pulled Addison's lips back to her own and turned, pushing her onto the bed. Lips attached and tongues entwined. They crawled up the bed to jumbled pillows. Passion firing her veins, Skyler lowered her hands to Addison's shirt. With a strong tug she pulled the buttons apart, ripping the forest green garment open. Addison gasped as her black satin bra was pushed up and her breasts were encased in searching hands and devouring lips. The solider writhed helplessly, Skyler's attention sending a pulsing pressure to her centre.

"Skyler," she gasped.

The blonde doctor looked up, breathing heavily. Addison cupped her cheeks, pulling her down for a deep kiss. When their lips connected Addison bucked, flipping Skyler over, fighting once again for the control they had been battling for from the moment they connected. Without breaking the kiss, Addison raised enough to reach her belt and unhooked its buckle. She released the pistols from her rear and dropped them carefully onto the floor. Rising to a sitting position she pulled the belt from her jeans and let the ripped shirt and bra fall from her shoulders. As Skyler's eyes connected with Addison's both women froze.

Addison's fevered breathing calmed slowly. She sat straight and pulled Skyler up in front of her. A moment of tranquillity and acknowledgement formed around both women. The air crackled between them as two hearts formed an invisible bond. Skyler reached out and softly caressed the soldier's cheek. Addison trailed the tips of her fingers over Skyler's lips. The almost urgent need that had engulfed them upon their initial kiss suddenly melted away and a deeper connection started to blossom.

Slowly and with sweet anticipation, Addison kissed Skyler. Their lips fluttered delicately over each other before opening to enhance the connection. Softly, Addison lowered Skyler back onto her bed. She allowed half her weight to rest upon the doctor and moaned as warm flesh and aroused breasts made contact. Skyler grazed blunt nails over her back and pleasant quivers assaulted her body.

"Addison," Skyler whispered.

The soldier's tongue licked a languid trail down Skyler's neck. "Hmm?"

Skyler writhed and groaned as Addison's mouth captured her nipple. The sensations caused her centre to pulse and desire to seep from her core. She couldn't speak until Addison refocused her attentions to the valley of her breasts. "Please tell me this isn't just about sex."

Shaking her head, Addison rose back up to face Skyler. "No... this is more... much more than even I have ever..." Without finishing her words Addison kissed Skyler again. She felt the blonde's hands unbutton her jeans and slip down her waist. Addison moved down Skyler's torso once again, past her breasts and on to the waist.

Skyler nodded. "Please... don't stop now."

With a light nod of her head, Addison unsnapped the button and lowered Skyler's zipper. She slipped her fingers into the waistband and began pulling Skyler's trousers down. "Are you okay?" she asked looking up at her soon to be lover's thighs, noticing she had been wearing no underwear at all. The knowledge caused a smile to quirk her lips and liquid anticipation to seep in a southerly direction. As the trousers slipped from her feet, Addison rose, standing beside the bed. Keeping her eyes linked with Skyler she lowered her jeans and thong underwear. Once both were fully naked, Addison descended upon Skyler.

They kissed again, unable to get enough of the sensual softness their explorations produced. Addison pushed her tongue further into Skyler's mouth, entwining with the blonde's in a silent quest for more. Hands moved effortlessly over bared flesh, searing paths of mounting desire. The temperature inside the room rose. The air was heavy with the scent of arousal and groans of desire. Addison moved her hips in a rhythm Skyler matched in pace and intensity. Thighs slipped between each other, the evidence of their passion appeared slick against hot flesh.

Addison broke the kiss. "God you feel so good," she moaned.

Skyler moaned as her hands encased Addison's breasts. "I can't get enough of you." Lifting her head she sucked one of Addison's nipples into her mouth. Addison cried out. Her clitoris was bombarded with stimuli and she ground harder against Skyler's thigh.

"God, Sky." Addison panted uncontrollably. "Don't stop... fuck don't stop." Her body trembled as the sensations rose within her. Addison's moans grew louder. She wasn't expecting such a quick release, but there was nothing stopping the inevitable.

"Skyler..." Addison's movements grew more intense. "I'm gonna come."

"Ugh!" Skyler sucked harder. "Yes," she mumbled around Addison's breast. The blonde pressed harder into Addison.

Addison writhed as her body reached its peak. "Ugh... Skyler... Yes." Her eyes squeezed shut tight as crests of explosive pleasure soared through her body. Addison shook, her back arched and her centre throbbed as she milked her released with a powerful need. Sweat beaded over her forehead and slipped down her brow. Skyler's name fell from her lips again and again.

Slowly the spasms calmed and so did Addison. Still holding herself upon her arms, she opened her eyes. Addison looked down at Skyler. Unexpectedly an errant tear fell from each eye.

"Hey..." Skyler whispered, wiping a finger under Addison's eyes. "What is it?"

Addison shook her head.

"No... come on."

Without answering, Addison lowered herself back down on top of Skyler and initiated a deep kiss. Skyler responded helplessly. She held onto Addison as the agent rolled over until Skyler was above her. Addison smoothed her hands down Skyler's back and cupped her behind. Releasing Skyler's lips she started to push the blonde up her body. Sky complied willingly until she realised what Addison intended.

"Addison, wait."

The agent stopped.

"This is something I've never done before."

Addison appeared confused. "You mean...?"

"No." Skyler smiled. "I just mean this... what you're intending."

Addison smiled. "Trust me," she said softly.

Licking her lips, Skyler nodded. With Addison's soft encouragement Skyler moved up her body to straddle her face.

Addison looked up to the swollen desire above her. The vision alone caused her stomach to clench with need. "Oh God," she groaned and ran a hand up either side of Skyler's thighs. Slowly, she lowered engorged lips to her mouth.

"Oh...OH!" Skyler hissed as she felt Addison's tongue sink into her. She felt the oral muscle glide along her centre before entering her thickly. "Yes... God!" Skyler leaned back and held on to Addison's thighs. She moved against the agent's mouth, tongue and lips.

"Addison, that feels so... so good."

Addison could only groan, thoroughly captured by the sights, sounds and taste of Skyler. She held onto the blonde's hips, coaxing and aiding her movements. Skyler moved slowly back and forth over Addison's mouth, enraptured by the blissful sensations. Liquid desire coated the soldier's tongue. Addison's own desire rose again.

Feeling her passion increase, Skyler adjusted her position and held onto the headboard behind Addison. Her grip tightened as Addison's focus turned to her tight bundle of nerves and her lips wrapped around it with a wonderful sensation of suction.

"Oh yes." Skyler ceased all movements, her entire world, for that one moment, focussed solely upon Addison's mouth and the wonderful sensations she was causing through her body. Her eyes fell shut as her head tipped back. Addison's hands glided up to her breasts. They manipulated and caressed her nipples to taught, ridged points then one hand slid back down her torso.

"Addison, please." Skyler resumed her grinding. She moved her clit back and forth over Addison's tongue. "Let me feel you. I need you inside me."

The agent could only comply and using two fingers she sunk inside Skyler.

287

"Oh... oh, Addison!" Skyler gasped as she began to ride Addison's fingers.

The soldier instantly began to detect a change as Skyler's arousal engulfed her fingers and clamped around them. Addison sucked harder, moving to the rhythm of Skyler's thrusts.

"Addison... that's it... just like... oh God...Addison!" Skyler screamed as her body yielded to the intense release that engulfed her body in a tumbling, shuddering climax. She groaned long and loud under the relentless force of Addison's manipulations. The agent feasted greedily, unable to get enough of Skyler. Strong pulsations gripped her fingers and throbbed around them.

Slowly, as the tremors lessened, Skyler released the headboard. Her head fell limply against the wall.

Addison caressed Skyler's back. She waited a moment before saying, "Sky?"

"Hmm?"

"You okay?"

"Hmm."

"Is that a yes?"

"Hmm."

With a smile, Addison coaxed Skyler down to lie upon the bed. She rolled onto her side and faced the doctor. Blonde hair lay in a haphazard tussle around her head and Addison ran her fingers through the golden locks, neatening the kinks.

"Will you tell me now?"

"Tell you what?" Addison asked evasively.

"Tell me why the tears."

Addison looked away momentarily and studied the ceiling for several seconds before turning back to Skyler. Noting the sincerity in her eyes, Addison spoke. "For the first time in... well, in ever... this didn't feel like it was an act of giving or taking... it was sharing... We were..."

"Making love," Skyler finished for her.

"Making love," Addison repeated. "Truly." Not sure of what else to say she kissed Skyler passionately. For endless moments they stayed locked in a loving embrace. It was Addison who pulled away first. "God, I don't want this to end."

Skyler smiled and pushed an errant lock of hair from Addison's eyes. "I'm not going anywhere."

Returning Skyler's smile, Addison winked. "Well that's good then."

"Oh, and by the way... yes, I would love to attend the Gala with you."

Addison smiled wider. Pulling the blonde close they kissed and formed a lasting connection that continued long into the night.

Chapter 26

General Blithe walked into his outer office where Antonia Bakersfield was busy on the phone.

"Yes, that's correct. Six dozen. You'll have them delivered to the Windsor Legacy no later than five on Saturday next? Very good… yes, thank you." She hung up and regarded the general.

"This gala is even more difficult to set up than the last one; the extra security for the possible attendance of the Prime Minister, the international flavor of the guests and the secrecy surrounding it all. It's a massive headache. Coordinating an attack while I was in the Royal Marines wasn't as much of a logistical nightmare."

"Now, Miss Bakersfield, you're doing a splendid job," Mark complimented. "I'm glad Quinton Zimmerman volunteered to help you finalize the arrangements though."

"He's been an enormous help, General. He's taken on the whole job of working with the hotel people on the set-up and entertainment. He's even arranged for a podium for the presentation of Addison Black's commendation," Antonia replied with relief. "It's taken such a load off me; all I had to deal with was the caterers, florists and…"

"Finding time to arrange for a certain general's formal uniform and the rest of the things to be made presentable? I do thank you for that, Antonia. You took on the extra work without complaint."

"It was no bother, General, I was happy to do it. I realize how special you wish this particular evening to be. I can see quite the attachment forming between you and Professor Tidwell."

Mark reddened slightly as he thought of Marlene. The previous night they had attended a play in the West End and enjoyed a late supper afterward. He had taken her home, to his home, at the end of the evening and it felt just right escorting her inside his house. It was almost as if she belonged there. The sweet kiss they had shared at the door of the guest room had been their first together, but Mark was under the distinct impression that both of them wished it to be the first of many. Now, in just two days he would have her on his arm as they attended a very formal, very public gala. Well, as public as a Special Operations gala could be. To have her there would be making a statement for everyone to see. You didn't bring a casual date to this type of affair.

"Yes, well, I know I won't be the only one escorting a member of that family."

Antonia covered her look of disappointment and asked in a professional tone. "Is there anything I can assist Agent Black with?"

"Nothing I can think of, Antonia. I spoke to her last night and asked if she needed anything and she replied in the negative. I have given her the remainder of the week off to let her injuries finish healing, but you know Black. She continues to go on working. She mentioned she was in the middle of a serious de-briefing when I called. That late in the day! No one is more dedicated to her job than Addison," he marveled.

"No, she has quite the work ethic," she replied, her tone shaded just a bit with sarcasm.

The general missed the inflection, but dropped three reports on Miss Bakersfield's desk.

"I hate to rush you on these, but I will need them by the end of the day for my early morning meeting," he said apologetically.

"It's no problem, General. It will be a pleasure to get back to some real work for a change."

Mark chuckled as he thanked her and headed back to his office, wondering if he had time to give Marlene a quick call before his next meeting.

****

Marlene Tidwell was at that moment asking her daughter her opinion about a dress to wear to the gala. It was approximately the fortieth time Marlene had done so in the last two hours and Skyler was growing weary of the hunt for the "perfect dress."

"Mom, look, why are you so worried? It's one party. What you wear won't make that big an impression on Mark Blithe's friends and colleagues."

Marlene paused in the middle of slipping the ivory sheath over

292

her head in order to return it to the saleswoman. "Make no mistake here, Skyler. I couldn't be less interested in what Mark's friends think, but I would like to make a certain general himself lose his breath and I only have two days left to find the dress to do it."

Skyler had to laugh as Marlene batted her eyelashes coquettishly. "I didn't realize you had stopped shopping for a dress and were just looking for a mantrap! Why didn't you say so in the first place? You could have made this so simple."

Marlene looked at her daughter in confusion. "Why simple?"

"Okay," Skyler began as she moved toward an enormous rack of dresses. "Harrod's has everything, right?" Marlene nodded. "So we know your dress is here somewhere. Let's narrow down the field. What is he wearing?"

"I think he said something about a formal uniform complete with sash and medals. He's not happy about it, but that is standard supposedly." He showed me a picture of himself attending an international conference and he is very handsome in it."

"A sash?" inquired Skyler. "What color sash?"

"Red. Why?" Marlene questioned in return.

"Because if you want every other female there to know that he is spoken for that evening, you get a dress color to match his sash. Now let me see." She moved to the area containing her mother's size and began moving hanger after hanger of red dresses past herself on the rack. "Nope, nope, too much material, whoa...too little material, nope..." Skyler sputtered to a stop mid-dismissal and lifted a floor length red evening gown from the rack. The lines were simple, tasteful and sexy. There was a small river of red sequins that ran the length of the dress from left shoulder to the floor in what appeared to be a gently descending waterfall. They sparkled as they moved and caught the light and the whole effect was sensual and elegant.

"That's it," Skyler breathed as she pictured her mother in the lovely attire. "Go ahead and try it on for any alterations, but **that** is the dress."

Marlene nodded. "Mark Blithe, with the help of this dress, and by the end of the evening, I do believe I'm going to have my way with you."

Skyler grimaced. "Mom! Too much information! I did not just hear that. Thanks for the visual of my mom being a sexual creature. I'm going to have to wash my brain out now!"

Marlene only laughed as she slipped the dress on. Maybe an inch needed to come off the hem, but otherwise it fit perfectly.

Marlene arranged for the dress to be delivered after the

alterations had been completed. She turned to her daughter. "Want to pick out something for you while we're here? I'm fairly certain you didn't pack a formal gown in anticipation of the excavation of Roman ruins in England."

"You're right about that," Skyler agreed, "But I don't need to pick something out. When I told Addison I didn't have anything with me, she insisted on making all the arrangements. I guess I know I can trust her by now so I'll just hope her good taste in women extends to good taste in clothes."

She paid for the purchase and hooked Skyler's arm in hers as they walked to the elevators. "Want to stop for some tea and a pastry? My treat for helping me."

"Sure," Skyler replied, "I've got nothing to do for the rest of the afternoon. Addison said she had some things that had to be taken care of today and needed some time to do that." They would still have the evening together.

Mother and daughter walked out of Harrod's and were immediately assisted in hailing a cab. Marlene gave the address of a teashop near Mark Blithe's house and they settled back for the short ride as the cab pulled into the London traffic.

As the black cab bearing Skyler and Marlene pulled away from the curb, another cab pulled in to the suddenly vacated space. Addison Black emerged and tossed a couple of notes at the driver.

"Thanks, mate," she said amiably as she looked up at the impressive store. Special Operative 2 was on a mission and like all other missions, she was certain this one would be completed swiftly and successfully. If she didn't have to take somebody down as she was doing it, so much the better. For just a moment she had a brief flash of insecurity, but it passed quickly and the steely resolve was back. Lifting her head and narrowing her eyes, she headed into the store.

****

One hour later, Addison Black was suffering from a bad case of shattered ego. The seeming morass of shoppers and the vision of the dozens of dresses she had seen were combining to make her head spin. She needed to stop the madness. Using her expert training, she spotted the weak one in the herd of salespeople and culled her out.

"Trina," Addison began smoothly, reading the older woman's name badge. "I am an official in the government and I require a bit of your time. You can do your country a great service here today or you can let the reputation of our beloved island suffer at the hands of foreigners."

The saleswoman bristled and leaned forward, darting her eyes to the left and right. "Bloody foreigners," she whispered before she stood straight again and asked, "How may I be of service?"

Addison lowered her voice and said, "I need a dress." The words were whispered in a manner that let the saleswoman know that she was being called upon to perform no less than her ancestors on the beaches of Normandy had.

"England expects every Harrod's saleswoman to do her duty," Trina said. "Come with me."

Another half hour later, Addison was pleased with the choice she had made. The gown was absolutely stunning. Trina was pleased that the government representative was happy with her work. Addison reached out and shook Trina's hand formally.

"Never has one agent owed so much to so few." Trina smiled in pride at the words.

"One last thing, Trina. Do you think I could get some fabric to match this dress?"

Trina considered the question. "I might have some that would match back in the storeroom. How much would you need?"

Addison calculated in her mind. "Three feet would do. I need a sash."

****

Marlene Tidwell had chosen a quaint teashop less than a ten-minute walk from the General's home. The lure of freshly baked pastries and aromatic teas had tempted her the past two times she had walked by the establishment. It was traditional, typically British and the kind of place visitors to the Isle would find hard to resist.

Skyler and her mother stepped up into the teashop. Though it was winter, local city inhabitants still used the shop as a meeting place to gossip with friends and neighbours. Already inside were two elderly women, wearing thick winter coats and discussing a friend's recent stay in hospital. The larger of the two, a woman with short, curly and blue rinsed hair had a small puppy upon her lap. She continuously stroked the chocolate brown canine as she and her friend conversed. Though there were only five tables in the shop, three were still empty. Skyler chose the table beside the window. Mother and daughter sat down, store bought purchases placed on the floor beside the window ledge.

From a small doorway, shrouded by a hanging beaded partition, a young woman emerged. Her mousy brown hair was held back in a tight bun and she wore a long white apron with lace edging. Noting two new customers she took her pad and pencil from a small waist high pocket and approached Skyler and her mother.

"Hello, darlings, what can I get you?"

"A pot of afternoon tea," Marlene replied. "I would also like a large fruit scone with clotted cream and strawberry jelly... I mean jam." Marlene looked to her daughter. "Skyler?"

Not quite knowing what to expect, but knowing she and her mother's tastes were similar, Skyler asked for the same. "But I'll have raspberry jam please."

"I'll be two ticks." The young woman ventured off with their order.

Left on their own Skyler traced her fingertip over the lacy design of the tablecloth and looked up at her mother. "Mom?"

Marlene looked away from her perusal of a table menu. "Hmm?"

"I want to ask you about Project Gemini."

"What is it?" Marlene placed down the menu.

Skyler paused before answering. She wasn't quite sure how she intended to deal with the issues she felt she had about her mother's project, after everything that had recently taken place. "Are you going to continue your work on Project Gemini?"

Marlene appeared confused by her daughter's question. "Of course I am, Skyler. We can't stop the tests we're doing. Do you know how close I was to creating a new drug for cancer patients? I have to finish this."

"But what about the Hyde application? I know you are contracted to work on both for the government, Mom. If you continue with this work, won't you still be in danger from terrorist organisations wanting Gemini?" Skyler had spent most of her early morning pondering over these thoughts and made a mental decision to talk about this to Marlene. Her concerns only deepened as time passed. Although Addison said General Blithe had begun an internal investigation into the possible traitor within M.I.5, Special Operations, while that person was still on the loose, Project Gemini was not safe and neither was Marlene or Skyler. "Mark has assured me security on the project has increased threefold. My team at this moment is being moved to a secured laboratory at Mindenhall RAF base." Marlene moved forward in her chair, crossing her arms upon the table. "Every precaution necessary to protect the sensitivity of Project Gemini is being taken."

"It still scares me, Mom."

"I know, Skyler, but..." Marlene paused as their waitress brought a tray containing the tea and scones. After placing down their order

296

Skyler and her mother were left alone. Marlene continued speaking. "I know you're scared, but we are doing all we can. I can't just pull the plug on **my** project. The possibilities are endless."

Picking up the white china teapot their waitress had provided, Skyler poured her and her mother a cup of tea. Her thoughts mulled over Marlene's words. She didn't want to argue with her, but Skyler knew she wouldn't feel content until the mysterious 'Dr. Kleein' was discovered.

"Let's just hope everything gets straightened out soon then."

"Yes." Marlene took a sip of her tea. "I have faith in Mark."

Skyler grinned. "Oh, I'm sure you do, Mom."

"Skyler Tidwell, what exactly are you implying?"

The blonde held up her hands. "Nothing... please believe me, there are some topics I can do without getting a visual on."

"And I shouldn't take offence by that because?"

"You're my mom!"

"Okay... I can accept that. I had a mother myself too." Taking a bite out of her scone, Marlene thought back to that morning when she had picked her daughter up to go shopping. "So, tell me more about how things are going with you and Addison."

****

Back at Special Operations HQ, Addison Black poked her head around the door to General Blithe's outer office. Sitting at her desk was Antonia Bakersfield, diligently working her way through a computerised document. She looked up at Addison's voice.

"Afternoon."

"Addison!" Antonia looked past Addison to the garment bag she held over her shoulder. "Been shopping?"

"Just a couple of things." Addison held up a dark green shopping bag containing her sash. "Reminded me how much I hate it though."

"I could have told you that... how many times have I had to do it for you!"

"Good point." Pulling the garment bag from over her shoulder, Addison draped it over her left arm. "The General in there?"

Miss Bakersfield rose from her desk. "No, he went down to Samuel's lab. He's testing a new project. I was going down there myself if you fancy a butchers?"

Addison shook her head. "You've spent way too long in the capitol, Miss Bakersfield. The first time I find you eating jellied eels I'm calling for help."

Laughing, Antonia shut down her computer and approached Addison. The agent held out her free arm and Antonia hooked hers through Addison's.

"Escort you to Sam's lab, Miss?"

"Thank you, kind ma'am." Antonia smiled as she and Addison made their way towards Samuel's laboratory.

Within the close confines of the elevator, Antonia lifted the corner of Addison's garment bag. "A dress? I thought you were wearing dress uniform?"

"I am. This is for Skyler Tidwell."

"Oh, I see."

The lift doors slid open and both women stepped out into the corridor towards Samuel's testing facility. Smaller rooms to the left and right of them were empty. Addison realised it was likely all scientists were in with Samuel and the General waiting to witness the unveiling of Samuel's new gadget. Of course, Addison was just as interest and sped up her gait to Samuel's lab. She opened the door allowing Antonia to enter first.

"Ma'am."

Antonia smiled as she tucked a lock of long dark hair behind her ear. "Thank you."

They walked into the laboratory, instantly finding Samuel's new source of attraction. Addison draped her garment bag over a nearby chair and placed the second bag on its seat. Addison approached the object, that although she considered visually stunning, she wondered what exactly it was. A crowd of men and women gathered around the attraction, General Blithe stood beside Samuel.

"Okay... you've got me," Addison called out. "What on earth is it?" She pointed to what she presumed was a helicopter only it held no rotating blades above and its whole shape appeared similar to that of a shark. *Or possibly a whale,* Addison thought. It was black, sleek and the windows were tinted dark and reflective.

"This is the first prototype," Samuel answered. He jotted notes onto a clipboard.

"Of?"

"A new type of transportation. It may take a few years before it can be used in the field, but this is the first working model."

Addison stepped closer. Tilting her head she bent her knees slightly and looked underneath the machine. What she found were intricately constructed panels surrounding four circular funnels. They appeared no more than two inches thick and the approximate diameter of each was that of a dinner plate. The agent frowned.

"What's it called?"

"I'm calling her 'The Air Shark, Grava-Force PT1'."

"Hmm... concise," Addison commented. "And how does it work?"

"Dr. Perkins was just about to explain," Mark Blithe said.

Addison held up a hand. "Sorry." She mimed locking her lips together and handed the invisible key to Miss Bakersfield. The secretary took it and placed the non-existent object down into her cleavage.

"You know where it is when you want it."

Addison winked and nodded in amusement. She turned back to look at Samuel when an approaching figure to her right caught her attention. Addison looked to see Quinton Zimmerman stand by her.

"What are you...?"

"Don't want to miss the show now do I."

Addison rolled her eyes. "That reminds me. I have a bone to pick with you."

"Hey... if it's about the Spas, it was one of those freak happenings."

"Yeah, freaky... I could have..."

"Shhh," Quinton said, cutting her off. "Have to be quiet, remember?"

With Antonia to her left, Quinton to her right and Blithe and Samuel in front of her, Addison silenced in order to listen to Perkins' presentation.

"Well guys and gals," Samuel began. "As I said I call this 'The Air Shark, Grava-Force PT1'. One day soon I hope it will replace the military's current use of the helicopter. It works by way of refracting the earths natural magnetic core to lift it above the ground. A super silent engine pushes Air Shark across the sky at a current speed of Mach One. At the moment she runs on the usual jet engine fuel, but I am designing a new type of engine unlike anything ever invented before." Samuel looked to General Blithe as though seeking permission to say more about that.

"What kind of engine?" Quinton asked.

Blithe nodded in affirmation, but something in the eye contact between Blithe and Perkins captured Addison's curiosity.

"Well," Samuel began. "I'm working on an engine that runs on a particular gas."

"What form of gas?" Antonia enquired.

"That is the amazing part." Samuel's expression grew with excitement. "It will be initially powered by solar energy; then the use

299

of a small capsule of the gas to start it up. This then turns to kinetic energy to establish the process of taking carbon dioxide out of the air and using that as a fuel. This pushes the machine through the atmosphere and the exhaust fumes released are nothing more than oxygen."

"That's amazing," said Giles Philips, a Special operation's agent.

"Incredible," said another.

Addison looked to Zimmerman who arched his eyebrows at her before asking Samuel, "And you have started tests on this?"

"It's in process."

The congregated group of scientists and agents seemed to hang on every word Samuel said. Addison's eyes scanned each face, suspecting that one of them was possibly their traitor and Agnes Brodie's superior in the plot to steal Project Gemini. Turning her eyes to the General, Addison stepped forward and stood behind him.

"In ten minutes I shall be commencing the first low level test flight of Air Shark." Samuel grinned as his colleagues began clapping.

Addison tapped General Blithe upon the shoulder. "A word?"

Mark turned to the agent. "Of course, Addison." Side by side General and Captain stepped away from the crowd. Once an adequate distance away, Addison stopped. "What is it?" Mark asked.

"That's what I'm wondering." Addison replied. "An engine that runs on solar power, a gas capsule, kinetic energy and a conversion process of carbon dioxide to oxygen? What's that all about? Is this even real?"

"It's parts of several ideas Samuel came to me with last month. All pretty much at the beginning drawing board stage but…"

"But you hope to feed false information to our traitor to see if this data is used for personal gain or power play."

"Although I'm conducting my own investigation, yes. Samuel came to me with the idea. It certainly won't do any harm."

"Yeah." Addison looked back to where Samuel, Quinton and Antonia stood off to one side conversing. "And what if Sam's the traitor?"

"I've not ignored that possibility." Mark pushed his hands into his pockets. "But I'm exploring every avenue possible. Right now everybody's a suspect. Even one percent of me suspects you, Addison."

The agent shrugged. "Natural caution. I'd say one percent of me suspects you too. As I know damn good and well it isn't myself, I feel like I should be offended you do suspect me… but I'm not. Everybody's a suspect." Addison looked back over at the groups of people. She scanned each one in turn until finishing with Sam, Quinton and Miss Bakersfield. "I know it isn't me and I only have a one percent suspicion it's you or even Skyler Tidwell. Apart from that, I suspect everybody. I have to."

"What about Marlene?" The General asked.

"I'm sorry, Mark, but to me she is a suspect too. What better way to regain control of her project than to take it underground? I mean...did Brodie really know whom she was working for? Marlene disappeared from our secure lodgings just a little too easily." Addison turned from watching her friends back to Mark. "However, saying that, I still believe the traitor is here with us right now."

Mark nodded as they both looked back at the conversing scientists and agents. "So do I, Addison. So do I."

M J Walker and Val Brown

Chapter 27

Just a short time now Dr. Kleein thought as the gloved fingers of the villain gently returned the sealed vial to its padded and secured nest. *Getting the vial into the gala will be no problem for someone as smart as I am.* Thoughts turned to how easy it had been to obtain the Ricin that had been inserted into the tuberculosis mycobacterium. *The right contacts with the right funding and you can get anything, even the world's deadliest poison.*

Although not outwardly affluent, "Dr. Kleein" had combined a substantial inheritance with inside information and currently had amassed an impressive portfolio of stocks, bonds, real estate in many countries and cash. The 'doctor's' real identity might be unknown, but the influence of the Kleein name was not.

Tonight the Hyde application of Project Gemini comes into full flower. Then I will be in a position to command the world's attention and destroy Addison Black and everything she holds dear. With that, the gloves were removed and preparations for the Special Operation's gala begun.

****

Addison Black was removing her dress uniform from the protective plastic bag it had inhabited for the past few months. She remembered wearing it to Jimmy Easton's funeral, a far different occasion than this evening. *I got my revenge for you, Jimmy. Agnes Brodie received exactly what she deserved and tonight I drink to her demise and your memory. No more bad memories though, Jimmy, because tonight I intend on making new memories. Very good memories with Skyler.*

Addison lifted the green sash she would wear across the uniform, the decoration changing the sombre nature of the garment to a celebratory one.

Yes, the good memories start tonight with her.

****

Skyler closed the door after generously tipping the delivery boy. The large box, clearly from Harrod's, was wrapped in the distinctive green color. She knew it was from Addison as the messenger had been fully screened and cleared by Security downstairs. Taking the large box to the kitchen table, she opened it to find a small white card. In a bold script it read,

This frock is very humble, but, like Cinderella, it would be transformed if you were to don it for the gala. Please wear it, Skyler.
Yours, Addison

Skyler spread the tissue paper to reveal a stunning emerald green gown with sophisticated lines and a daring neckline. *Humble frock, my backside!* Skyler knew high fashion when she saw it and the gown she held was as far from humble as caviar was from turnips. She brought the gown up in front of her, catching her reflection in the mirror situated on the wall across the room. Her breath caught at the sheer beauty of the garment.

Oh Addison, it's spectacular she thought. *You are undoubtedly the most generous, most wonderful and most romantic person I've ever met. This dress is even going to outshine the one Mom picked out. I just love it* she admitted to herself as she twirled the gown around the living room. *I love the color... I love...* The thought caused Skyler to stop her dance and look at herself in the mirror again.

****

Marlene was smoothing a fragrant cream into her skin after stepping from a rose scented bath mere minutes before. She hoped Mark Blithe's would replace her hands later and a trail of gooseflesh lifted in the wake of her fingers.

The professor decided this special night was going to be even more special. Tonight she would go with her feelings and invite Mark into her bed and her heart. She had every indication and hope that he would accept. They had grown ever closer and she could no longer deny the powerful pull of the very attractive man.

She swallowed nervously with the revelation that she was on a path she had not taken in a very long time. She resumed applying the cream to her skin as she glanced over to the red dress she would be wearing to the gala. *I hope you recognize the significance of the sash tonight, Mark, because I'm staking my claim on you. I think I'm about to give everyone the surprise of their lives at the gala.*

****

Mark Blithe fumbled with the decorations on his black jacket, wishing for at least the tenth time that battle ribbons and medals weren't part of the dress uniform. Securing the last of them, he surveyed his work. *Not bad for an old bachelor soldier* he mused. He had never enjoyed official functions, but this time he looked forward to it with anticipation. He allowed himself the luxury of thinking about the ball ahead and pictured the scene of his triumph.

As he began to dress for the occasion, he frowned. Addison's comments earlier in the week about the traitor were disturbing. She was nearing the truth, he was certain and he had his suspicion that he was not immune to her questions. He would need to do something to turn her attention elsewhere, someplace more productive. *The search for the traitor needs to be directed, and directed by me* he thought. *Maybe Miss Bakersfield can be of some assistance.*

****

Antonia Bakersfield was leaning forward across her vanity table making little kissing motions with her lips and adjusting her lipstick according to the look she saw in the mirror.

Got to look my best tonight she thought as she slipped on her earrings. They complimented her choice of black satin gown perfectly. *I'm glad I decided not to wear my uniform. I'm sure Addison will give me much more notice in this.*

A large orange tabby cat leaped up onto the vanity and watched her mistress spritz perfume behind each ear, along her neck and into her cleavage. Antonia turned her head from side to side with an appraising look. *Addison Black, you're in for a few surprises tonight.* She rose from the vanity table and left her bedroom, picking up her evening bag on the way. Dropping in a few necessities, she checked her watch. Her escort for the evening, Quinton Zimmerman, was due to arrive any minute

****

In one of London's innumerable black cabs, Quinton Zimmerman settled comfortably into the back seat. He was relaxed and confident. His target was in sight and he wouldn't let the night end without completing his mission. He gave an amused chuckle, earning him a glance from the driver in the rear view mirror.

Quinton glanced at the man and winked. *Too bad you aren't in my shoes tonight, mate,* he thought. *There will be a few raised eyebrows when I make my move.*

As the streets slowly passed he reviewed the past several days. He had been impressed with the presentation he had witnessed regarding the new transportation device. He thought the invention could potentially be worth millions or even billions of pounds. It was a sum of money he wouldn't mind having at his disposal. Maybe Special Operations didn't know what a genius they had in Samuel Perkins, but Quinton did.

****

Samuel Perkins was extremely annoyed. Whether it was at Addison Black or her infernal tiny black menace, Spike, he wasn't sure. Once again Addison had expected him to baby-sit that spawn from hell, that terror with tiny teeth, the demon in a dog's body. Well, I am a respected scientist and government agent and it's time everybody realized that. It's way past time.

Tonight Samuel had shed his role of Special Ops' resident nerd and was resplendent in his uniform. Tonight Samuel was going to the gala and he didn't care who wanted their dog watched. Addison had found other accommodations for her mongrel.

You've always underestimated me, Addison. Maybe tonight you'll learn that was a big mistake.

****

Addison had made a big mistake and she realized it the moment Skyler opened the door. The gown she bought that she figured would compliment her lover's look did a lot more than that. The green dress gave an emerald fire to Skyler's eyes and the plunging neckline gave an ample view of the blonde's assets.

Addison swallowed thickly, unable to tear her eyes from Skyler.

If Skyler noticed the stare she said nothing about it. Actually she might not have noticed because she was completing a visual survey of her escort at the same time. It was Addison who first snapped back to the realization that they were staring at each other through an open doorway.

"You look stunning, Skyler, absolutely beautiful." The tone of the agent's voice left no room for doubt that she was speaking her very thoughts. Skyler blushed, both pleased and a little embarrassed at the compliments.

"I don't know if you can call a soldier beautiful when she wears her uniform, but if you can, she is."

Addison smiled at the slightly awkward comment.

"Your carriage to the ball awaits, Madam," the agent said gallantly as she offered her arm to Skyler. It was as the arm was extended toward her that she noticed the sash slashing diagonally across Addison's chest.

Skyler stopped, as she was just about to step out the door.

"Your sash..." she said and then faltered as she remembered the conversation with her mother a few days before.

Addison looked down at the sash then back at Skyler.

"Yeah, quite the coincidence the dress and sash being the same color. It's almost like it was planned." The American nearly believed Addison's innocent expression until the agent winked at her.

The romantic gesture touched Skyler deeply for a reason she couldn't name and she moved forward a few steps to plant a light kiss directly on Addison's lips. The Brit raised her eyebrows, but was obviously pleased by Skyler's response.

"What was that for?" Addison asked.

Skyler reached back to pull the door shut and slipped her arm through the agent's. "Nothing, just a small preview of the real celebration after the ball."

Addison smiled in surprise as Skyler tugged her down the hall.

****

It was only half an hour's journey to the secure location of the gala. Starting at half past eight, all guests were expected to arrive at least twenty minutes before hand. Addison had left to pick up Skyler with plenty of time to spare. The young doctor had pre-warned her that she needed time to get ready. Addison had simply rolled her eyes neglecting to mention it would probably take her the same amount of time to prepare herself. She had a reputation to maintain after all.

Sitting beside Skyler in the back of their chauffer driven Rover, Addison observed the scenery as their navy car steered its way towards the gala's entrance. Feeling the car begin to slow, Addison turned to Skyler. Once again she acknowledged how stunning the doctor looked. She smiled as Skyler looked at her.

"Are you ready?"

"Well," Skyler pondered the question. "Yes, although I'm still not completely sure what to expect."

Addison's features twisted to an ironic smile. "Ah, you know... your typical military bash. That is unless we do get a couple of posh-knobs attending; then you throw in a bit of pomp and pretentiousness for good measure." Addison looked out through the driver's window to where uniformed and civilian dressed guests were entering a highly guarded building. "There will be a high level of security due to recent eventualities. The P.M. was said to be attending, but I was told that had been cancelled. I've heard no different so far."

"That's a shame," Skyler remarked. "I was looking forward to meeting your uncle Tony."

Addison grinned. "Some other time?"

Skyler nodded as their car pulled up outside the entrance. Addison opened the door. Climbing out of the car she walked around the Rover and opened Skyler's passenger door. "Ma'am."

"Thank you." Skyler slipped effortlessly out of the car and Addison pushed the door closed. With a proud smile the soldier held out her arm and Skyler hooked her own through it. They turned to face the building. It was a relevantly new structure, built in the early sixties and owned by the government. Standing on only two floors its slightly weathered brick structure had been painted a bright white. Addison could tell a fresh coat of paint had been applied within the last fortnight.

Ascending six steps, Addison and Skyler approached an arched entrance. Two soldiers stood either side of the door and just beyond that stood a third soldier holding a list of guest names. Addison took an I.D. wallet from her pocket.

"Captain Black and guest, Skyler Tidwell."

The young officer, although he knew Addison, checked her identification against the guest list. "Welcome to the festivities, Captain. You are some of the last few to arrive."

"Thanks, Miller." Addison led Skyler over to an identification gel pad; it was very much the same as the one that allowed access to her armoury back at home. She pushed her fingertips into the electronic print register and then urged Skyler to do the same. "It's just a log to record the entrance and exit of all guests for the evening."

Skyler pushed her fingers into the device and slid the tips onto its copying pad. It was cool against her skin. She saw a red light move down the screen, recording her prints. "Do you have to do this at all army functions?"

"No," the soldier replied. "Just for M.I.5, Special Operation's functions." They began walking together down the wide, maroon carpeted corridor. "Believe it or not, there are surveillance devices all over Special Ops. They are often a lot harder to locate than you would realise. At the moment we have fingerprint and retinal scans, but General Blithe is waiting on approval for some new inter-monitoring equipment."

To further improve the security, Mark Blithe had begun proceedings to install a new form of security device. Samuel Perkins had recently designed and built a working model. It was a system incorporating voice and implant recognition. Every operational agent within M.I.5 that bore an implant would be monitored, even within headquarters itself.

Stopping in front of a set of wide double doors, decorated with the Regimental Crest carved into old English oak, both women could hear soft music and conversation from within the main ballroom. With a feeling of anticipation, Skyler looked to Addison. The soldier smirked, the right side of her lips quirking upwards.

"Ready for a night to remember?"

"Bring it on," Skyler replied.

Addison nodded as she pushed the doors open onto a night neither of them would ever forget.

****

Almost the size of a soccer pitch, the ballroom was a hive of festivities. Upon a small stage at the front of the room a regimental band played easy listening music. In one corner a disc jockey station had been set up for late night dancing. Before that was a large dance floor on which several groups of people conversed. The remainder of the room was filled with circular tables, each one draped in maroon cloth and set ready for dining. A vase containing a single, fresh rose stood centre display upon each six-seated table.

Like the stereotypical German said to claim their sun-bed with a towel, so Addison knew Mark Blithe would claim his table in a similar way. Remembering his preference for front and centre, Addison scanned the first row of tables. Sure enough she saw the General's large coat draped over the back of a chair. Not more than ten feet away stood the man himself, conversing with Marlene Tidwell and Major Thompson.

"I suppose we're somewhere over there," Addison acknowledged as she began leading Skyler towards her mother and the General. They got less than half way before a tall striking man with dark brown hair and eyes stopped Addison. Flecks of grey peppered his temple, making him appear older than his years.

He held out his hand to Addison. "Congratulations on the Israel Operation, Black. I heard you completed your mission to destroy Agnes Brodie once and for all. Wish I could have been there to see that."

Addison shook his hand. "Thanks, Brian. It was well overdue."

Brian Cooling, also known as S.O.7, was an ex-desert rat. He lived and breathed the military. Though it was common for operatives to have very few ties, Brian Cooling took that to the extreme. Upon first joining the army he had cut off all links with civilian life and made the military his world. He lived in the barracks and socialised only with fellow soldiers and agents. Addison occasionally wondered what Sergeant Cooling would do when age led to his departure from the service.

"Congratulations to you too," added Addison. "Blithe said you retrieved the Defence Data Files without detection and police capture." Addison looked to Skyler then back at the Sergeant. "Brian I would like you to meet Doctor Skyler Tidwell... Skyler this is Sergeant Brian Cooling."

"Hello," Skyler greeted, shaking Cooling's hand.

"American," Brian said, and then realisation dawned. "Tidwell... oh of course. Your mother must be the professor with General Blithe I assume."

Skyler looked over to where her mother remained beside Mark Blithe. "That would be me."

Brian smiled charmingly. "It's a pleasure to meet you."

"Oh, you too," replied Skyler, though there was something about the man that made her feel a little uneasy.

"If you will excuse me. I'm making the rounds and there's a certain person over there," Brian pointed to Samuel Perkins standing in the far corner of the room beside an exit sign, "I need to speak to. Catch you later," he said as he made his way towards Perkins.

Addison and Skyler continued to make their way through the groups of soldiers. There were nowhere near as many civilian dressed bodies. Even those without uniform were in some way involved with

310

Special Operations in a high-ranking position. It was doubtful Skyler herself would have been allowed access to the knowledge of Special Operations if it were not for her mother's work and Brodie's supplied information about the clandestine network.

"I have a question," Skyler said.

"What's that?"

"Why would what Brian was doing possibly land him in trouble with the police?"

Addison stopped walking. "Ah, well you see..." She thought for a moment on how best to explain their situation. "Sometimes our assignments can be targeted at people who appear to be living within the law. We can know differently. In order to carry out our mission it may involve entering a situation that is quite literally considered breaking the law." Addison thought of a non-related example. "For instance, it could involve breaking into the residence of a high profile establishment to gain access to illegally held information. There are many situations where we just cannot admit or provide any knowledge of who we work for. If we did, our time in the army would be denied or the military would even say a soldier was given a dishonourable discharge years earlier, rather than admit to any knowledge of our actions. Quite simply, we could and would be sent to prison under justified laws."

Skyler was less than impressed. "That's way too harsh; all for serving your country? How can you work under so many possible threats?"

"Because we all believe what we are fighting for is the right thing. Far more good is done to want an end to Special Operations, Sky."

The doctor wasn't convinced with Addison's reply. She held little doubt what Addison said was true. What she did believe, however, was that Addison's motives might hold different undertones of reason. "That may be true, Addison, but I have a feeling the guilt you still feel for the bad things you did as a kid pushes you to work selflessly for the good of others now. There are people today, even kids, who get up to a lot worse than you ever did with petty theft."

"Maybe," Addison replied. "You're right, I know, but as long as I believe what I'm doing is right, then I shall continue." The soldier pondered her response. For the first time she felt she had another person to consider in her actions. "Does um... does it bother you? I mean... I know how you felt about your dad's line of work and his death... I..."

"Addison!"

Addison turned in the direction that her name had been called. Quinton Zimmerman approached, Miss Bakersfield on his arm.

"You're a dark horse," Addison said to Quinton. "I didn't know you two were going together."

"I would ask if you were jealous, but I think we both won out on this one." Quinton took Skyler's hand and kissed it. "It's a pleasure once again Miss Tidwell. Nice to see you under less tense circumstances."

Skyler beamed. "You too, Quinton." She looked to Miss Bakersfield noticing the curious appraisal she was being given. "Um... Addison?"

Being jolted back into remembering her manners, Addison spoke up saying, "Skyler Tidwell this is Miss Bakersfield, Miss B... Skyler Tidwell."

The brunette shook her head. "Antonia, please," she said to Skyler. "This one has always called me 'Miss Bakersfield'... unless she wants something." Antonia winked. "Anyway, I'm the General's assistant."

The women shook hands as Skyler's eyes took in the slinky black dress Antonia was wearing. It was satin and low cut, hugging her figure in a very flattering manner. Her look was finished off beautifully with a unique necklace. Black and green, round cut stones lay around her neck, resting delicately over her collar bone and joining with a square cut black stone just above her breast bone. Skyler also noticed earrings that matched.

"That's an interesting necklace you have," Skyler complimented.

Antonia ran her fingers over the stones. "I know... it's amazing what you can find in a charity shop. It's only costume jewellery, but I thought it would go well with this dress. I just had to find the right occasion to wear them."

"Oh I know what you mean. I've done the same thing," Skyler admitted. "I found a beautiful bracelet at a back street bazaar in Egypt. It was second hand, but in astounding condition."

"Egypt!" Antonia gushed. "What a place to shop. I wager that was a wonderful place to find interesting bargains and peculiar finds."

"I found the most beautiful woven bed spread while in Cairo," Skyler continued.

"Really?"

"That's it," Quinton interrupted. "If you two are going to talk shopping all evening Addison and I are going to prop up the bar."

Antonia held up her hands. "Subtle hint taken. Besides, if you are going to the bar you can buy me a stiff one!"

"It's free, remember?" said Addison.

"Oh of course. Well in that case I'll have two!"

Quinton chuckled as he led Antonia towards the bar. Skyler watched them leave with a smile. She knew she would be meeting many of Addison's friends and work colleagues. So far they had all made varying degrees of impression on her. However, the underlying fear that one of them may well be the unknown 'Dr. Kleein' was never far away from her mind. It did serve to bother her a great deal, especially considering this person had ordered her death, but Skyler knew she couldn't allow it to cloud her evening. She had Addison and her faith in the agent was immeasurable. They had both agreed, on their car journey to the gala, not to allow remaining issues mar their enjoyment of the night.

"So..." Addison turned to Skyler. "Are you feeling okay so far?"

"I'm doing fine. Looking forward to a fun evening and then maybe a **very** enjoyable night?"

"Ooh!" Addison took a step closer to Skyler and slid one hand around her waist. "You read my mind." She leaned in further to kiss Skyler. Their lips connected for a soft, brief moment; just enough time for one set of eyes with malicious intent to capture their act.

Skyler heard the distinctive sound of her mother calling her name. "Mom!" the blonde said, making an expeditious turn away from Addison's tempting lips.

"Honey, you look beautiful." Marlene looked her daughter up and down. She ran a hand over the fabric of Skyler's dress. "Very soft!" Marlene looked to Addison. "A good choice."

"Thanks Prof... Marlene."

Mark Blithe nodded at Addison. He took her arm and pulled her to the side while Skyler and her mother spoke. They stood close to talk quietly.

"Security seem efficient to you?"

"I'd say." Addison looked around them. "How many do you have posted?"

"Three on the door, four outside, six located inside the building plus an extra five here as guests."

"Final guest count?"

"Ninety-six. All arrived and accounted for as well." Blithe nodded with satisfaction. "Everything is going to plan and running like clock work. Your presentation is to be held at eleven. The waiters begin serving dinner at nine o'clock. People are already beginning to take their seats."

Addison looked around her and sure enough tables were being

filled. Each setting was allocated with a nameplate and there were six seats to a table. Ignoring the knowledge of her forthcoming presentation she asked, "Where are Skyler and myself sitting?"

"With Marlene and myself, of course." General Blithe inclined his head to their table where it was already occupied by two bodies. "And Major Thompson and his wife."

The agent groaned. "Ugh... not 'Miss Majorette'. That woman barks out orders more than you."

"Well be nice," Mark reprimanded playfully. "Don't go feeding her any fairytales this year about suspicious extraterrestrial, U.F.O. sightings while on night watch as a young marine."

Addison had to chuckle. "You were trying not to laugh as well."

"Yes, but you didn't have Major Thompson asking you why his wife had developed such a sudden interest in Astronomy. She spent almost eleven hundred pounds on a telescope."

The soldier burst out laughing as General Blithe checked his watch. Right on schedule a bell sounded, giving everybody fifteen minutes to get seated before dinner was served.

"Come on," Addison said. "Let's get the food out of the way so we can start the D.J. and get in some dancing."

Mark followed Addison to their table. "Just for the record, Addison. I'm on to you this year. I've remembered to make sure there is no 'Birdie Song, Agadoo, Superman, Conga or The Okey Cokey' tunes in the mix, so there is no way you are paying off the D.J. to play one of those embarrassing songs when I agree to get up and dance."

"Damn it," Addison said. "I suppose you had to get me eventually." The soldier crossed her fingers as she tapped the compact disc tucked into the waistband of her trousers. *Got to move with the times,* she thought, making a mental note to hand the disc she had made the day before over to the D.J. *Should I go with The Macarena,* Addison pondered, *or go full out and shock them all with The Gang Bang song?* Addison chuckled mischievously to herself as she followed Mark to their table. She always made sure to have a night they would all remember. Unfortunately, this time it was no longer in Addison's hands.

Chapter 28

Dinner, as always, was a plentiful affair with four delicious courses. An option of three dishes was available for each course and all had been pre-chosen through invitations. As was usual, Addison found the dinner to be far too much. Through the course of many years her body had re-conditioned itself to survive and function with the small, nutritious meals soldiers often ate in the field. Addison sampled each course brought before her, but she never completed a dish. Instead the agent chose to talk while the other members of her table continued to dine. She entertained them with amusing stories and proceeded to further enthral Mrs. Thompson with tales of a pilot friend's mysterious sighting while on a routine night flight from Heathrow to Edinburgh. Mark Blithe had simply shaken his head in controlled amusement.

By the time dessert was ready to be served, Addison's appetite had taken a sudden growth. Not in the least hindered by the added three glasses of wine she had consumed, the soldier readied herself as a chocolate cheesecake, tiramisu and fruit crumble were placed upon their table.

"Bugger me!" Addison exclaimed. "Choices, choices. Which one to try first."

"Which one?" Skyler said in bemusement. "You no more than picked at the other three courses. Were you just saving yourself for dessert?"

"Well not really." Addison studied the dishes before them. "But look at the options. So... people," she addressed the other occupants of her table. "Tell me now which one you are all least likely to eat because I love them all and could do serious damage to any one of them." She sensed Skyler sidle up beside her.

"Personally," Skyler started in a low voice. "I'm having wonderful visions which include that chocolate cheesecake, but don't include you with clothes."

The soldier swallowed a sudden lump, which had unexpectedly formed in her throat. "Umm…"

"Marlene," Mark enquired. "What would you like?"

Marlene pursed her lips. "I'm not that fussy. What are you having?"

Mark checked his watch. "I don't generally eat desserts... besides it is five minutes past eleven. I think I should get up there and start my speech. I don't think anybody will mind if it is during dessert. Although these functions can go on until four or even five in the morning, only the trouble makers," Mark nodded towards Addison, causing her to stop munching on the flake of chocolate she had picked from the cheesecake decoration. "Stay until the end."

"What exactly are you implying?"

Mark shrugged. "Oh nothing, Addison."

Addison leaned to her side, towards Skyler. She spoke in a low voice, but loud enough for Mark to hear. "Sometimes I feel I should trust him as far as I can throw him."

"Don't you mean **could** throw him?" Major Thompson asked.

"Oh no," Blithe answered. "She means **can** throw. During a game of Rugby not very long ago, I made the mistake of opting to play on the opposing team in a friendly match. We got involved in a rough tackle and Addison wasn't too happy about losing the ball. She tackled me back for the ball and sent me flying. I've only just got rid of the cane I was walking with."

"Use dirty tactics to get the ball and so will I to win it back."

"It did make me remember a very important fact."

Addison frowned. "Which is?"

"It's better to be fighting with you than against you," Skyler guessed.

General Blithe tapped the side of his nose then pointed to Skyler. "The lady is spot on. It's much safer to stand with you than against you."

With a shrug Addison swiped her finger through the corner of the tiramisu. "It's not that I'm a sore loser. I just don't like to be beaten!"

Marlene arched her eyebrows and smiled. Chuckling lightly she began to cut the cheesecake.

"Look at the time," Mark commented as he checked his watch

once again. "I need to get up on the stage." The General rose to his feet. "Be ready for when I call you, Addison." Giving Marlene a loving smile, Mark walked away from the table. Samuel Perkins stopped him halfway on his approach to the stage. Addison watched their conversation for a brief moment before a tap on her shoulder diverted her attention. She turned to see one of the immaculately dressed waiters, clothed in black and white, standing beside her.

"Captain Black?" The young man asked.

"Yes."

"Captain, you are wanted at the front security desk. There is an Agent Alon Yamburg who is asking to see you urgently. Corporal Miller wouldn't allow him passage as his name isn't on the guest list."

"Really?" Addison asked, more surprised to hear Alon was here than she was that he hadn't been allowed admittance to the gala. "Okay, I'm coming." Drinking down the remainder of her wine Addison turned to Skyler. "I won't be but a moment." Rising, she followed the waiter out of the ballroom.

A feeling of foreboding settled into Addison's mind. She wondered what possible reason could Alon have for travelling all the way from Israel to speak with her. Why not a phone call? Something was wrong and she knew it. Her instincts were never wrong. Walking through the doorway and turning to the security room, Addison could see Alon standing beside Corporal Miller. Her feeling of dread increased as she took note of Alon's agitated stance and concerned expression. Addison increased her stride, eating up the distance between her and the Mossad agent in seconds.

"Alon, nice to see you, but what's going on?" she asked cautiously.

"Addison, my friend. We have to talk urgently. We discovered some alarming information while continuing our own investigation into what happened in Israel."

"You have been conducting an investigation?" This was something Addison hadn't been made aware of.

"Of course we have," Alon, replied "Do you think my government was happy when they discovered what had been going on?" Alon looked around him. Two soldiers were still within hearing distance. "I need to speak with you alone."

Nodding, Addison said, "Okay," and led Alon into a small security office. A teak table stood by the wall and Addison sat upon its edge. She was anxious to find out what it was that seemed to concern Alon so much. Whatever it was, his uneasy disposition was beginning to rub off on her. "What is it?"

"Addison, I believe you still may be in serious danger."

"Explain."

"Through my investigations I managed to discover the full name of the mysterious owner of the compound Brodie was using." Alon handed Addison a sheet of paper. "His name is Dr. Tobias F. Kleein. Is that name familiar to you? At all?"

Addison studied the name, shaking her head. "No, not at all. Never heard of it." She tapped her lip as her mind tried the possibility of another anagram. Going through every colleagues name she could think of, including, Mark, Quinton, Antonia, Samuel and Marlene, Addison came up clueless. Not one name she tried seemed to fit into the name of Dr. Tobias F. Kleein. "I don't know, Alon. This name means nothing to me at all. I just…" Addison ran a hand through her hair; the soft locks trickling through her fingers. "Don't know."

Alon sighed. "Okay. Anyway… that is not the worst of the information I must deliver to you."

"Not the worst of it? What else do you have for me, Alon?"

"I came here because I wanted to see you in person. I didn't want to risk speaking with you over the phone or leaving a message. I needed to speak with only you, Addison."

"Okay?"

"When I landed at Heathrow this evening, I received word from my superior. Addison we recently apprehended a man suspected of illegal weapons trading. He tried to make a deal with a promise of information. Basically, I discovered he'd put a 'Sadie Bregon' in contact with a scientist who supplied her with a large quantity of the poison Ricin."

"Ricin?" Addison asked in elevated alarm.

"Yes. He said he was put into contact with Sadie Bregon through a Dr. Kleein. He worked for her through the duration of Agnes Brodie's time in Israel."

Addison blew out a strained breath. "Jesus. Ricin is one nasty bugger."

"Addison?"

"It's a good job I destroyed that place because I…"

"Addison," Alon interrupted loudly. "At first I didn't know whether I could believe his information. Then he told me something I could verify myself."

"Which was?"

"He said he was paid to take a delivery from Kleein's compound to a courier at the airport. He said he drove a food delivery truck on the morning of the day you destroyed the place. Addison, I witnessed the vehicle leave that morning. He described it to me perfectly; it was a vending machine supply truck. He certainly was there that morning, Addison. Everything fits."

The feeling of dread, Addison experienced upon hearing Alon had come to speak with her, increased ten fold. She took a deep breath. Needing to be sure she was on the same wavelength as Alon, she asked, "Exactly what is it you are saying?"

"I'm saying Brodie sent out a vial of the bacilli... before you destroyed the compound."

"Fuck... oh, fuck!" Addison's heart rate increased and she rose to her feet as the implications of Alon's words sunk in. A vial of Gemini's Hyde application had left Israel? That information was only half as alarming as was the fact that they had used the well-known, deadly poison Ricin. It was a poison for which there was no cure for its deadly effects. "Jeez, Alon, do you know what you are saying? Do you know what this means?" Addison headed towards the door and then stopped. She turned back to Alon. "We're in the middle of a dinner for gods sake. Almost a hundred guests, not including the band and waiting staff."

"Prime target."

"Exactly," Addison replied. "Kleein is here. I know it, Alon. I just know it." Addison opened the door swiftly. "Corporal Miller?"

"Yes, Captain?"

"Call the guards in from off the door."

"Goff... Murray," Miller shouted. The guards appeared in the doorway before him.

Addison took charge. "We may have a possible threat, men. I need you to alert the troops on guard outside. We might have a situation here, guys. I don't want anybody leaving this building, at all. I need you to make sure of that. Tell them to make sure nobody gets in or out of here and anybody seen within the vicinity, whether they seem suspicious or not, I want them detained. Understand?"

"Yes, Captain Black." Both men left to follow Addison's orders. The soldier turned to Miller.

"Has anybody left the building since all guests arrived?"

"No, ma'am."

"There is a very real chance we may have a traitor here tonight with a highly contagious chemical weapon. An air-born variation of the poison Ricin with the contagious ability of tuberculosis."

"Captain, is that..."

"Possible? Yes. We need to..."

"*Corporal Miller, come in.*" Goff's voice sounded through the

319

radio attached to Miller's hip.

Corporal Miller answered, "Roger, Goff."

"Captain Black needs to come out here right away. We've located the soldiers on guard. They're dead. Gunshot wounds."

Addison took the radio from Miller's hand. "All of them?" she asked.

"Yes, Captain."

"Shagging hell." Ignoring common sense, that stated she should stay within the building, Addison ran from the security office, needing to see the bodies for herself. "Stay there, Miller," she ordered as she ran down the concrete steps. Alon followed her, turning right and following her around to the side of the building. They spotted Goff standing by the far exit. He was illuminated by a green light and Addison could clearly see two bodies slumped together upon the ground. She jogged towards them.

Looking down at the bodies she said, "Kleein's here, Alon. Damn it." Addison paced around the bodies seeing Miller standing further away with a body either side of him. "Shit!" The agent's mind wandered back to Skyler and the festivities commencing in the main ballroom. "I've got to get back in there." Addison took off again. "You two guard the back exits," she ordered. "Alon, come with me."

Running around to the entrance, Addison took the six steps two at a time. Miller stood dutifully by the door awaiting orders.

"Don't let anybody in or out of this door, got it?"

"Yes, Captain."

Addison and Alon ran back into the main ballroom, slowing down as they entered the doors together.

"Ah... and just in time," General Blithe said. He stood on centre stage, a microphone resting lightly in his hand. He placed it back upon its stand as he said, "Ladies and gentlemen, fellow officers..." he held out his hand, "Captain Addison Black."

Addison looked around her as the occupants of the ballroom began to applaud. Heart hammering in her chest, the agent's eyes moved around the guests' faces, trying to ascertain who may be currently missing. There were too many to accurately determine. Addison turned to Alon. "I have to go up there. We know nothing, okay? I don't want to cause any alarm. Not yet anyway. Nobody can leave here until we access the situation."

"Got it."

Taking a deep breath, Addison turned back to the applauding room of guests and began making her way to the stage. As she wove her way around the tables she passed Skyler. Their eyes connected, the doctor seeing something hidden behind Addison's façade. Skyler's clapping slowed, her eyebrows drawing together. Addison smiled reassuringly, but Skyler wasn't convinced.

Reaching the stage, Addison stepped up to the platform. She approached Mark and shook his hand. The applause continued. Addison looked out among the sea of faces. She tried once again to gauge any form of suspicious action. Alon walked around the edge of the room, watching the guests.

As the applause died, General Blithe began to speak. "Captain Black, in a career that so far has spanned almost thirteen years, your record has been exceptional. In working for the Military and Ministry of Defence you have successfully completed your missions gallantly and with honour."

Addison felt awkward standing in the spotlight. Her only thought was to get off the stage and find Dr. Kleein. Four men were already dead. She didn't have time for this, but what concerned her more was the fact that she wasn't sure whom she could trust.

"Now although usual ceremonies of this kind are held at Buckingham Palace, circumstances, and the nature of our work make that impossible. So instead, we are here today to honour you with not one, but two medals... for gallantry and distinguished conduct."

Addison looked at Mark, stunned by his revelation. Her main concern was whether the presentation of two medals would take longer than one. The soldier tried to smile and appear surprised, but on looking back at Skyler she saw the same confused expression. Kleein was out there, probably watching right now, one step ahead of her. She felt her anger rise.

"So in respect of the situation and resolution of your mission... here today to present you with these medals is the wife of the soldier whose life was taken so tragically and before his time... by the very person you dealt with and put an end to..."

No! Addison's eyes widened. *Not Jenny. Not now.*

"Jennifer Easton," Mark introduced.

Feeling the situation couldn't possibly get any worse; Addison scanned the room until she located Jenny Easton climbing the steps to the stage. James Easton's wife smiled proudly. She looked well, Addison acknowledged. Her red hair was cut into a short bob. She had put on some weight, filling out the fragile frame Addison had been concerned about after James' death. The pressure to find Dr. Kleein increased with the guilt ridden realisation that she had already been the cause of Jimmy's children losing their father; she would be damned if anything happened to Jenny as well.

321

The applause continued and Addison looked across the room to Alon. The Israeli Mossad agent maintained his position by the far exit. She looked to Mark Blithe and for the first time the general seemed to register something of concern etched into her features. He frowned, giving her the same look Skyler was.

Jenny reached Addison and they hugged affectionately.

"I didn't know you were even here," Addison said.

"It wouldn't be a surprise otherwise. They kept me hidden."

The applause finally stopped and Jennifer stood in front of the microphone. She spoke softly. "I know I'm not as prestigious as the Queen presenting these medals, but I was asked and am honoured to do so. Captain Black... Addison... you brought to justice the person who took my husband's life." Jenny paused and took a breath, gaining hold of her emotions. Addison's mind felt swamped with frustration and the urgent need to flee the stage and find Kleein. The terrifying knowledge that Gemini might very well be in the room with them, hung over her like a pressurised, dreadful weight.

Jennifer continued. "So it is my honour to present you with these medals." Blithe handed her two cases, each approximately the size of her palm, and open portraying the medals. "For distinguished service and gallantry... myself... and more importantly, your country thank you, Captain Black, for your service and loyalty to the realm."

Applause echoed out once again as Addison accepted the medals with one hand. She hugged Jenny and shook Mark's hand, knowing she would have to make a short speech. She needed to get off the stage as soon as possible, but knew she had to act as calm and clueless to the events that were unravelling around them.

As the guests calmed, Addison stood before the microphone. "I'm not going to draw this out. I'm sure you all want to finish your desserts and abuse the free bar!" She continued to scan the guests and officers through their light laughter. "I just want to say that what I do is nothing more than is in the hearts and minds of everybody. No matter what situation we hold in life we all take chances. It's just that some of us get more recognition than others. So saying that... I dedicate this honour to everybody who stands for what is right in this world."

Again applause rang out through the room and Addison decided that was her cue to depart the stage. With a smile and slight nod, she placed her hand upon Jenny's back and escorted her from the platform. Walking beside Jennifer she led her straight to the table in which Skyler, her mother and the Major were occupying. People began talking quietly amongst themselves and the D.J. started a simple melody.

Addison addressed Skyler. "Sky, I need you to look after Jenny for a while." She turned to James' wife. "Can you stay at my table? You don't have to leave just yet do you?"

"Of course I can and no... I don't have to leave yet." Jenny sat in Addison's abandoned seat. The soldier made to leave the table when Skyler stopped her.

"Addison, what's going on?"

Addison looked around the room. Alon was no longer standing by the far exit. In fact, she could no longer see him at all. "Sky, I'll explain in a moment. I have to go and check on something."

"Something's happened," Skyler insisted. "What is it, damn it?"

"Look..." catching a movement in the corner of her eye, Addison looked to the exit and saw Alon slip through the doors. He made clear eye contact with Addison and beckoned her over. "Listen... I'm going over to the bar. I'm going to be speaking with Alon Yamburgh..."

"Alon?" What's he doing...? Addison?"

"When he leaves me alone at the bar come over to me, okay?"

"Okay... but..."

"Act like everything is cool." Addison smiled. "We are having a good night, remember?"

Although she was still confused and concerned by Addison's actions, Skyler nodded. She took the boxed medals Addison handed her and kissed the agent softly. "Everything is okay."

"Good... I'll speak to you in a moment." Winking, Addison wove her way back around the tables and left the room through the main entrance. She knew Alon would meet her around the back of the ballroom. Sure enough, she headed down the corridor and turned right to where Alon was waiting for her by the ballroom's far exit.

"Where the hell did you go? I asked you to stay by the exit." Addison didn't want to consider the possibility Alon may be the enemy.

"I went to Corporal Miller and got us a radio each from the security office. Now we can keep in touch with the men outside as well as Miller. We've altered the frequency." Alon handed Addison a tiny transmitter, earpiece and voice sensor. The soldier slipped the transmitter into her breast pocket. She placed the, practically invisible earpiece into her ear and clipped the microphone to the inside of her shirt collar.

"Okay... good idea," she acknowledged. Watching Alon activate his own radio, she contacted the men outside. "Goff... Murray... what's your status?"

"All is quiet this side," Goff replied.

"Same here Captain," responded Murray.

"Miller?"

Corporal Miller answered saying, *"Nobody has attempted to leave, Captain Black."*

"Roger that." Addison placed her arm over Alon's shoulders. "Okay buddy, let's get back in there and act like we're having a good time."

"How are we going to figure out who Kleein is?" Alon asked. He entered the ballroom with Addison and they walked directly to the bar.

"I have that in hand. Trust me, Alon." Taking a seat at the bar, Addison ordered two   double shots of Jack Daniels.   A barman, dressed identical to the waiters, handed her the order and Addison pushed one glass over to Alon. She waited until the server left before speaking. "Alon, I want you to go back out into the foyer. Check the rooms down here and then upstairs. Are you armed?"

"Yes."

"Good."

"Are you?"

"No..." Addison looked across the room. She could see Skyler watching her. "I'll meet you in a moment. First of all I need to work out exactly who Kleein is."

"Okay, my friend." Alon rose from his stool and picked up his glass. Speaking in a louder voice he said, "And congratulations again, Captain Black."

"Thanks, Alon." Addison turned to the bar as the Mossad agent disappeared from the ballroom. She looked down into her glass, swirling the dark, amber liquid around the container. *Who are you, Dr. Kleein? What do you have planned?* Addison looked up and into the mirror behind the bar. She could see Skyler approach. The doctor sidled up behind her, placing her chin on Addison's shoulder.

Maintaining an outer image of calm, Skyler asked, "What is it, Addison? You're making me nervous."

"I'm sorry." Taking Skyler's hand, Addison ushered her around to sit down upon Alon's vacated stool. "Sky..." Addison peered around them. There were far too many people around to risk speaking with Skyler about the situation when she wasn't sure what her reaction would be. Addison rose. Drinking down her whiskey she leaned into Skyler's ear. "Come with me."

Skyler was confused by the seductive tone in Addison's voice. "Pardon?"

Taking the blonde doctor's hand Addison pulled her to her feet. Maintaining eye contact with a secretive smile, Addison led her out of the ballroom. The soldier walked backwards until she hit the bathroom door. Pulling Skyler inside and after checking to make sure it was empty, Addison turned to Skyler.

"Sky... there is no easy way to say this... Dr. Kleein is here."

"What?"

"Kleein is here. I've just discovered a vial of Gemini's Hyde application made it out of Israel before Brodie's compound was destroyed."

"What?" Skyler placed a hand over her chest, hoping she was hearing wrong. "Are you sure?"

"Of course. We've already discovered four soldiers killed outside."

Skyler's heart rate increased as sparks of alarm shot to her nerve endings. "No! Oh my God. We've got to warn everybody. We've got to evacuate."

"No!" Addison placed her hand on the bathroom door, slamming it shut as Skyler tried to open it. "We don't know who Kleein is. Causing any degree of alarm could either force Kleein to release the bacilli ahead of any pre-arranged plan and infect us all... or it will help Kleein to escape with everybody else. Four soldiers are already dead. We have to figure out who Kleein is."

"How?"

Addison took the paper Alon had given her from her side pocket. "This is the full name of Kleein. It's Dr. Tobias F. Kleein. I've tried all the names I know but can't find any that fit... I was under the impression that it was another anagram like Sadie Bregon, but I think not."

"Maybe." Skyler's sharp mind studied the name. "You've tried all the names of the people you suspect?"

"Yes."

"Even General Blithe?"

"Mark, Quinton, Antonia... even your mother." At Skyler's surprised expression Addison added, "I have to be thorough. The trouble is that I'm not seeing a thing. There is nothing. If the name isn't an anagram what is it? Sky, you've met a lot of people here tonight. You have one of the best analytical minds I've ever known. You read people instinctively. I need your input on this... and fast."

Skyler placed Addison's sheet of paper down beside a sink. Her eyes moved swiftly over the letters, her subconscious mind working to decipher Kleein's name as she spoke... "Miss Bakersfield lied to me."

She didn't look up from her analysing.

"Pardon?"

"She lied. The necklace she was wearing... it certainly wasn't costume jewellery. In fact, even her dress was..."

"Hold on," Addison interrupted. "What are you saying?"

Skyler continued to study the name. "I'm saying I know gems. Her necklace was a truly beautiful combination with a stunning contrast of black and green gems. But Addison, those green stones were emeralds and the black stones were diamonds." Skyler looked up at Addison. "Black diamonds; the most rare of diamonds you can find. Serious money."

"The type of money you don't earn working as a General's assistant?"

"Try top-billing movie star or monarch of the realm. Addison, they are priceless. Lord only knows how she got a hold of them."

Addison rubbed her chin, blowing out a weary breath through her lips. "How can you be sure they were really gems?"

"I know a diamond when I see one. I studied them in Amsterdam at a cutting factory. Addison, those stones weren't costume jewellery and they aren't a television shopping channel imitation."

The agent began pacing around the bathroom. She strode up the walkway, past a row of green doors on either side of her. Walking back to Skyler she stood by the exit just as it began to open. Addison thrust her hand onto it, slamming the barrier shut. "There's been an accident... you have to use the restroom upstairs," she called out. Keeping her hand upon the door, Addison stared into space and thought for a brief moment. She looked back to Skyler. "That isn't enough evidence."

"How about 'Toni Bakersfield'?"

"Huh?"

"Kleein," Skyler answered. "You never got Miss Bakersfield's name because you used Antonia. If you shortened it to 'Toni Bakersfield' you get Dr. Tobias F. Kleein."

Addison snatched the paper from the tiled surface of the vanity unit and mentally re-arranged the letters in Kleein's name. "Fuck me!" Her mind drifted to snippets of conversations she'd had with Antonia. Questions the secretary had asked. Who else had more access to General Blithe's information, intimate knowledge of Special Operations and more importantly, Addison's career history? "Bloody hell." Addison took Skyler's hand. "We've got to warn the General." They fled the bathroom, making a beeline for the ballroom. "I've got to find her, Skyler. She's combined Gemini with Ricin."

"Ricin! Addison… that's deadly."

"And if it's released **we** are dead." With added urgency Addison burst through the doors desperate to locate Mark Blithe.

M J Walker and Val Brown

Chapter 29

Within the main ballroom the lights had been lowered and music increased in tempo. Uniformed officers had discarded their jackets to the backs of chairs and loosened their collars for comfort. It was time to have some fun and many guests were taking advantage of the fact. Already, a quarter of the room's inhabitants had migrated to the dance floor. A well-known, top forty hit was playing and the atmosphere was one of relaxed enjoyment.

General Blithe sat beside Marlene at their table. They spoke in raised voices, trying to be heard over the music. Mark, too, had abandoned his jacket. He sat, pleasantly relaxed, tapping his foot to the beat. The night had been enjoyable. Dinner was superb as always and his companion had been, *wonderful*, Mark thought, *beautiful and wonderful*. He leaned close to Marlene's ear.

"I'm not expected to stay through the whole bash," he said.

"Really?" Marlene replied, a smile brightening her features.

The General nodded. "Just let me know when you've had enough and I..." Mark took Marlene's hand, kissing it softly, "will escort you home."

A pleasant shiver tickled Marlene's senses. "Well actually..."

"Blithe, my good man!"

Mark looked to his left finding Major Thompson beside him. The Major's ruddy complexion and handlebar moustache was his long time trademark. His cheeks had turned a little too flushed from over-consumption of alcohol and Mrs. Thompson had decided her husband had enough for the evening and was going to take him home.

"Major," Mark greeted, disappointed to miss the rest of Marlene's words.

"Want to fill me in on what's going on? We just went to leave, but your man on the door said we weren't permitted, orders from Captain Black. Do you know something I don't?"

Blithe appeared confused. "Not permitted to leave? No, I have no idea what Addison's up to."

From the other side of the room Addison had seen General Blithe and Major Thompson converse. With Skyler beside her, she approached their table swiftly, desperately needing answers. Skyler scanned the room as they went. She was unsure whether she wanted to catch a glimpse of Miss Bakersfield or not. Within the throng of dancers she could be lost in a sea of moving bodies.

"General," Addison greeted.

"Addison, just the person I was about to look for. Would you mind telling me…?"

"In a moment, Sir. I have an important question I must ask you first."

Mark was intrigued, but concerned by the looking in her eyes. It was the same expression she held upon the stage only now there seemed to be more urgency in her mannerism. "What is it?"

"Have you seen Miss Bakersfield?"

"That's it?"

"It's important, Sir."

Simply by the sheer fact Addison was addressing him in such a respectful manor, Mark knew she was serious. "Yes, I have seen her. The poor thing accidentally knocked a glass of tomato juice down her dress. She was so upset. Something about Tabasco sauce staining? Hell if I know but anyway, she just went to change into something a little dryer. They have spare server suits here. I think she was donning a waitress skirt and blouse."

Addison's eyes connected with Skyler briefly. "And Quinton?"

Mark nodded to the dance floor. "Living it up with Samuel, Kate, Jenny and a few others. Samuel had been looking for you, but Kate lured him onto the dance floor."

The agent leaned into General Blithe. "Mark, I need to speak with you right now. Dr. Kleein is here. A vial of Gemini's Hyde application left Israel. It contains Ricin. I believe the intention is to, at the very least, use its release here tonight as a threat for some form of gain. That is best case scenario."

Mark looked at Skyler. Fear was easily evident in her eyes. He shot to his feet and turned to Marlene. "I want you to stay here. I need to attend to a matter with Addison." He looked to Skyler. "Will you stay with your mum?"

Skyler sat down beside Marlene. "I need to speak with her, yes."
"Bear with us," Mark said to Major Thompson before charging off with Addison. They exited the ballroom. "What aren't you telling me, Black?"

Addison directed General Blithe to the security office. "Evidence points to Antonia, Mark."

The general paused mid-stride. He was silent for several moments as Addison's words registered in his mind. "Antonia!" He sighed and a pained expression twisted his features. "You're sure?"

"Yes, Sir."

Commencing walking, Blithe increased his stride as a flash of anger coloured his cheeks. Addison led him to the security office. Pushing the door open she stopped in her tracks, Mark walking into her.

"What are you...?" Marks words froze as he discovered what Addison had found. Lying in the middle of the room was the lifeless body of Corporal Miller. Addison crouched to her knees and checked his pulse.

"He's dead." She checked over his body. "Two shots to the chest. His weapon is missing as well."

Blithe picked up a phone. "I need to issue a warning and declare an emergency. The anti-contamination unit will need to be alerted and dispatched."

"Mark, we can't risk alerting Kleein... err, Antonia to the fact we know what's going on. We can't risk making her panic and act before she has a chance to put whatever plan she has into action."

"I'll advise caution and discretion." The general began dialling a secure line. "Worst case scenario, they need to section this building off under quarantine." Blithe's call was answered. "This is General Blithe..."

Addison stepped across the room. "Worse case scenario, we all die." Placing her finger on her ear Addison said, "Murray, come in, this is Captain Black..."

There was no reply.

"Murray?"

Nothing.

"Come in Goff, this is Addison Black."

Again there was no response. The agent's concern began to grow. With Miller dead and no response from either Goff or Murray, there didn't seem to be anybody guarding the exits. With faltering hope, Addison called one more time.

"Alon, hey man it's Addison." The soldier waited, but again

there was no response. "Alon, please come in… Alon? Alon?" The transmission was dead. "No!" Addison pulled the transmitter from her jacket. Raising her hand she made to throw it across the room, but paused just short of releasing the radio. "Bugger it. Fuck it. Fuck it. No, damn it!" Addison dashed towards the door. "I'm going to find Antonia."

Mark placed down the phone's receiver. "Addison," Bending down he took the radio from Miller. "Don't get rid of your radio. I want you in contact with me."

"Got it," Addison said and left the room. Looking both ways the soldier headed up the corridor. Reaching a small hallway to her left she turned down the narrow passageway, with two doors. The first door was a side entrance to the kitchen. A surveillance of that room resulted with little findings. Addison tried the second door. It was a utility room. Two silver, industrial washing machines stood side by side. Spotting a slip of black material, Addison pulled it from the top of the closest appliance. Instantly she recognised it as Antonia's dress. The scent of tomato juice and Tabasco was strong. Addison scanned the room for any further clues. After finding nothing she continued her search for Antonia. She headed to the main corridor and towards the rear of the ground floor where she came across the ladies' and gents' toilets. Addison checked inside both rooms. Entering the gents she stopped short of walking fully into the room as she saw Brian Cooling standing at a urinal.

"Oh, Brian, sorry, I was just looking for…" Addison poked her head further into the toilet. All the stalls were empty; Brian was its only occupant. "Nope… okay… carry on." Addison made a swift exit, leaving Brian watching her departure with a suspicious glare.

A wide set of stairs stood beside an elevator. Ignoring the lift, Addison opted for the steps. Taking the maroon carpeted stairs two at a time Addison reached the second floor, arriving in a seating area. Six black, leather sofas were strategically placed around three glass top coffee tables. Reproduction prints of Monet paintings adorned the walls reminding Addison of a student's dormitory room. The agent ventured towards a shorter corridor. A set of double doors to her right led into a smaller function room. To her left was another door, the entrance to an informal meeting room. Addison slipped inside. Though she could hear music coming from the ground floor ballroom, on the first floor it was calm and relatively still. Many of the main rooms were shrouded in a blanket of darkness. A dull light came from under a second door in the meeting room. Addison knew it was an office. Moving as silently as possible the soldier crept towards the light. She held her ear by the door, listening for movement. Not hearing a sound, she peered through a gap between the door and its frame. Alarm shot through her as she spotted a hand lying upon the floor. Recognising the wearer's watch Addison pushed the door open urgently. There, upon the floor, Addison found Alon lying in a pool of his own blood. One arm lay strewn above his head.

"Alon!" Addison knelt down beside him. A quick survey of his body found two bullet wounds, one in this thigh, the other in his ribcage. "Al, man, I'm so, so, sorry." Addison attempted to stop the blood flow. She placed her hand upon his side, applying pressure to the wound. Warm, sticky blood oozed between her fingers.

"Addison," Alon whispered.

"Alon! Stay with me, okay?"

"She's... here..." The Mossad agent coughed and a flash of pain racked his body. "Get her."

"You don't go anywhere, okay?" Addison pulled off her jacket. She draped it over Alon's body. "Stay with me, Alon."

Alon nodded weakly. "Ankle," he whispered in a rough, strained voice.

Unsure what he meant, Addison frowned. "What do you mean?" Looking down she inspected his feet, seeing nothing, but she reached down nonetheless. Lifting his left trouser leg to check his ankle, she discovered what Alon was referring to. Strapped to his ankle was a small pistol. She pulled it from its holster. "I'll be back, okay? Hang on." With a final look of assurance Addison rose to her feet and left the room. She wiped her bloody hand on her dark dress trousers and gripped Alon's pistol.

Making her way back to the hallway Addison began a vigilant trek down the corridor. She changed her mind to a frame of logical thinking. If Kleein did want to release Gemini into the atmosphere, what would be the best way to accomplish that? *Air conditioner!* Addison thought.

Having utilized the function building many times before and having attended several meetings within its four walls, Addison was familiar with its layout. As such she made a beeline straight towards the female toilets. Addison knew the main unit, for the system was located and contained within a small room that was only accessible through the female bathroom. Light shone from around the doorframe. That was nothing conspicuous in itself as all bathrooms were in use during any gathering.

Feeling her feet slightly slide underfoot, Addison looked to the ground. Though the carpet, like throughout the building's main passageways, was maroon, a dark contrast of blood was highly visible. Addison realised at least one body had been dragged into the bathroom. A dark trail led from the doors of the second, smaller function room. The agent presumed it had been one of the guards Blithe had placed within the building for the evening.

Addison placed her ear to the door and listened carefully. A sick feeling of anger curdled her stomach at the thought of what the traitor intended to do. Addison found it difficult to acknowledge Antonia as Kleein. She hoped she was wrong, however unlikely she knew she would be.

From inside the bathroom the agent heard definite movement. Harsh breathing was clear, as was the sound of metal clanking against metal. Steeling her resolve and readying the pistol Alon had given her, Addison pushed the door open. With no handle, the green barrier was a simple swing door. Addison thankfully acknowledged the hinges didn't squeak with movement.

The first sight Addison happened upon was a haphazardly deposited pile of bodies. She counted five in total. All but one of the bodies were soldiers who had been on guard that evening and all had been shot in the chest. It would have been easy for the traitor to incapacitate them if they knew and trusted their assailant. Two of the bodies were women and Addison realised one was still alive. It was her breathing that had echoed from within the room.

Placing her forefinger upon her lips, Addison whispered, "Shush!" She then pointed to the open door at the far end of the bathroom. The female soldier nodded.

Addison looked down the rectanglulr room. Seven blue toilet doors lined each side. At the end of the room several dispensing machines faced the open door to the air conditioner's maintenance room. Pointing her gun towards the door, Addison walked forwards. She was careful not to make any sound, leaving bloody footprints in her wake. The soldier slowed her breathing, finger poised upon the trigger. She drew closer knowing the inhabitant inside the cupboard would soon be visible. There was only just enough space for one person to stand. Gradually the infamous 'Dr. Kleein' appeared. A mane of thick dark hair came into view and Addison knew instantly it was Antonia. She was dressed almost precisely as Addison had expected in black trousers and a white button down shirt. A handgun was tucked into the back of her belt. It was Alon's, the pistol's make was that of the Israeli governments standard issue.

Short, sharp beeps came from the unit and it appeared to Addison that Antonia was programming its computer. The unit's casing had been removed and it was, at that moment, powered down. The soldier realised, with sudden impact, what Antonia intended to do. She planned on programming the air conditioning unit to come on after she had left. Three fans, fairly close to each other, were inside the main chamber of the unit. When the air conditioner was activated by the timer, the fans would start and presumably release Gemini into the circulating air. After that happened... Addison didn't know if there was any known antidote. There sure wasn't a cure for Ricin, but Skyler intended to ask her mother about that side of her work, if it existed.

"Don't move, Antonia."

The woman froze. She seemed to ponder Addison's words before slowly turning around. "Wonders will never cease," she said. "The great Addison Black does actually remember my name after all."

Addison looked down at Antonia's hand seeing the pistol, complete with attached muffler, aimed at her. "It's over, Dr. Kleein! Drop it."

Antonia gave a smile, oozing with self-importance. "It will soon be over and don't worry, I intend to drop it and when I do, you will all drop like flies... little, weak, pathetic flies."

Disturbed by Antonia's almost random sentences, Addison asked, "Why? Why are you doing this?" She didn't understand what could and obviously had turned Antonia against her country in such a vile, hateful way. "**How** can you do this?"

"Why? How? Addison, tell me. How would you feel if your career had been taken from you by some fuck up's stupid mistake? Forced to take a desk job. Not able to do anything more than sit there and watch others... LIKE YOU... succeed."

"But..."

"But nothing... what do you do? Sit back and swallow the bitter pill you are given? That's what I was expected to do." Antonia scratched her temple with the extended barrel of her gun. "But I didn't. I still crave the danger and excitement. Who wouldn't? I mean, surely you can understand. This way not only do I get that, but I also get tons of money as well. This little demonstration of Gemini's capabilities is going to earn me over two and a half million pounds."

Both women continued to aim their guns at each other.

"And the safety of this country... the lives of possibly thousands if not millions of people? That is worth the money?"

"The myth's a lie, Agent Black. Money **can** buy you happiness." Antonia ran her fingers over her emerald and diamond necklace. "It can buy you lots of happiness."

Anger rising, Addison directed her gun to Antonia's head, the secretary mirroring her action. "I hate to be a kill joy and all, but I have to end that. Tell me, Antonia, where's Gemini?"

Antonia shrugged. "That should be the least of your worries."

"What do you mean?"

"What do I mean?" Antonia pretended to ponder her question. "What do I mean? Well... put it this way... I've been up here far too long now. My man's going to know something's fallen foul if I am behind schedule. I had to be prepared for any eventuality. Tell me, Addison. Was Brodie right in saying Miss Tidwell holds a special place in your heart?"

A cold chill of fear slithered down Addison's spine. The urge to run back to the ballroom slammed into her instincts, but she remained standing. "Hand over Gemini."

"You're not worried about Miss Tidwell?"

"Give it to me, Antonia. While you are still able to do so."

Antonia knew Addison wasn't bluffing. "Alright... alright." She held out her hand. "Slowly, okay?" Slipping the free hand into her trouser pocket she withdrew holding a slim black case. It was the approximate size of an executive pen case. "Here you go." She placed the case upon the floor and slid it across the ground. It hit Addison's boot. The agent bent down cautiously, gun still trained upon Antonia as she picked up the container. Using her thumb the soldier flipped open its lid. It was empty.

"What the..." Addison looked up finding Antonia's wickedly grinning face.

"Oh, I'm sorry... I forgot... I've already planted it."

From the bodies upon the floor Addison heard the unexpected voice of the female guard she had encountered upon entering the bathroom.

"In... the unit..." she forced out causing Antonia to growl with anger. She spun around ready to fire a final shot into the woman, but as she began to squeeze the trigger Addison fired, shooting the gun from her hand. Sparks fluttered around them as the bullet hit metal and the pistol flew from her hand, hit the wall and dropped to the floor. Its clatter echoed around the sanitary walls of the bathroom. Addison aimed her pistol back at Antonia.

"Look what we have here!" The soldier grinned. "**Now...** hand over Gemini."

"You really don't get this do you, Addison!"

"Get what? That you are an insane, money hungry bitch. Don't worry, I've figured that out."

Antonia shook her head. "No, no, no... I'm talking about the initial motivation." She took a step closer. "It was you. It was always you, Addison. I despise you." Antonia's eyes took on an icy glare. "You have EVERYTHING that should have been mine; just because I lost my hearing in ONE ear?" Again Antonia stepped closer, shocking Addison with her venomous words and raised voice. "You get the action, adventure, glory, and the fucking medals. I am better than you. I have always been better than you, but have I ever been allowed to prove myself? No."

"Look, Antonia," Addison said calmly. "I'm sorry fate dealt you such a shitty card, but how can you say this is anybody's fault?"

"You would say that considering it's yours."

"Then explain to me how."

"You're an S.O. Agent... I'm an S.O. GOD DAMN secretary. While you sharpen knives, I sharpen pencils." Antonia moved ever closer. She didn't stop until her chest pushed into the barrel of Addison's gun. "While you terminate an enemy I cancel an appointment. You travel around the world; I drive to work every day... the same boring route. It should have been ME."

"Antonia, I'm sorry the way things turned out, but that isn't my fault. It isn't anybody's fault."

"You have everything you want, Addison." Antonia's words dripped with resentment and sarcasm. "I offered you me, but you didn't want that did you. Not good enough, huh? Damaged goods."

"You..." Addison paused. She refused to believe Antonia started all of this simply because she had turned down her advances. As far as she was concerned, it was all innocent flirting. Antonia wasn't going to blame Addison for her own misdeeds. "You have nothing left, Antonia, get down onto your knees, hands behind your head."

Shoulders slumping in defeat, Antonia said, "There's no use anymore. The air conditioning should come on any second now. You won't detain me. I would rather die and I will."

Shocked by her statement, Addison's eyes switched to the air conditioning unit. It was a brief moment, but enough time for Antonia to make a move. She knocked Addison's gun away from her and struck the agent hard across the face. Lip catching upon a tooth, blood flew from Addison's mouth. Antonia kicked her hand and she dropped Alon's pistol, feeling a bone break in her little finger. The ex-marine attack didn't last long, however, as Addison struck back with several moves of her own. Punches were traded and blocked until Addison lashed out with a kick to Antonia's stomach, knocking her to the floor.

Once Antonia was down, Addison ran to the air conditioning unit. She looked inside, spying the sealed glass vial. Within the vial was another container, a misty coiled glass tube containing Gemini. Addison reached into the unit swiftly. She slipped her hand between the fan blades and grasped the vial. Her nerve endings were alight with sparks of nervous energy as she prayed the programmer wouldn't automatically start the fan. So easily she could lose her fingers.

Addison pulled the vial out. With the deadly container in her hand she turned back to Antonia. The brunette stood by the door, gun aimed upon Addison.

"Tell me, Agent Black, what do you hold most dear to you?" With those words Antonia fled the room.

Addison looked around. Locating her weapon she retrieved it speedily and followed Antonia back out into the corridor. She heard footsteps descending rapidly down the stairs and took chase. Addison looked over the banister.

"Stop... now!"

In reply, Antonia fired several shots up the winding steps. Addison darted away from target and continued the chase; within her left hand Gemini's Hyde application and in her right, Alon's pistol. She reached the bottom step and Addison saw the back of Antonia disappear into the ballroom. She followed, running as fast as she was able.

Bursting through the double doors, Addison stopped dead in her tracks. She hadn't been aware of when it happened, but the music had died and the entire room was in silence. Her first sight was that of the guests standing on the dance floor. They stood in silence, hands upon their heads. Secondly, Addison realised Antonia really did have a partner. Brian Cooling stood atop Blithe's table. He held a submachine gun aimed towards the crowd. Antonia was situated to the side of the crowd, away from them. She held Skyler with one arm around her chest, a gun pressed against her temple.

"You must both be sick of this by now," Antonia taunted. "Drop the gun, Addison. Now."

Addison did so, immediately. "Let her go, Antonia."

"Oh... um... no. I want a trade."

Shaking her head the agent wrapped her hand a little tighter around Gemini. "No way."

Switching her hate filled glare from Addison, Antonia spoke calmly to Skyler. "Are you willing to forfeit your life for Gemini?"

"If I have to," Skyler replied confidently. She felt too much anger at Antonia to feel fear.

The brunette smiled. "Your faith is misplaced. Let me try something else." Antonia looked over to the crowd of guests. At the front of the group, standing off to one side, was General Blithe, Marlene and Jenny. "Brian," she called.

Brian smirked at Mark before replying, "Yes, boss?"

"Aim at the mother."

"No!" Mark ordered.

Brian shook his head at the General and aimed directly at Marlene.

"Please no," Skyler pleaded.

"Antonia!" Addison loosened her grip on Gemini. "Let's talk about this."

"Now you want to talk?" Antonia turned her focus back to Skyler. "Would you beg for your mother's life? Would you beg for Addison to hand over the vial now?"

Skyler looked at her mother. Marlene trembled noticeably, but she shook her head. The blonde turned to Addison. She gazed deep into her eyes, desperate for help. "Please don't do this."

"Wrong answer," said Antonia.

With a flick of her wrist, Antonia turned her gun onto Marlene. She fired two shots into her chest then switched the gun back to Skyler.

"NO!" Skyler screamed. "NO... MOM, NO!"

Shrieks echoed from the hostages as they scattered to the far walls and stage.

"MARLENE!" Mark called as he caught her falling body

. "FREEZE!" Brian yelled at the guests and they did so immediately. "Next person to move dies."

"NO... ANTONIA, YOU..." Addison seethed with anger, "YOU..." At a loss for words she clenched her fists, feeling powerless in the face of Skyler's heartache.

The blonde cried helplessly. Tears of fear and overwhelming grief fell from her eyes. She sagged against Antonia, despising the woman behind her yet unable to gain the strength to fight against her captor. Her eyes remained fixed upon her mother who lay lifelessly upon the floor. Mark crouched above her, pressing his hands upon the wounds but blood pumped freely from severed arteries. Skyler attempted to free herself, needing to help her mother, but Antonia held her firm.

"Mom," Skyler cried. "How could you?" she sobbed to Antonia. "How could you?"

Addison breathed heavily, her chest rising and falling as she controlled her desire to charge Antonia. She felt helpless, impotent in the face of such evil. The soldier thought rapidly.

"Fuck you, Antonia," Addison said, shaking her head. "You

want Gemini? YOU CAN HAVE IT!" With bubbling rage she threw the vial across the room towards Antonia. Addison knew Skyler's life would momentarily become of no importance as Antonia focused on the vial... and she was right. Pushing Skyler to the side, Antonia reached for Gemini. At the same time, and with a roar of rage, Mark leapt to his feet and charged Brian, taking him completely by surprise as he watched the events unfolding between Addison and Antonia. It was too late for the traitor to act as Mark knocked the table from beneath him and Brian fell to the floor. Glasses smashed and plates clattered upon the floor. Mark Blithe was upon him.

Vaguely aware of Mark's attack, Addison unleashed her own upon Antonia. She launched herself across the room before Antonia could react. They came together in a blur of fast, violent blows. Punches traded; kicks delivered.

Addison took Antonia by the collar and threw her against the wall. She flew over a table, rolling over its top and onto the floor where she hit the bottom of the wall. Addison jumped up over the table to Antonia. She took the ex-marine again, lifting her from the floor and holding her against the wall. Both their weapons had become lost to them, scattering in opposite directions across the ground as they fought.

Taking the hand holding Gemini, Addison thrust it against the wall, never forgetting the potentially dangerous capability of the bacilli. Although it was strong glass containing Gemini, it was not unbreakable. Addison never forgot that as she delivered a chain of bone breaking punches to Antonia. The soldier weakened her immensely until she was able to pry her fingers away from the vial. She placed the glass tube lightly between her teeth and then threw Antonia over another table. The brunette collided with an assortment of glasses and bottles of wine before hitting the floor.

All around them people scattered, running from the room. Mark Blithe had gained the upper hand over Brian and was binding his hands together behind his back. Skyler bent over her mother. Though she felt a faint pulse, there was no response from Marlene.

Sensing Addison's approach, Antonia tried to shake her dazed mind. She spotted the soldier's gun and lunged upon it, jumping to her feet as the agent neared.

"Stop," she seethed, blood spitting from her mouth as she spoke. "Screw you, Addison. You may think you have won this round, but now you die." Antonia saw movement to her side. Mark attempted to reach for Brian's submachine gun but he froze as she said, "I wouldn't if I were you, Mark. You let me leave here and I let Addison live."

"No deal," replied Addison.

"I DIDN'T ASK YOU," screamed the brunette. "Mark?"

A sudden and disturbing thought occurred to Addison. "You wanted to be caught, didn't you? I mean, why else would you anagram the name?"

"Very clever, Addison. Of course I wanted to be caught. How else was I supposed to get out of the miserable situation my life was in? Brodie left behind a large pair of shoes and I intend on filling them." Antonia turned from Addison. "Now stop stalling me, Mark. I assume you will make the right decision."

Mark shook his head and said, "No."

Antonia's eyes widened then she smiled with a blasé air. "Okay, fine." Pulling the trigger, she fired at Addison. A shot ricocheted across the room, followed by three more.

Addison lurched as pain stormed through her body. She grasped the side of her stomach, warm blood flowed again between her fingers, only this time it was her own. Looking back in shock, Addison stared at Antonia. The brunette's face was feral yet stunned. Her demeanour seemed to calm abruptly. She smiled and blood seeped past her lips like flowing wine. Her body crumpled and she fell to the ground. Behind her stood Skyler, the brunette's smoking gun still grasped within her hand. She stared down at the lifeless body of Antonia Bakersfield.

"Sky?" Addison whispered painfully.

"Mom's dead," the blonde replied hollowly.

"No." Rushing back to Marlene, Mark's composure shattered as he fell to his knees beside her body. He swept a hand through her hair. "Marlene... no." A chocked sob erupted from his throat as he broke down and cried.

Amongst the commotion around them Addison attempted to walk to Skyler. The blonde doctor seemed lost in a haze. She staggered half way before her knees buckled and she fell to the floor, landing on her side. Tears of excruciating pain stung her eyes. She felt faint, light headed and distant.

It was at that moment Skyler's foggy mind cleared. The gun fell from her hand as she spotted Addison. "No... Addison... not you too." She ran to the agent's side, dropping to the floor and cradled her head. "Stay with me, Addison, please."

Addison smiled. She attempted to raise her hand and handed the vial over to Skyler, wrapping her hand around the blonde's, sealing Gemini safely between them. "I love you," she muttered as she slipped into unconsciousness.

"No..." Skyler cried. Her head fell to Addison's chest

completely unaware of the men, dressed in full protection suits, charging into the ballroom. Pressing her hand to the agent's wound she sobbed hot, salty tears. "Don't leave me, Addison, please," she begged. Upon the floor beside them, Skyler saw Addison's medals. Splashes of the agent's blood covered both of them. Squeezing her eyes tightly shut, Skyler held Addison close and whispered, "I love you too."

Chapter 30

Two months later...

In the converted lighthouse on Cornwall's rugged coast, Spike danced outside the bedroom door. It had been several hours since her mistress had disappeared inside with the blonde woman and the tiny black dog was getting desperate for a visit outside.

It was only impeccable training that assured Spike had not had an accident up to that point, but even the best-trained animals had their limit. She stood on her hind feet and pawed rapidly on the thick oak door emitting a low keening whine. The door flew open suddenly and Addison appeared pulling a black shirt on as she emerged.

"All right, all right, Spike I hear you. I'm sorry, girl, I know you're desperate for a waz, so let's get going." The small dog led the way to the door leading outside and sat waiting patiently as Addison disabled the alarm and allowed the mongrel the freedom she craved. As Spike galloped happily along the cliff top stopping occasionally to mark her territory, Addison settled on the top step and reflected on the events of the previous two months.

Her recovery from Antonia's nearly fatal gunshot was painful and laborious. There had not been a time previously when the agent had come so close to losing her life, even in the most pitched battle. She remembered the searing agony she had felt as the traitor's bullet entered her flesh and very little else after that. She pieced the story together from snippets Mark Blithe, Samuel, and Quinton Zimmerman had given her. They told her how Skyler had fired the fatal shot into Antonia Bakersfield after her mother had died in her arms and Addison was about to be her next victim.

Addison marveled at, and would always be humbled by, the

knowledge that a woman like Skyler, so previously unsure of her ability to kill was prompted to defend a woman, such as herself, to the death. Through a dim fog Addison thought she recalled confessing her true feelings just prior to slipping into unconsciousness, but she could not be certain. Perhaps it had only been wishful thinking. Certainly when Skyler had arrived back in England a scant week ago, no mention of love had been made just as there had been no mention of it when Addison had regained consciousness in the hospital.

It had been understandable, at that time, that Skyler was still in shock from the loss of her mother; the last blood relative she had left and Addison felt that it was no time to push Skyler for a commitment of any kind. Only days after regaining consciousness Addison held back the tears as Skyler said goodbye to join Mark Blithe in returning her mother's body to the States. She was to be laid to rest beside her father. Though Addison understood the necessity of the action, she had never felt more alone in her life.

Several weeks had passed, but as Addison recovered her physical strength her emotional strength dwindled as she received only short mails and truncated phone calls from the American. Just as Addison despaired of ever seeing Skyler again, a messenger had arrived with word that she was returning to Britain with General Blithe and wanted to see her immediately.

That had been a week ago. Addison remembered their meeting very clearly. Mark Blithe had delivered Skyler to Cornwall personally, but he slipped away again with barely a word to the agent and only a cryptic comment to Skyler about checking into "the matter we discussed". Addison hadn't asked what the General meant as the blonde had flown into her arms causing most rational thought to flee from the Brit's mind; the few days since then had been spent in each other's arms finally and fully recovering from their separate wounds.

Spike broke into Addison's thoughts with an excited yapping as she raced toward the lighthouse steps. The agent didn't need to be told Skyler had joined her, as this was Spike's reaction anytime the American was in her proximity.

"Spike, you're such a fickle little tart. You used to only respond to me like that. Now it seems you've developed quite an affinity for my overnight guests."

"And how many overnight guests have there been since I've been gone?" asked Skyler as she handed the agent a mug of tea and sat next to her on the step. Addison recognized the heavy olive green, cable knit sweater that Skyler wore as one of her own from her days in the Marines. As the blonde leaned her head against the agent's shoulder,

Addison answered her with the honesty that had become the hallmark of their relationship.

"There's been none but you Skyler and if you leave there will never be one again." Skyler started at the words and drew back to look into Addison's eyes to look for the truth in them. The unusual combination of Addison's eye color did nothing to disguise the fact that her words were sincere and heartfelt. Skyler hesitated only a moment, drew in a deep breath and addressed the agent.

"Addison there are a few things I need to talk to you about, but it had to wait until today. I needed to wait until a few things were settled before I felt confident enough to speak to you about us." Addison was concerned, but knew she could do no more than listen to what the American had to say.

"It was the most difficult thing I had to do, going home and laying my mother to rest. If Mark hadn't been with me, I might have fallen apart completely. With you in the hospital and having had such a close call with that traitor, I wasn't sure if I could go through losing somebody I loved like I lost my father. I know that every time you go out on a mission that possibility will always exist." Addison felt a chill pass over her heart. Spike, sensing her mistresses' discomfort, clambered up the lighthouse steps and settled into Addison's lap, placing her small muzzle on her thigh. Automatically the Brit's hand moved to stroke the scruffy black fur.

Skyler continued. "I knew right then, standing at my father's grave that I had a serious choice to make. It was either accept and support your work in any way I could or cut myself off and lose the woman that I love forever." Addison glanced up anxiously into Skyler's green eyes.

"You do love me then?" Addison asked softly.

Skyler smiled, "I would think my being here with you would have answered that question, but yes, Agent Black, I do love you with all my heart." Just as Addison would have replied, a low tone was heard coming from her wristwatch.

"Damn this new technology of Samuel's! I've been waiting for the new communication device to activate and I might have known the timing would be this rotten. This had better be important or there will be hell to pay," Addison said as she rose, tucking Spike under one arm and draping the other over Skyler's shoulder. "Come on, you might as well see the rest of my little hideaway."

Addison led the way through the garage, setting Spike down to process herself and Skyler through the security system, allowing their admittance to the armory. Addison's watch beeped insistently again as they made their way over to the recently installed equipment, placed there by Perkins a mere two weeks earlier. Spike contented herself with slipping in behind her two mistresses and returning to the large bone she had left there for safekeeping and began to gnaw on it with gusto.

Flipping a short series of switches, the image of General Blithe appeared on the satellite videophone. "Addison! Good to see you looking so chipper! I suspect the lovely Doctor Tidwell has had something to do with your improved appearance and enhanced recovery." He smiled. "Good to see you again, Skyler. I've missed you."

"I missed you too, Mark. I don't think I could have handled the trip home under the circumstances if you hadn't been there with me to lend your support and keep me apprised of Addison's hospital course everyday." The Brit was amazed. She had felt unremembered and a little neglected, but now she was learning that Skyler had known everything that was happening with her during her return to the States.

"It was my pleasure, Skyler. You are much your mother's daughter and she was a remarkable woman. I...well, I ...I shall miss her very much." Addison looked down as Skyler took her hand and squeezed it, seeking strength from the agent that she was most willing to give.

General Blithe cleared his throat and composed himself. "I have been doing some research into your request Skyler and with my contacts in the government and within S.A.S. itself, I am now able to give you news regarding it."

Addison glanced at Skyler, but the American's full attention was on the image of General Blithe. "What is the decision, Mark?" she asked anxiously.

Mark opened his mouth to reply, but Addison had stood by long enough without knowing what was going on. "Hold it, Mark! What are you two going on about? What request and what decision? I have a feeling this is going to concern me in some way and I think I have the right to know what is being done without my knowledge. Now, who is going to enlighten me?" She moved her glance from Mark to Skyler and then back again.

The general shrugged. "No need to get up a head of steam, Addison. This whole business started on the plane ride from London to the States. Neither Skyler nor I felt much like sleeping so we talked. I complimented her on figuring out the anagram of the name Tobias F. Kleein and also for spotting the jewelry that didn't fit in with Miss Bakersfield's story. Skyler's capacity for knowledge is quite extraordinary." This was not news to Addison and she nodded at the general's observation.

"Skyler was very worried about you, Addison, and she commented more than once that she wished some of the knowledge she has picked up over the remarkable course of her studies would have done you some good prior to you being nearly...well, severely wounded by that demented traitor." Addison looked again at Skyler who now had moisture collecting in the corners of her green eyes.

"If I had lost you, Addison..." she began.

"You didn't and you won't," the agent replied with conviction. "Ever."

Mark cleared his throat and said, "Like any outstanding administrator, I have an eye for whatever may benefit my group and I saw the potential in Skyler. I have been trying to think for quite a while now of a way to bridge that gap between the advance sciences we are developing in the labs and the practical use and knowledge of our agents in the field. It took a bit of wrangling, but Addison, I'd like you to meet the newest member of the Special Ops team, Doctor Skyler Tidwell. She will be working as our contact between the agents and the research, science and development sectors to provide the operatives in the field with the best information possible."

"Skyler in the field?" Addison nearly shouted. "No way! First Agnes Brodie then Antonia Bakersfield and God knows who else might turn out to be involved when we're done questioning Brian Cooling. I'm not having Skyler exposed to that sort of danger ever again!"

Skyler sighed and smiled at her protective partner. "Technology, Addison, that's the key. Think about what an advantage it would be to have an operative, a control if you will, at your disposal throughout a mission. A miniaturized camera on your person, a device like a cochlear implant in your ear and it would be as if you were taking all the resources of Special Operations with you every time you went into the field. You already have the bio-chip in you, this would be just taking that concept one step further."

Addison thought about it as the consummate professional that she was and was able to see the distinct edge something like the general and Skyler were talking about, would be. Although Alon and the female guard were recovering from their wounds, it had been close for both of them. This was an edge that might save lives and anything on that order was worth checking into.

"But what about your own work?" Addison asked, suddenly concerned that Skyler may be giving up her own dreams to be with her.

Skyler turned fully to the agent now. "Addison, I love you. Do you think there is anything in the world that interests me as much as you now? I knew standing at my parent's graves that the only way I could bear to know about you leaving to go on a mission would be to go 'with' you. So, when we come back from our well-deserved holiday in Egypt, you and I are going to be the prototype of the new Special Ops team. The question is... are you up for it, Agent?"

General Blithe watched the exchange between the women with interest. Unselfconsciously, Addison pulled Skyler to her and kissed her with undisguised enthusiasm. "I love you, Skyler Tidwell, and with you, I'm up for anything." She kissed Skyler again and her arm reached out to the controls of the videophone as she did so. The screen in Mark's office went blank.

The general chuckled as he leaned back in his chair. "Science, technology and Black's Magic. Now **this** should be interesting."

The End...?

About the Authors

Val Brown is a healthcare professional with many years in Nursing. Her current job takes her to all parts of the United States.

Writing was only just a fantasy until she met a certain British poet online and started a writing partnership and friendship that has led to the publishing of this first novel.

Though she enjoys exploring and traveling, family and friends will always be her main interest.

M.J. Walker is a 27-year-old living in a rural setting in middle England. When not working she spends her time writing novels and poetry. She collects old coins and makes jewellery using beads and artefacts from ancient times. An avid collector of ancient items herself she has a keen interest in all things historical.

She was first published as a poet at age seventeen in the United States followed by her inclusion in many anthologies in her native country. Through her offerings on the web, MJ met and teamed up with Val Brown, an American nurse.

M.J. is a part-time numismatist and currently studying Journalism.

She will soon be moving to Cornwall, birthplace of the legendary King Arthur.

Order These Great Books Directly From Limitless, Dare 2 Dream Publishing

The Amazon Queen by L M Townsend	20.00	
Define Destiny by J M Dragon	20.00	The one that started it all…
Desert Hawk,revised by Katherine E. Standelll	18.00	Many new scenes
Golden Gate by Erin Jennifer Mar	18.00	
The Brass Ring By Mavis Applewater	18.00	HOT
Haunting Shadows by J M Dragon	18.00	
Spirit Harvest by Trish Shields	15.00	
PWP: Plot? What Plot? by Mavis Applewater	18.00	HOT
Journeys By Anne Azel	18.00	NEW
Memories Kill By S. B. Zarben	20.00	
Up The River, revised By Sam Ruskin	18.00	Many new scenes
	Total	

South Carolina residents add 5% sales tax.
Domestic shipping is $3.50 per book

Visit our website at: http://limitlessd2d.net

Please mail your orders with credit card info, check or money order to:

Limitless, Dare 2 Dream Publishing
100 Pin Oak Ct.
Lexington, SC 29073-7911

Please make checks or money orders payable to: Limitless.

I

Order More Great Books Directly From Limitless, Dare 2 Dream Publishing

Daughters of Artemis by L M Townsend	18.00	
Connecting Hearts By Val Brown and MJ Walker	18.00	
Mysti: Mistress of Dreams By Sam Ruskin	18.00	HOT
Family Connections By Val Brown & MJ Walker	18.00	Sequel to Connecting Hearts
A Thousand Shades of Feeling by Carolyn McBride	18.00	
The Amazon Nation By Carla Osborne	18.00	Great for research
Poetry from the Featherbed By pinfeather	18.00	If you think you hate poetry you haven't read this
None So Blind, 3rd Edition By LJ Maas	16.00	NEW
A Saving Solace By DS Bauden	18.00	NEW
Return of the Warrior By Katherine E. Standell	20.00	Sequel to Desert Hawk
Journey's End By LJ Maas	18.00	NEW
	Total	

South Carolina residents add 5% sales tax.
Domestic shipping is $3.50 per book
Please mail your orders with credit card info, check or money order to:
Limitless, Dare 2 Dream Publishing
100 Pin Oak Ct.
Lexington, SC 29073-7911
Please make checks or money orders payable to: Limitless.

II

Introducing...

Art By Joy

By Joy Argento

Hi, allow me to introduce myself. My name is Joy Argento and I am the artist on all of these pieces. I have been doing artwork since I was a small child. That gives me about 35 years of experience. I majored in art in high school and took a few college art courses. Most of my work is done in either pencil or airbrush mixed with color pencils. I have recently added designing and creating artwork on the computer. Some of the work featured on these pages were created and "painted" on the computer. I am self taught in this as well as in the use of the airbrush.

I have been selling my art for the last 15 years and have had my work featured on trading cards, prints and in magazines. I have sold in galleries and to private collectors from all around the world.

I live in Western New York with my three kids, four cats, one dog and the love of my life. It is definitely a full house. I appreciate you taking the time to check out my artwork. Please feel free to email me with your thoughts or questions. Custom orders are always welcomed too.

Contact me at ArtByJoy@aol.com . I look forward to hearing from you.

Motorcycle Women

Joy Argento

Check out her work at
LimitlessD2D or at her website.
Remember: ArtByJoy@aol.com !